Discover other books by

Sheron Wood McCartha

Available in print and eBook on Amazon

The Alysian Universe Series

Caught in Time: Book 1

A Dangerous Talent for Time: Book 2

Cosmic Entanglement: Book 3

Past the Event Horizon: Book 4

Space Song: Book 5

Touching Crystal: Book 6

Time's Equation: Book 8

Terran Series

A World Too Far: The Ship

Someone's Clone

Alysian Universe: book 7

By

Sheron Wood McCartha

Digital Imagination Publishing
Beaverton, Oregon

Copyright 2014 by Sheron Wood McCartha

SOMEONE'S CLONE

This is a work of fiction. All characters, organizations, or events in this novel are inventions of the author's imagination. Any resemblance to anyone living or dead is entirely coincidental.

Cover art by Toni Boudreault

Published by Digital Imagination Publishing
Beaverton, Oregon

ISBN 978-09891599-5-1

Printed in the United States of America

Acknowledgements

Rarely do we go it alone. Usually *someone* helps us to our goals or destination. So, it is with this book, my main character, and me. For almost a year, my writers group inspected this, one of my favorite stories, every two weeks, chapter by chapter, helping me make it better. Thanks to: Diana, Clayton, Ted and Chelsea.

Once I went through that journey, I turned the story over to my Beta readers. The startling discovery was that each one focused on a different aspect of the novel.

Veronica Sicoe is a writer who has a great blog at Veronicasicoe.com that I recommend to any science fiction fan. She is a new mother with limited time due. So, the meticulous detail and time she spent making suggestions reflected a true professional.

Cathy Reynolds also did a phenomenal job. Her attention to the mechanics of the story was much appreciated. She is an enthusiastic reader, and I am lucky to have her as a fan.

Finally, Beta reader Lea Day, with her vast experience and deep knowledge of the genre added much to the result.

Often we don't go it alone, as this story points out. As life tosses us obstacles and challenge, others come forward to help us cross that finish line and complete our story. Thank you every one

Not shown, D'Ankanque is south of map

<u>Chapter 1</u>

"You must never, ever, tell anyone where you got this child or that it's not yours. Do you understand?" Elissandra Telluria brushed her short sandy-blond hair away from sky-blue eyes with one hand, while cradling the wiggling young boy with her other. The new parents nodded vigorously, having recognized her famous face.

"You were chosen because of your loyalty to the Democratic Union and because you're considered intelligent, good people. Your grandfather, Admiral Stone, served his country well, bringing honor to this family. In addition, his connections may afford some protection for you and the child. Please realize this is a risky adoption. It is important he favors both of you, so few will question that he's yours. Never say otherwise."

The young woman nodded at her, tears brimming in her eyes. "We'll take good care of him. We'll protect him and do all you say. We wanted a child of our own, but it's not possible."

She reached out for the squirming child with gray-blue eyes and sandy brown hair who put out his chubby hands toward her and waved eagerly in response. Her husband patted her on the shoulder as she took the boy and placed him in the curve of her hip. They looked proudly at each other and then fondly at the child. They'd already forgotten her presence, so powerful was the youngster's charm.

Elissandra sighed. She knew what they felt, had experienced the child's charisma in her own past. "Then it's done. We'll never meet here at the Med Center again, but I'll send a young man named Trey Lyne who'll give you your final papers. Heed his advice and call on him if you need help."

They nodded. The husband put his arms around his wife, including the child in his protective embrace.

Gratified by their eagerness, she counseled, "Be firm with him. He has a way of..." She stopped speaking, since they were already wrapped up in the child and barely listening to her anyway. Let them find out all about him for themselves she thought, as a wry smile formed.

But as she remembered, the smile faded and a frown knit her brow. Some still argued for destroying the child. Yet neither she nor Brett Telluria, an important congressman in the Democratic Union, and brother, could agree in good conscience with that choice. Together, they had pursued an alternative plan: this adoption. She hoped there'd be no regrets. Yet this innocent couple did not comprehend the possible danger they faced.

The new parents looked up and smiled at her.

Time to go. She swung around, gathered up her coat and slipped through the door of the bare walled adoption room. She stopped to cast one last glance inside and heard the wife murmur to her husband, "She's so famous that she probably has no time to raise a child. I think we're most likely the beneficiaries of an indiscretion."

Startled by the comment, Elissandra paused in the doorway. *They considered the child hers?* She shook her head, knowing she could never reveal how wrong they were.

<u>Chapter 2</u>

Ailain Stone hurriedly washed his hands and shook them in the air, causing tiny droplets to splatter all about him. Thrusting them under the blower, he impatiently pulled them out, still damp. Peering into the refresher's mirror, an adolescent of seventeen with sandy brown hair smirked back at him. The chubby cheeks made him vow once again to give up extra desserts. Still, it wasn't a bad mug. The dimples helped.

He felt lucky. Winning this trip to visit the Space Center near the capitol of Tygel with his friend Jeremy was the coolest thing that had ever happened to him. So far, the best exhibit had been the movie talking about possible alien worlds. Yet, no one had discovered any aliens, so sometimes he enjoyed trying to imagine what they might look like, conjuring up lots of interesting and weird images.

Having just finished lunch at the Center's cafeteria, his group was next scheduled for a private tour of a replica of the spaceship that now followed a mysterious signal in outer space. He was eager to see it, possibly do an extra credit report. The others in his group: his parents, his friend Jeremy and Jeremy's mother, Kate, all waited outside in the hallway. He needed to hurry.

Shaking out his hands one last time, he slicked back an unruly curl and gave a final nod at the mirror. His image nodded back, reflecting serious gray-blue eyes alight with anticipation. The wayward curl sprang back out. He brushed it in place once more, pleased with his life and excited about his future. So far, the trip had been ripping, and he didn't want to waste time lingering in the can.

He heard a loud shout and paused to listen. Terrified cries abruptly penetrated the refresher's door. As he opened it, it wasn't so much the volume or frightened tone of the voice, but its familiarity that alarmed him the most. Loud angry shouts that sounded like his father's fell abruptly silent, while his mother's hysterical screams grew louder.

What was happening out there?

He pushed through the door and froze. Down the walkway, he saw his father slumped lifelessly on the Space Center's smooth plascrete floor, blood oozing from a gaping wound.

Frantic, Ailain dashed forward.

Next to his father, his mother struggled to fend off a knife-wielding assailant. She staggered backwards, blood staining her blouse.

He saw the attacker signal his accomplice who held a terrified Jeremy by one arm while Jeremy's mother pulled on the other in a desperate tug of war. The assailant was stronger, and Ailain heard a sickening crack. When he shrieked in pain, Jeremy's mother released him with a horrified gasp. The accomplice gathered up a now moaning Jeremy, slung him over his shoulder, strode off into a side corridor, and disappeared. By now, various bystanders had taken notice and become alarmed.

Between sobs, Kate croaked, "Help us! Help us!" A few took confused halting steps toward her; one or two pulled out a caller and punched in an emergency number.

Ailain pushed past a gathering of spectators as he ran to reach his mother, now staring in disbelief at the blood blotting her formerly immaculate white blouse. The attacker watched his accomplice disappear, not noticing

Ailain rushing forward, weaving through stunned bystanders.

"No! Murderers! Stop them!" Ailain screamed at the milling group.

His mother turned at the sound of his voice. Anguish lit her face as she gestured frantically for him to go back. Lurching forward, she yanked off a pendant from around her neck and tossed it to him, screaming, "Take it! Run! Hide!"

Swinging back around, the attacker growled and stabbed her to silence.

His mother collapsed next to his father. Blood, spilling from her neck, stained the floor's smooth surface and mixed with his father's, making an accumulating red puddle swell in size.

The pendant skittered toward him across the plascrete floor just beyond reach. He stared at it, and looked up.

The assailant's gaze also followed the bright gem, then lifted to stare directly into Ailain's terrified eyes. Dark anger flashed in the young tough's face. Something electronic along the side of his cheek sparked blue, and he put a hand up to his ear and muttered unintelligible words. Then, he glanced backward, following the path to the point where his partner had disappeared. He whirled around to study Ailain, and comprehension flared across his face. Treading forward over the still bodies, lying like broken marionettes beneath his feet, the assailant stepped toward Ailain, tracking a path of bloody footsteps behind him. As he left, a few brave visitors rushed to aid the stricken victims.

Ailain glanced toward the sparkling crystal necklace lying tangled on the shiny floor.

Commotion in the corridor increased, but now the assailant moved purposefully toward Ailain and the bright gem, ignoring all else.

Fear coursed through Ailain's body as a rush of adrenaline kicked him into overdrive. He jerked forward, snatched up the pendant, and dodged left toward an exit. The advancing killer slid sideways in front of him to block, a scowl on his face. Ailain edged right, but his opponent blocked that path too. Muttering into the blinking blue light, the assassin fumbled in his coat, pulled out a wicked looking knife, and aimed it at Ailain.

Clear thinking fled his mind as panic set in. Spinning around, he noticed his path led back into the refresher. He plunged through the door, hearing it slam shut behind him. A *thunk* sounded against the outside frame.

What a stupid mistake! This room is a trap.

He frantically tried to spot a window and found none. *Where can I go? What can I do?*

No way out. The waste can was too small to hide inside, and the duct pipes hung too high to reach. He had to do something. *Had to.* Otherwise, he was as good as dead.

Why? Why did those men kill my parents? What do they want with me? Or Jeremy?

Heavy footsteps thumped just outside the door.

The heavy crystal necklace sparked in his hand. The room began to vibrate around him, making him dizzy. He staggered to a washbasin. His head exploded in pain as something overtook all thought. His body felt light and insubstantial, as if he were dissolving. He touched the mirror, seeking a solution, but only found his reflection fading before him. Sliding toward the floor, down past basins and pipes, he felt the stirring air from the door as it crashed open, but a dark nothingness swirled around him and tossed him far away out of time.

Chapter 3

A hard floor beneath his aching body. Cold. Pain. More pain. His head throbbed. His body felt bruised all over. Sensory information flooded his brain as conscious thought returned. Ailain lay on a cold smooth floor. Water dripped nearby. Murmuring sounds filtered in from somewhere outside. Groggily, he wondered where the frag he was.

Memory surfaced like a flash fire, burning through his brain. It wasn't true, couldn't be true. Reaching upwards, feeling a washbasin's edge, he pulled himself painfully from the hard floor as every muscle screamed at the effort. He must have fainted and knocked himself out. A large knot swelled on his forehead. Staring at the door, he expected the assassin to come plunging in with knife held high, but all stayed quiet. Going to the door, he leaned and put an ear against it. Nothing but small common noises came through. No screaming voices, no panicked knot of people, no wailing sirens, or shouts sounded on the other side. He opened the door to peek out. A few desultory strangers ambled along the hallway. A child licked a candy treat as its mother yanked its chubby arm to hurry it along. No blood on the floor. No weapon-wielding ferocious assassins. Everything appeared unbelievably peaceful.

Pulling the door open further, he saw a man slouched on a far bench calmly munching on a food bar with the air of someone who had been waiting for a long time. The man seemed familiar, and Ailain was puzzling out who he was when the man looked up and waved in excitement, half rising from the bench.

Confused, Ailain thought he recognized the face of a distant cousin who had visited their home upon occasion during his early childhood. The man appeared older, different, but then it had been a while since he'd last seen Trey Lyne. Apprehensively, he scanned the area, but everything still appeared quiet.

"Trey, is that you?" he whispered, not sure.

"Ailain!"

"Yeah?"

The man rose from his seat. "Thank the Creator, it's finally you. Come here." A hand gestured him over.

Relieved, Ailain stepped forth on rubbery legs still shaky from fright. A million questions and a ferocious headache pounded his foggy brain. As he advanced, the whole Space Center felt strange, somehow out of synch, but he felt groggy and bewildered by his recent experience and put the confusion down to a banged up head. "What are you doing here?" he asked, looking around, bewildered.

Where is everyone?

"I'm here, waiting for you." Trey patted a spot on the bench next to him and peered up and down the corridor. He handed Ailain an energy bar. Ailain realized he was ravenous and devoured it gratefully.

As he sank down, he rubbed his head and winced. "I bumped my head and knocked myself unconscious. Stupid me." He smiled at Trey, glad for a familiar face.

Trey Lyne had been in and out of his life since Ailain was a small child. Trey's overall complexion mirrored Ailain's but with darker hair, most likely from his mother's side of the family. His eyes were the same pale blue-gray color. Many commented on how Trey and Ailain favored each other, except Trey looked twenty something annuals older with more mature facial features. The man didn't have an ounce of fat on him, and Ailain envied him that. Both produced the same killer dimples that flashed whenever they smiled. Now his usually all-knowing face appeared older and tired, but he smiled reassuringly, nonetheless. Ailain felt an intense relief at seeing him.

"I can't find mom and dad." Ailain leaned forward and peered down the corridor, frantic at their disappearance.

Trey's dark eyebrows slanted down into a frown.

Struggling to remember, Ailain recounted, "I came out and saw…" Waving an arm, he mumbled, "It must've been a bad dream." Distraught, he jumped up from the bench. "They've just gone to the space ship. I need to catch up."

Trey put out a hand to hold him from leaving. "No, wait, Ailain, listen. I have to tell you something that's going to be hard to understand." He paused, searching for words. "Your parents are gone. They're dead. Someone attacked and killed them. You were there. Think about what happened. You must have seen something. Tell me exactly what you saw." Again, Trey scanned the corridor, then bent his head toward the boy as if to listen intently.

Ailain blinked back threatening tears brought on by an overwhelming surge of grief. "No! That can't be true. We were going to see the ship. I just have to catch up." He took a step forward as Trey grabbed his arm and tugged him back.

"No, they're not there." Trey spun him around so he stared directly into Ailain's eyes. Strong fingers gripped his shoulders. "Your parents are dead, and there's nothing you or I can do to change it."

"It's all my fault." Ailain choked out his guilt. "If I'd been there and not fooling around in the refresher, I might have stopped them."

Trey shook his shoulders. "No! You are not to blame. But help me find them." He pulled Ailain down onto the bench, Ailain slumped there as Trey growled at him, saying, "Tell me exactly what you saw…every detail."

He tried to concentrate in order to describe accurately what he remembered. "I saw a man." He stopped to think. "He was dressed in black pants, black shirt, and carried a knife. He didn't appear old, almost a kid. It all happened so fast. Part of his face was covered, but I saw his eyes."

"Go on."

"He had dark eyebrows and black as coal scary eyes."

"Yes. Was there anything unusual about him?"

"There was a blue, flashing, electronic thing near his cheek."

A hissing sound came from Trey. "I.N.Sys equipment. I'd bet the house on it."

"Why would I.N.Sys hurt my parents? The Information Network System is supposed to protect us."

"So they say. But sometimes I wonder. What else?"

"There was another guy who took Jeremy away. Is Jeremy all right?"

Trey's eyes softened, revealing anguish, forewarning the pain of his next words. "No, I'm sorry."

Ailain inhaled with a gasp and clapped a hand over his mouth to stifle a sob. Dropping the hand, he asked, "Why would anyone want to hurt Jeremy or my parents? They were good people."

"A good question."

"Is he…?"

"Afraid so."

"He was my best friend—just like a brother. We liked the same things and, and…" Tears brimmed in his eyes as despair gripped him again.

A grimace crossed Trey's face. He gazed away, murmuring, "You both look a lot alike. Someone could easily mistake Jeremy for you if they weren't paying attention." He swung back around and eyed him intently.

Confused, Ailain asked, "Why would they want me?"

"Why indeed? I think they did, though."

"I hid in the refresher. The man followed me. I thought he would come in and kill me, but he didn't. No one came. Where did he go? Why didn't anyone come and find me?" He broke out in a sweat and started to shake all over.

"They looked everywhere for you. You weren't there."

"I was. I was. I just came from there." He pointed behind him, but continued to stare at Trey's grim face. An uneasy feeling enveloped him. Something was very wrong. Things weren't adding up. "Why didn't anyone come get me? Kate knew I went in there. Is she dead too?"

"No, she's alive." Trey flashed a brief smile and then rubbed his hand through his hair. "They did try to find you. You just weren't there anymore."

"Where was I?"

"That's what everyone wants to know."

"Did they get the men who did it?"

"No, they got away."

"I was there. Why didn't they come get me?" panted Ailain. The room started to waver, throbbing with light and dark. He felt dizzy.

"Stop!" Trey grabbed his arm and shook him. "Listen to me, Ailain. I think you did a trick, a very clever and difficult trick. You did it to get away from the killer. You didn't mean to do anything wrong, but things have changed because of what you did. I need to tell you something else." Trey patted him as if to comfort him. Ailain suddenly decided he didn't want to hear what Trey was about to say.

But Trey said it anyway.

"All of this feels like it just happened, but that's not the case. It happened a long time ago. It's now Maire, the fifth phase, of eleven sixty-four, twenty-eight annuals into your future. Remember it when you have to send me."

Feeling like he was in a surreal dream, Ailain studied the area, noticing how things appeared differently. The Space Center looked larger and shinier with more people, new equipment, and displays that he hadn't noticed before. He put his face into his hands. He didn't want to see any more.

Trey sighed. "We're okay here for now, but we can't linger long. We have to get you somewhere safe."

Ailain grabbed at Trey's arm. "That guy knows about me. He knows Jeremy is the wrong boy. He looked at me and saw his mistake. He was coming to get *me*, wasn't he?"

"They may still come for you even after all this time, and we don't want you found. We have to hide you until we can figure out who they are and how to stop them."

"Why don't we go to Security? We need to have them arrested. I can give a good description of them."

A snort sounded from Trey. "Most likely they look very different now. Remember, twenty-eight annuals have passed. Besides, I don't trust anyone. If I.N.Sys is involved, telling them might be dangerous. They would put you somewhere, convincing you that you were safe, but you might become trapped in a place where the assassin could find you. After what's happened, I suspect I.N.Sys of collusion. Someone from the inside has hindered the investigation. They're calling the case closed, but I didn't see them trying too hard to find the murders even at the beginning. Makes me suspicious. You need to have the freedom to move around. You need to get away from here and disappear."

"No! I want to go back. I can't walk away from my life."

"Do you know how to go back? Can you control where you go?"

Anguish swept over him as he whispered, "No."

Trey picked up a bag. "Then, we have no choice but to move forward, and quickly. Can you, at least, walk? We need to reach the Terran space station called Earth2."

Ailain stared down the corridor, taking one last look, hoping to see his group, hoping it was all a mistake. But they weren't there, and everything stayed different. Small hairs stood up along his arms, and he had trouble catching his breath. Eleven sixty-four? He was twenty-eight annuals in the future? With no idea how to return.

"Yeah, I can walk." He stood on shaky legs but steeled his resolve and stumbled forward.

Trey flipped a switch on a nearby hidden panel. Opening it led them to an interior corridor. The panel shut, and Trey breathed out a sigh of relief. Then he took a jacket out of a bag and handed it to Ailain.

"Put this on," he said. "You're my size. It should fit."

Ailain glanced at a jacket with tools in its pockets. A badge with the word, "Maintenance" was pinned on it. He hoped he wouldn't be required to fix anything.

Trey took off his jacket, turned it inside out and re-buttoned it. Now his jacket also resembled a mechanic's with a badge and tools tucked into pockets. Adjusting his badge and smoothing down the collar, Trey tapped Kayse's arm. "Follow me and don't talk to anyone. We're two Terran maintenance men heading to the Earth2 Station."

"Terran? Earth2? What are you talking about?"

"You've missed a lot due to your jump. We found out we're a colony from another world called Earth. Advanced aliens, called Enjelise, seeded our planet to disperse the human species. Recently, these Earth people, called Terrans, discovered this planet. That's why the Terrans are so upset about the way we treat them. Technically, they're distant ancestors. According to the natives here, they're alien invaders. Both sides are looking down their noses at each other. Some bad feelings are going around."

Ailain stared at him, gap-mouthed. "Are you saying all the unbelievable stuff you've been telling me is true?"

Trey huffed. "Haven't you listened? Look, we need to move fast, so stay close. Don't say your name; in fact, don't say anything. Monitors have face identifiers, but it'll take time to identify us through ASSIST. If we move now, we can get away before they stop us."

"ASSIST? Never heard of it."

"Yeah, Alysian Synchronized Satellite Information System Technology known as ASSIST. It's a worldwide communication and information network."

"So, what's this outfit I'm wearing?"

"You're a Terran maintenance worker."

"Terran? Didn't you just tell me they're aliens? And now I have to pretend to be one? Ugh. Aliens are weird. Some have tentacles or..."

"Have you ever met one?"

"Ah..."

"Have you?"

"Well, no. But I've imagined some that were...."

"Thought so." Trey frowned at him.

"Will I have to wear an extra eye or attach a sixth finger?"

Trey rolled his eyes. "They're different, but not as different as you might expect. Once you meet one, then you can tell me what you think. Until then, keep quiet and do as I say. Now follow me."

<u>Chapter 4</u>

Ailain's mind whirled as he sat next to Trey in a jitney chugging its way to the spaceport. They were headed into fricking space. Jeremy would be blasted, except…except… he was dead. Ailain tried not to think any more about it. A wave of inconsolable grief threatened to overwhelm him. By closing his eyes and holding his breath, he managed to gather back control. *Mom and dad dead.* It didn't seem real. They'd *always* been there for him. He felt the onslaught of brimming tears again, and agony gushed forth.

It just can't be true.

Maybe this was one of those funny programs where everyone would pop up and say, "Got you. Surprise!" Shows like that aired all over the vid. He also had second thoughts about just going along with Trey. Maybe he should call a guard, but what if Trey was right? Mom had warned him constantly about stranger danger, only Trey was no stranger, and she'd made a big deal about trusting him if anything bad ever happened. Well, something bad had happened. Something very bad.

At least, that's what Trey had said. Maybe he was wrong. Then Ailain remembered the pendant and reached into his pocket. There it sat, proof that it had really happened; that it was all true.

Anger quickly overpowered his grief. He would make those men pay for what they did, even if it took him the rest of his life. He would take revenge, and they would be sorry.

Trey gazed over at Ailain and gave him a quick sympathetic glance. "I'll keep you safe" was all he said and immediately returned to concentrating on his personal communicator. Trey had never been one for long emotional conversation, but the brief words made Ailain feel better. He didn't want to talk anyway. His mother always drove him mad, asking pointless questions when all he wanted was to be left alone. *Well, she wouldn't be bothering him anymore.* His throat suddenly ached. *This was stupid. He couldn't keep crying like some baby.* Wiping his face with his sleeve, he took a deep breath, flipped the pendant over in his hands and tapped the bright crystal. The jewel glowed with a rainbow gleam, and a button popped out at the bottom. He pushed at it.

A strange noise and flash emitted from Trey's neck area. Jerking forward, Trey peered at him. "What are you doing? Is that the beacon?"

"This thing? Mom threw it at me when she told me to run."

Trey heaved a sigh of relief. "Good for her. Probably saved your life. The Talent Crystal signals me when activated like an emergency beacon. Anytime you're in danger, you tap the crystal and push that button. I'll try to come help you, but it must be serious trouble. It's not a toy." Trey touched the necklace. "This was our link. This was supposed to keep her safe."

"Didn't work too well, did it?"

Trey looked up abruptly and scowled. "I tried, but I couldn't get there quick enough. I tried to make it right, but fate dictated otherwise."

"That's just an excuse," Ailain grumbled.

"No, it's the hard reality. Now I'm trying to keep you safe, whether you believe it or not."

"I can't wear a girl's necklace," Ailain complained, sidetracking further discussion of the incident.

"It might come in handy." Trey squinted his eyes and inclined his head. "If it makes you too uncomfortable that way, we can remake it into a wrist band or a pin, but a necklace is easier to wear."

"I'd prefer a wrist band."

"Let me think about it. But for now, wear the necklace."

The jitney slowed to a stop as passengers hurried out. In front of them stood a gleaming, white, modern building that contained a mass of people, all heading for various transportation desks and destinations.

"Okay, we're here and you're to keep quiet and let me do the talking. Follow my lead. We're going to the Earth2 Station and after we arrive, I'm going to call on an old friend who just happens to be visiting there."

***

Shuffling along with a bunch of travelers, jamming into a crowded shuttle, and then sitting without talking for a solid two duros was not the fun Ailain had envisioned space travel to be. His mind kept replaying the attack and wondering what came next in his life of awful events. Again, he rewound the tape of his memory, reviewing the terrifying images he found there.

Their small window afforded a limited view. From a distance, the Terran station looked like a tinker toy floating in space. Its fat cylindrical body rotated to provide a low gravity and several large solar array panels fanned out in all angles, resembling petals trying to catch the sun's rays. Several additions jutted out around the center and provided a number of docking bays for arriving and departing shuttles. Other protuberances and jutting parts looked as if some giant had stuck on bits and pieces randomly.

Attached to the station, a large spaceship floated in tandem.

Trey explained that it had formerly been owned by a Senator Brandon, which the government had confiscated after he went to prison. They had completed it just in time to use it as a quarantine to prevent the aliens bringing in any diseases or alien fauna that could damage the planet's ecosystem. There was still another, the original space station, the Alysian Station, where many lived or worked on space experiments and other low gravity projects, but it orbited farther out from Alysia.

Inside the shuttle, Alain sat stuffed into a small seat. Trey lounged next to him in an aisle seat, his legs dangling out. The lack of gravity played havoc on Ailain's body. His head ached and his stomach felt as if he was going to throw up at any moment. In addition to his physical discomfort, a mixture of grief, hopelessness, and finally anger marched back and forth through his thoughts until only the hard, cold anger remained. He closed his eyes in exhaustion and collapsed into unconsciousness.

After a time, Trey tapped him on the shoulder to let him know they'd be docking soon. They entered the orbiting space station, one that hadn't existed before. He knew he would wake up soon and find it all a crazy dream. He pinched himself hard, but nothing changed, except for the added pain. He stood up stretching out cramped muscles and tagged behind Trey as they disembarked.

Getting through entry at Earth2 Station proved easy as someone influential had pulled strings. Trey jerked out a caller and started to argue with whoever was on the other end; probably trying to convince someone to provide lodging.

Once inside the station's habitat, Ailain surveyed the area with interest. He felt the lightness of the gravity, although everything stayed down on what passed for the ground. Still, the extra bounce in his step threw him off balance. He noticed Trey adopt the shuffling glide used by others, and Ailain copied the gait, finding it easier to walk that way.

Inside, corridors twisted and turned in surprising directions, made even more confusing by the unfamiliar gravity. Out on the loading docks, all had appeared quiet, but as they moved inside, away from the docks, life stirred. Rundown storefronts sold used and shoddy looking wares. Various odors of unfamiliar chemicals, stale oxygen and human stink mingled in the air. He caught a whiff of cooking food that set his stomach growling with hunger as they passed several flashy eateries.

Then he saw the Terrans. They didn't look so very alien, yet somehow they were. They possessed a human form: two eyes, a center nose, two arms with a hand at each end, a torso, and long legs containing feet at the bottom. The basic configuration appeared the same as any Alysian. They all tended to be pale of skin and almost spindly thin with hardly any body hair except on their head. If they had hair at all, it was close-cropped. At first, they seemed all the same, but then he noticed the subtle differences between individuals. Small and neat, they walked with a gliding shuffle that spoke of an extended knowledge of maneuvering in low gravity. Some of them clustered in groups where everyone wore the same outfit and looked exactly alike.

Several females slouched along the corridors in neon bright skirts that barely covered their personal parts. Heavy makeup masked their faces, and they wore elaborate earrings hanging from humanlike ears, while jangling bracelets encircled two slender arms. These female Terrans acted much friendlier than the others acted and often would stop a male to smile and talk to him.

"Hey, are they…?" his voice trailed off.

"What do you think?" Trey grunted, embarrassed. A few called out to them, but Trey picked up his pace, dragging him away as he tried to sneak another peek.

The cacophony of an alien language reached his ears as they approached the busier parts of the station. The odd guttural speech sounded like barking arks to Ailain. Surprisingly, he didn't see any children or old people anywhere. Many Terrans wore a vacant, vapid expression he found disconcerting. He didn't know if it was their mental state or the effect of various attachments worn about their bodies. Just about everyone he saw carried some sort of electronic apparatus plugged in somewhere on their body. The whole scene made him feel as though he walked through a surreal science fiction vidcast.

Trey still argued on his caller as Ailain slowed down to linger at a display of food just inside a glass window. The food looked odd—as if it weren't real, but delicious smells wafted out onto the streets and set his saliva glands gushing. Inviting music resonated from inside the store and streamed outside, to snatch for his attention. He stopped, mesmerized by the compelling music and delicious smells.

Trey kept striding on at a fast clip but then whirled around when he noticed the boy's absence. Angrily, he rushed back, grabbed Ailain by the arm, and dragged him along next to him without missing a beat of his conversation.

A wave of weariness swept over Ailain. He just wanted to sit down and rest.

Pocketing his caller, Trey eased up the pace. "We'll take the TC and then the elevator. Just a little further and we'll be there."

"TC?"

"Transit car."

They arrived at some tracks where a series of small, open rail cars approached. "Hey, looks like a roller coaster! Cool." Ailain's interest sparked.

"But hopefully not as exciting. Hop in." Trey swiped a card through a slot on the arm of their seat."

Once they were settled, Trey leaned back in his seat. "We're going to have to change your name." He inclined his head forward and peered at him anxiously. "Someone has put red flags all over the name 'Ailain Stone.' Why don't we call you Kayse? That's a good alias for you."

"Kayse?" Ailain wrinkled his nose. "Why the frag would I want to change my name? Why red flags? Kayse?"

Trey paused. "Okay, you need to know a few things in order to understand what's happening."

"Gee whiz, that'd be just great; because right now you've got me totally confused about my entire life."

Giving him a sharp look, Trey explained. "Actually, you were adopted. Those people you saw killed weren't your biological parents. They took care of you just like real parents, mind you, but they weren't. The Stones liked the name Ailain and named you that when they adopted you. Now, we need to change it to protect you, and Kayse is as good as any. Okay?" Trey stared at him, a strange unidentifiable emotion flitting across his face. It held pain but also caring.

Ailain blinked in shock. *Adopted? Not his real parents?* The world tilted crazily. He glared at Trey. "I don't believe you. They were my real mom and dad. I don't care what you say." Yet deep down, he knew Trey was right. "I should be called Ailain. That's my given name." A stubborn streak emerged. He desperately wanted this to all go away.

In a firm tone, Trey disagreed. "Too dangerous. Better to call you something else. Kayse is a cool name. You got a better one? Give me something better then."

"Never thought about it. Why would I ever think I would need another name?" But for some reason, Kayse sounded good. It sounded cooler than Ailain.

"No, I suppose you wouldn't have had a reason until now." Trey rubbed his forehead. "Let's use the name Kayse until it's safe and talk about the other stuff later."

"Sure, okay, Kayse is fine if it's so life and death. I'm just not used to it."

"Great. Kayse it is." Trey let out a relieved sigh. "Now remember not to tell anyone your other name, and I mean anyone. Don't say a word about your former life. Especially not about what you did—you know the trick."

Through a haze of exhaustion, Ailain noticed an improvement in the surroundings as they rode up higher, or maybe inwards, or was it outwards? He kept getting confused about direction, due to gravitational differences, and disoriented because of the station's spinning motion.

Finally, Trey tapped him, and they exited the Transfer Car before a series of residential entrances. Trey coded in a number on a panel at one entrance. A door opened onto a long hallway with plush carpet and live greenery at various points along the wall. Greenery on a space station would be hard to maintain, so he expected it was a sign of prestige. They walked down the carpeted hall until they came to a panel with an engraved gold plate that said: Captain Elise Fujeint Steele and Dr. Richard DeVane Steele.

An argument appeared to be in full-blown progress on the other side.

Chapter 5

Trey palmed the guest plate. The argument stopped abruptly, and the door eased open. A tall, slender, dark-haired man with a long-nosed aristocratic face peered out at them. His narrowed gray-blue eyes took in the pair of them as he irritably waved them in. Ailain recognized him as an Alysian, most likely from the Democratic Union, and probably from the Glendalia region with that pale complexion and the sharp facial features. His mother had come from that area, or his adopted mother, he amended.

Oh Fate! No. They'd been his parents and they'd always be, no matter what anyone said. He took a deep breath to ready himself.

The man looked familiar, and Ailain felt positive he'd seen him before, somewhere on a vid program or in a flash profile. Something political. Someone famous. Next to him stood a trim, no nonsense woman. She wore short-cropped auburn hair and had a refined, well-balanced, almost perfect face. Her outstanding feature was a pair of stunning violet eyes fringed with lush eyelashes. She appeared small and dainty, but her eyes reflected intelligence and strength.

"Have you lost your mind?" was their host's inhospitable greeting. He spoke perfect Unis. Ailain understood every word, and suddenly he felt on familiar ground. Straining to understand the language spoken on the station had been disorienting and stressful. Here was someone from home, someone he could understand. He almost wanted to cry in sheer relief.

"Lost my mind and everything else," Trey responded, waving Ailain, now Kayse, into a comfortable chair for which he stumbled gratefully forward. He sat down with a sigh, rubbing his eyes. The station air must have irritated them to make them so red and watery.

"Kayse, this is Dr. Richard Steele and his wife, Captain Elise Fujeint."

"Elise Fujeint *Steele*," she corrected. Both paused and nodded at him.

"And this is Kayse." Trey waved grandly at him, as if presenting some great gift. Kayse wiped his nose with a sleeve and peered up at the looming man who frowned down at him.

"You need to take him to the authorities," their disgruntled host advised. No welcoming smile graced his face. "When I offered to locate him through the Timelab for you, I didn't think you would dump him on my doorstep as a thank you."

"I believe I.N.Sys is compromised," Trey shot back. "Richard, those guys snatched Jeremy right in the middle of Tygel's Space Center, for Fate's sake. They must have had important connections to make so nervy a grab and then carry out a double murder. For me, the truly astounding part is that we haven't caught them yet."

Trey paced back and forth and then stopped in front of the dark-haired man. "No one, after all this time, knows who did it, nor do they seem to care. He was supposed to be the Admiral's grandson. You would think that would give some pause. I'd say only someone high up in government or on the inside of I.N.Sys; someone desperate enough to attempt it might have managed it—or a maniac, perhaps. Or all of the above. I've done some of my own poking about, and for over twenty-eight annuals, I.N.Sys has been ineffective in finding out who the perpetrators were. I find that fact incredible."

Putting his hand out, Richard tried to calm his guest down. His eyes flicked to Kayse, revealing concern, and then focused back on Trey. "Hey, remember that other events took precedent. Alysia is still trying to sort out all the environmental problems and weather tantrums brought about by the comet hitting our moon. Trace did his best to find the killers, but the case got overruled by other more urgent matters."

"Conveniently."

Richard paused and took a deep breath. "Maybe the kid should wait in another room while we sort stuff out."

Rubbing his forehead, Kayse spoke up. "I'd prefer to stay, sir, and understand what's happened, maybe have a say. It's my life here you're deciding."

With a focused gaze on Kayse, Richard said, "You must realize that I'm not in a stable political position right now, and it's going to get worse, which may cause further problems for all of us. Director Walker can take you under his wing and use I.N.Sys to protect you."

Trey shook his head. "The notorious Trace Walker is losing control of I.N.Sys, and I'm not so sure he would be able to protect Kayse. Trace does things by the book to a fault sometimes. He would be required by the law to remand the kid and put him in protective custody, which would tie Kayse up right where someone could walk in and grab him. If they are as brazen as I suspect, they'd certainly try."

"It wouldn't be that easy."

"A double assassination and kidnapping in the middle of a busy Space Center didn't appear too difficult for them."

That gave their host pause.

Kayse caught his breath and stared down at the floor, blanking out the anger and frustration that threatened to engulf him.

With a concerned glance his way, Trey continued, "Besides, Trace is tied up in those blasted committee hearings and distracted. Someone is out to shake up the current government and take control away from President Sean Courtland's bunch—and Trace is Sean's man to the core. You've seen the hearings. I'm surprised you haven't testified."

Grimacing, Richard nodded. "Most likely they're saving me for last, a final nail in the coffin. It's one of the reasons I can't keep him."

The Steele name began ringing bells in Kayse's memory. Then he caught his breath. Yes, Richard Steele, known as one of the most famous and wealthiest men in the Democratic Union, was the very person who stood in front of him. Kayse stared at a living icon of Alysian history. The icon appeared distraught.

"Look at him; really look at him." Trey gestured at Kayse. "Does he remind you of anyone?"

Suddenly, Kayse felt put on display, which made him uncomfortable. He brushed at the ridiculous maintenance uniform, ran his hand through his hair, and squinted at them.

Richard's eyes widened at the gesture and turned away. He angled a worried glance at his wife who stood next to them, listening with an avid interest. Returning his gaze to Trey, he said, "I *am* looking at him. I see *him* all too clearly. He was like a father to me. But you can't possibly know what you ask. It's not the same."

"It's *exactly* the same, and I'm suggesting nothing more than what he did for you when you were this kid's age." Trey pointed at Kayse, then faced Richard. "You're experienced in the Timelab and understand this better than anyone…. you know the situation, and you have resources very few do."

Elise's eyebrows rose.

"But he," Richard waved a hand in the air, "needed a gate for the transfer. You're telling me this happened without a gate?" Richard stared at Kayse, making him feel like some alien mutant. "*That is* different. Besides, I only worked as his assistant in the lab until he died. Afterwards, I took it over. Frag, Trey, I've put all that behind me. I'm trying to be a quiet man now."

"Balls! You went and married a Terran." Trey pointed to the petite woman who narrowed her eyes at him. "Not just any common Terran, but a starship captain type of Terran. According to some Alysians, you married an invading alien. You're right in the thick of things, just like always. Trace warned me about you ages ago. Said you always landed in the middle of any current crisis."

Straightening up and putting her hands on her hips, Elise replied indignantly, "Slow down, Trey. Just back off. We have a right to choose how we live our lives and not be pressured by others with their ignorant prejudices and demands. The reality is that I don't have time to care for another child, especially if he comes with heavy baggage. My work is critical, and the politics right now are explosive. It's too bad we have to refuse your request, but we have a young daughter to think about."

Kayse glanced at the attractive woman who stood next to Richard and detected a powerhouse of determination wrapped in a misleading package of dainty femininity until you studied her closer or heard her speak.

Richard made a random gesture toward the ceiling. "Elise, honey, I understand. It's just I owe the man so much…but you're right. Keeping the kid would be insane. I wouldn't know what to do with him. And I couldn't even begin to ask you to…" His voice dropped off.

She rolled her eyes at him.

Still confused by the conversation and growing tired of being constantly referred to as "the kid," Kayse jerked forward, ready to walk out on these people who obviously didn't want him. Trey shook his head and gestured him to stay.

Frustrated, Richard turned to Trey. "Okay, come to my study with me, and I'll make a few calls. Surely there must be someone who can take him…" his voice trailed off as the panel closed behind them.

Immediately, a loud argument burst forth on the other side. Kayse could barely make out the angry words. The shouting subsided as Richard started talking on a caller.

Kayse gazed at the woman who stared back in frustration. She didn't say another word, but she looked as if she was ready to yell at someone or throw something at the closed panel door. After observing him for a while, she finally heaved a sigh. Her face relaxed.

"Tough time?" she asked sympathetically.

He nodded and hiccupped.

"Me, too. It must have been scary by what I heard."

"Yeah, I saw two men murder my mom and dad. Now it appears they weren't my real parents. My whole life so far feels like a lie."

"Not a lie, just maybe an unsuspected path." She ran her hands down the sides of her slacks as if to smooth them out.

Closing his eyes, Kayse added, "There was lots of blood. And screaming and yelling." He shuddered at the admission, which made it so vividly real. He put his face into his hands to hide from everything around him, but it only made the disturbing images more intense. "That man is going to pay," Kayse said, through gritted teeth as he raised his face to her. "I'll see him dead for what he did to them if it's the last thing I do."

"You're far too young to be saying stuff like that," she said firmly, but he noticed an underlying tone of sympathy in the comment.

A tear slid down his cheek. He didn't even try to wipe it away. He rubbed his knee with a hand and heard his stomach growl.

"You sound hungry," she said briskly. "How about a nice bowl of soup? I have some soup in the galley." She considered him, a frown crossing her face. He could sense a battle going on within her.

She motioned with her hand, and he followed her to a table in a section lined with cabinets and cooking tops. She pulled two bowls out of a cabinet and lifted the lid to a pot sitting on a warmer. His mouth watered as he watched her ladle a steaming concoction of something with a wonderful yeasty smell into two bowls and place one in front of him on the table. Reaching into another compartment, she handed him a piece of warm bread. She gathered two lidded tumblers, added ice cubes and poured a beverage that caused a fizzing noise. Next, she pulled out a chair, sat down next to him, and handed him one of the drinks. She watched bemusedly as he hungrily devoured the meal.

Before she spooned soup into her own mouth, she murmured, "It's nothing personal. It's just a bad time to be taking on someone like you. There is a lot happening around us right now."

"Yeah, well," he said around a mouthful of bread. "A few things have been happening to me too, you know."

Sympathy flooded her face. "I have an idea. Angel mentioned that he was ready for a mission. He might take us on. To be safe, we should alter your appearance." She slanted her head to one side and gave him a thoughtful stare.

He knew when to shut up, so he just sat there and finished his soup.

As he was spooning in the last bit, Richard and Trey returned, still arguing. Richard cleared his throat, "Elise darling…"

Elise lifted her face toward him. "Did you find *anyone* who will take him?"

"I called everyone I dared." He shook his head.

"Why?"

"He's an unusual Alysian with a rare genetic condition. He could be dangerous. Certain people would like him dead while others want to use him. We won't keep him, if you don't want to."

She eyed him, a strange expression crossing her face. "I wish I could believe that, but you'd never forgive me, or yourself, if something happened to him; I see it now." She straightened up. "Okay, he'll stay, but I have conditions."

"Whatever you want." Richard smiled in relief and leaned in as if to kiss her.

Her hand went up in front of his face. "You'll have to arrange for several Terrans to be sponsored on Alysia if I do this. I want you to help accelerate Terran immigration to the planet. Then, we'll have to alter his appearance and make up a story about some cousin who is visiting. I want Jay Luttrell to do the operation. He'll do it right."

Trey and Richard glanced at each other. Something passed between them that made Richard frown.

Elise pursed her lips. "It appears he's at risk without our help, so we can't abandon him, but I'll need to know what makes him so dangerous in order to protect us. I won't leave him open to killers without trying to help, but he can't stay around long, not with our daughter living with us."

"He'll only stay for a short time while I sort it out," Richard assured her.

"Okay," she consented. "But I'll need to contact Angel and ask for help." She smiled.

He nodded mutely. In one way, Kayse felt relieved to have a place to stay, but in another, he felt as if he'd stepped into an even more dangerous situation…but it was his only option right now.

Richard winked at Trey. "This is what I get for marrying a spaceship captain who knows how to take charge."

Elise put an arm around him. "Not true. I used to be a ship's captain; now, I'm just a dutiful wife to a very famous and important Alysian who is occasionally foolish but always kind-hearted."

"This man is not fooled one bit," Richard retorted, kissing her on the cheek.

Past Richard's shoulder, Kayse noticed her eyes widened at the comment.

Richard pulled away with a grin. "I know who is boss around here."

Her shoulders relaxed just the littlest bit as she laughed.

The door chimed. Elise and Richard exchanged indecipherable looks. He went over to check the door monitor and said, "It's Tempest. She's come back from her tutoring."

<u>Chapter 6</u>

The door opened to reveal a harried looking young woman and a serene pre-pubescent girl blithely licking some sort of sweet. The girl's dark curly hair stuck out in a wild riot, and her brilliant violet eyes were rimmed with the longest black eyelashes Kayse had ever seen. They blinked at him and then widened. She gave him a slow smile as if she knew a secret. He felt suddenly uneasy under her intense gaze.

"I have to run." The out of breath tutor practically threw schoolbooks and a jacket at Richard and beat a hasty retreat down the corridor.

"Bye," said Tempest, not glancing back as she continued to stare at Kayse. "Who's he?" she asked as she came sauntering into the room.

Richard was hanging up the jacket and putting the books on a shelf. "This is…" Richard stopped and looked at his wife and then Trey.

Jumping in, Trey said, "This is Kayse Kiare, your father's second cousin." Kayse stared at him in disbelief. Trey made patting motions at him with his hand. It seemed he now had a new weird *last* name, too.

The amazing thing was both Dr. Steele and Captain Fujeint nodded at this introduction as if it didn't seem surprising at all. Kayse's mouth opened and then shut.

Tempest gave him the once over. "What's he doing here?" She nibbled on her sweet, leaving a bit of chocolate on an upper lip.

Good question. He wanted to know the answer himself, actually. He was curious as to why he was here and not down at Headquarters, giving a detailed description of how his father and mother had been murdered, not to mention his best friend kidnapped, oh say, twenty-eight annuals ago. He paused. They might question why he was just reporting it now. Yeah, well, that would be hard to explain and sound convincing.

"Er, Trey and I need to go over to the station administration to check out a few things." Dr. Steele delved back into the closet, pulled out two jackets and handed one to Trey. He paused and glanced at Kayse. "Kayse may be staying with us for a bit. So, maybe, you two kids could get to know each other, eh? We won't be gone long." He gave Elise a brief kiss on the cheek and hurried out.

Never had two men left a room so fast.

Kayse studied Tempest while she glared back.

"I'm really thirsty," she said to her mother without even looking at her.

Elise smiled. "I'll get you both some juice and let the two of you get acquainted. I'll be in the kitchen."

Alone with the kid, he didn't know what to say, but Tempest had no problem there.

"So how old are you?" she demanded.

"Why don't we sit down?" he responded, feeling awkward standing in the middle of the room during what was beginning to feel like an interrogation.

"You're taller than me." She stared up at him and didn't budge an inch.

"Yeah. I'm older too. I'm seventeen. And I'm trained in martial arts, so don't mess with me." He thought that might give him an advantage in the situation. Start strong. Let her know you're older and wiser and know some moves. Begin with an edge.

"Seventeen ain't that old. Besides, you're kinda chunky for being that old. Most guys at seventeen have more muscles from sports and stuff." She poked him in the midriff.

He winced. *Chunky!* He felt as if her sharp finger punctured his ego rather than poked his chest. Inhaling sharply, he realized this was not going to be easy. He gestured toward the chair again.

"So, I'm a work in progress, not perfection like you, huh. How old are *you*, hot stuff?"

"I'm almost thirteen."

"Almost! You're really twelve then," he shot back. "Some would consider that a child."

"Not if they knew what was good for them," she retorted, undaunted. "You're Alysian. My dad's from the Democratic Union. He's an important man there, and my mom was once captain of a real spaceship. She's important too, even though she's a Terran."

He wasn't sure what "even though she's a Terran" implied, and he didn't know what he should talk about with this kid. Trey had warned him not to reveal anything about himself or his background.

"Yeah?" he countered. Brief, succinct, and no information given. Although, it did sound a bit lame.

She smiled and fluttered those long, incredibly thick lashes. "Great. I want you to explain some things to me, then. Mary Ellen was talking about Alysian boys and the thing girls don't have, and I wanted to see one. Eddie showed me his, but he's just a Terran. It was ugly and not interesting at all. The way he talked about it, you'd have thought that it was something special. I wanted to see if Alysian boys were different. Alysian boys are always acting as if they're hot stuff. People keep saying Terrans are not as good, but I sure can't see how. Maybe their skin is paler, and they run toward a smaller size with not much hair on their heads, but I can't figure out what the fuss is all about. I figure it has to do with those private parts no one talks about. Maybe you could show me yours sometime—that's if you really are an Alysian. You look mostly normal to me, not like my Uncle Braden who some say can hear people thinking. Mom says some Alysians are unusual, too." She studied him curiously. "You weird like that?"

His jaw dropped open. A twitch developed in the corner of his eye. He tried to get his thoughts under control. "Let's sit down and talk about you instead. I'm sure you're far more interesting." Taking her by the arm, he practically pushed her into a large comfortable chair and sank down nearby, relieved to be sitting. He crossed his legs firmly and took a big breath. No stupid girl was going to make him into a peep show if he had anything to say about it.

As she squirmed into her chair, she chattered brightly, "Not really. I'm pretty boring, but we could talk about my mom and dad; they're famous."

He did want to know more about these people, since it seemed like he might be staying with them for a while, so he decided to encourage the conversation in that direction.

"So tell me about your parents," he ventured cautiously. He gave her a small smile—one you would give a very dangerous animal that you didn't want to excite.

"They don't say anything interesting in front of me, you know. It's like they want to be careful." She took another bite of the chocolate and deposited it into a pocket somewhere.

"What are they like?" he asked. It seemed like an innocent enough question.

"At night after they think I'm in bed, they like to play this game," she started.

He wasn't sure he wanted to hear this, but he didn't know what to say, so he didn't say anything.

His mistake.

"My dad tries to hide something in mom and mom makes a lot of noise about it."

His eyes widened in astonishment. She took it as a sign of encouragement.

"Sometimes, I don't think she wants him to hide it because she makes all these moaning noises, but then sometimes she yells, 'Yes. Yes.' I think that means she has won, and it's the end of the game, because he usually stops trying to hide it, and mom stops making the weird sounds." She eyed him and smiled.

He went all red and couldn't catch his breath, or maybe all his blood just left his brain for somewhere else. The image of the two of them having sex caused a strange reaction in his body. Panic was setting in when Captain Fujeint called from the dining area, saying the juice and muffins were ready.

"I don't think you should go into their bedroom at night," he choked out. "You really shouldn't be there. It's not a place for girls your age."

"Nothing's wrong with their bedroom," she announced firmly.

"No, no. I just think you should stay out of your parent's private room, especially at night," he ventured. Images of Elise and Richard started to fill his mind, and he had to get moving or soon the conversation would return to parts he didn't want to discuss, thank you. He'd learned way more than he'd wanted and nothing of what he'd hoped.

With a shrug, she agreed. "Okay. The game's getting boring anyway, but I bet tonight that they'll have lots of interesting things to say about you. A girl could find out some neat stuff if she listened in. I could come into your bedroom later and tell you all about it."

"No, no. You're not to come into my bedroom!" he yelled a little louder than he needed to with Captain Fujeint so close by.

"You sure are touchy about people being in bedrooms." she huffed.

"Come have a snack, kids." Her mother used her "captain's" voice to get them in.

Kayse practically ran out of the room toward what he hoped was some protection. Tempest trailed behind him.

Elise smiled at him as they entered, but he couldn't erase the image of her and Richard in a compromising position, thanks to Tempest. Elise's eyebrows arched, and she gave Tempest a sidelong glance. "I hope you two are getting along nicely," she commented.

"Kayse has some kind of problem in bedrooms," Tempest mumbled around a mouthful of muffin.

Elise eyed him speculatively. He could imagine all kinds of thoughts going through her head, none of them good.

"No, you don't understand," he protested. "It's not the bedroom particularly; it's about spying on people in bedrooms…" He stopped. The words had come out all wrong. Grabbing his juice, he drank it down in one gulp before he could say anything worse.

Elise gaped at him. "You and Tempest don't need to be talking about spying in bedrooms or even what happens in bedrooms," she said, attempting to sound stern but coming off flustered. Did the deepening furrows on her forehead mean she was reassessing his suitability as a houseguest?

"I didn't mean…" he fairly shouted. "Captain Fujeint, I…I didn't start the conversation."

"Please call me Elise. If we're going to be living together, it would make me uncomfortable if you called me Captain Fujeint all the time. Besides, I'm a Steele now. Elise Steele. And you should call my husband, Richard." She studied Tempest. "Who started this talk of bedrooms anyway?"

Tempest swung her legs. "I did, but he has the problem. I don't mind bedrooms. I thought he would like to know a little bit about you guys since he's going to be staying here. So, I told him about being near your bedroom the other night and what you said...and did." Tempest shrugged.

Elise's mouth dropped open and several expressions danced across her face, each more intense than the last and ending with anger. "Young lady, you're to stay out of our bedroom and not listen to private conversations!"

"Jeesh, don't tell me you're touchy about bedrooms too. What's with everyone?"

Elise glared at Tempest as the kid innocently munched a muffin.

Not much later, the men returned with grim faces. Soon after, Tempest and Elise left with Richard for a dinner engagement, promising not make a late night of it.

Trey seemed almost relieved to see them go.

Alone with Trey, Kayse finally got a chance to ask a few questions. Gesturing him over to a seating area, Trey fidgeted a bit, sat down, then cleared his throat. "Look, I have some business I've got to do, and you'll be safe here for a while." He tapped the arm of his chair. "You will need to keep your head down and stay out of sight. Someone is still searching for you. Elise is right. With all the surveillance vids here on the station, we'll have to do something to disguise you. Consider it a protective measure."

"All this has to do with that 'trick' you said I did, doesn't it?" he asked.

"Yah, the trick." Trey hesitated.

Staring at a far wall, Kayse blurted out, "Trey, I'm not stupid. I traveled in time. Somehow, I managed to jump forward twenty-eight fricking annuals, but I don't see why anyone would want to kill me for that."

"Think about it, kid." Trey raised an eyebrow. "Some are afraid if you can travel into the past, you might change everything. Others would like to use you in order to change events to benefit them. Knowing the future means knowing what companies get rich, what politicians win elections, and what stocks gain value. That kind of knowledge can make a man, or a group of men, very wealthy and powerful."

Trey rubbed an arm and gave Kayse a direct look. "They tried to kidnap Jeremy, not kill him. They only killed him because he wasn't you and could identify them." His gaze shifted around. "You are sort of unique. Well not unique, but not like most Alysians. Sorry, but I must leave you here with Richard for a while. He'll take care of you and, if you find you're in trouble, activate the beacon. I haven't had time to remake it, so just wear it around your neck and hide it under a shirt. I'll be back in touch after you return to Alysia. Meanwhile listen to Elise and Richard. If they want to change your appearance, or tell you to act a different way, then do it. Listen to them; it might just save your life."

"You're abandoning me?" An uneasiness surged through him.

Trey squeezed his shoulder to calm him down. "Hey, I'll see you before you know it. I got stuff I gotta do. Some of it will help us. Besides, I've gone to a lot of trouble already and called in a few favors for you, this place being one of them. So, behave and do what they say. Richard, he's okay, but he has his hands full at the moment with stuff. Keep a low profile and we'll figure this out."

Looking away, Kayse grumbled, "Just lay low until you straighten everything out, is that what you're saying?"

"Yeah, that'd be good." A relieved expression crossed Trey's face.

"Okay, I'll try."

The two sat in silence for a bit. Trey left for Richard's office to handle some business, and after a while, the Steeles returned. Trey bid a hurried farewell, accompanied by an acknowledging nod from Richard. Shortly after, over strenuous objections, Tempest headed to bed.

Kayse followed soon after. He found his sleep cubicle small and spare, but he was so tired neither his earlier brush with death nor a too candid young girl could keep him awake.

<u>Chapter 7</u>

He awoke in the middle of the night with someone tugging at his blankets. He sat up suddenly, not knowing where he was, or what time, or even what had happened. Then in a rush, it all came back. Maybe he'd had a bad dream, but when he studied the room, he wasn't home or in his old bed. He slept in a different bed, in some strange place that contained weird air and low gravity.

Scanning the darkened room, he sensed someone nearby. Could it be the murderer come to kill him already? A shadowy figure stirred by his bed, and he felt mounting dread, until he recognized the outline of a young girl. Tempest was fulfilling her threat of invading his bedroom.

"What are you doing here?" he hissed. "I told you not to come here in the middle of the night. Or any time for that matter."

"I have something important to tell you. I know how touchy you are about bedrooms, but this couldn't wait." She eased up onto the bed and sat down next to him. Eyeing him speculatively, she took a sip from a glass of water.

"You can't be in here with me," he said emphasizing each word.

"I couldn't help but wonder what kind of nightclothes you wear."

In disbelief, he peered at her through the dim light. "I usually wear regular pajamas, but I borrowed some because I didn't bring any with me." He peeped under the covers to make sure it was true, since he didn't remember too much about dressing for bed. He breathed a sigh of relief when he saw he wore a pair of oversized men's pajamas, probably Dr. Steele's; Richard, he amended. It felt awkward to call such a famous man by his first name. He'd need to get used to it.

"Mary Ellen said some guys don't wear clothes to bed at all. She said they sleep in the raw. It sounds gruesome, so I wondered if you did that or if Alysian guys wore something else weird when they slept."

"This is what couldn't wait?"

"Sure, in the morning you'll be all dressed. It would have been interesting if you were sleeping naked or did that raw thing. Eddie says most Alysian boys wear nightclothes, but then he said some don't. We usually live down on Alysia in a fancy house near Tygel, but I don't know much neat stuff about the boys there. Mary Ellen knows lots of stuff since she has two brothers and lots of boyfriends. She's older than me. More near your age. I don't have a boyfriend yet. She says when I'm older, I'll know a lot more and maybe have my own boyfriend too. If you play your cards right, I'll let you be my very first one."

"Get outta here," he shrieked.

Tempest put her hand over his mouth and leaned in. "Don't wake my parents. They need their sleep. They were up late talking about you."

"I need my sleep too," he mumbled.

"You should hear what they said. It was all about you."

He admitted to himself that he wanted to know what they were talking about, so he took a deep breath and nodded okay. She removed her hand.

Her curly hair tickled his face as she leaned in to whisper. "I think because they're bringing you into our family, they want to make sure you're going to look okay. I mean you look okay to me, but maybe not so good to my parents who may want some improvements since they're really famous and have to consider what people think."

His eyes widened, but he didn't say anything.

She went on, taking his silence for permission to continue. "I heard them say that they're going to change your hair, maybe your eye color and some other weird stuff. I thought you might like it if I gave you some pointers."

He didn't know what to say, so he just kept a dumbfounded silence and tried to shut his open mouth.

Wiggling in closer, she touched his eyelid. "You should go with green eyes. Mary Ellen's boyfriend has green eyes and he's dreamy. Also, I don't think you should let them change your cute dimples. Although I don't know how anyone can take out dimples. They're holes in your face, and you would look funny if they filled them with plaster or something. You should consider red hair. It makes a statement, you know. I've always wanted red hair myself, but since I'm pretty okay the way I am, I guess I'll wait at least until I'm as old as Mary Ellen before I ask mom again to let me dye my hair. She wasn't keen on red hair the first time I mentioned it…or the other times, either."

She stopped to take a breath and see how he was taking all this advice. He must have appeared thoughtful because she smiled. He was beginning to realize he hadn't thought much about what might be changed. It was worth a thought before they railroaded him into something more than a new name.

"I appreciate all your suggestions," he said trying to keep the tension out of his voice. "But you need to get off my bed and out of my room."

"I shouldn't tell you this part," she said leaning in.

"It's like I'm on a runaway train," he murmured.

"Since I'm half Terran, I have a certain obligation but I heard there's a really big secret on the Terran Space Station. Something they don't want Alysians to know about. I'm also half Alysian, so I'll admit to certain interests in that direction. That's why I'm going to tell you."

"So tell me," he said curiously.

"I don't know very much about it, only it's near where they're going to take you tomorrow, and there was some argument about whether to do something to you or give you something only Terrans can get. That's all I know. I'll listen in and see if I can find out more."

"No, that's okay. You really should stop sneaking around in their bedroom."

"How in the heck am I ever going to know what's going on around here if I don't do a little listening?"

He heaved a big sigh. She had a point.

"Are you sure you don't want to show me your thing while I'm here?"

"No!" he shouted.

A voice came down the hall. "Tempest, are you up?"

She rolled her eyes as he started to break out in a sweat. If they found her here in bed with him… She eased off the bed and tiptoed to the door.

"Go," he said hoarsely.

She leaned out the door into the hall corridor. "I'm just getting a drink and going to the bathroom, Mom," she whispered. "Better not be too loud or you'll wake up Kayse. He needs his sleep, you know."

"Okay, darling, get to bed," returned the sleepy reply.

He groaned and put a pillow over his head to better suffocate himself.

Chapter 8

The next morning, Kayse was making his way out of his room, dressed and ready, when murmuring voices drifted in from the kitchen. Wonderful smells of cooking mingled with tense whispers. Sidling past the living room furniture, he felt much like Tempest as he angled his way to the kitchen panel and waited, not wanting to interrupt.

"Finally, they want me to come testify before their fragging review committee," Richard commented, as he bit down hard on a wedge of toast. He stood helping Elise put together breakfast while venting loudly. "Those political cronies of Klaymore Townsend have assembled a hangman's committee to inquire into the governmental procedures used in dealing with the aftermath of that comet's collision. They're accusing former President Armstrong of improprieties in office, but they're actually going after Sean Courtland, since they don't want his party in office a second term. These so-called "inquiries" are nothing more than attempts to discredit the whole conservative side of Democratic Union politics, so Klaymore and his buddies can get a foot in the door."

Nodding at him, Elise poured another tumbler of kauf, offering a sympathetic noise.

Picking up his drink, Richard flourished it around. "I would like to know what they'd have done. We had to deal with two moons on a collision course because of that comet hitting one and changing its orbit. So then, our weather went wonky. We found out about a black market in wild crystal and, if that wasn't enough, an impending invasion of aliens. The people should be grateful Alysia is still intact; but no, they want an investigation so they can crucify those who did do something. I don't remember their political cronies doing anything significant at the time. Sat around with their thumbs up their—"

"Richard…" Elise warned, casting a glance around.

Taking a quick gulp of his drink, he continued his tirade. "Certain areas which have not rebounded as fast are saying Sean Courtland is discriminating politically when distributing disaster funds, and they want increased compensation. The committee is a sham!" Richard's voice inched up in volume.

"Calm down. You'll wake the kids," Elise said, sliding over a plate of food Kayse couldn't identify.

Richard stared down at the plate. "Now I have to drop everything and put a team together to account for every move I made from the time I first presented the crisis report until we finally cleared Thanos from orbit. I don't remember what I did yesterday, much less what I did fourteen annuals ago. It's a political maneuver, I'm telling you." Richard grabbed a fork and scooped up a yellow mass of something resembling scrambled eggs, but Kayse couldn't be sure. He'd no idea what these people ate.

"You'll do fine," she soothed.

Richard swallowed and waved his fork at her. "No, I won't. I always freeze up under interrogation. Experience says I don't do well. I get so nervous; I blurt out anything. What about you? I can't leave you here on this space station by yourself."

Patting his face, Elise answered, "I'll be fine here until I finish, and then I'll take the kids back down to Alysia."

"Your fellow Terrans never did stuff like that, did they?" Richard pushed some more food around and tore off a piece of toast as he glanced over at her.

Shaking her head, Elise laughed. "Of course not, we were always one big happy family. That's why over half the original members of the fleet didn't survive. At first, food and energy shortages on board the ships brought on by overpopulation created riots. Sterilization was a real popular solution, by the way, and caused lots of dissent. We implemented a lottery to defuse things, but people still protested. Next, disease almost put an end to the whole convoy before Jay found a cure. That left us with not enough people to run all the ships, and, most of the population now proved sterile. We needed to find our way out of situations just as dire, if not worse, and you better believe politics raised its ugly head." She tapped her plate. "I wouldn't want to be hauled in front of some investigative committee for some of the harsh decisions I made in order to ensure our survival. You go for the common good; eventually someone gets the short end of the stick and wants your head on a platter so they can punish someone for their pain."

Kayse noted she was getting heated as she described her own experiences.

After a sip of his drink and a nod of agreement, Richard added, "People are starting to believe all the ark dung they're dishing out, and now they're going to drag me into it and make me look like an idiot." Richard stared moodily at his wife. "As if that isn't enough, Trey has dumped Kayse in my lap, and I'm worried. That kid, considering his background, is explosive."

"We can change his appearance and think up a cover story. Something about me wanting a second child and legally not cleared to have another one biologically."

Richard leaned into his wife. "We could discuss that some more," he murmured. "You know, practice a little bit?" He sidled in. "I know some people who might waive the requirements if you want a second child. I could pull strings for us, Elise."

"Richard…" Her tone held warning.

"I'm not getting any younger, Elise."

"Well, right now you're acting awfully juvenile. We have our hands full with this new addition. Let me take Kayse to the lab and see what Jay can do."

Shifting back and grinning at her, Richard laughed, "Dr. Jay Luttrell, the miracle worker. He sure fixed me up. You're right; I've never felt healthier or better. That injection of his worked like a charm." Richard patted his chest. "I even think my hair is getting darker." He ruffled the hair on his head. "At least it stopped going gray so fast, and I've been feeling pretty frisky lately. Let's find some time tonight to be alone for a change."

"Mmmm, maybe I could arrange something," she murmured, kissing him on the forehead.

"I love you," he blurted out and reached for her.

Kayse decided maybe now was the time to stroll on into the kitchen and see what was cooking before things got too hot in there. He interrupted them in a clinch that was developing into some serious groping. When he coughed, they both jumped apart. Elise smoothed down her blouse while Richard adjusted his shirt.

"K…K…ayse, I, er, didn't see you there," Richard stuttered. He cleared his throat and ran a hand through his hair.

"I was just wondering what was for breakfast," Kayse answered nonchalantly.

"Why don't you grab a plate and cup out of the pantry over there?" Elise pointed to a nearby panel. "Breakfast is just about ready."

He walked over to a small storage room, slid open the door, and leaned down to grab a plate, only to come nose to nose with a grinning Tempest.

"That fragging door jammed shut on me," she said stomping out. "I just went in to find some cereal, and the next thing I know, it locked on me." She brushed her hair back and glared at him. Kayse let a small smile curve his lips.

"Watch your language, young lady." Elise shook her head.

Richard walked over to the panel and slid it back and forth. "It's not supposed to lock," he said uncertainly.

Giving the panel a rap, Tempest commented, "Stuff on this space station breaks all the time. They built it in a hurry and didn't use quality material. No matter, Mom has breakfast going. What's cooking, Mom?"

"They are," Kayse muttered and grabbed a piece of toast.

Richard tossed him a quelling look. Elsie's face took on a blush color.

"Go get dressed first, young lady, and then I'll feed you breakfast," Elise ordered.

"I'm gone," she threw over her shoulder as she departed.

"I'll have someone come fix that panel." Elise ran it back and forth, frowning at it. "It's dangerous. Anyone could get stuck in there, and no one might find them for a long time."

"You believe her?" Kayse retorted in amazement. He sat down with a thunk. "You really believe her?"

"What do you mean?" Richard asked, puzzled.

Kayse stared at Richard who was helping himself to what Kayse dubbed "lumpy scrambled eggs." If he hadn't been so hungry himself, he would have passed on it, but his stomach was ready to eat soggy cardboard if necessary. With a deep breath, Kayse asked, "Does anyone around here ever pay serious attention to that girl?"

Richard snorted. "We listen way too much to her. In fact, I should warn you, she talks nonstop." He tapped a finger on the counter for emphasis.

"Yeah, that I figured out. No, I mean, have either one of you talked to her about stuff?"

"Stuff?" Richard gazed at him, wearing a confused expression.

"Yeah, you know, stuff a girl her age should know."

Elise and Richard stared at each other, perplexed.

"What stuff are you talking about exactly, Kayse?"

"Girl stuff, boy stuff," he said, plunging a fork down into the pale, yellow mass of food and filling his mouth.

Actually, it tasted good.

Understanding dawned on their faces.

Frowning at Richard, Elise said, "The school teaches all that biology stuff. I saw it in the curriculum. She's too young right now. Shipboard doesn't teach sex until…until…" She turned to question Richard. "No one has explained sex to her yet?"

"Elise, honey, we took her out of school to come here. My guess is her current tutor isn't covering it. She's still too young to know about sex," he said confidently. "She's only ten. Or is she already eleven?" He glanced over at Elise.

"She says she's almost thirteen," Kayse countered. "She wants me to be her show and tell, and I, I don't want to. Until someone explains to her, she will keep asking me." He blushed. "I refuse to be her means of sexual research."

Richard choked and Elise blinked. They stared at Kayse who continued his argument. "I'm grateful you took me in, but she wanted to examine me naked. It was embarrassing. I won't do it." Kayse picked up his juice and gulped it down. He didn't know what he would do if they threw him out. He couldn't think of another place to go, much less what he would need to know to cope with a world twenty-eight annuals into the future. The idea terrified him.

"She isn't ten?" Richard asked. "I thought she was only ten, or possibly eleven."

"I'm almost thirteen," Tempest said, coming through the door, now dressed. "What are we talking about anyhow?"

"None of your business, young lady. We're getting our breakfast and getting ready for the tutor." Elise tossed a warning glance at Richard.

"You said I could go with you to fix Kayse," Tempest protested indignantly.

"I said no such thing. Besides, we're not 'fixing' him; we're just going to alter a few things to make him look a little different."

"You promised," Tempest wailed, a stubborn expression developing on her face. "You told me I could go. I remember you saying it. You're just getting old and forgetting things," she grumped.

Elise inhaled sharply. Her voice tightened as she said, "I promised no such thing, and I don't forget! My memory is functioning just fine. Finish your breakfast. Amy's due any time now."

"Getting old and forgetting stuff, I'm telling you. You're scaring me," Tempest muttered under her breath.

Elise glared at her. She looked like she might burst into flames at any moment.

Just then, the entrance chimed and an attractive young woman with bright blue eyes and golden brown hair swept in. Kayse gazed up appreciatively and bestowed a warm smile on her. Tempest slammed her drink down on the table, and Amy's sunny smile dimmed. Kayse saw Tempest glare at him. He decided to put his head down and finish off whatever it was he was eating.

Thankfully, they soon left.

"Elise, are you sure you're going to be all right without me for a few rotations? You could go with me now, you know." Richard said with concern edging his voice.

"No, I need a few days. I must finish the paperwork on my final selections. Ailey De Vey hasn't finished her interview with Jay and I have to inform Admin about some routine maintenance issues that concern the ship. I'll need your signature on the immigration papers, by the way. Finally, I should take care of Kayse. They don't have the expertise to do what has to be done down there on Alysia."

"We're pretty advanced in plastic surgery," Richard protested. "Besides, I don't know if I should leave you alone with Luttrell up here. I heard rumors about you and him."

A snort came from Elise. "You can trust me, Richard. I'm a happily married woman now, but I'd rather Jay take care of this. Let's keep the surgery away from Tygel Med Center. That's the only place on your planet advanced enough to do such an operation, and Jay mentioned that he'd rather not go there. My ship is secure, and no one knows anything about Kayse there. We'll be fine. I'll join you in a few. Don't worry. Remember, I used to captain that ship. I'm safer there than down on Alysia."

"I can get Trace to send up some security," he offered. "I'm uneasy putting Kayse solely in Terran hands."

"Richard, these are my people. I'll see that no harm comes to Tempest or Kayse. As an extra precaution, I'll get in touch with Angel to watch over them. After we return home to Alysia, then we might need Trace's help."

She put her hands on her hips. "You meet with Trace and Sean. Devise a package that will get the President's constituency back on a firm footing. If Klaymore Townsend gets into office, Terrans will be facing serious problems."

Richard nodded and said, "I know Townsend hates Terrans. He's stirring up the whole Democratic Union against them with wild accusations, like saying they plan to take over the planet. It's one of the main platforms he's running his election on."

She narrowed her eyes. "I wouldn't put it past him to try to exterminate us completely if he gets elected. He keeps forgetting we're the original stock. He should have more respect for his ancestors." She sniffed.

Richard grinned. "You're one tough lady, darling. No wonder they made you a captain." He kissed her on the forehead, passed through the living room, and gathered some luggage sitting by the door.

"Make sure you keep in touch," she said. "And sign those papers."

"Don't worry," he responded, waving at her and blowing a kiss.

She shooed him out the door and closed it. Leaning on it, she wiped her brow. "Two down and one to go," she muttered as she turned to consider Kayse.

He gazed innocently back at her.

"You do understand why we have to do this procedure, don't you?"

"Not really. You say that I'm in danger. How do I know I can trust any of you? Trey seemed awful eager I not say anything and rushed me here for a new identity."

"Sit down, Kayse." She motioned to a comfortable chair in their small living room just off the kitchen. "Richard said that you know you're not the biological son of Anjie and Brad Stone."

The world wavered a little around him at the chilling confirmation. "Trey said something along those lines, but I wasn't sure that he was telling the truth."

"He was."

"Then who are my real mother and father? Why are they too afraid to tell me? Were they criminals? Monsters?"

"I don't know about that, but I will tell you what I do know, if it helps."

"And what is that?"

"Richard only told me part of it, but what he explained was that you're valuable because of some genetic condition." Elise leaned in toward him. "What is this special genetic condition you have? What can you do, that no one can?"

He froze. Trey had been emphatic that he tell no one about his Talent. Now, here she was protecting him, yet something held him back from disclosing to her his time traveling stunt. "I don't know," he lied.

Her brows furrowed as she sat back. "You can come and go around here, but be careful and avoid attracting undue attention. The alterations I have proposed to Dr. Jay will make you physically different—and only you, Trey, Richard, and I will know who you were from before."

"Tempest will know."

Shaking her head, she answered, "Not really. She only knows you as Kayse. You'll need to learn to cope with the changes, but you'll adapt. Many of my people have received enhanced bionics and have done very well. You won't be changed inside. You'll still be the same person you always were."

He shrugged. *Yeah, and how well did I know that person, anyway?*

She continued, "Take that for a mercy. Several had other ideas. Some talked about a mind-wipe, and others wanted you dead."

"Who *were* my parents?" He stared at her. "What did they do that was so terrible?"

"Richard didn't tell me all the details. It's connected to some deep Alysian secret. I think it has to do with you having a special ability. There are rumors of people on Alysia who carry what they call "Talent." You may be a unique gene line out of the Alysian gene pool, and what people don't understand, they fear. Take it from one who knows." She smiled at him coolly. "Jay has never seen an Alysian with Talent; he's only heard the rumors, so I think he'll be very interested to meet you and study your DNA."

"Is there any information that I could find on these Talents?" he asked.

"If I were a curious lad, I'd use the web and start with Tygel's Med Center. The Med Center was founded to study and protect Talents. I know they keep records on genetic lines there, but I would be very cautious when poking around their system. Lures and traps might be programmed into that database. Trey suspects someone is out there waiting and watching for you to make a move. When you do, you can bet they'll try to come after you. So, be careful." She dusted off her hands and went to the kitchen to put away the breakfast leavings.

He trailed after her. Setting elbows on the counter, chin cupped in his hands, he said, "Smoky green eyes then."

"What?" She turned around.

"If you're going to change me, then change me for something better. Give me smoky green eyes and a thinner, more refined nose. Dark hair, of course. Tempest said I was flabby, so I'd like to have muscles and not be so fat."

"You've got a shopping list? Should I be writing all this down somewhere?"

"Oh, that would be great!"

She glared at him. "Listen to me, Kayse. Don't ever forget that I used to be a starship captain. No matter what I say to Richard, I don't take orders from an out-of-nowhere kid."

He leaned back a bit, daunted by her ferocity. "Haven't forgotten you're in charge," he said with delicacy. "I'm just putting in some hopeful requests. It isn't often a kid can go shopping for a new look. I want to make sure that this doctor friend of yours doesn't turn me into a weirdo."

A thoughtful expression crossed her face. "I'll think about your suggestions," was all she said. She downed her drink, finished wiping off the counter, and grabbed a jacket. "I'm going to make arrangements. Use the teacher module. Richard showed you earlier how it works. Catch up on Terran and Alysian history. Learn the Terran language too. There is a tutorial there. I'll be back later if you have any questions. Remember, knowledge is power."

He watched her leave.

And then, sometimes… well, sometimes it just causes pain.

Chapter 9

Elise was gone no more than a few intervals when the chime sounded. Kayse looked up as Tempest breezed in. Taking off his headset, he quirked an eyebrow at her.

"Ready for lunch? she asked. "I have some time available, and I thought I could show you around the station. You probably have cubicle fever already so stretching your legs will do you good. Gravity's light here, and your bones will leach if you don't exercise them."

He stood up from the chair and scrunched up his eyebrows at her. "Does your mother know you're loose?"

With a casual shrug, she opened a clothes closet and said over her shoulder, "Hey, don't look a gift ark in the mouth, Bud." Her eyes glinted, by which he suspected Elise had no clue that her child had wandered off the leash. Tempest needed a babysitter to watch out for her unless he planned to leap at her, wrestle her to the ground, and then lock her in that closet…. followed by a boot out the airlock when Elise found her there. He'd no idea where Elise was or how to locate her to let her know Tempest was out wandering loose. Besides, the idea of getting out and doing a looksee sounded very attractive.

"Here's a jacket." Tempest flipped him a dark blue top. "They keep the public area cool to save on the heating cost, so usually you need a jacket or coat outside of living quarters."

"Thanks," he said as he slipped it on. The sleeves ran long, but otherwise, it did the job.

As they descended in the elevator, their surroundings became dingier and rougher. The soft carpeting gave way to hard plascrete. The greenery grew sparser and the smell got ranker. Soon the stink of sweat and unidentifiable chemicals permeated the air. A cacophony of sounds caught his attention. An air blower coughed in the distance, nearby voices murmured in clustered groups, feet shuffled on the moving walkway, while an open-roofed TC whizzed by on metal tracks, heading for the next station.

Tempest waved for a ride, and a Transfer Car carrying two Terrans in the back slid to a halt in front of them. She angled an eyebrow at him and gestured that he should step into the front car.

He climbed in.

She bent over to slide a plastic disc through a slot and, with a lurch, they took off.

He reached to grip a hand bar and tumbled into a seat beside her as she laughed. "I've always wanted to eat at the Ship Captain's Lounge, but Amy won't take me there. Good thing she had a medical appointment, or so she says." She winked at him. "She seemed anxious about the time, so I told her that mom was on her way to pick me up and she should go on and not be late."

"You lied!"

"I was being creative. I didn't want Amy to be late, and mom *will* be picking me up…just a little later than Amy thinks. I'd rather be here with you than sitting in some doctor's office. This will be a grand adventure. Besides, you can protect me if anything happens. You bragged that you knew some martial art moves."

"If you think something could go wrong, then we shouldn't go," he replied as he stared at blurred scenery whipping past.

"Nonsense. It's perfectly safe. They have the wildest drinks and the music is frantic. The floor is clear, right on through, and all you can see, if you glance down, is deep space. They say if you can stay in the Captain's bar for more than fifteen intervals without getting space sick, then you can fly in a space ship. My dad can't do it. He gets sick in space, even in low orbit."

"You want to fly a spaceship?"

"Of course. I'm my mother's daughter, aren't I?" She fluttered her long lashes at him.

"Yes, you are," he said tight-lipped. "It carries a responsibility for how you behave. I was an Admiral's grandson and…" He stopped and closed his eyes. "Never mind. Maybe not," he whispered.

"Hey, quit ruining our fun."

Not saying anything further, as the TC started to slow in the more congested areas, he returned to studying the station and its inhabitants. Terrans appeared to be a pale-skinned people with odd rounded eyes. They were smaller than Alysians and frailer looking. Delicate. They moved with an easy grace in the lighter gravity. One appeared to glower at him as the car slowed, nearing its destination. He sensed hostility in the gaze and was disturbed when the TC stopped to deposit them in front of a raucous dining establishment. As he got off, he could hear the buzz of conversation and the sound of loud music coming out of the place. Standing in front of the entrance, his anxiety increased as he studied the place.

"I'm not carrying any credits," he said, abruptly.

"Then you better stick with me." She flashed a wide grin, "Because I have lots."

"Is there an age limit?" He became suddenly nervous about escorting a young girl into what appeared to be a more adult establishment than he'd expected.

"I'm the Captain's daughter. That's her ship attached to this station. They'll let me in, if I insist."

Oh, great.

They pushed their way in, as several eyes centered on both of them. He was remembering Trey's admonition not to call attention to himself. They'd have him out on the streets in no time at this rate. The bartender blinked and waggled a few frantic fingers at the hostess while Tempest nonchalantly inspected the room. A slim, pale girl with short red hair and dimples came up to them and indicated she would escort them to their table. It was in the back in a dimly lit corner.

Good.

The music had an offbeat tempo and sounded edgy, but no one seemed to be paying much attention to it anyway.

"They serve fresh hydroponic stuff here," Tempest enthused, scrolling through a screen on a nearby wall that displayed an array of food choices. "Mary Ellen said they serve the best salads here." She tapped an image of leafy goodness. "Also, I'm thinking of drinking 'the Bomb Blast.' Cool name. Bonus is that they speak Unis. My Terran is a bit rusty, to tell the truth, and I don't know a lot of words."

A rare thing.

With a hand to his chin, he leaned in to study the menu with her. "Better not drink anything your mother wouldn't approve of," he admonished, squinting at the drinks and wondering what was in them. By the look of the vivid names on most of them, he wasn't too sure *he* should order any.

Their waitress returned immediately with what appeared to be an appetizer. Tempest hummed as she read the menu, while Kayse asked about the specials. The waitress mentioned a soy dish that mimicked beef. That didn't sound too appetizing. The image showed a brown lump with gravy oozing over it. Tempest pointed to something on the menu, which caused the waitress to pale. She gave a small shake of her head. "There is an age requirement on that order," the waitress said stiffly.

Wrinkling her nose and frowning, Tempest huffed. "Well, maybe not. I'll just have the 'Garden of Eden Salad' and cold filtered water."

The waitress raised an eyebrow toward Kayse. Not knowing what to order, he said, "I'll have the same."

Suddenly all smiles, she strode away before they had time to change their minds.

"Next time, I'll have the 'Deep Space Explosion.' I should be old enough then," Tempest grumbled. Tapping the table, she gave a smile. "It doesn't matter because Mary Ellen especially suggested the salads, and she'll be *so* jealous if I eat one; even more, when I tell her that I had it with a real live date." Tempest grinned at him.

The thought startled him. He hadn't considered this a date. It was more like a babysitting arrangement, as far as he was concerned. The music stopped and as the set began changing, the door opened again. Kayse turned to stare at the view of stars through the floor, almost hypnotized by the brilliant points of light, when he realized the room had suddenly gone quiet.

Raising his head, he saw four burly men swagger in, obviously Alysian. One sported a hooked nose and shifty eyes, another had a receding hairline with a small earring in one ear, while the third kept nervously glancing around and tossing dirty brown hair back over his shoulder. The fourth, and scariest of the gang, hooked a leg around a barstool as he checked out the place. He surveyed the room until his hard, dark eyes locked on Tempest. His big size and bulging muscles threatened violence. The ugly jagged scar over his right temple, along with a partially smashed nose, gave him a menacing appearance that indicated he had probably been in a few brawls during his life.

Kayse's stomach clenched and his heart began drumming rapidly. He jerked his eyes away and gazed deliberately elsewhere.

No refined gentleman there. And on top of all that, the ruffian showed an interest in Kayse's corner, causing the hair to rise on the back of Kayse's neck as the tough continued staring at them.

Scanning the room, Kayse noticed several Terrans paying their bill and leaving. A few wandered in, saw the four at the bar and left. The place began to thin out, and Kayse broke out in a nervous sweat.

With a wide grin, the one with the scar picked up his drink from the bar, nudged a companion, and started to amble over in their direction.

A few more patrons left, and the restaurant got quiet. The bartender waved at the band, encouraging them to start up again, and a few strands of music warbled out.

"You're a bit young to be hanging around here, girlie," the thug drawled as he sauntered up to their table and stopped to sip his drink. He spoke Unis and gave Kayse a wink. Kayse eyed him askance. The thug appeared part Alysian but mostly bad.

Tempest had been going on about something to do with Mary Ellen when she stopped abruptly, cocked her head and scowled at the intruder. "Excuse me, we're talking here," she said imperiously.

Ignoring her comment, the interloper focused on Kayse and rumbled, "You're a mighty brave little boy to be bringing such a pretty young thing like her in here. These folks don't like Alysians around here, and by the looks of things, you're out of your neighborhood."

"My mother owns this bar," Tempest interrupted haughtily. "It's called the Ship Captain's Lounge, and she is the ship's captain. We have a perfect right to be here."

"Tempest…" Kayse warned.

"Your mother knows you're here?" He shook his head. "I bet not. Maybe she don't worry much about slave traders abducting you."

"Slave traders?" Kayse croaked. "No one said anything about that to me." He glared at Tempest.

The man sloshed his drink around, spilling some on Tempest. She pulled out a napkin and dabbed at her outfit. "Hey, watch it, bub," she said angrily. "The garb's new."

He gave out a nasty laugh. "Yeah, all kinds of ruffians prowl this place. You need to be careful. A pretty little thing like her would fetch a nice price." He pointed at Tempest who looked up and narrowed her eyes at the blunt finger, almost going cross-eyed as it landed on the tip of her nose. "In fact, my own Terran mother was abducted near here right in front of me when I was this girl's age. Alysian slavers beat and raped her. So, I have a special reason to find a few nice Alysian girls and return the favor."

"No thank you," Tempest responded, turning back to Kayse. "Besides, I'm half Terran. Try someone else." She fluttered fingers at him.

"Part Terran? Even better. The Terran slave trade is always looking for pretty, young girls. They like a little spunk and energy too… so fun to work it out of them," he said, wrapping his fingers around her arm.

"Let go of me, scumbag." Tempest jerked her arm back.

The attacker, outraged, leaned in and snatched her around the waist, tucking her up under his arm. Tempest let out a blood-curdling scream and kicked about wildly.

With a colorful curse, their attacker jerked her away and shook her. "Hold fragging still. Stop that!"

Shaking with half anger and half fright, Kayse stood up and shoved back his chair. "Put her down," he demanded. Two of the gang, who now followed their leader over, closed in threateningly on either side of him. The thug laughed harshly and swung around to leave, but was blocked by a black form emerging out of the shadows of a dark corner.

The being wore a black silk jacket with dark pants tucked into black boots. A black hood fell back off the head, revealing a crown of short-cropped tousled hair that glowed a pale color. Brilliant golden eyes glared at their attackers. Whether it was male or female, Kayse couldn't tell. Shadowed light played over a half-hidden face. The apparition smiled slightly, but the eyes remained cold. The voice, while soft of tone, held unwavering authority.

"He said put her down," the apparition ordered. "You're out of line once again, Kurt my friend, and if you don't start behaving properly, you're going to be a line edit in the station's registry."

"You don't scare me, Angel," Kurt blustered as he pushed his way past, trying to juggle a struggling Tempest. "Frag!" the bully shouted as Tempest bit down on an exposed arm.

"Put. Her. Down. Now!" spat out Angel.

"Make me," the arrogant response came as Kurt shifted Tempest and gestured for backup.

A quick step and the arm holding Tempest twisted to an odd angle. With a yelp, Kurt dropped her ungraciously onto the floor. In one smooth motion, Angel swept her deftly out of the way and faced her abductor.

She lay there, smart enough to stay put.

Two attackers came forward and grabbed at Kayse, but he ducked under their reaching hands and whirled with a roundhouse kick at the back of a set of legs that buckled and collapsed.

He rotated and delivered a chop against the neck of the second attacker, causing him to stagger back and grab his throat, gasping. The bartender reached out, caught the stumbling bully, and placed a gun to his head. He muttered a few choice words that Kayse couldn't translate completely, though the meaning appeared crystal clear.

A knife appeared in Kurt's hand as he lunged forward, but Angel merely sidestepped his attack and tripped him. The momentum of the large man kept him going as Angel danced around to his back and hefted a booted foot, shoving him to the floor with it.

Kurt fell, the breath going out of his lungs. His hand twisted and, as his body met the hard, smooth floor and slid, the knife dug deep into his chest. Blood oozed out, creating a red smear on the floor.

The bald bully tried to twist out of the barkeep's hold. They wrestled for the gun. But when the gun went off, the barkeep had a firm grip on the gun, as the other's body sank to the floor. The barkeep gave the ruffian a rough kick, but the body didn't move.

Their waitress started screaming as the remaining customers leaped from their tables to huddle against a back wall.

Farther down the bar, the hooked-nosed Alysian scampered out the door.

Rising from the floor, the long brown-haired attacker reached for a knife; but a shot rang out, and he slumped forward, a bullet in his forehead. Everyone left in the room gazed around, bewildered, but no one owned up to the kill.

Angel sighed as the body, formerly known as Kurt, took a final heave and went still. Shaking his head, Angel toed the body. "Not the way I wanted it to end, but karma will get you every time. Manny, clean this mess up and recycle the bodies. Do what you think is necessary. Maybe pass it off as a disagreement among criminal elements. Might save you and your sniper friend from a disagreeable arrest and trial experience. Up to you." A moneycard slid across the top of the bar. The bartender nodded, abruptly. Angel continued, "If anyone asks, they weren't here." He pointed at Tempest and Kayse. "I doubt anyone will even inquire, but if the authorities do, let me know. I'll be available." Again, the bartender nodded rapidly.

"Waste. Such a waste." Angel motioned to Kayse. "We take her back, *now*."

Kayse nodded with wide eyes and reached to lift Tempest off the floor. For once, she didn't speak. Kayse felt chilled at the thought that his ignorance of the bar and circumstances had just cost lives, and he didn't want to even think about what Elise might say when she found out.

Outside, silence prevailed as a car slid up to a stop, and Angel gestured them in. Sitting inside, he pulled out his caller saying, "Amy said for me to pick you up and call her when I'm ready to deliver you to the school's stop."

"Do I have to go back?"

"Troublesome child," Angel said it softly, but his disappointment came through loud and clear.

Tempest pouted. "I'm not a child."

A staring war ensued. Finally, Tempest glanced away as Angel shook his head.

Silence. Kayse felt Tempest shiver next to him. Recalling the dead bodies on the floor, ignited the memory of his parent's own bloodied and crumpled bodies, sending chills through him. The idea of Tempest being abducted shocked him. He started shaking and couldn't stop.

"Very stupid," Angel said louder.

Tempest gazed away. "I'm impetuous," she protested, rubbing an arm. "Everyone says so. I'll be thirteen soon, so I'm not a child."

"Then quit acting like one." This time Angel said it with an edge to his words. "Did you even stop to think about what you were doing?"

"I was hungry." Tempest sniffed and gazed out the side of the rumbling car.

"And did that ever include what the consequences might be?" Angel arched an eyebrow. "You knew what that place was."

"All right, so I wasn't thinking of the consequences." Tempest's eyes started to fill up with tears. "I just wanted to have some fun. Mary Ellen said…said that they served a great hydroponic salad. I didn't expect anyone to be *killed* there." Tears rolled down her cheeks.

Angel remained impassive. "Don't drop your tears on me. Those deaths are on your scorecard, not mine. I'm not responsible for the event; I was clean-up. Do you understand what happened there, and what else could have happened?"

"I was just sitting and eating lunch. I wasn't messing with anyone." Now the tears ran in rivulets.

"You went there for lunch?" Angel faced Kayse, his stare penetrating Kayse's very soul. "And just what were you thinking to take her there?" The golden eyes turned a stormy bronze. "What if those brutes had taken her? They almost did and would have, if I hadn't been there. Do you have any clue as to what might have happened to either of you? No, of course you don't. How could you and do what you did?" Angel crossed his arms and glared at them.

"It was her idea," Kayse protested. "I didn't know anything about the place." He turned to Tempest. "You almost got us killed."

Gone was the brash young girl. "I'm sorry. I won't do it again. Promise."

Angel nodded. "Most definitely you won't."

In the distance, a young woman jumped up and down, waving her arms wildly at them.

"Please don't tell mom," Tempest pleaded.

"Too late. Don't you know that, as far as you're concerned, she gets informed immediately?"

Tempest chewed her lip, and a frown creased her forehead. The TC pulled onto a sidetrack and, with a smooth motion, stopped in front of the waiting tutor.

Angel pulled what appeared to be a bracelet out of his pocket.

"Thank the Creator you're safe! I was frantic," Amy reached in to help Tempest out. Angel snapped the bracelet on Amy's wrist and then placed the other end onto Tempest's wrist. Startled, both girls jerked their hands away as they gaped at a pair of handcuffs.

"I don't have time to keep track of her on your watch too," Angel growled at Amy. "That's your job. Luckily, you called Elise, and she called me, or *your responsibility* would be slave material by now."

Amy's eyes widened. She jerked at the link, forcing Tempest to lurch forward.

"Oooww!" Tempest exclaimed.

"I'll give Captain Fujeint the key so you can unlock yourselves when you drop her off." Angel gestured to Kayse. "Fun's over. Go home."

"I can't. I don't know how to get there."

Tempest brushed hair back out of her face. "He's new here, Angel. You'll have to show him the way."

"So this fiasco *was* your call. Okay, where am I taking him?"

"To my dad's apartment. He's living with us. I just wanted to show him around... be a courteous hostess."

"So you decided to take him to The *Ship Captain's Lounge*?" Angel glowered at her.

"Poor choice, now that I think about it," Tempest admitted contritely as she jangled her manacles.

"Grievously poor," Angel spat out.

"We need to get going," Amy interrupted. She gave a murderous wrench on the bracelet as Tempest staggered after her, gazing back over her shoulder at them.

"Captain Fujeint's apartment it is," Angel said, settling back into a seat. "I hope neither she nor Dr. Steele are home. I don't want to go into the sordid details about what happened face to face with either one of them. That will be your job." A harsh smile turned his way.

"Tempest invited me to lunch. I thought she needed someone to watch her." Kayse tried to explain his actions. "She gave no indication that the place would be dangerous. She even hinted it was named after her mother."

"You hardly seem the bodyguard type," Angel mused. Abruptly, a soft smile lit his features, turning them almost feminine. Angel trailed a finger on Kayse's cheek, leaving a warm line down the side of his face. A low chuckle emitted from the mesmerizing creature's refined mouth. Kayse became aware of golden eyes with dark pupils rimmed in a faint lavender color. Once seemingly sharp cheekbones became more rounded and refined. The change in demeanor unsettled Kayse. He shivered, becoming uncomfortable, confused.

"You handled yourself well in the fight." Angel tilted his head to one side. "Surprised me, and I'm not easily surprised."

The comment made Kayse's heart thump in his chest. Suddenly Angel was morphing into something different, disorienting Kayse. His cheek burned where Angel had touched it. He blushed as Angel laughed, leaned over, and put a card through the slot, activating the TC. The car leaped forward as Kayse whacked back into his seat.

Leaning sideways, Angel studied him for a moment and then closed his eyes, cutting off any further discussion.

Exiting the TC, Kayse followed Angel to the apartment's entrance. Studying him, he noticed the enigmatic being stood taller and appeared gracefully built. An other-worldly air suffused him; something in the glowing eyes and the fluid grace of his movements caught Kayse's attention. The body, although slender, held slight curves yet appeared as hard as drawn steel.

At first, he'd been certain Angel was male, but now he wasn't sure what gender this creature was. It was alien, something not quite human, different. Kayse was shaken by his attraction to a creature whose gender he didn't even know; especially when he knew he liked girls.

"What are you?" he asked as they reached the door. "You aren't Alysian, and you're not Terran."

"Ah, such an innocent." Angel gave a soft laugh. "I'm Enjelise. I'm probably the only purebred Enjelise left on Alysia, except for my mother."

"Enjelise? What's that?"

"Do you know nothing of the Enjelise and our ways? Where have you been the last twenty annuals?"

"Somewhere else." Kayse studied the exotic alien. "I'm sorry I don't know about you, but I would like to. Where do you come from?"

"My species comes from another world. My line is from the Guardians, sworn to protect Alysia," Angel said. "But now most have gone, changed, evolved. They brought humans here to colonize Alysia in order to disseminate the species. However, *I* was born on Alysia under the protection of Mother Kat and Richard Steele. My mother is Ariel Truthsayer. My father, Darius Avarric. They are kind and gentle, unlike me. I struggle to reach the next ring of life and will probably never see the face of the Creator or reach spiritual fulfillment at the rate I'm going."

"You saved our lives back there," Kayse said thoughtfully. "I would think that would move you up a notch on your spiritual ring of life." Kayse placed his hand on the doorplate and watched in surprise as it slid open. He rotated to face the Enjelise for one last look.

The smile on Angel's face was luminous. "I'm supposed to; it's my job. I'm pledged to the Steele family." The Enjelise leaned in and kissed Kayse on the forehead. "But thanks for the praise." It pressed the keys to the handcuffs into Kayse's hand, spun around and departed.

The soft kiss burned Kayse's forehead and warmed him all the way in as he stumbled through the living room.

That was until he saw Elise's face and heard her voice thunder full throttle in Captain's Mode. "What in all Destinies did you think you were doing taking my daughter to that god-forsaken hell-hole of criminals and dead beats? I'm going to petition to have that bar's name changed."

Standing firm, he lifted his chin. "I didn't take her; she dragged me there. If you'd think about it, you'd realize I'd no idea what it was like. How could I know it would be dangerous? She kept saying you owned the place."

"Where did she ever get that idea?"

"It's called *The Ship Captain's Lounge*, for Fate's sake! Even so, I went because I thought she might need protection. I'm skilled in martial arts. And by the way, I don't relish the job of babysitter, if that's what you have in mind for me."

The furious face changed to a thoughtful frown. Eventually, a smile crinkled her mouth. "I like it better than the other duties you suggested she had in mind."

He blushed.

"If you ever get permission to leave this apartment again, someone other than Tempest must accompany you. How long did you think you could last out there?"

He grimaced. "Now that I know better, not very long." He thought it over. "But she made it quite the experience."

"A nanosecond at best," Elise countered. She heaved a sigh and doused the emerging grin. "Kayse, we're going to a great deal of trouble for you. Both Richard and I could be put in danger. We can't have you jaunting all over the station. I don't have the time or resources to deal with the consequences." She put up her hand before he could protest. "I know you weren't to blame, but you'll have to find a way to restrain Tempest's impulses."

"She made it sound like a fun walk in the park."

"She gets it from her father's side," Elise retorted. "All that charm." She rubbed her forehead. "Go get cleaned up. I've made an appointment for you for tomorrow. I can't afford to have anyone recognize you here."

He nodded and dragged his body into the refresher, then slipped on clean clothes, not soaked in terror sweat and dotted with someone else's blood. Images of blood and dead people flipped through his mind, and it was a while before he could think of anything else and stop his shaking.

Chapter 10

The next morning Kayse rose early and dressed. Today he would get a new look. He heard Elise speaking firmly to Tempest in the kitchen while she started breakfast. Tempest's voice started to shout in protest, so he decided to avoid any battles between mother and daughter. As Tempest stomped off with her tutor, he was relieved that she wasn't coming along for the procedure; although, he almost wished her nearby as a distraction. The whole idea unnerved him. Fate, he felt terrified. He'd never liked people poking at his body, never mind making fundamental changes to his looks.

Before he could object or let some frantic state overwhelmed him, Elise marched him out the door, down the hall, and into an enclosed private TC that slid up just as they stepped to the curb. They angled into the backseat where a beefy bodyguard greeted them.

Moving quickly, the TC whizzed along the station's outer rim, eventually diverting into an enclosed tube-like structure connected to the attached ship. There it stopped. Kayse grappled with second thoughts about his impending changes and putting his life into Terran hands on Trey's say so. He felt herded into an action that he wasn't sure was in his best interests. Still, his mother had trusted the man and the trouble was, right now, he could think of no other alternatives. He felt like a small piece of flotsam struggling to stay afloat in a rampaging tide of other's intentions.

"Captain's ready to board," Elise said next to him. She gave him what she might have considered a comforting pat on the shoulder, but to him, it felt more like a prod.

"Attention, *New Found Hope*. Captain coming on board," a voice announced.

"Captain coming on board," a nearby speaker boomed out. The door slid open, and two people stood stiffly at the ship's entry, saluting a welcome.

"Welcome to the Captain. What is the Captain's wish?" the one on their right asked without expression.

"I'm here to see Dr. Luttrell."

"Please enter."

Elise strode forward. Several knowing glances and winks were exchanged behind her back after she passed. Kayse followed, wondering what that was all about.

An eerie dim light bathed the smooth surfaced corridor and made everything difficult to see clearly. Strange sounds pelted his ears. Gurgles from pipes or water containment units reverberated softly in the background. Distant machinery hummed while air circulated in gentle breezes throughout the ship. The slap and shuffle of cushioned footwear came toward them as he eased his way down the corridor. He watched someone approach, snap a salute, murmur a greeting, and continue.

The smell of ozone mingled with the tang of recycled air and the pungent stink of Terran bodies living too close together. They passed an area, and he sniffed, trying to identify the fragrance. A kitchen perhaps? The aroma of cooking food wafted out of an open hatch.

All the while, they advanced deeper inward. At last, Elise stopped and a door slid open. A pleasant deep voice greeted them. "Elise dear, so good to see you again. What have you brought me this time?"

"Hello, Jay." Elise entered to give a compact Terran male a hug and cheek kiss. She faced Kayse. "This is Kayse Kiare. Kayse, this is Dr. Jay Luttrell. He's going to change you so no one will recognize you and make you better than you could ever imagine." She faced Jay again. "Are you ready for us?"

The doctor looked interestedly at Kayse. As Kayse returned the gaze, he noticed that Dr. Luttrell's face contained symmetrically precise features, topped by curly, light brown hair that tumbled about in the lighter gravity. A pleasing smile sat on the doctor's lips as he nodded at Kayse. "We're set. I stayed up half the night implementing your revisions to the software, and I think it's all ready. You inspired me to add a few additional programs."

"Sounds exciting," Elise responded.

"So let's get to it." Luttrell gestured Kayse to a table, where the boy disrobed. Kayse felt the prick of a needle and then nothing.

***

Distant fuzzy noises ticked at his consciousness. Slowly, voices clawed their way into his thoughts. He fought against intermittent grogginess that tossed him in and out of wakefulness. Words sounded blurry at first. He remembered Elise and some Terran doctor were going to radically alter him so that no one would recognize him.

Soft voices rose and fell around him. Words gained meaning, but then fell back into garble. Someone left and someone entered.

Overhead a masculine voice announced, "You can come in now. I'm almost done. Can you stay over tonight?"

A female voice drifted in. "I've lots to do," she said. "But I'll stay a bit so we can catch up. I don't know when

I'll be able to get up again. They're going after Richard, and travel arrangements could prove difficult."

Kayse hazily wondered where Richard might be traveling. He imagined a balmy ocean beach with swaying trees and booming waves until a deeper masculine voice jarred him out of his reverie with a complaining tone.

"I didn't sign up for this cruise to be sitting on a decaying hunk of metal for the rest of my very long life."

Kayse found himself perched on a huge slag of metal on a beach somewhere. Their words tickled his thoughts and drifted through his mind.

"No, Jay. None of us did. We let the others go on, and we stayed for the greener pastures right in front of us."

"Swaying trees in warm breezes was the pitch you made to me," he replied. "Fourteen Earth years are too long to wait, no matter how bright the dream."

Kayse felt a soft breeze brush his cheek and tried to call back his swaying trees.

"I copy you," she answered roughly. "But fourteen years should be nothing to you. Keep the sweet breezes and swaying trees in mind. We'll get what we want if we're patient."

Kayse floated on a swelling sea, searching for land.

A throat cleared roughly, disrupting the dream. "If Townsend stops your husband, that stops emigration and we'll be locked up here for a long time, bet on it. The ship will vote to go if that's the case. An underground group is already trying to separate the ship from the station and ready it for travel. Where does the Captain go then?"

"The Captain goes with the ship, Jay. It's always been that way."

Kayse's boat became a ship where he tried to catch flickering star-words as they drifted by him.

"Would it be a hard choice for you?"

The female voice answered. "Yes, very hard. We might not find another habitable planet in my lifetime. The universe is vast and not much of it is agreeable to humans. We may not survive. Then, Earth will be a forgotten dream. And Richard…"

"Yes, dear Richard. Knowing you, I'm thinking abduction would be your choice of alternatives, if it came to it."

This line of discussion jerked Kayse sharply awake. He tried to focus better. *Someone was talking about abducting Richard Steele.* His hazy dream vanished like mist over sea. He tried to listen harder.

"Richard would be angry for a long time, but eventually he would get over it. Those nanobots you inoculated him with will give him plenty of time to get over just about anything. I think his love would eventually triumph over any hard feelings."

"There's always me, you know." The masculine voice sounded petulant.

"You come with a lab attached."

"I'm trying to learn to disengage."

"Let me know when you succeed, if ever." A long pause followed, and Kayse almost fell back asleep. "Now he's brought Kayse into the mix."

Kayse jerked to semi-consciousness again at the mention of his name.

"You said I would be interested in taking a look."

The female voice sighed. "Consider him an opportunity. He's an Alysian Talent you can inoculate, augment and possibly study. These Alysians may be distant relatives, but they're different in significant ways. We need to find out what those ways are. Getting the DNA of a confirmed *Talent* will give us a better idea of what we're up against."

Kayse forced himself to become alert and focused.

"I hear rumors of telekinesis, teleportation, telepathy…but I don't know what *this boy* can do. I just know they're terrified of him. No one will give me specifics. They only mumble generalities."

The man countered, "He comes with a provenance, an original. We have to discover who. The work is amateur. Yet, I haven't found a word in their database about the procedure or a hint it was ever done. Whoever created him kept it tightly under wraps. The Alysians have strong taboos against experimenting in this field of science."

"If he is what we suspect, then Richard knew the original. Although I've only the histories and rumors to rely on, you can bet the original wasn't your average Alysian."

Kayse's mind blurred, and then focused on the word "original."

"Remember, he's most likely not a perfect copy if an amateur did this.

Copy? Kayse's heart beat faster.

"I'm doing a lot of augmenting here. What I plan to do could make him even more dangerous. Have you considered that aspect? He could turn against us."

A rustling noise distracted Kayse.

"Whoa! His heart rate just spiked. I thought I gave him the right dosage. He's Alysian, not Terran…could be different…Ah, it's back down again."

A female sigh answered that comment.

Skin rubbed skin somewhere nearby. "He's okay. Relax. Elise. If they would kill the kid for what they suspect he is, then they doubly don't need to know the extent of our scientific abilities. They'd slaughter us all for freaks if they knew what we really are. Or they'd kill to get our technology."

"You will take care, won't you, Jay?"

"Always, my dear. Never fear," the doctor assured her. "I have upped his odds quite a bit with my nanobots and the Electronic Secretary Assistant insertion. He can now understand Terran through the translator program, and eventually have access to the ASSIST network. When you get to Alysia, contact your brother, Elija. If he can activate the ESA…" The words drifted off as Kayse felt tired and his mind sluggish. The words bumped and bounced. He struggled to focus on hearing more.

The female voice said, "It's amazing, Jay. You say it will enable internal communication between them? This one may be our answer if handled correctly."

"I've never done this many protocols in one body. I'm on the experimental side here."

A vision of him as a rat running through a maze flashed into Kayse's mind, and the image started to scuttle away. *The words…I must pay attention…* The rat scampered back.

Fingers tapped and prodded him.

"According to Richard, someone is trying to kill him. Trey scared Richard with wild talk about several attempts on his own life. I want Kayse augmented, not only to protect him, but to protect us."

"No one here would let anyone hurt you."

"Wrong. Tempest maneuvered Kayse into taking her for lunch on the sly. They tangled with Kurt and his gang of cutthroats. I asked Angel to watch over her and within one rotation, the Enjelise is fighting for her life."

"Any repercussions?"

"Kurt and most of his gang are dead."

"What were they thinking?"

"They tried to kidnap her, for what I shudder to guess. I thought being my daughter would afford her some protection and, with Angel for backup, I was sure they would be safe. Now, Angel may have to face the consequences for her thoughtless action."

Kayse heard a lab coat crinkling, and then felt a hand brush by his arm. "Angel will survive. My feelings about Kurt are 'Good riddance to bad rubbish.' Recycle him with the rest of the trash." A pause in conversation followed. "Hmmm...I better check the dosage so he doesn't regain consciousness too soon."

A waft of air and the smell of a light perfume as someone, Elise most likely, leaned over him. He felt the warmth of her body against him. An urgent tone came into her voice as she said, "Jay, you can't say that. Three men are dead because we wanted to protect our own. That's just what we accuse the Alysians of doing—being judge, jury, and executioners all in a row. I refuse to be a hypocrite."

"Hey, be careful. Don't lean on him."

The weight eased off. "Sorry."

"Kurt did his fair share of killing and slave trading that no one stopped, even though some tried. We can't have that. It gives Terrans a bad name. So, I'm glad Angel finally put him away."

"Angel said he accidentally fell on his knife."

Someone started fiddling with instruments and gave out a surprised grunt. The room fell silent. Kayse began drifting back to unconsciousness, but then Elise started talking again.

"Raising a kid isn't what I expected. Most of the time it's not all the cuddles and warm smiles some would lead you to believe."

"A lot were angry that you were able to have a child and they couldn't. Did you ever thank me? The fertility serum was limited. You owe me, you know."

"Yes, I know, but I suspect you're keeping track and will exact payment eventually. She's just so daring, and she doesn't stop to think of consequences."

"That behavior has a familiar ring to it. I remember a young girl always getting into trouble aboard this ship."

"I've settled down since we were cribmates."

"Elise, why did you marry him? Was it diplomacy, or was it truly for love?" Betrayal and hurt coated his voice.

Kayse fought drowsiness, wanting to hear her answer, but he slowly was losing the battle.

"Ah Jay, I saw the advantage and, at first glance, he wasn't repellent. The man took an interest. You warded off all suitors, and anything male wouldn't look at me. Being the Captain, I was isolated. You discouraged others from paying me any attention while showing a lack of care yourself."

"Huh!"

"I realized Richard loved me. A girl could do far worse. Besides, he offered me a ticket down to the planet."

"And me? We were the ship's favorite couple."

"With your lab, you had no time for me."

A soft rustle intruded into the haze of Kayse's mind, and he felt a hand slid over his sheet to the other side. "Direful neglect?" The male voice sounded overhead, the weight of a body pushing against Kayse's side. "I'm sorry Elise, but if you'll remember, disease was decimating the convoy, and dad was perfecting the cloning technique that would save us all. Finding a solution was a stronger priority than you and sex, unfortunately. You, of all people, should know where duty lies." A rueful tone laced the words.

"Sex! I forgot. Jay, do me a favor?"

The body backed up and weight lifted.

The word sex peaked Kayse's interest. Wanting to hear what might be said, he fought the growing darkness.

"Something to do with sex? Glad to."

"Not that. Give Tempest a biology lesson."

"How do you want me to do it? Soft and gentle, with talk of love? Is there a lab class involved?"

"Fate, no! Don't touch her, Jay. I'll have your head on a slab if you do. No, give her the hard, cruel, head under the pillow story. Tell her the gruesome details. List diseases. I want her cringing at the thought. However, I want strictly hands off. If I hear otherwise, you'll pay dearly."

"You're a tough woman, Elise."

"She's harassing the poor boy. He's trying to cope, but he's at his sexual peak and has no outlet. Then add in all the conflicting feelings of being abandoned and hunted. He's ripe for anything she might offer. Fate help me, I can hardly cope with what I already have on my plate."

"Well then, I've loaded the dice for you. I took your list and added my own."

"What do you mean?"

"Let's see what takes first, and then I'll run you through the protocols."

"Let me know soon."

"Alysians have a certain chromosome that Terrans lack. I took DNA samples while he was under."

"Something happened to him. Richard knows but won't tell. Fate! He has secrets; I have secrets. Some marriage. We each keep deep dark secrets from the other."

"Ahhh, the boy's gaining consciousness. I need to increase the drip. I shouldn't have been talking so much…it's just it's been so long since we've talked. There's a lot I want to say. I do miss you. And, I still love you."

Kayse wanted to hear more, but the darkness descended. When he finally regained consciousness, Elise was gone, replaced by a nurse. Then he was out again.

Chapter 11

When he awoke the next time, his senses erupted into awareness. First, there was sound. Voices murmured outside his cubicle. Pipes from the ship groaned as they expanded and contracted. Somewhere metal screeched as if it was being wrenched apart. Paper slippers worn by medical staff made swishing noises scurrying down the hall outside his room. Then he noticed smells. The odor of burning from a blowtorch mixed with the sharp tang of medicines. Finally, feeling blasted in. Dull aches and pains rippled throughout his body, making him groan in protest.

His face felt like someone had taken a mallet to it. Terrifying darkness continued as he tried to open his eyes but couldn't. Raising a hand, he encountered a swath of bandages over both eyes. Relief washed through him when he realized the bandages prevented his sight, not blindness. Noises outside the room resolved into the sounds of a young girl giggling and another older voice hushing her up. The door panel slid open while he pretended to be unconscious.

"Jay says he should be awake soon." A light feminine voice moved closer to him.

"Adjust the dosage a little more to bring him back up. As soon as he wakes, let Jay know."

The two made rustling noises. His head started to clear but still felt a bit groggy.

"Have you heard the latest rumors?" the higher, younger voice questioned.

"What now?"

"They say the Alysians want to bomb the station here to kill off the Terrans once and for all. Everyone I know has petitioned the Oversight Committee for planetside sponsors, but they won't let anyone on planet unless one of their stinking Alysians acts as a supervisor. They keep control that way. Word is they use Terrans for hard labor and porn."

"Are you going?" the older voice asked.

"Hell no, Jay won't let me go. He says his team stays here until he goes. He doesn't want to go down there because the Alysians get too curious about his work, and that's dangerous. Because I've worked in the lab since consciousness, he insists I stay up here with him."

"They don't want us on Alysia, plain and simple. They're afraid we'll contaminate the planet or try to take it over. Leave them to come up with stupid ideas like that."

"Not so stupid, if you think about it. Rumor says we're building a rebellion down there already. The Alysians are afraid to let any more go down for fear we'll all join up. The captain is finding it harder and harder to convince them to let any stationer leave here. Meanwhile, we have an underground forming here on Earth2 that plans to ready the spaceship and leave. They're tired of waiting."

The older voice snorted. "Fools! Speaking of which, our patient should be conscious. The monitor says his vital signs are up. I'll call Jay and get him in here." Kayse heard a rustling sound at his bedside as someone moved off toward the door.

"Caitlin?"

"Yes."

"Let me know if you hear anything more, okay?"

"Yeah, same here."

Then the person moved on, stirring the air as they opened the door panel, and all that was left was the sound of one person breathing and muttering to herself.

Soon the slide opened again, and he hear someone enter. He soon recognized the deeper tones of Dr. Jay. Delicate fingers peeled away the bandages, and the room blurred into existence.

"So you're alive, aren't you boy?" The voice oozed satisfaction.

He pretended to wake and stretch. "It appears so," he answered, blinking into the bright light. Relief swept through him as his vision cleared, and the room came into focus.

"You go easy now," Dr. Jay warned, taking a pulse and peering under his eyelids. "You're a bit of an experiment, I'll admit. You're the first Alysian I've tried this many operations on all at once. So, take it easy. I'll want to monitor you closely. You'll feel fatigued as your body adapts to the new protocols. It's to be expected with this many changes."

Kayse caught his breath at the word "many." He hadn't expected a lot of changes.

"So what did you do?"

Dr. Jay patted his arm, sporting a wide grin. "The green eyes you requested were easy. I also darkened and straightened the hair along with thinning out the nose. I programmed internal nanobots to take care of any diseases and repair most bodily harms. You carry the longevity gene already and could live a very long life, barring an accident or someone killing you. That part will be up to you."

"Great."

"Then I added my own touches."

"Such as…"

"I inserted an ESA that communicates with the Alysian Satellite System and Information Support Technology network, known as ASSIST. It works via satellites and Comsat towers. You'll be able to access any information that you might need once you activate it. Right now, it's not on. It contains a GPS system so you can locate just about anything through our satellite network.

"Could be useful. I don't want to get lost around here."

Luttrell snorted at the comment. "I've injected a carbide ceramic ossification catalyst that will make your bones as tough as steel."

"Seriously?"

A smile tugged the doctor's lips. "Not to mention there's a fibroid muscle protein complex to boost muscle density along with a colloidal neural stimulation solution to increase reaction time."

"So I'll be really fast?"

"Yep. Might take a bit of getting used to, though." Dr. Jay leaned back. "The icing on the cake, however, is my personal experiment with pheromones. Everyone's going to be subliminally influenced by your smell. They'll want to please you because you smell nice. It's a new program I wanted to try out."

"On the lab rat."

Luttrell shrugged. "Joke now, but you'll thank me later."

Kayse tried to process all the information. Finally, he said, "So, you're saying that I'll be stronger, faster, never sick, and smell good?"

"Pretty much." Jay nodded.

"Wow!"

"Yeah, exceptionally awesome."

"So what do I look like?"

"Right now, you look a pretty mess. Give yourself a few rotations so you won't terrify yourself when you look in the mirror."

A harsh laugh filled the room. Kayse glanced over and noticed a stern-faced woman clothed in a white uniform. He guessed she was the older voice from before.

Jay Luttrell waved her over. "Dora here, however, has seen it all. She can stomach just about anything—even your ugly mug. You saw more than your share of horror on the *New Found Hope* after the pandemic, eh Dora?"

The stiff older woman nodded grimly.

"Now you'll move quicker than you're used to," he told Kayse. "So take everything slow, or you'll damage yourself and everything around you. You can go home soon but move carefully. Stay calm; don't get excited. I mean it. You need to learn what your body is capable of and how to control it. Try things out in small easy steps." Jay smiled. "Good luck. If you need anything, the nurses will get it and, if they can't, I'll be available. After you get settled, I'll come by the apartment, in say, a few days."

Kayse wondered what he meant. He blinked.

Dr. Jay frowned at what may have been his puzzled expression, and then the frown cleared. "Ah, Alysians say rotations. In a couple of weeks…er, cycles…you'll be feeling much better, and in a month…that's a phase, isn't it, you'll feel completely healed." He muttered, "And why can't they use meters? It only makes sense. But they have to name measurements differently, too, and make extra work for me." He smiled wanly and returned to his subject. "For now, get some rest and get used to your new body. Don't look into any mirrors for a while, or you'll be scared witless at what you see. Eventually, you'll be a pretty boy with green eyes and an aristocratic nose. Have faith." Dr. Jay handed him a cup of liquid to swallow, then left.

Two rotations later they dressed him, bundled him out of sickbay, and back to the apartment. Elise's face appeared drawn and her skin pale. On the apartment's vidscreen, Richard sat in front of the Investigation Committee as they interrogated him, probing every little hiccup that happened during the Armstrong administration, searching for errors in governing.

Richard had been lead crisis manager during John Armstrong's presidency so the opposition party now gleefully put him on the hot seat, trying to discredit any of their actions.

As Kayse watched Richard on the vid, the man displayed dark circles under his eyes and a tired demeanor.

After several rotations recuperating in the apartment, Kayse mustered enough courage to look in a mirror and saw a thinner version of himself with pale skin, dark hair, thank goodness not red hair, and a swollen nose. A slight bump bothered him at the back of his head, but he soon forgot about it, since the itchiness and soreness there didn't last.

The adolescent pudginess melted away. With regular workouts, his body shape soon reflected a muscled leanness. He saw smoky green eyes and dark arched eyebrows on a strange bruised face. The results were rather compelling, if you took away the bruises and swelling. He kept his dimples, but the dark, straight hair was a welcome change from the unruly light brown of before.

Aside from the physical differences, he also noticed a phenomenal speed and strength, which required some getting used to. In his first few clumsy attempts to exercise at the apartment, several uncoordinated maneuvers almost demolished Richard's workout equipment there.

Elise grunted when she saw him and nodded. She appeared pre-occupied with other things—that was when she even visited the apartment. They discussed his "cousin" cover story again and added more details.

However, Tempest reacted differently. She'd been kept away, so he could recuperate. Finally, she reappeared, hurrying in through the front door to stop suddenly in front of him. He raised an eyebrow at her, expecting the usual torrent of words, but all he got was a mouth forming a round circle. She reached for a chair and sat with a plop.

"So?" he said with a swagger in his voice.

"Erk," she replied. "Kayse? That you in there?"

"Yep. What do you think?"

"Ah…"

She was having trouble speaking.

"Need more feedback than 'erk'," he replied. Walking to the chair, he leaned over in front of her and furrowed his brows. "Okay, let's start with short, *understandable* adjectives."

"Whoa," she whispered. "You look dangerous."

"I am. Remember that. Keep it in mind when you're harassing me. I am not to be messed with."

"I liked it better the other way. You were more fun."

"For you, maybe; for me, not so much."

"When those bruises and bumps heal, you're going to be really hot. Wait until Mary Ellen sees you. She's going to shit in her pants."

"Watch the language."

"You even *act* different. I really like the eyes, though. You look like dad …especially his younger pictures."

"Not so chubby, eh?"

Tempest left the comment floating, then changed tack. "Mom says soon we will be leaving for Tygel. She'll probably make me go back to that stupid school, but at least I'll have something interesting to show Mary Ellen."

"I am not your show and tell," he said firmly.

As he started to walk away, heading for bed, she murmured, "Don't bet on it." He smiled. He suspected she thought he hadn't heard, but then he hadn't mentioned the enhanced hearing. He needed a few secrets.

***

Sound asleep, a noise woke him up. As he peered through the dark, a pair of eyes stared at him. He whipped out of bed and crouched in a combat ready stance until he realized it was only Tempest... again.

"Wow!" she said, startled. "You move fast. I wasn't trying to bother you; I just wanted to watch you sleep."

"You *are not* to enter my bedroom anymore," he said, grabbing her by the wrist.

"Shush, you don't want to wake Mom," she said. "What if she discovers me in your bedroom?"

He growled, "I plan to wake her up. I want her to know you're here." He marched Tempest to Elise's room.

Outside Elise's door panel, with a firm grip on Tempest, he shouted, "Your daughter is in my bedroom, bothering me again!"

A rustle came from the other side and a heavy sigh. Elise padded out, a robe wrapped around her. Her eyes narrowed in irritation at her daughter.

"Tempest, what were you doing?"

He turned to the wayward girl. "Don't say you got confused. You know where your room is."

"I did get confused."

"Liar." He eyed Tempest with disgust.

"Get back to bed and leave Kayse alone!"

"I needed a drink of water," she whined.

They both glared at her. "Okay, I'm going, I'm going." She tossed an angry look at him over her shoulder. "You're no fun anymore."

Chapter 12

Most mornings after Tempest left for tutoring, and Elise did whatever Elise did, Kayse would hang around the apartment, absorbing the learning modules and working out. Dr. Jay had told him to gather strength and ease into his new powers. After noting his response time on various computer sports competitions and games, he found them fricking amazing. He wished Jeremy could see what he could do now, except Jeremy wasn't alive—because of him.

Grief flooded in, threatening to overwhelm him. He took a deep breath, trying to get back control of his emotions. The loneliness proved hard to deal with, and everything confused him. This future frightened him. He would find out who had killed his parents and make them pay, if it took the rest of his life.

After a while, when his emotions cooled a little, he became bored and actually started to miss Tempest with her antics. Never thinking he would feel that way, he finally admitted that she did make life more interesting. In a weird sort of way, he now looked forward to bantering with her, but she stormed in and blew by him with hardly a word in passing. He didn't need his acute hearing to catch the loud slam of her bedroom door panel. He glanced inquiringly at Elise who trailed behind.

"She was with Dr. Jay," Elise muttered, hanging up a short tan jacket.

"She's talking a lot less and moving pretty fast. Did he remove her vocal chords and accelerate her metabolism like he did mine?" he asked with a big grin. "It would be really great if he has given her a vocal cord removal operation."

Offering a wan smile, Elise moved to the kitchen and opened the storage cubicle. "Sorry, didn't happen; maybe next time. Dr. Jay Luttrell spent the entire rotation educating her on sex and biology. I hope you put your time here to good use." She took out a tumbler. She hit the ice dispenser and two cubes clinked in. Next, she poured herself something liquid from a very sinister looking bottle. Sweeping the drink toward him with a nod, she brought it back and drained a large amount down her throat. That done, she took a step back and blinked. A smile popped out on her face.

"Ahh, that tasted good. Too bad Richard isn't here to join me, but unfortunately he's down on that fate-wracked planet, battling power hungry idiots." She raised the drink again and knocked back another large gulp. Then, she poured some more.

"Exactly how much detail did Dr. Jay go into with Tempest?" he inquired archly. The liquor was disappearing at an alarming rate.

"I told Jay to be pretty graphic and explain all of it. He may have overdone it a bit. She's quite upset, but you can rest easy about her making any midnight visits in the near future until the visual images clear, and the hormones kick back in. By then, I hope we'll be safely on Alysia where I'll have more resources available, and you'll have recuperated more. The Lady knows, I can't deal with her by myself."

She stared a bit glassy-eyed at her drink, lifted it, and took another long swallow.

Not knowing what to say, he was relieved in one sense, and in another, saddened at Tempest's loss of innocence. Already he missed her easy banter. He expected it would be uneasy silences and angry grimaces for a while. But this was Tempest, and not much could keep her down.

With a confident and encouraging expression on his face, he said, "She'll be fine, Elise. She's a tough kid, and now at least she knows. I think the not knowing made her crazy. This way, she won't ask me to be a visual explanation of what a male is."

Elise snorted a laugh as she rubbed her forehead. "And I considered being captain of a space ship complicated. This parenting stuff is harder than I expected."

He nodded. "She's certainly a handful."

"To say the least." Elise continued, "We leave tomorrow for Alysia." Her hand stabbed the air. "I have to get a few more forms signed and organize some Terrans for the trip down. I'll introduce you to Jemma, my assistant. You most likely will have some more questions about Terrans, and she would be a good resource for you onboard the shuttle. Maybe you two could sit together."

She knocked back the rest of her drink, nodded at the glass, and sighed deeply. The air coming out of her sounded like a deflating balloon. Clicking nails on the rim of her drink, she said, "Then tomorrow, I have to sign papers and get a contingent of people organized. Oh, yeah, I already said that. I'm too tired to think straight." Giving him a bleary stare, she heaved another sigh and added, "Do not, under any circumstances, leave this apartment. Tempest will be busy all morning, so you won't have to worry about her, but we'll return in the afternoon. So, here's your last chance for some quiet study."

She put the glass in the sink and glanced around. "I'm going to bed. I'm exhausted." She flipped a light and started with a slight stagger toward her bedroom.

He surveyed the quiet emptiness and thought maybe he would turn in early, as any party or lively entertainment around this place just wasn't going to happen.

***

The next morning, he expected to meet Tempest at breakfast, but she fled the kitchen when he arrived, picking up something that looked like food and running back to her room. He eyed Elise, who shrugged. "She's still mad at me for making her a woman, I suppose. She already told me that she's furious she's female. She can't believe how people have sex. One more rotation with Dr. Jay and then we leave. Should be a fun trip sitting next to her."

"Yeah, thanks."

Elise leaned over and turned on a vid box. Richard's face appeared on the screen. "This ought to be fun too," she commented dryly. "They've started the committee hearings again, and Richard's been called to testify because he managed the plans for handling the comet crisis."

The committee interrogation appeared on a worldwide vid with a feed to both Alysian and Terran orbiting space stations. A stern looking, pinched-faced politico was talking. "Dr. Steele." The man shuffled papers and squinted at Richard over his spectacles. "Twenty thousand died in the flood that swept over the Norlands. Thousands were homeless because of weather changes. The Democratic Union declared a state of emergency, but President Armstrong acted with too little, too late. His successor, Sean Courtland, didn't do much more to alleviate the desperate conditions of many regions. On the contrary, he teamed up with other nations, such as the Ching T'Karre, and added to the space station instead. You wrote the paper warning Alysians of the impending disaster, and yet even some of your solutions proved faulty.

What defense do you offer about the administration's lack of effectiveness in controlling the crisis?"

A camera panned from the chairman's accusing look to the pained expression on Richard's face. He cleared his throat. "Both presidents tried to work with other leaders so they could make a united effort at handling the problem, rather than each country going it alone. The space station provided an attempt to pool efforts to confront a crisis or offer a safe haven if the planet became unlivable. This committee has made it sound as if it was my fault Thanos and Kracta were on a collision course. I just alerted the world to the impending threat and proposed a solution."

Shaking a finger at him, the committee member continued, "But when the science in your plan proved faulty, you abandoned the whole project. Thanos was breaking up and debris rained down on Alysia while you got distracted—by an invading alien woman, as it turns out." Several chuckles went through the committee, while others just looked upset.

"I got distracted because our telescopes revealed an impending alien incursion, not any single being." Richard blushed, glanced down, and started shuffling papers.

Glancing over her shoulder from the vid broadcast, Elise frowned. "He does that when he's flustered and mad. He'll start shuffling papers. Watch, he'll go for a drink of water next." Sure enough, Richard glared at the speaker and reached for a glass of water, shuffling a few more papers.

"I would think that a disintegrating Thanos would capture your attention, not a pretty alien face, Dr. Steele," the speaker said wryly.

Rubbing his face in exasperation, Richard answered, "At the time, the debris was burning up in the atmosphere with very little damage to Alysia. However, new data indicated the alien space ship had changed course and was heading toward our world at an unheard of speed. Originally, we thought we had plenty of time to worry about any invasion crisis, but new data changed our thinking."

Richard took a sip of water, then continued. "When we first spotted them, they were still way out beyond the solar system, and we thought nothing could go faster than the speed of light. At speeds we were familiar with, we figured it would take more than ten annuals before they would even approach the inner planets. Then suddenly, they were two planets away and headed toward Alysia. They had a means of travel totally unknown to us." He stopped to sigh heavily. "I had no idea about the alien woman at the time, but I have since been enlightened." Here he gazed into the camera and gave a wink.

Elise barked a laugh.

"So your science was faulty again, Dr. Steele. You keep coming up with bad science."

"I change my science when direct observation changes it. Every scientist operates that way. I think if you study science, you'll see that good science is open to revision as new or different information becomes available."

"So, now we have these invaders to deal with."

Richard leaned forward. "Don't forget it was the Terrans who saved us by helping move Thanos out of the way before it collided with Kracta. What Alysia doesn't realize yet is that they have advanced science and technology that may be useful to us if we can learn to work with them and stop these hostilities. On the other hand, they could become extremely dangerous if we make them our enemy. My relationship with Elise was one of the main reasons we survived. Things were looking dire, and Captain

Fujeint persuaded them to help. We should thank them rather than treating them as badly as we do."

"How can you say that, Dr. Steele, when we still have worldwide problems, and the Terrans are compounding them?" a different voice interrupted.

"At least we have a world left in which to have those problems." Richard glanced down, checking his notes. "Dr. D'Enaude," he responded and nodded at the man. "Their science has already helped us. Thanos is no longer a threat. The weather is finally stabilizing, and people are coping with the changes in their lives. I imagine before long; Alysia will be thriving once more."

A sour expression passed over the committee member's face. "Unemployment is at an all-time high, resources are in a critical state, and we're supposed to house and feed these *invaders*. The current president's legislation supports additional immigration onto our planet. Soon we'll be overrun."

"This panel is not about the Terran situation." Richard tapped the table before him. "This panel was convened to evaluate our response to the Thanos crisis and to investigate developing strategies to cope with any possible future comet or asteroid threats. I submit that we did the best we could at the time, but I'm willing to hear constructive ideas on how we could improve, if ever such a confluence of events were to appear again." He put a hand over the microphone and muttered to an assistant.

A new committee member signaled for attention and leaned into her mic. "Mr. Chairman, a word?" A middle-aged brunette with red lipstick and hair in a tight bun interrupted.

"Yes, Miss De Grace?"

"Mr. Chairman, I submit to Dr. Steele that the Terran situation *is* our next crisis and, once again, the situation is being mishandled. The Terrans are not the same as Alysians, and I have some disturbing scientific data that says they are even more different than we might imagine them to be. Their advanced technology threatens us. We better wake up and protect ourselves before we find Alysia in alien hands." She sat back in a huff as chaos erupted around her.

"Well." Elise clicked off the vid. "Richard is tied up in committee now, so he can't do anything for us, and they are turning us into the boogeyman."

"Who?"

"It's an old Earth phrase for something scary. When my people see this, they're going to be upset, possibly turn violent. Alysians may get their alien attack after all, if they keep verbally attacking us and treating us like inferiors. It just won't come from the skies; it will erupt here on the ground. There's work to do, and right now Richard needs me. I'm glad I'm heading back down."

With that, Kayse went to pack and help Elise and Tempest close up the apartment. Not sure what work she talked about or how she could help, he did acknowledge that Richard probably needed her.

Earth2 Station had lost all appeal, and Kayse longed for familiar territory. He wanted to go home to green trees, familiar scenery, and comfortable faces. Tomorrow he'd be on a shuttle headed toward Alysia, living in a household with Terrans. Unfortunately, he had discovered that most Alysians hated Terrans.

Chapter 13

Kayse checked in at the station's desk and again at the boarding gate, before finally walking through the long narrow corridor that led toward the shuttle. The noise and jostling of boarding passengers unsettled him as he threaded his way, eventually arriving.

Before he entered the shuttle, they issued him antistatic slippers and searched every indignant inch of his body before wishing him a successful trip to Alysia. He tried to filter out the noise and the odd smell of Terran bodies crammed into too small a space, but it was impossible. Voices all spoke at once, luggage thumped as the passengers stowed their possessions, the shuttle engines rumbled and then changed pitch, and the grapplers clanked and grated as they strained against the dock's edge.

A headache started to bloom, aided by a blast of a strong perfume that made his eyes water. On top of that, the body odor of a passing maintenance worker made him grateful for the perfume's heavy floral fragrance. At least he wasn't stowed in the back like most of the Terrans. Then he noticed Tempest in a disagreement with an attractive blonde female who stood in front of his assigned seat. He slowed down. At the moment, he wasn't ready to deal with any more hassles.

"I thought that you would *want* to sit next to Jahn." The girl pointed to an extremely handsome, Alysian who smiled back engagingly and waved.

Tempest's lips firmed into a familiar stubborn expression. "Jahn's very nice, but this is my seat, and this is where I plan to sit, thank you very much." She angled her head toward the subject under discussion. "I know I told Jahn that I liked him, but now I like Kayse better."

Oh, Fate.

"Yeah, but Jahn would be good company for you. He's closer to your age. Maybe Kayse would rather have someone his own age sit next to him," the stunning girl suggested. The female version of this brother and sister pair caught the eye. Gradually Kayse advanced toward them. The blonde looked like a delightful female who was all ready to be friendly company, very different from the glowering Tempest who stood next to her with her arms crossed, and a frown furrowing her face.

He sighed, knowing that he would pay dearly if he indicated he preferred any other company than Tempest's. That much he knew about that female. Little enough, but it might be a long voyage if he didn't act smart here.

He arranged a pleasant expression on his face, saying to the newcomer, "While I'm flattered by your gracious offer, let's just keep to our assigned seats for now." It was diplomatically said, but Tempest still didn't crack a smile or even a pleasant expression. She arched an eyebrow at the older blonde girl and fluttered a hand to shoo her away.

"Your call." The charming young female shrugged. "I'll just be over there. Come by later. I'm Jemma Telluria, by the way." She gave him a bright smile and wiggled a finger in the brother's direction. "And that's my brother, Jahn."

"Nice to meet you both," Kayse acknowledged, still aware of Tempest glowering next to him. "I'll try to drop by your seat later." He put on what he hoped was a sincere expression.

Jemma's nostrils flared, and then she winked.

As an afterthought, he recalled her last name—Telluria. Ever since reading about the Tellurian name in his lesson module, he'd been curious to learn more. Studying her, he imagined she might have additional Talents even more interesting than any so-called time Talent. He gave a silly smile thinking of it. Jemma caught the look and responded with a grin of her own. She turned to sashay back to her seat.

Tempest punched him in the arm.

"What?" he growled, rubbing the now sore spot and frowning in indignation. His muscles hadn't healed totally yet.

She snorted at him and plunked down into her seat, hooking her seatbelt with a sharp, angry tug. She glanced up at Kayse and made a face. "Guys," she said in disgust, "have one track minds."

"No argument there," he responded glibly.

She huffed.

With a shrug, he sat and plugged into the console where he accessed a playlist of songs he'd set up earlier. He hoped the music would soothe and distract him, as he didn't want to fight with Tempest the whole trip.

Elise had given them medication to help counteract the discomfort of weightlessness, but she warned it would also make them feel drowsy. Thinking about it, he was beginning to feel more relaxed than he should, given the commotion going on around him.

Behind half-closed eyes, he studied his fellow passengers in attempt to stay awake. Ten appeared to be Terran emigrants, and ten were most likely returning Alysians he didn't know, possibly traveling on business. Kayse stared at three Terrans who looked like identical triplets. They were extraordinarily beautiful, almost too perfect. A shiver rippled through his body for some unknown reason.

Then he saw an interesting, dark-haired, Alysian girl coming through the hatch alongside Elise, using extensive hand gestures as she chatted enthusiastically about something. Intermittently, she'd brush a mop of wayward curls away from her lively brown eyes, but inevitably, the curls would flop back. Elise laughed at something she said, and they stopped across the aisle to chat like old friends.

Leaving them to their conversation, his eyes alighted on a petite Terran girl. She appeared scared to death. Her wide aqua eyes stared transfixed at all the commotion. He smiled at her, and then turned to notice Tempest glaring at him again. Aggravated by her behavior, he closed his eyes, studiously ignoring her. Her possessive attitude irritated him. He had a right to look at whomever and whatever he wanted without her making a fuss.

Soon enough, Elise joined them. She heaved a large sigh as she settled into her seat on the other side of Tempest by a small window. Without opening his eyes, Kayse could sense her restlessness. Something bothered her. He opened his eyes to watch her, and she gave him a tight little smile as she clicked her seatbelt in place.

He felt the shuttle bump against something, and his stomach lurched, as they prepared to leave the docking gate. He pulled out some chewing gum and turned the music up louder in his earjacks. The engines rumbled louder. Several heavy metal clamps clanged loose. With a jerk, the shuttle finally shook free and rotated onto its flight path. An acceleration boost pushed him deep into his seat, as they finally set forth toward Alysia.

Once they were away from the Earth2 Station, everyone settled down and the turmoil in the cabin calmed. He felt the soothing feeling of meds kicking in. Nothing mattered anymore. At first, the shuttle maintained a light gravity, helped by forward acceleration. However, once they achieved the required velocity, the engines cut out and gravity lifted. The cushions and straps held them in, but the experience of weightlessness disconcerted him. His sinuses started to clog up, and the blood began pooling up toward his head. His eyes fluttered shut as the meds took complete hold, so he lowered the music and floated into sleep.

He awoke suddenly as he felt Elise jostle him and pass in front of his seat murmuring, "Something's not right." He opened his eyes and looked questioningly over at her.

"The pilot has changed our flight path." She tapped the window that displayed a starry universe. All he could see was a sprinkling of stars and Alysia rotating beneath them. Blue seas, green land, and white-whipped clouds covered her surface. The planet loomed larger and larger as they approached. Everything appeared fine to him. Beautiful, in fact.

Elise frowned and stood up. "I'm going to check with the pilot. I'll be right back." She eyed a sleeping Tempest. "Watch her," she ordered as she eased her way forward.

Now awake, Kayse grew restless. The cabin lights were turned to dim, and the rest of the passengers either were in a drugged sleep or wrapped up in a virtual reality program. Several intervals passed, and still Elise didn't return. He decided to call up the shuttle's course on the seatback's computer and study its route. They would orbit Alysia three times coming in on a downward spiral toward Tygel Space Center. With one orbit already completed, they now entered the second.

He decided to access a Terran language program, but soon, he became bored. He unhooked his headset and scanned the cabin, wondering when they would hit the edge of Alysia's outer atmospheric layer.

As if on cue, the edge of the first layer buffeted the shuttle. Body fluids started a downward flow and pressure built up in his inner ear. Muscles still trying to heal from the operation protested. Other passengers began to come out of their stupor and clutch various body parts as they protested the growing gravity. Many had never known the full weight of a planet's pull. He leaned across Tempest to peer out the window.

One eye popped opened as she groaned, "Are we there yet?" She stretched and yawned.

"We're coming down into the first atmospheric layer. It'll still be a while."

He gazed out the window and saw frothy clouds dancing over a deep blue ocean. Browns and greens splotched the land. He'd never seen Alysia from this vantage point before. The colors were intense and beautiful. A tug of homesickness washed over him. What would going home be like now?

The shuttle swooped forward toward a world of semi twilight. Lights began winking on over the planet as they flew past vast areas on the darkening planet, now lit up, that marked out both large cities and lesser towns. As they flew toward night, below them black empty land, lakes, or uninhabited regions contrasted with clusters of twinkling lights that signified life. He felt the buffeting of the shuttle, which indicated contact with a heavier layer of atmosphere. They plunged toward the planet's surface.

Beneath his gaze, the scene began to change as they traveled over the planet out of night into morning. The monitor showed their flight path as the shuttle looped around and flew closer and closer toward the spinning planet.

As they grew nearer, he searched for signs of population, but only saw high mountains, rough terrain, and a deep green jungle. He hadn't been the best student in geography, but that kind of terrain was a long way from Tygel Space Center. And where was Elise? She hadn't returned. A niggle of worry began to build. They were descending at a rapid rate and all he saw were treetops and mountain ridges.

The monitor on the chair in front of him went blank.

"Geesh!" Tempest complained. "I hate to travel on the shuttle." She reached into her bag for gum, unwrapped it, popped it into her mouth, and started to chew vigorously.

Unbuckling, Kayse clambered over Tempest into Elise's seat by the window. Tempest inspected him, arched an eyebrow, and commented, "Getting pretty friendly, aren't we?"

He ignored the comment and the accompanying smirk. "Where's Tygel? It was a big city when I left it. Why haven't we seen any buildings or roads, huh? I know there should be lots of outlying towns down there. Also, what happened to the monitor? It's stopped functioning." He turned to her.

She wrinkled her nose in concern and looked from him to peer out the window.

An escalating murmur of voices echoed around him as others began to rouse and wonder what was happening.

Tempest swiveled back around and gazed at him. "Where's Mom?"

With a sigh, he said, "That's worrying me. She left a while ago, saying she would be back soon, and she hasn't returned. I think I need to go find her."

With a touch on his arm, she shook her head. "Don't bother. She's probably the one flying this thing. She always tries to con the shuttle crew into letting her put a hand on the helm. When she's in space, she wants to be in the cockpit where the action is. She's probably fine."

Just then, a light came on overhead.

"This is your captain speaking. All passengers are to strap in. We'll be landing soon. I repeat, please remain seated for your own safety. Everyone prepare for landing."

The shuttle began vibrating and shaking as it hit the cloud layers and thermal winds. Uneasiness filled the cabin.

"Tighten your seatbelts, we're in for mild turbulence, but it will pass. The situation is under control."

A murmur rose from several passengers.

"Everyone sit down and be calm." A burly Terran eased into the center aisle and glowered around the cabin.

"What's going on?" a girl shouted, whose name he dredged up from introductions. *Jemma*. She started to unbuckle her seatbelt.

"I said, just relax." The large Terran pulled out a gun and aimed it at her.

"What's he doing?" a nervous voice added to the growing unquiet.

"We'll be landing soon. Everyone should just remain calm."

"Where are we? I demand to know what's happening." An Alysian male to his left asked, "Where are you taking us?" He stood up and moved toward the Terran who aimed the gun at him. A small pop sounded as the man stared at the Terran and then at the small dart stuck in his chest. He crumpled forward, his body falling onto several screaming Terrans.

"It's a hijacking," one woman shrieked and shoved the unconscious man into an empty seat next to her.

"I said to be calm and get ready for our landing," the muscled Terran shouted. He leveled the gun and swept it over the frightened passengers. "Or you'll be next."

Besides Kayse, Tempest snorted. "He's the one doing all the yelling. He can't just start ordering people around like that." She began unbuckling her seatbelt to rise.

"Put your seatbelt back on and remain quiet," Kayse ordered. "I don't want to hear another word out of you." He tugged her back down.

Tempest's mouth opened and closed. She stared at him. He glared back. Then, she clicked her belt back into place and gave a rebellious snort. She looked the other way, but she stayed put. He breathed a sigh of relief. Nothing could be done right now. Once they landed, maybe some opportunity to escape might open up. He wasn't going to get them both hurt by acting stupid at the wrong time.

They were now low enough to see the landscape in greater detail. He searched for signs of civilization, but all he saw was a small village surrounded by jungle with a few rough roads extending outward. It sure wasn't Tygel down there.

The shuttle swooped over treetops, edging closer and closer to swaying branches, until Kayse thought they would land in the very trees under them and then, at the last moment, the shuttle glided onto a narrow, hard-packed landing strip. The wheels screamed as they bit the rough ground and roared down a long runway, bouncing and shuddering. Kayse smelled burning rubber and scorched metal as the shuttle braked.

Finally, they came to a halt in what felt more like a controlled crash than a landing. He wanted to get out and kiss the ground. A number of passengers seemed to have the same idea and were unbuckling and grabbing baggage as they rushed toward the hatch. But a burly Terran stood there with his arms crossed, casually blocking the exit. Finally, a knock sounded on the other side, and he grabbed the latch to open it.

Voices murmured in excitement, "Where are we?" Frantically, Kayse sought his medallion and pushed the emergency signal to send out a message to Trey. Then he slipped it off his neck and into an inside pocket of his jacket.

Large leafy trees and dense foliage greeted his sight as he exited the shuttle. He heard several intakes of breath as the magnificent vegetation swayed before them. Green plants were considered a luxury on the station, and most likely many station dwellers had never seen living, growing plants this large and varied.

A strong, fecund odor of soil and plant material rose from the ground. He'd never experienced the musky aroma of a jungle, but the rich, loamy earth and the fragrant blooms called back memories of a planet bound childhood almost forgotten.

Makeshift tents and hastily built concrete buildings nestled within a cleared era not far from the runway. Several armed Terrans waited as passengers got off the shuttle. The guards directed them in single file to a large, block concrete building. Hard-faced Terrans with weapons stood at the door.

Just before he got to the building, Kayse glanced over his shoulder and saw Elise limned in the hatch with a look of anger on her face, and a gun pointed at her head. He swung back around to find a gun waved in his face as a harsh voice demanded all his valuables. A searcher's wand beeped out the secret hiding place of his medallion. Reluctantly, he handed it over, along with his caller, wrist computer, and music pod.

He watched as they march Elise past him. As she went by, she murmured, "Watch over Tempest, and don't do anything rash. I'm going to see what this is all about." The guard grabbed her away from him and pushed her toward the concrete building. He followed.

Everyone was forced into a, sparsely furnished room where one long table piled with papers stood on a hard plascrete floor against a cement wall. A room with a large window and door occupied the far corner. As Kayse looked through the glass window into the room, he noticed a man pacing back and forth on the other side. Obviously, an office, it held a desk, a table, a cluster of chairs and a built-in cabinet with sink. Elise glared at the guard and entered.

Kayse lingered outside by the office's door while the rest of the soldiers stripped valuables from passengers and segregated them into groups. He peered around and spied Tempest not far away, pouting in a nearby corner with a group of kids. Leaving the guards busy with the others, he strained to pick up snippets of the conversation between an officer and Elise, going on inside the office.

"After all we've accomplished, you're going to ruin everything with this fool stunt," an indignant Elise spouted. Kayse recognized her "Captain's Voice."

"Ruin? It's been fourteen annuals. Many are tired of being treated like second class citizens by arrogant Alysians."

Elise's voice rose in irritation. "You call the Alysians arrogant when you assume you have a right to their planet? I repeat, *their planet!* We are the strangers here. You expect because we are from Earth, they should welcome us with open arms? You expect plum jobs, high status, and all due reverence? Guess again, *Earthling.*" She emphasized the slur. "You don't want to do this."

"I want them to know that if they don't let us off that prison of a space station soon; your life is forfeit. With you as a hostage, your husband will persuade them to act now."

"Rather you'll persuade them we're everything they fear.

"You have married our enemy."

"Have you lost your mind? You will start a war here. They will label us terrorists because of this stupidity and hold all Terrans responsible. How are we ever going to get along with them if this is the way we act?"

"I'm not a terrorist. I'm a father who wants his daughter to grow up with dirt under her feet and blue skies above, but if I have to use threats, I will."

"This way you forfeit both your lives."

His hand went up as if to hit her, but just in time, he got control of his temper and the hand dropped. He spun around and strode over to his desk to gather some calm.

At the door, a Terran soldier came up to Kayse and pushed him away, waving him to the other side of the room where several guards were assigning sleeping tents.

Tempest sidled over to him with frightened eyes. "Kayse, what are they doing to my mother?" she asked.

"Arguing with her. But, she's holding her own for now," he said tightly. "What do you say to a little spying? I think we've discovered the base camp of rebel Terrans. Let's see what we can find out about them. My experience has been that you're good at spying. What do you think?"

A sly grin appeared on her face. "I may have a few abilities in that direction."

"Just be careful," was his answer as Terran soldiers led her away with the women.

Chapter 14

The makeshift cot was uncomfortable and the company restless. Still, he slept due to total exhaustion and a body trying to come to terms with new changes. Over the protests of every muscle in his body, the gravity of Alysia bore down on him. Outside, the wind disturbed his sleep. Trees and bushes rustled and slapped their leaves in a wild unfettered dance.

He dreamt of miniature robots running up and down carrying microscopic buckets of blood to various areas of his body. Invading nanobot armies hammered away at his bones, molding him into a new form. His mind morphed into a computer, as he became something other than human, with no emotion or feeling. He awoke with a start and a blinding headache.

So much for no feeling.

Light leaked in from the windows and heat clogged the room. The sky outside brooded overhead. He felt that if he stepped outside, the sky would fall on him. How would those born and bred on spaceships cope with the effects of planetfall?

Lying still, the dream dissipated while he gathered his wits and listened to voices murmuring about the room. Gradually, he became aware of something crawling along his arm and jerked upright, swatting wildly. He sat up on the edge of his bed, shaking his arms and legs. Several small dark critters dropped to the floor and skittered away. He rested his head in his hands as he sat slumped on the cot.

In that position, he could hear the hushed voices of others talking around him. For some reason, he understood the Terran words and, even more amazing, he had spoken it fluently without any effort a few times last night. Those few lessons under the learning hood seemed to have taken hold.

As he listened to their whispered conversations, he discovered several fellow passengers very happy to be here. They'd expected to end up on Alysia as indentured slaves in some private home or institution and, now, they might have better prospects.

Still, many complained about the gravity and the heat, while others commented on the dense wet air. They expected someone to regulate the weather to a cooler temperature and a lower humidity. They weren't used to an uncontrolled environment. Several continued to lie in bed, reluctant to get up. Indigenous wildlife seeking bodily fluids would soon solve that problem. He scratched at several bites rapidly swelling into burning, itching, red bumps around his legs and ankles.

One of the Terrans, excited at making planetfall, exclaimed, "Did you see the trees? I never thought trees could grow so big. Each one is a different shape and color, even those within the same species."

"Did you smell them?" another responded. "They smell exotic and strange."

"So? You and your buddies always smelled rather exotic and strange when on Terran Station," a friend retorted, followed by smothered chuckles.

"Lankford's here. I saw him. He came down earlier. Someone said that buddy of yours, David what's-his-name, is here too."

"Then let's go and see what's up," a nearby voice suggested. "Joe said they have a cafeteria where we can get breakfast."

Kayse decided it was time to get out of bed. The idea of food became a powerful motivator to go and check out the place. He found the refresher and splashed water on his face, then discovered his bag had been searched and placed back next to his sleeping cot. He gave a quick rummage through to find some clothes to wear, but noticed his medicine and data pads were missing. Shaking out his bedding caused a few more wiggling bodies to flop out and scurry away toward dark crevices.

Time to go.

Leaving the sleeping tent, he ambled toward a central clearing where he saw a line of people jostling each other near an eating area. Several Terrans stood by, casually holding weapons and chatting with the new arrivals. These captors appeared quite cordial, as long as everyone did what they requested.

Kayse edged his way behind a milling group and found himself at the end of a serving line where he grabbed both tray and utensils. Finally, wending his way inside the cafeteria, he arrived at the serving area. A quivering mass of a yellow substance landed on his plate along with some bread that a server handed to him. They crammed a glass of bright yellow juice into his free hand.

Across the room, Tempest sat at a corner table talking to one of the guards. The guard placed a hand on her shoulder and said something with a smarmy laugh. Angrily, she shrugged off the hand and tossed her hair.

Kayse could see the conversation going downhill fast, so he decided to get over there before a scene developed. Accelerating, he tried to navigate through the press of bodies but found it slow going.

Abruptly, the guard gripped Tempest's arm, brought her up out of her chair and pressed his body against hers, as he whispered something into her ear. Tempest stomped on the guard's foot hard and cursed.

An angry bellow issued from the guard's mouth.

"Leave the young lady alone," Kayse said as casually and as firmly as he dared upon arriving.

Surprised, the guard whirled around with an angry expression on his face, followed by a brief wince. Gathering himself, he glowered at Kayse and growled, "Just who do you think you're talking to, boy?"

The muscled guard stood larger than most Terrans and appeared quite imposing. He now focused on Kayse, who was still balancing his tray and trying to avoid bumping into others. Pushing Tempest aside, the guard swept out his hand and knocked Kayse's tray onto the floor. "I said are you talking to me, *boy*?"

As the guard started to raise his gun and aim, Kayse acted without thinking and knocked the gun aside, punching the guard squarely in the nose. Astonished, the man grabbed his nose with a roar as blood spurted out. He sucked in his breath. "Why you little…" He started a charge, but Kayse stepped aside and tripped him. The guard fell heavily to the floor as screaming and shouting people jumped out of their way. An area suddenly opened around the two of them. A few fled the building for help.

Kayse watched the attacker gather his wits about him and scan the floor for the dropped gun. Both spied it at the same time. The man dove for it, but Kayse was faster by far, and got to the gun first, picked it up, and stepped aside, waving it in the air.

The guard tried to get up but fell back down, holding his bleeding nose and shaking his head.

By now, they had everyone's attention. "Tom, Jack, shoot him," the guard shouted from the floor and pointed at Kayse. In his peripheral vision, Kayse saw two men approach, pulling out guns.

"Everyone stop right there," a commanding voice rang out. Kayse turned to glance at a tall, stern-faced man who entered the room. Everyone fell back, opening a path for him. He had burning green eyes and a chiseled face that revealed a small scar at the side of one cheek. As people scrambled out of his way, he strode to the center of the room and stopped before Kayse. The two other guards stepped back.

"There'll be no fighting in here," the newcomer ordered. "We have enough battles to fight without fighting each other." He stared in disgust at their attacker who was wiping a bloody nose and blinking dazedly. "Get up off the floor, Dan. Wipe the blood from your face. You look a mess." He glared at the struggling man. "You should know how I feel about fighting with newcomers. We're here to welcome them, not beat them up. We want them as friends, not enemies." Their leader reached down to help the man up.

"I was just talking to the little lady when he started the fight," Dan protested as he rose to stand, holding his nose.

"He kept touching me." Tempest edged forward, eager to put in a word. "He wouldn't leave me alone even though I asked nicely at first."

Up close, Kayse recognized the man who had argued with Elise in the office. This person must run the camp.

The man clenched his jaw and fisted a hand, saying, "Dan, when will you learn manners around young girls?"

"Sir…"

"Report to my office in ten minutes, but first, go get your face cleaned up. Move." He waved his hand and turned his back on the disgruntled antagonist, swinging around to face Kayse.

"So what happened here?"

With a heavy breath, Kayse answered, "I saw him bothering her. I came over to protect her, and he waved a gun in my face. Then he knocked my tray to the floor."

"Tom, Jack, get this mess cleaned up and put those guns away. Dan Smith's a Degrade and an idiot, but you two should know better." The man shook his head and stuck out his hand to Kayse.

"I'm Commander Jeb Brock. I run this camp. This is not the way I expect our newcomers to be greeted," he apologized.

Kayse studied the hand, puzzled. He'd been told shaking hands was some sort of Terran first contact ritual. He put out his hand and tried to imitate the firm shake of the Commander. His fist still felt sore from the thrown punch, and he tried not to wince as the man squeezed it.

"I'm Kayse Kiare and this is Tempest Steele." Kayse introduced them with as polite a tone as he could muster.

The man blinked and withdrew his hand.

"Steele! Blast! She's the captain's daughter, isn't she? Oh, better and better. I'm going to kill the man for his stupidity. Her mother is already in a temper. That damn fool should know better than to mess with the captain's kid."

"I'm not a kid. I'm thirteen," Tempest interrupted, rising onto her tiptoes.

Commander Brock narrowed his eyes. "I'll speak to him. He shouldn't be bothering any girls her age. Unfortunately, this isn't the first time for him. He's a good soldier, but he's walking a thin line here. So, are you her bodyguard or something? I saw how you moved. It was quite impressive. We need to talk. Come to my office in, ah, fifteen minutes."

Kayse frowned, not knowing the measurement.

Jeb Brock caught his hesitation. "Right. Alysians say fifteen intervals." He spun on the balls of his feet and strode out of the room, not waiting for a refusal.

***

Within the allotted time, Kayse arrived outside the Commander's office. Immediately, a guard ushered him into the room.

Inside, Commander Jeb Brock ranted at Dan, but stopped as soon as Kayse entered. The Commander signaled him to come over. "Dan is leaving now, but first he has something to say to you." Commander Brock glanced pointedly at the guard.

Dan took a deep breath, struggled a bit, but finally managed to say, "I didn't mean to rile the girl any. I just wanted to get to know her, friendly like. Never dreamed she was only twelve. She looks older. She's a bit touchy too." He shuffled his feet a bit and shot a glare at Commander Brock who narrowed his eyes. "She stomped my foot."

"Dan," the Commander murmured.

Dan blinked and shuffled his feet some more, gazing downward. "Sorry 'bout it. I won't bother her no more."

The Commander's eyebrows rose and a grin appeared on his face. He clapped Dan on the back. "It takes a man to admit a mistake and apologize." Dan made a noise in his throat, but swallowed it as Commander Brock walked him to the door. As they passed Kayse, Dan tossed him a murderous look over his left shoulder.

"Try to behave, Dan, and keep your hands off the young girls. You understand that if I hear any more about this sort of thing, I'm going to act, and I can guarantee you won't like it. Howard's going to need help processing new arrivals. Why don't you go see what you can do over there?"

The Commander pushed him out the door and came back toward Kayse, shaking his head. "Dan can't help what he is. He was made rough."

That sounded curious to Kayse.

"It's a problem, but he's a damned fine soldier, and I need him. I've warned him before, but he has a hard time hearing me. With that broken nose, he won't be able to smell anything, but maybe he'll be able to hear a little better."

Motioning Kayse over to a simple sitting area, the commander gestured for him to take a seat. He turned to an alcove where he reached in for a rough earthenware mug and a thermos and started to pour out a dark liquid. He lifted the mug and asked, "Would you like some coffee? We Terrans drink a lot of it. You probably didn't get a chance to get any due to Dan's bad behavior." He sighed. "Again, I apologize for my men. I try to explain proper conduct to them. I've had to deal with more pressing matters recently and, consequently, discipline has slid some.

He poured the coffee and handed it to Kayse, who took it with a mumbled, "Thank you, sir."

After a brief silence, during which they both sipped their drinks, Commander Brock said, "Appears you know how to handle yourself, though." He eyed Kayse speculatively. "Nice moves back there."

"I've taken a few lessons." Kayse smiled at him tightly.

The coffee was hot, strong, and tasted good. Commander Brock poured some more for himself and took a satisfying sip. He smiled. "So how did you get tangled up with Captain Fujeint's daughter?"

"Elise and Richard sort of adopted me."

"Elise and Richard?" Commander Brock let out a heavy breath. He shook his head and rubbed his free hand over his forehead. "First name basis. Damn, why me?"

"That is their names."

"Yes, I know," Commander Brock sighed. "And how old are you, son?"

Kayse hesitated to offer too many details. Trey had warned him, so he said, "Too young to be fighting that guard, but old enough to know better—now."

Brock grinned and poured some more coffee for Kayse, then sat down. "We Terrans never like to talk about our age either—especially near Alysians. You act young, whatever your age."

Kayse pondered an appropriate response as he took another sip.

Commander Brock chuckled. "Rumor was Captain Fujeint claimed she was over five hundred years old, but I told her she didn't look a day over two hundred." He appeared to wait for a laughing response.

Instead, Kayse choked as the time span registered. Catching his breath, he said, "Are Terran years anywhere near Alysian annuals?"

Startled by his reaction, the Commander rubbed his chin in chagrin. "Oh…just a joke. Forget it. Yes, very close, but forget what I said." His arms attempted to shoo away the thought.

Changing the subject, Kayse muttered something about the coffee being hot.

"I like my coffee hot, even in this damned climate," Brock responded, smiling.

Kayse thought now might be the time to ask the burning question. "Ah, where are we, anyway, sir?"

"You'll learn after you're vetted."

"Vetted?" *That sounded sinister.*

"Checked out. You're a bit of a mystery. You talk funny. You have amazing reflexes and, for a youngster, you handle yourself well in a fight. You're too big for a ship's boy. The pale skin and chiseled face don't fool me. My bet's that you're an Alysian. The question is: who are you exactly?"

"My parents are dead. Killed in an attack, as I said. Elise and Richard recently adopted me. They knew my parents and were kind enough to take me on."

Which was close to the truth.

"You're a most interesting boy, and I welcome you to our humble little camp. Maybe you could be of some use here. Cooperation would benefit you."

"A difficult step for me to consider since the shuttle was highjacked, and I was kidnapped against my will."

The Commander barked a laugh. "Hijacked is a strong word. 'Detoured' would describe it better. What I'm doing is trying to carve out a spot for Terrans where they can have a choice in their lives. I offer a place where there's dirt beneath their feet and blue skies above. Here, they can feel the wind in their face and stand up free and out from under Alysian tyranny."

"You're raising an army to fight the Alysians, aren't you?"

Commander Brock frowned.

Kayse continued, "This is an Alysian planet. Don't you think we have a right to decide who we want here?"

"Yes, but there's plenty of room." The Commander shrugged. "You don't know what it's like to live on Alysia as a Terran."

"Are they your enemy?"

The Commander grimaced as he set down his drink. "Not unless they want to be. Pure and simple."

"Richard Steele isn't going to be too happy you've abducted his wife and daughter. He's going to come looking for them."

"Steele's done a lot for us, and I appreciate his efforts, but it's been over fourteen bloody years, and we're still under Alysian domination and treated like dirt. It's time we put some backbone into our demands. You'll see what I'm talking about after you've been there a while. They despise Terrans and anyone associated with them. If you live with Captain Fujeint, you'll be treated differently. Do not doubt that. Here, I offer you a place of your own among equals. You'll be treated with respect and dignity. Think about it."

"I *was* treated with dignity and respect," Kayse retorted as he handed his cup back. He clenched his jaw. "It's only since I've been here, that I've been treated poorly. Richard won't like his wife kidnapped. He'll turn this planet upside down until he finds her. He has the means. He values his wife and will want her back; that much I know already. Innocent people could be hurt or killed. You have antagonized the one man who championed your cause and that can't be good."

Commander Brock pursed his lips and narrowed his eyes. Kayse realized people probably didn't talk back to this man often, and most tried not to disagree with him to his face. Kayse might regret his candor.

"That supposes Captain Fujeint wants to go back. I'm not so stupid that I'd expose this camp. Everyone who fights with me does so because he or she volunteered. I've taken precautions to protect the people under my care, rest assured. Elise went and married a powerful Alysian, now our enemy. I fear she's under his influence; so lately, I find it hard to trust even her."

"Elise can be trusted."

With a grunt, Commander Brock said, "I would like to believe that, but nowadays one can't be too careful. Experience often leaves a bad taste and a doubting heart on this world, if you're Terran."

Commander Brock stood up and put out his hand. Kayse hesitated. He felt fairly certain Terrans shook hands when they met, but now he was leaving. Brock frowned at the hesitation, so Kayse decided it must be an important ritual and put out his hand to shake again. That brought a smile to the man's face. A knock sounded on the door, and a guard came in to escort Kayse back to his barracks.

As he walked along, pondering the recent conversation, someone came past and gave Kayse a rough shove. Startled, he looked up into Dan's snarling face. "Watch yourself, kid. You'll regret making me appear a fool in front of the Commander."

Before Kayse could answer, Dan strode past into a nearby building, leaving him to stare disconcertedly after his new enemy.

***

He found Elise in a separate tent alongside the women's main tent, a bit of a walk from the square, cement central building. She was talking to Tempest and two other girls standing beside her. One was the attractive blonde from the shuttle. Jemma Telluria, he remembered. He wanted to get to know her better. The other girl he'd seen talking to Elise, also on the shuttle. Giving her a closer appraisal, he admired her short, dark, curly hair and lively smile, all wrapped in an attractive package. He guessed she was near his age, possibly older. However, the intelligence in her eyes attracted him the most.

"There you are!" Elise strode over to him, with Tempest in her wake.

Tossing him a questioning look, Tempest said, "I'm glad you're all right." She turned to her mother. "Kayse came to my rescue when that guard bothered me." She grinned at him. "You really gave him a good punch in the nose."

Elise glared at her, and she subsided. "Tempest has this wild story about you getting into a fight with one of the camp guards." Elise ran a hand through her hair. It appeared it hadn't been the first time she'd done so. "Kayse, we don't want to antagonize these people."

"He was bullying Tempest, for Fate's sake."

Elise crossed her arms. "Let me deal with them."

"When that bully was harassing Tempest, I didn't see you anywhere nearby to 'deal' with them," he said stiffly.

Elise frowned. "Well, let me know if he bothers her again and be careful around here. I'll talk to Jeb about it."

The dark-haired girl cleared her throat.

Elise nodded and faced her. "Oh yes, Kayse, this is Ailey DeVey. She came up with us on the shuttle when we came from Alysia to the Earth2 Station. She's doing a paper on electrobiological interfacing and works at Tygel Med Center. I arranged for her to interview Dr. Luttrell."

He nodded at her.

Elise gestured to the familiar blonde standing next to her. "And you remember Jemma Telluria from the shuttle? I believe you've already met. Her family and Richard are good friends. Plus, she and her brother are helping me." The girl broke into a wide smile.

Kayse acknowledged her carefully, along with a sideways glance at Tempest, who thankfully remained calm.

Elise left the entrance, walking toward the concrete building and Commander Brock's office. "I'll be back soon. I'm going to talk to Jeb about that guard and get a few things straightened out."

Kayse swung around and found himself staring at three female faces, who simultaneously threw him feral grins. He backed up, stumbling a bit. Suddenly, he felt like a gibbet in the presence of hungry raptors. He could feel his face heating up and his hands began to trembling.

Not surprisingly, Tempest spoke first. "You were pretty impressive with those moves. That man kept pestering me. He wouldn't go away."

An incomprehensible anger flooded him at her foot stomping stunt. "Do you know how much trouble I'm in because of you? That guard's hates me because I made him look like a fool in front of his buddies."

"He is a fool. A bozo."

"A bozo?" Kayse scrunched up his face as the meaning came clear. "That's another Terran term, isn't it? I can understand Terran well and speak it fluently. That's scary."

"You've gotten pretty scary, Kayse, let's admit it," Tempest said. "But whatever dear Dr. Jay did come in handy in that fight." She grinned. "Of course, you're an Alysian and so it seems reasonable that you're scary and bossy." She wiggled her eyebrows at him.

He made a noise through his nose, and then observed all the listening females. Assuming an indignant tone, he said, "Where can I get a bite to eat? I'm starving. I missed my breakfast, remember?"

"We'll take you," the three chimed in. Feeling like a prisoner surrounded by guards, he fell in step and headed out toward the cafeteria.

By the time they got in line for food again, they were serving lunch.

Chapter 15

The heat beat down without mercy. Flexing sore muscles, Kayse squinted up into the sun-blazed sky and wondered if rescue would ever come. Five cycles, or what the Terrans referred to as weeks, had passed and still no Trey. The medallion might be defective, or else Trey couldn't rescue him for some reason. Maybe he lied; maybe he died.

Due to the heat, he'd stripped to just his work pants, and his bare chest and arms glistened with sweat. After working all day clearing the jungle, Kayse felt hot, tired, and thirsty. Glad to be finally finished, he leaned over and lifted the freshly filled bucket, pouring water over his now bronzed and muscled chest. The cool, spring-fresh liquid felt wonderful sluicing over his hot, gritty body. Water splashed into a parched mouth and the rest he rubbed over his face.

Out of the corner of his eye, he caught movement and noticed Tempest off in the distance by the rail fence, staring at him. He waved as Jemma joined her, and they both waved back. That meant dinner tonight with the two of them, and most likely, Ailey also. Finally, Tempest had turned thirteen and now expected the world to consider her a teenager. A small party, organized by Jemma, had marked the momentous occasion, and Tempest already was making plans for her fourteenth.

Kayse's thoughts turned to his decision to work for Commander Brock, but to delay a commitment on joining any Terran resistance. He actually enjoyed the rough labor.

It distracted his mind from going crazy wondering who he was and gave him time to get used to how his new body worked. Usually he completed his job before the others. He liked pushing his body's limits and making his body stronger every day. Being among the workers also gave him an opportunity to learn more about the Terrans.

Gazing around, he noticed the girls leaving and the rest of the team finishing up. As more water buckets arrived, his group joined him under some trees.

"Damn, you were quick diverting those falling logs," a Terran named Pete who had red curly hair commented. "You probably saved my life."

"No probably about it," offered a second fellow by the name of Ted. He nodded a polite greeting as he walked over.

Pete picked up a bucket and poured half the water over his head, then shook out the dripping moisture.

"Gah, Pete," exclaimed the more fastidious Grant who stood next to him. His gaunt face scrunched up in distaste. "You're shaking water all over us like some damn cur."

Squinting at Kayse, Ted commented, "How do you manage to get it all done so quick? My muscles are killing me."

With a shrug, Kayse admitted, "My muscles ache too. In fact, my whole body aches, but I actually like the work. When I'm done, I feel like I've accomplished something."

"Yeah," choked Pete, coughing on inhaled water from the bucket sluicing. "Raising blisters is my big accomplishment." He displayed several prominent ones on both hands.

"Well, the work is doing me some good at least," bragged Ted with a smirk. "I'm getting tan and buff. The babes are noticing me, not so sure about you losers."

"Ack!" someone choked. "Dream on."

"I'd rather be at home, relaxing in air conditioning with my wife," countered Frank. "This sucks." He pushed hair out of his face and swung a sunburned Alysian arm, trying to loosen some tight muscles.

Pete and Ted scowled at him as they picked up towels to wipe off moisture and exchanged quick angry glances.

"They lashed one of the Alysians who refused to work. Wasn't a pretty sight," Pete commented.

Glaring at the suddenly tight expression on Pete's face, Frank grabbed a towel and stormed off, leaving the others to stare uneasily after him.

"Arrogant Alysian," Pete muttered.

Kayse noticed the sun setting behind the trees. He wanted to get going for a real shower and change into clean, dry clothes before dinner. And he didn't want to get into a fight. "Gotta go," he said to the group around him as they grumbled, stomped, and rinsed themselves off in the clearing.

Pete plucked at Kayse's arm. "Thanks again, I owe you."

"Glad I could save a life." He grinned at the grateful Terran.

"You'll be regretting that soon enough," shouted a voice from out of the group. Everyone laughed, the tension breaking up, as Pete protested loudly.

A feeling of pleasant camaraderie rolled over Kayse as he headed off for his shower. His thoughts turned to his upcoming dinner companions. He smiled, thinking of Jemma who often asked what he was doing and how things were going. He liked that she showed an interest.

He remembered when recently, she'd put her hand on his arm, rubbing it reassuringly, and his breath had stopped at her touch. Her hand had felt silken soft compared to his callused mitt, and her blonde hair had looked beautiful all tumbled down around her face. He smiled thinking of her. She always smelled like fresh green grass. She'd stared into his eyes and said that if he ever needed anything to let her know. He wondered exactly what she might be talking about and found himself lost in fantasies of wild sex.

Arriving near their living quarters, he stopped outside the tent where Jemma and the other girls slept. Exhaustion and tired muscles kept him from moving forward, except for a bit of swaying. His thoughts slid into oblivion as he stared at nothing, too tired to move.

That was until Tempest stomped out. "You know you're standing out here like some zombie? You coming in or what?"

Her voice startled him out of his reverie, and he blinked. She appeared distressed. He wondered if anything had happened. "Is that Dan guy bothering you again?"

Her eyes flicked away, and she ducked her head. "Sometimes. But I can handle that bozo guard." She lifted her chin and gave him a defiant stare, her eyes glistening.

Scowling at her, he said, "I saw you two arguing the other day. It looked like he was going to hit you, but then he just waved his arms and shouted before stomping off."

She grimaced. "He likes to shout and hit. He has anger management issues." She closed her eyes. "Actually, he does scare me a little. Something's not right with him," she whispered. "I did a little investigating and found out he likes to bully and hurt young girls. I'm in the category. He's careful how he does it and makes them too frightened to say anything for fear of what he might do to them."

"You will let me know if you want me to stop him, won't you?"

"Yeah, I'll let you know if he crosses the line."

"Tell your mom so she can talk to Commander Brock. She'll persuade him to get Dan under control."

"Yeah, okay. Gotta get ready for dinner. We on?"

"Heading to the tent to get ready right now."

***

The next afternoon while he was coming back from working on yet another building, he felt a rough shove from behind. Stumbling forward, he whirled around to see the smirking face of Dan Smith.

"I haven't forgotten you, boy," Dan said with a sneer. "I paid a visit to your little friend the other night, and she said to give you my regards. I'm thinking she could be a lot of fun now that the Commander has his mind on other things."

Kayse wondered momentarily what "other things" the Commander might be concerned about, but then narrowed his eyes and glared at the man, remembering Tempest's comments.

"Leave Tempest alone," Kayse growled. "If I hear you're bothering her, I'll…"

"You'll what?" Dan slid a wicked looking knife out of its sheath. "You're forgetting your place here. You Alysians aren't allowed to carry weapons, are you? Sometime it won't be a push; it'll be a blade between your back ribs when no one's watching. This is Terran territory. You got no say here. Think on that, kid."

Reaching over with lightning speed, Kayse whacked Dan's wrist, causing the guard to drop the blade. "You're just the type to stab a man in the back rather than face him, I bet," Kayse snarled as he reached to snatch up the knife before Dan could react. "I'd be careful around sharp instruments if I were you. You could hurt yourself." He waved the weapon in the guard's face as Dan cradled his wrist and glared.

"You better watch your back," Dan retorted. Abruptly, he made a lunge for the knife, which Kayse easily sidestepped.

Recovering his balance, Dan threatened, "Next time I'll bring my buddies, and you won't be smiling so much." Without further bravado, he strode off.

For a while, Kayse kept a wary eye out, but none of Dan's friends showed up or threatened him.

That night, tired from the day's work, Kayse fell hard asleep. He found himself dreaming that he was lost and wandering through a musty, moss-covered corridor in an old castle, searching for something. Opening a hidden door, he discovered a high platform lit by a web of flashing lights. Stumbling forward, he climbed onto the platform and teetered at its brink while arcing lights surrounded him. The platform grew higher and higher, reaching far out into space, past galaxies of whirling stars and planets. As he looked down over the edge, he felt himself start to tumble forward and cartwheel through the void. He floated about until a shuttle swooped under him, and he landed inside. Panicked, he strained to identify the shadowy figure of the pilot. He felt he desperately needed to know who the person was, but couldn't quite make out the face no matter how hard he tried.

Dimly, he heard a voice chanting, "Humpty Dumpty sat on a wall. Humpty Dumpty had a great fall. All the king's horses and all the king's men couldn't put Humpty together again."

Humpty Dumpty? What kind of name is that? I won't be named Humpty Dumpty. It's an awful name, and I refuse to use it!

As he woke up, he was protesting, "No, no," but then realized it was only a dream. Relief swept through him. Kayse sounded so much better than 'Humpty Dumpty.' He'd fallen a great long way into the distant future, now in pieces, with no one able to put him back together. Like the subject of the rhyme, he would never be the same again. Then he wondered idly where all the king's horses and all the king's men were because they weren't nearby, and he needed saving. Why would he think that?

The odd thought made him shiver.

He opened his eyes and saw Tempest in the dark, looming over him.

"What are you doing here?" He surveyed the darkened room nervously and sat up.

She brushed a hand over his face, pushing back a strand of hair. "Reciting a famous Terran nursery rhyme for you. I came for a visit. I figured you needed cheering up."

"How did you get past the sentries? Do you know the trouble you'll get me into if they find you here? Your mother…"

Tempest sat on the cot and pushed some hair out of her face. "I was scared and lonely. That Dan person came by and said scary things to me. You said to let you know."

"Not in the dead of night!"

She shrugged. "I just wanted to be somewhere safe, that's all. I couldn't sleep. I knew that if you were next to me, everything would be all right. I was scared, and only you make me feel safe."

He blew out a breath. "Okay, we're going to tell your mom first thing in the morning." He stood up.

"Hey, where are you going?" She grabbed his arm.

"I'm pulling over an empty cot so I'll be right here, but you have to promise to go to sleep as I'm exhausted. And you must promise to tell your mother in the morning."

"And Dan?"

"I'll have a little chat with him tomorrow. This has gone on for too long. But now, let's get some sleep."

***

He awoke with Tempest nowhere to be seen, but the rumpled sheets proved it hadn't been another dream. Someone had to stop Dan, and he was the best one available. Or maybe Elise could do something. He would talk to her so she could notify Commander Brock that Dan's harassment hadn't stopped.

After breakfast, he went searching for Dan and found him arguing with someone. It seemed the man liked to argue with just about everyone. He didn't recognize the person as he was standing with his back to him, but Dan's eyes shifted to his, peering past the stranger's broad shoulder.

"Ah, Kayse. There you are, boy." Dan nodded at him, then scanned his surroundings. Kayse moved purposefully toward him. Dan fumbled for his knife, but Kayse still carried it. Dan's eyes widened as he saw Kayse pull out the blade and glare at him.

Suddenly, the stranger whirled around, and Kayse felt a blow to his hand that sent the knife skittering to the ground. The stranger then spun back around to deliver a hard punch to Dan, whose eyes rolled back into his head as he collapsed onto the ground.

Kayse stopped, shocked. No one had ever moved that fast on him. He studied the fellow more closely. The man stood at an even height to his with a dark, neatly trimmed beard that covered a large portion of his face. A straw hat sat canted on his head. He wore a white shirt and dark jeans. Although dressed like most men in camp, the guy moved differently.

The stranger turned to Kayse. "What the frag do you think you're doing? You planning to kill me?" The stranger bent over and picked up the weapon.

Shaking his head, Kayse pointed at Dan, now sprawled on the ground. "Not you, him. He's threatening a friend of mine, and I needed to have a serious personal conversation with him. The knife was to get his attention."

The man wiped sweat from his forehead. Scanning the area, he said, "I'm searching for a Kayse Kiare." His eyes squinted and then widened. "Kayse? Is that you?"

With a frown, Kayse answered, "Yes, who wants to know?" He eyed the man as something familiar about him rang a bell.

"Wow! I would never have...wow!" The man shook his head as if clearing it. Then, the man's hands gripped his shoulders. "Are you out of your mind? Carrying a knife and threatening a guard! Do you want to die? If his friends don't slit your throat, the Commander will have you strung up, flogged or just quietly disposed of somewhere in the jungle under some tree. Your life would be over, no matter what, and that's not an option here."

Kayse listened to the voice, looked past the beard, and then relaxed in the man's iron grip. "Trey! Where have you been? I thought you said you'd come right away if I activated the beacon."

"Do you have any idea how difficult it was to find you? And by the way, why aren't you wearing the medallion? I can't find you if you just leave it lying around where anyone can pick it up." He threw the necklace at Kayse, who reached out and caught it. "Some muscle-bound guard was wearing it, and he wasn't too happy to hand it over to me. In fact, he's downright pissed. My time is limited here, because soon someone will discover him and untie him. Then, he'll come looking for me." He squinted at Kayse. "You really have changed, though, totally unrecognizable. It also makes you extra hard to locate...which probably is a good thing."

Kayse waved away his words. "They highjacked the shuttle. They took all my stuff from me with a gun in my face to persuade me to hand it over. I barely had time to activate the beacon. Now, this goon threatens Tempest and is after me because I interfered when he tried to molest her. He means to hurt her, and now he wants to kill me." He gathered breath, suddenly realizing that there was a lot of anger inside of him now bursting forth.

Trey stepped back from Kayse's barrage of outraged emotion and put a hand up. "Yes, well, this place is lined with dense jungle to the south, on the north high impassable mountains, and on the east, a broad river with lots of trees and brush. Give me a break, will you? It took a while to get here, but now that I'm here, I may be able to help you. What's going on, anyway?"

"They call us guests, but some of us are really little more than prisoners." Kayse heaved a sigh. "I'm not sure about their Commander, Jeb Brock. He talks a nice line, but he has a bunch of goons running the place, and they are not stellar people. One's a real asshole." Kayse glared at the still unconscious Dan.

Checking the area to make sure the coast was clear, Trey motioned Kayse to follow him. He led him to a dense stand of trees and motioned him in. The close-growing vegetation protected them from being noticed too easily.

Trey brought his voice down to a whisper. "Commander Brock may be willing to look the other way for that guard to pursue his dream of an independent Terran state. He needs every strong arm he can collect who is willing to fight for his cause. Brock is not going to get rid of someone like him unless he's forced to do so."

Pausing to stop and survey the area again, Trey continued, "Trace is trying to put together a rescue mission, but he keeps getting tied up in committee hearings. Therefore, that leaves Deuce Card to lead any rescue. He's part of I.N.Sys, but someone I trust. However, I.N.Sys is suspect. I believe there's a traitor in the organization. So, it's important not to reveal who you are to anyone in the rescue mission, or anyone who could talk to your rescuers."

"Oh, that's great. As if things aren't bad enough, I have to worry someone in the rescue may want me kidnapped or dead. Your list of would-be assassins is getting awfully long, and I'm not the bad guy here. I haven't done anything."

"So far," countered Trey.

"I'm not planning on doing anything."

"A lot of people are afraid of you. You present a potential threat to them or potential power."

"I haven't done anything that would hurt anyone." Kayse ran a hand through his hair in exasperation.

"You just tried to attack him." Trey pointed to Dan who was still out like a light.

"He deserved it. He's been harassing Tempest, and I thought ...just to scare him some."

Frowning, Trey tapped him on the chest with the knife. "Hold on a little longer. We're not sure who's after you. Let's just leave it for now that certain people are frightened and might do something drastic if they knew who or where you were. So, we have to proceed carefully." He handed the knife back.

"I'm surrounded by angry Terrans."

"Then infiltrate them. Learn what they plan and what their strengths are."

"You want me to be a spy?"

"With caution. This is the first off-the-grid installation I.N.Sys has located, and Trace wants to see if there are others, how strong an army they have, and what their intentions are."

"What happens when Dan complains to their Commander?" He pointed at the unconscious guard on the ground. "My life's not going to be worth much then." Kayse hunched his shoulders and stared.

"So go right to Brock now. Get there before your friend here does. Make a preemptive strike. Tell him how Dan is acting and what a danger it is to the whole camp. Say some stranger punched him and act ignorant. Blame me. I did do it. I'm betting that Commander Brock knows what Dan is like. Meanwhile, I'll help Deuce gather a rescue team. Give us four cycles. This place is buried in jungle. Have Elise gather anyone who wants to leave with her and put them on alert. Someone will contact you when the time is right."

Trey left without another word, leaving Kayse staring into trees, holding the knife, and finally glancing down at an unconscious Dan Smith.

Chapter 16

Four cycles, a little over a Terran month as the camp calculated it, passed with everything pretty much the same. Kayse wondered if Trey had gotten lost in the jungle or died trying to get out. Fortunately, Dan subsided in his harassment of Tempest. Commander Brock occupied him with other things and put him on a short leash, thanks to Elise's protests and his complaints. During that time, Kayse managed to make a favorable impression on several people in the camp through his willingness to work and his camaraderie. As a result, only a few listened or sympathized with Dan. Then, Kayse noticed a shift in the camp's atmosphere. People acted as if they expected something to happen.

That afternoon, Kayse and Tempest sat eating lunch at the canteen. Puzzled, he said, "Something's up. Commander Brock has an all-out call on every able-bodied man to clear and extend the runway. So, I'm on a short shift to get back because I'm one of their better workers." He smirked at her. "Want to feel my muscles? I'm not your chunky boy anymore."

Exhausted beyond endurance, his muscles ached fiercely almost every night, but he wasn't about to mention that to her. She eyed him and the bulging arm muscle he painfully flexed for her.

"No thanks, I can see what a mighty man you are from here." She took a spoonful of soup and blew on it, studiously avoiding any further appraisal of his musculature.

Shrugging, he tore off a chunk of bread. "Why are they clearing the airstrip?"

"Perhaps so the shuttle can take off," she said, giving him a disgusted look, as if he were some moron. She dabbed a piece of bread meticulously in the soup and grinned at him with a superior expression. "Or land a large plane in order to get any arriving stationers away to somewhere else."

"Where would they get a large plane?"

"I imagine they stole one right out from under the dumbass military's nose. Before we left the station to head home, Dad said there was some flap going on that delayed the committee hearings. I got the feeling it was a military crisis since dad mentioned General Moore's name."

"I wonder when it's coming."

"Soon is the chatter." Tempest chewed on her bread a while. "I noticed a lot of people packing their stuff on the sly. Commander Brock is getting his people ready to move, and mom has put the word out to some trusted Alysians to be ready."

Running a hand through his hair, Kayse nervously murmured, "The runway won't be ready tomorrow, but maybe if the commander keeps pushing really hard, we'll get it finished within the next cycle." Gazing past her to some distant point, he murmured, "Any rescue team might find an empty camp."

"I don't think they're quite that organized here," she countered, rolling her eyes.

"According to Trey, this isn't an easy place to get to. It's well hidden and well protected. It could be close."

"Yes, well, let me see what I can find out. I'll come by tonight to let you know. Dan meets his cronies for drinks at some hangout almost every night. Maybe I can spy on them and find something out. Then I'll drop by your tent around midnight if I have any news."

He leaned forward abruptly. "No, it's too dangerous. I don't want you anywhere near that brute and his buddies."

"Yeah, but then how am I ever going to find out things? *You* were the one who told me to spy on people. Besides, I like the midnight rendezvous idea. I haven't done that in a while." She stood up.

"No! Don't!" He half rose from his seat and reached out.

Avoiding his grasp, she picked up her tray and swung around to leave, waving fingers at him over her left shoulder.

No more breaks were allowed, and the weather became brutally hot. Rumor flew around camp that a plane or another shuttle would be landing, which could launch to the space station and return with a load of unauthorized Terran immigrants. Commander Brock would then disperse the arrivals to Terran hideouts around Alysia. It was an unprecedented move. Terrans had never done anything so brazen before. Everyone was abuzz.

Kayse's team worked hard until dusk. Commander Brock even dropped by the airstrip to commend his unit on the fine job they were doing. He went from man to man, encouraging them, but stopped often to gaze skyward with a worried expression. Nothing arrived, except nightfall. Too tired to care, Kayse wolfed down his dinner in a blur of pain and exhaustion and then stumbled off to bed. He was glad to hear Elise had acted on his rescue alert comments. Hopefully she took care of who she talked to, as Commander Brock didn't need to find out about any Alysian rescue before it happened.

***

Deep in the night, a light tap on his arm woke him. His muscles ached in protest as he rolled over. Waking up in the dim light left him confused as to where he was and what was happening. Blinking out sleep, he recalled the camp and his precarious situation. A stifled groan escaped his mouth. The looming black shape above him didn't appear to be either Tempest or Trey. He jerked up onto an elbow, trying to focus, when he recognized Angel's luminous golden eyes gazing at him in the dim light. As he started to say something, a quick hand over his mouth prevented any sound.

"Tempest?" the soft voice questioned.

"Tent next to Elise," he whispered back.

Angel shook his head.

Their lunch discussion came to mind, and Kayse wondered if she'd gone to eavesdrop on Dan. They'd kept him so busy working on the airstrip, he'd found no time to check in on her that evening. She might get in trouble...most likely already was. Sudden concern caused him to clench his jaw as adrenaline rushed through his body.

A finger crooked at him, and he rose noiselessly to dress, glad that his clothes lay in a carryall at the foot of his bed. Thinking about Tempest, several thoughts raced through his mind. One was Dan Smith. What if he'd caught her spying on him? The thought sent an anxious shiver through him.

An eyebrow lifted on Angel's face. The Enjelise pointed a forefinger toward the door where an unconscious guard lay slumped. His own eyebrows rose, and Angel grinned back, putting a finger to his lips.

Kayse gestured for them to go out and waggled an index finger for Angel to follow. He tried to remember where Dan's bunk was located. Then he recalled it sat at the outer edge of the camp in a small cabin where most of the guards slept.

Angel tapped his watch and flashed five fingers, three times at him. Fifteen. That didn't give them much time. Kayse nodded. Around him in the dark, other figures began moving in stealth.

"Tempest," he mouthed her name at the Enjelise. Angel nodded and gestured him forward. Kayse took off at a hard run, listening for Angel's tread behind him.

In no time, they found the cabin. A dim light glimmered inside and peering through a window, he saw Tempest gagged and bound to a chair with a scowling Dan standing in front of her.

It appeared as if they both had stopped to gather some energy after a recent struggle. Her top was torn. A fresh red splotch swelled on her left cheek. Then she banged around in the chair, trying to get loose while making angry grunting noises. She paused, breathing hard and glaring harder. Dan stood with his fists clenched, trying to catch his breath. Red bite marks lined one arm and hand.

Angel pointed at the front and then at Kayse. Circling a finger, Angel pointed at himself. Kayse noticed the cabin was otherwise empty.

When might Dan's friends return?

As he waited for Angel to circle around to the back, he worried over the limited amount of time that remained. Finally, estimating that Angel had moved into place, Kayse kicked the door open with an angry grunt and bellowed, "What's going on, Smith?"

Dan whipped around to face Kayse. His gaze moved from Tempest to Kayse, and widened in alarm. Angel crept up behind him, a dart gun in his hand. He fired.

Pivoting around, Dan grabbed the back of his neck and shot a baleful glare at Angel as he slid down to the floor and passed out.

Angel waved the gun triumphantly.

Kayse knelt at Tempest's side. "Are you all right?"

"Do I look all right?"

"Dan didn't rape you, did he?"

Tempest leaned her head forward, closed her eyes, and whispered, "No."

"You're sure?"

She lifted her head and her eyes flew open. "I think I would know something like that. He touched me. He touched me in places where he shouldn't, but he didn't rape me? He just wanted to scare me into keeping quiet. It's the way he gets away with stuff, but you got here before he did anything really bad...so no, he hasn't raped me or killed me yet...He just scared the heck out of me and said a lot of nasty things."

Angel pocketed his gun and pulled out a knife. He took one look at Tempest and shook his head.

"Child, you're trouble."

"Not my fault."

"If only I could believe it."

"Let's get out of here," Kayse hissed at them.

Angel nodded curtly and cut the ropes that tied her to the chair. She put out her hands so Angel could cut off the ropes at her wrists.

Rubbing her arms, she murmured, "Thanks."

Kayse motioned them forward and tapped at his chrono.

"I'm on a tracking monitor," Angel said, flexing his wrist. "But we need to get going."

Kayse nodded.

Overhead, a *thwump, thwump* of whirling blades announced their ride coming in. The noise caused the camp to swirl into confused action. People came pouring out of tents and buildings, some half asleep. Three arriving helios made enough racket to wake the dead.

Tempest stumbled, and Kayse realized that she was barefoot. She would never make it running barefoot in the dark through the jungle. He picked her up and threw her over his right shoulder, then took off for an open area where the helios had paused to hover. She gave a squeak of protest at first, but quickly subsided.

Her flailing arms banged against his back, jolting already sore muscles, while her breath woofed in and out. As she bounced along over his shoulder, her knees pounded on his chest and stomach. His leg muscles started to burn as he raced toward the sound of whirling blades, and he found catching his breath difficult.

Lights went on all over the camp, and shouts erupted from various buildings and tents. Streaks of laser beams began to light up the night sky as Terran guards took aim at the incoming aircrafts. A wild scramble of Alysians emerged from nearby tents as one helio picked up a load and took off immediately, rising above the growing commotion of people. Dirt and debris whirled everywhere.

Not far ahead of Kayse, a black whirring form hovered in the air, while all around, slashes of light sliced the night. A bullet whizzed past his ear. A *thunk* sounded, and a grunt from Angel made him worry the Enjelise was hit. Out of the sides of his eyes, he noticed laser lights flaring extremely close by.

He increased his speed.

Tempest cried out as he felt a sharp shove on his back. She whimpered and thrashed, endangering his grip, until he thought he might drop her. Shifting her body, he tried to ease the pressure off an aching shoulder and balance his load better. With a sudden strangled cough, she slumped against him into a heavy unconscious bundle. He listened for a faltering tread behind him, but Angel kept up the blistering pace, even though his breathing began to sound hoarse and labored.

They reached the helio and peered up into a red-lit maw as the aircraft lowered, kicking up a whirlwind of dirt and vegetation. A bullet pinged off a stanchion, and a rope ladder rolled out of the black monster like a ridged tongue coming out to lick him up. Positioning Tempest on his left shoulder and blinking dirt out of his eyes, he leaped and grabbed a hold of the ladder with his right hand. Angel breathed heavily behind him. Something wet slid down his back, but he had no time to pay attention to it. He pulled himself up, rung by rung, until hands reached out and snatched Tempest from him. Several other hands grabbed and hauled him on board. He rolled in, relieved to be out of the range of direct fire.

Next to them, a second whirring aircraft took off as voices sounded ominously nearby. He sat up to peer outside. Loud shouting broke out in the cockpit as one of the Terrans began to climb the ladder. Still hanging from the ladder, Angel kicked at him, attempting to dislodge the threat. The black metal monster struggled to lift even as Angel dangled below. A shot pinged off the side in a shower of sparks, uncomfortably close. Several others shots followed, but Angel hung on tight while the ladder gyrated around in the whirling wind. The helio lifted away from grasping hands, and the Enjelise crawled upwards, scrambling into the cockpit.

Looking out the cockpit window, Kayse squinted down at the camp, which now resembled a disturbed anthill. Men ran around wildly still shouting and shooting weapons.

Hands pushed him away from the door and reached for Angel as a laser hit scored the helio's side. The smell of scorched metal and burnt paint invaded the cockpit. Finally, Angel rolled completely in and the door slammed shut.

Kayse felt gravity shove him down hard onto the metal floor as the big bird lifted straight up and then canted sharply. The heavy swing to the left caused him to lose his balance sideways, and he banged against a metal seat, as the craft gained altitude and flew off into a dark still sky.

Dragging himself up into the seat, he peered out the bubble-like window and watched the camp shrink into the distance. Soon gigantic trees hid it from view, and only a small swath of the raw airstrip remained visible. Finally, that too disappeared, swallowed up by the dense jungle.

In the dim light of the cockpit, Kayse checked on Angel, who lay on his back with his eyes closed and hands clasped as if in prayer.

"We made it, Angel. We made it!" His hand patted the Enjelise who had rescued them.

Angel's eyes fluttered open, and a small smile flickered over curving lips. "That we did." A liquid oozed down a magnificent curved cheek. *Blood or tears?* In the semi-dawning light, it was hard to tell. Then the Enjelise went quiet with only harsh breathing to say he was still alive. Kayse moved aside for the paramedic to attend him.

Next, he examined Tempest. Blood smeared down the back of her left arm, and her pale face looked as if she were in shock. A paramedic in the crew had already examined her for injuries, placing an oxygen mask over her nose and mouth. Applied bandages soon stanched bleeding wounds and a shot looked to have tamped down her pain.

A sudden terror that she'd been fatally shot washed through Kayse. Startled, he realized how much she mattered to him. Over the short span of time he'd gotten to know her and experience her irritating, quirky self, he'd grown fond of her.

"Is she going to be all right?" he inquired.

"Depends on if we can get her to the Med Center in time."

He overheard the pilot say into his headset, "I'm helio two four two Juliet enroute to Tygel Medical Center with medical emergency on board. Request direct. Contact Richard Steele to apprise." The microphone clicked off.

The paramedic shot a grim look at Kayse as the whirring helio flew rapidly away in a brightening dawn.

Chapter 17

The flight seemed to take forever. Wherever they'd been, it was a long way from Tygel. Kayse watched Tempest's face, her long thick lashes fluttering against her pale skin. He reached out to grab her hand, and it squeezed back briefly in a feeble response. But she mostly lay there limp and unresponsive.

Gazing out the window, the landscape rolled by beneath the helio as night turned to morning. Jungle foliage gave way to rough mountainous terrain and then to wide blue sea. After a time, rocky beaches edged the water, soon leading to towering trees in a dense forest. Eventually, the forest changed to farmland and orchards, until suddenly, the rooftops of Tygel glimmered on the horizon.

He saw impossibly tall, angular buildings with sleek lines that pushed higher against the sky than he ever remembered. If he'd ever doubted that he was in the future, viewing Tygel erased that doubt. As they got closer, he became aware of traffic clogging the streets and pedestrians hurrying along like ants on forage.

Finally, the Med Center's rooftop appeared beneath them. A large circle indicated their landing spot. Exhausted, bruised, and emotionally fried, Kayse stared downward as the Center grew closer. A splash of green caught his eye, and he saw a lush garden with trees and a simple fountain nestled in a corner of the otherwise utilitarian concrete roof. Dizziness overwhelmed him.

The garden's vulnerability frightened him. He stared at trees that whipped in the turbulent currents of prop wash, and his mind fell into memory. He remembered the same trees, but much smaller, swaying around a gurgling fountain that sheltered giggling and shouting kids. An image came to him of splashing water, shrieking children, and a man in the shadows watching it all.

"He's going into shock," a voice said near his ear. A needle plunged into his arm. He felt the jolt of the helio landing, and a burst of clarity flooded his senses at the same time. He opened his eyes and sat up straighter in his seat. The cockpit door opened to reveal a wave of doctors and nurses erupting from the rooftop door. They were pushing gurneys and hoisting small plastic bags.

Nearby, the trees of the garden whipped themselves into a frenzy and the flowers danced, but there was no laughter, no children, only the dark figure of a man lurking in the shadows.

The shadow man resolved himself and came into the sunlight, revealing Richard Steele, calm and poised, amidst the frantic activity. The second helio landed, causing the trees to bend and sway even more violently. Richard moved eagerly forward, his arms opening up as Elise bounded out of the hatch before the craft even touched down. Her last jump landed into his open arms, which enveloped her in a joyous embrace.

Kayse amped up his hearing to listen over the whirring blades.

"She'll be fine, darling. She'll be fine." Richard uttered the words in a tone of absolute certainty that made Kayse shiver at its prediction. The husband put his arm around his wife's shoulders as he led her into the calmer interior of the Med Center and waited by the door.

"I'm fine." Kayse brushed aside a solicitous hand. "Take care of Angel and Tempest first. I'm fine."

Following those two, Kayse wobbled shakily down the helio's steps as the twirling blades wound down to a stop, and the trees gradually subsided from their manic dance. The bright flowers nodded at him, but the children's laughter no longer sounded in his ears, and the dark shadow had disappeared to tend to his wife and daughter.

They kept Kayse in the Med Center for three rotations. A couple of doctors took an intense interest in him, and for the first two rotations, they had him pretty drugged up while they did a lot of poking and prodding amid muttered comments. Finally, Richard showed up and ordered them all away.

By the third rotation, he'd recovered enough to check on Tempest, but she was resting and not taking visitors. Feeling stiff and groggy himself, he returned to his room. He tried again at the next shift.

This time he found her awake. Pale, with her hair sticking out in all directions, Tempest managed a wan smile. Long lashes, edged with teardrops, fluttered wetly. "Kayse," she whispered as she reached up to touch his arm. "You saved my life. The others left me tied to that chair while they ran to save themselves. I saw several people setting fires near that cabin. So most likely by now, I'd be barbecued."

Other than deny his heroics, he asked, "What's a barbecue?"

She gazed to one side. "It's a Terran dish where raw meat is skewered on a stick and cooked over a hot fire."

Making a face, he replied, "Arrgh, I just lost my appetite."

She coughed out a laugh.

He let her thank him profusely, all the while remembering her flapping on his back as a bullet buried itself into the fleshy part of her arm and not a vulnerable part of his back. Maybe he owed her his life, but he held back from saying it aloud. He might need the obligation she felt to provide him leverage sometime in the future, if experience was any teacher.

She recovered, just as Richard Steele had predicted. More to the point, Kayse didn't get a chance to say anything as Tempest returned to normal behavior and went on and on about school, and how he would meet her amazing friend, Mary Ellen. All Kayse needed to do was nod and grunt in the right places as the conversation continued. He was beginning to wish he *had* left her attached to the chair where everyone would blame Dan Smith for the loss.

A rumor circulated that a military raid on the Terran camp had been attempted. However, a second shuttle or transport plane never appeared. Led by General Moore, the military currently combed the jungle and mountains, searching for any signs of aircraft. Kayse didn't think they would have much success.

The Terrans were also gone from the camp, having escaped into the trees and nearby secret caves, leaving only abandoned buildings and tents to greet General Moore and his men. Kayse was glad. The Terrans were only struggling for survival. He'd seen and heard their plight and gotten a glimpse of their side of the story. Now, he would get an earful of the Alysian side.

So, bored to distraction from hearing about her friends, he bowed out of Tempest's presence and took to wandering the corridors. Since Ailey DeVey now had returned to her lab, he thought of paying her a visit there, but he wasn't sure of the location.

Lines on the floor soon captured his attention. *Purple.* A purple path came out of Tempest's room, trodden on by busy doctors and nurses on their way to healing the sick. Everyone walked briskly, as if on his or her way to something important and urgent. Then, *Green.* Along the green path, the pace became more leisurely as collars were unbuttoned and hands grabbed cool drinks rather than clipboards and stethoscopes. Green went to the garden or lounge. He loved the garden, but now he wanted to explore new places. Crossing over from the green that headed up the stairs, his eye caught a red line. Red? Now the red took him… home? *What a strange thought.*

Kayse veered off onto the red path and followed the convoluted route through heavy metal doors that said, "Keep out" or "Private." With a push to open one, a camera mounted high overhead blinked a red light twice. Most likely, he had set off an alarm somewhere, but curiosity kept him moving forward.

Then he entered a room and he was there. A memory came wandering back to him like a lost child. A few cribs, wallpaper with ludicrous animals, and a deep pile rug where a very young child once rolled and laughed while being tickled. His hair stood straight up along his arms. He couldn't breathe.

He knew this place from some long ago vague memory. Quickly backing out of the room and shutting the door, he looked around and noticed the sign "Genetics Lab." He grabbed the latch to that door, heart pounding in expectation. As he was about to enter, a harsh voice startled him.

"What are you doing here?"

With a jerk, he whirled around to see a man breathing heavily as if from a hard run. A frown wrinkled the stranger's forehead, and he held a gun loosely in his hand.

"I got lost," Kayse countered apprehensively, staring at the gun.

"This is a restricted area."

Kayse examined the security badge on the man's shirt. "No one told me that," he said. "I must have made a wrong turn."

"Who are you?" The voice became terse and demanding. "Do I know you?"

"I'm a friend of Richard Steele's. I came in the helios just recently."

The man pointed the gun at him. "You know Richard Steele?"

"Yes."

The man studied him intently. "Do you know this place?" He waved his gun at the door. "They do genetic experiments here." Pointing to the sign, he growled, "It's restricted. In there they tinker with human DNA. Scientists attempt to take the place of the Creator and design abominations." The man stopped and blinked. He waved the gun in a threatening manner. "No one is allowed in there anymore."

The man's eyes didn't look very sane to Kayse, so he backed up until he felt the hard wall behind him, all the while scanning the area for a quick way out.

"I just got lost," Kayse insisted. "I'm a patient and decided to visit a friend while I was here. I'm trying to find where Ailey DeVey works." He tried to tamp down the terror that rose in his gut. No one was around but the two of them, and the guard was acting very scary. They were alone. No one to see. No one to witness a death and lots of places to hide a corpse.

Kayse's breath almost stopped. The man seemed familiar as he studied him. Taking a hard line, he repeated,

"I have a right to be here, well, at least in the hospital." He looked around, noticing the sign that said "Restricted."

The gun lowered. Hesitation appeared on the guard's face. "This place is off limits." The man took on a cunning expression. "This is Arwoyn Telluria's *secret* lab. My father worked here with him. I thought you might know him, being Richard's friend and all. My father was Dr. Warner Straung, a great geneticist, who made groundbreaking discoveries, but he still loved me, his son, more than his *experiments.* I know he did." Tears welled up in the man's eyes.

"Never met the man." Kayse shifted uneasily.

A frown appeared on the guard's face. "They knew each other. Richard Steele worked with my father. He was part of the great plan, but they didn't kill him, did they? No, not him. It was my father who sacrificed himself for the greater good."

"Do you want to call Dr. Steele and ask him personally? Or I'm sure I.N.Sys would be interested. Should we call I.N.Sys?"

Anything to get you and me out of here. Now.

The man hesitated again as if making up his mind. "Okay, maybe you're right, and I've made a mistake. I did once before. However, if you're trying to find Ailey DeVey's office, I'll escort you there just so you won't get lost again. Then I'll check out if you're telling the truth about your meeting. If you're lying about that, then you're coming with me. We don't like liars here. They get punished."

Together the guard led him back to the lobby where they consulted a directory. He insisted on accompanying Kayse to her office.

Nervously, he opened the door to find Ailey in the midst of relocating. She apologized for the mix-up.

Furrowing his brow, the guard spun away angrily. He turned back around and pointed a finger at Kayse. "I'll be watching you, kid. And I'll be checking out your cockeyed story of being Steele's friend." He strode out, leaving the two of them breathing heavily. After the door closed, they both collapsed against her desk.

"Phew! He's a scary one." She gazed at him questioningly. "I'll alert security and check him out. Not everyone who pins a badge on his chest is necessarily authorized. I don't recognize him as one of the regulars, but I have been away."

"Yeah, please do that. I'll owe you. Thanks."

"Sorry you got lost, but I'm glad that you came. Since I've been gone, everything's a mess. I advertised for additional help, but they haven't found anyone yet, so I'm pretty much on my own with a couple of temps who come in sporadically." She combed her fingers through her hair.

An idea began to form in Kayse's mind. "I have some more schooling to do at home, but maybe I can come in afternoons and help? I need the work and the distraction."

Joy flooded her features as she nodded vigorously. "That'd be great. I could use the help. I only think of you swinging an axe and cutting down big jungle trees. I can't imagine you in a white lab gown, pouring over statistics and poking lab rats."

"I'm a multi-talented guy; what can I say? There's a lot I can do that you don't even know about."

The comment seemed to amuse her. She gave him a funny look and sniffed. "Are you any good at these...other things I don't know about?" She leered at him and delighted in his bright blush.

Chapter 18

As soon as the Med Center released him, Kayse found himself staring into the stern face of a man introduced as Director Trace Walker and someone named Jak Fields. They sat in Trace's office that had a simple but tasteful décor. A thick burgundy rug lay on the floor. Three chairs faced an elegant heartwood desk. Bookshelves graced one wall, expensive artwork two others, and a window behind Trace's desk looked out over the city.

The third man in the room, sitting next to him, was Richard Steele. The name, Trace Walker, sounded familiar, and Kayse realized that he regarded the elusive head of I.N.Sys, and a man on the hot seat from the investigative committee, currently airing on all the vids.

Director Walker, considered to be one of the more powerful men in the Democratic Union, wore the same harried expression as Richard. Both looked like they needed sleep. Director Walker's curly, dark, hair lay tousled about as if he had run his hand through it repeatedly, and indeed, as Richard murmured something to him, he brushed several strands out of his eyes and glowered from under dark eyebrows.

Trace introduced the other man as Jak Fields, Director of I.N.Sys' National Operations. He appeared older than Trace or Richard and had a hard-worn face and iron-gray hair. He narrowed his eyes at Kayse as if he suspected him of some horrible wrongdoing. Gaunt and tough, Jak Fields looked like someone you wouldn't want to cross.

Kayse tossed Richard a weak smile. At least there, he found a friendly face. Richard had warned him to expect a debriefing concerning his experience at the camp and to be careful of what he said. Several suspected him of collusion with the Terrans. Neither should he utter a word about his former identity, nor anything concerning his parents' murder. Kayse figured the conversation might be short.

Shifting in his chair, Trace leaned forward and asked, "Did you at any time hear Captain Fujeint and this Commander Brock speak to each other?"

"Yes, sir," Kayse replied, trying to appear earnest and truthful. "More than once."

A look passed between Jak and Trace, while Richard frowned, crossed his arms over his chest, and leaned back.

"What did they say?" interrupted Jak.

Kayse cleared his throat. "Elise was chewing out Commander Brock for hijacking our shuttle."

A smile went from Richard to Trace. He also tossed a smirk toward Jak, who just grunted in response and turned his head away.

"Did they sound like they were working together?" Trace asked as he looked down and fiddled with paperwork on his desk. The casual attitude didn't fool Kayse. They were going after Elise, but right now, she and Richard were his meal ticket and shelter for the foreseeable future. He had to be careful what he said.

"Sounded more like arguing." Kayse ran damp palms down his pants. "No, I'd say they definitely weren't on the same side, although the Commander did treat Elise with proper respect."

"What is your opinion of Commander Brock?" Trace wanted to know.

"Actually, the guy has a gripe." Kayse took a deep breath. "The word on Terran Station is that Alysians treat the Terrans pretty lousy. They're sick and tired of the long waiting times to come down to Alysia, only to be treated badly when they get here. More and more are coming around to Commander Brock's point of view, seeing the need to get more aggressive with their demands."

"We've got trouble already," Jak grumbled.

"Jak…" Trace warned.

Glaring at Jak, Richard leaned forward toward Trace. "Conditions on the station aren't good. Frag, they're not even hygienic, and it's getting worse."

Trace nodded. "If it were left up to me, I'd get rid of that piece of junk and bring them all down. We put them there originally as a precaution against them bringing alien diseases and adverse fauna onto Alysia. Sort of a quarantine station left to us by Senator Brandon. We completed it to accommodate the Terrans. But after all these years, we've eliminated most of those threats. The cost of keeping that thing operating is a big hole in the government's budget."

"They'll try to take over Alysia if you bring all of them down!" Jak growled.

With a shake of his head, Kayse disagreed. "I don't think the Terrans want the whole planet. They just want a piece where they can live free. The Commander said so himself."

"Sounds like you have some sympathy for their little takeover," Jak accused.

"Not really." Kayse leaned back and shot a glance over at Richard. "But Trey suggested I should volunteer to be in their Militia to find out what they're up to."

"No!" Richard slammed down a hand on the desktop. "You're not going to even think such a thing."

A look of interest passed between Jak and Trace as the idea floated between them.

"It's not a bad idea, Richard," Trace began hesitantly.

"It's a terrible idea. No, as his guardian I absolutely forbid it. It's too dangerous."

"Easy, Richard." A short staring contest between Trace and Richard ensued. Finally, Trace glanced away.

"Do you know what this Terran Militia is planning?" Trace asked Kayse, raising an eyebrow.

"I think they stole a larger shuttle and unloaded the Earth2 Station. That would be my guess," Kayse answered calmly. "There's a rumor going around that the military plans to blow up the space station and kill everyone on it."

Jak leaned forward. "And waste a space station?"

Trace frowned at his subordinate. "Jak, you're not serious."

"No, but I like the idea of using the kid as a spy to see what they're up to."

"No!"

"Richard, it's not such a bad idea," Trace argued. "We could learn a lot. Why are you blocking this so hard? It's our best chance yet to find out what they're planning." Trace gave Richard a puzzled frown.

But Richard didn't budge. "He's *not* on the table for any of your spying games in that camp. Too dangerous there. He almost got killed the last time he was there. End of argument."

"Jeb already likes Kayse," Jak said. "He could be inserted easily."

"Richard, I could..." Kayse leaned forward.

"No you can't, and that's final. Trace can pick someone else. Not you." Richard looked stubborn. At that moment, Kayse realized his importance to Richard. It had to do with his father, and he wanted to know what Richard knew but wouldn't tell him. *Who was my father? Had he been such a monster that people wanted his son dead too? How much am I like him? What does Richard know that he wants to protect me?*

"All right," Trace said, pushing away from his desk.

"I have more questions," Jak protested.

"We're done for now," Trace said evenly. "Get the kid some schooling and keep an eye on him. I'm sure we'll have more questions down the road." Then he turned to Jak. "And I want you and your men all over that camp. I want to find where they've gone. Dismissed."

"Yes, sir." Jak stood up, nodded, and left the room.

Richard started to follow suit, but Trace gestured him back into his chair and pointed Kayse to a chair in a corner by a small table. Kayse activated his amplified hearing.

Trace murmured to Richard, "Is the kid Elise's? Someone said that she and some hotshot doctor had a relationship on board the ship a while back."

Richard rose to his feet. Leaning across the desk, he hissed, "That was long ago." He glanced at Kayse, who got busy reading a magazine from the table.

"Yeah, so, the kid was born before your marriage, but I'm curious about all this concern. Anything you want to tell me?" Trace stood up, almost nose to nose with Richard.

"You're hunting the wrong krell there, Trace. Take a good look at the kid. They aren't related."

Trying to appear inconspicuous, Kayse continued his pretend read. He scratched his nose, ignoring the stares.

Trace continued, "I could use him, but for now, if you say so, he's off the hook. It's just that your wife's a well-connected Terran." Trace paused. "You usually don't keep secrets from me. I hope you're not starting now."

"Well, I hope she doesn't keep secrets." Trace shrugged. "The kid does resemble you, however. Similar ugly mug. He isn't some forgotten by-blow of yours, is he? A result of a former romantic adventure?"

"Trace!"

"Okay, okay." Trace put up his hands and warded him off. "Just trying to figure it out. Can't see you taking in a distant nephew, but then if you say that's the way it is, that's the way it is. We're done for now, but keep in touch."

After they left Trace's office, as they were walking down the corridor, Richard came to a sudden stop and stared at a woman who was entering the main lobby.

"Frag! That's Liana. She's come down from Alysia Station. We've got to get out before she notices us."

Curiously, Kayse peered down the hall to see a tall, slender, sandy-haired woman talking to Jak.

"Think of a black wall—now!" Richard urged.

Puzzled, Kayse imagined a black wall as he felt a tickle at the back of his brain. Richard thrust him out of the I.N.Sys lobby. Richard opened the car door and pushed Kayse into the passenger seat.

"Bastards are playing dirty."

"Who is she?" Kayse peered back through the lobby window, trying to identify her. Then he remembered her picture as part of the returning space crew. What was she doing at I.N.Sys? Richard acted as if she could read their minds, and then he remembered the rumor saying the crew had developed that ability out in space.

Kayse followed Richard into the parked car. Richard jumped into the driver's seat and accelerated the car out of the parking lot as if chased by demons.

Distracted and sweating, Richard shouted, "Buckle up, Arwoyn. We're getting out of here right now."

"Who?" Kayse mumbled.

Chapter 19

School. Kayse shuddered. School had been fun before. He'd been sort of a teacher's pet. The thrill of new knowledge, the excitement of projects…he had radiated enthusiasm and they had favored him for it, but so much had changed since then. Now he wasn't the same person. He didn't fit in. Somehow, twenty-eight annuals had disappeared in a flash and when he looked out across the street toward the jostling, noisy crowd of kids going into the white, austere building, he felt like an outsider treading on alien turf. However, he was glad to be out of the jungle, on solid ground, and ready for some company his own age. He closed the automatic car's door and inhaled a deep breath as he studied the milling students across the street. A driving test and a pre-programmed car enabled him to have the limited freedom of driving Tempest to school. Now, here he was feeling like the old man of the group.

First off, he noticed how differently they dressed. The latest fad appeared to be clothes constructed from a metallic fabric that shifted colors as the wearer moved. Brightly colored pants with long tops or short dresses with neon colored leggings formed the current fashion. Hair cropped in jagged lines or styled in odd shapes and accented with streaks of fantastical colors decorated a few heads.

They didn't carry books, but only small thin electronic notepads like the one Tempest now carried. The compact device communicated with ASSIST and accessed any book ever written or any piece of information ever encoded. An electronic device, no bigger than a pack of smokes, stuck out of many pockets and winking earpieces were attached to most ears like exotic jewelry. Many listened to music or conversed over electronic gadgets with friends while ignoring all else around them.

The school offered a tailored curriculum, although nobody yet had offered him a clue as to what courses he should take. This future presented an alien world with kids Tempest's age using technology far beyond Kayse's understanding. He couldn't imagine what he would find at Sunpointe Academy where he planned to go two terms from now.

However, these teenage students carried the same air of rebellion about them that he remembered from his own school days. And the girls still congregated at one end of the building while the boys lounged at the other, trying not to be obvious as they exchanged furtive glances.

Tempest jumped up and down in front of him. "Come on," she complained, grabbing his hand. "I want to introduce you to Mary Ellen. I talked to her last night and told her you were bringing me to school today. We planned to meet before classes, and now you've made us late."

"Whoa girl, I'm not that anxious to meet this Mary Ellen of yours."

Tempest flipped her hair back and shifted her tablet from one hand to the other. "Oh, you have to. I told her so much about you. She wants to meet you. She's already sixteen and knows absolutely everybody. She's really rad, and besides, it's important to me. Come on, Kayse."

She stopped to shout, "Hey Mary Ellen, yahoo, over here." Tempest waved frantically at someone.

Kayse looked across the street at a tall, attractive female surrounded by five other girls who were giggling and smirking at a couple of boys across the way. He recognized the pattern of behavior.

Okay, so some things never change.

Tempest practically dragged him up to the group. The other girls made room and the giggles took on a frenetic note. They all gazed at him as if he were some exotic creature or a tasty dessert.

"Mary Ellen, this is *Kayse*," Tempest gushed. She waved her arm with a flourish. Mary Ellen nodded like a queen acknowledging a subject.

Scrutinizing him from head to toe, the brunette batted eyelashes at him while chewing away on a wad of something he supposed was gum. He stared back, causing her to blink. She stopped in mid chew as if in contemplation of his worth. Then she smiled lazily at him. "Welcome to our institute of higher learning," she said with a casual wave of her hand. "Tempest mentioned you were new around here." She focused a laser stare on him and began chewing more rapidly.

"He's living with me," Tempest chortled triumphantly.

"So you consider him part of the family, do you?" Mary Ellen asked, staring intently at him.

"Yep." Tempest bounced on her toes. She beamed at Kayse who didn't feel like returning the bright smile so much. He gave a tight grin to Mary Ellen strictly for politeness sake.

"Kinda like a big brother, is he?" Mary Ellen asked, blazing a big smile in his direction.

He didn't trust the fake camaraderie. She reminded him of a shark eyeing her prey. "It's just for a short while," he answered carefully.

"We don't know how long exactly." Tempest grabbed at his arm possessively while he stood and scowled at everyone.

"Interesting," Mary Ellen murmured.

Great, now he was on her radar because of Tempest. He felt a sudden urge to get clear of the whole scene.

"Nice to meet you," he said, tugging at Tempest's arm. "But, I don't want us to be late for class."

"You know," Mary Ellen drawled as she put a finger on his other arm to stop him. "There's a Rave Party coming up next weekend on West Street. Why don't we hook up there, and I'll introduce you around to a few of the more important kids at school. You can be my date while you check out the locals. You'll meet the older kids, more on our level, who have similar interests. Tempest hangs out with such babies that they will bore you silly. Kids our age have so much more to offer, wouldn't you say?" She tilted her head and raised an eyebrow.

Well, he was still two annuals older than this paragon, but he would be a fool to pass up the opportunity to meet new kids. Tempest stood there opened-mouthed. He imagined that she had planned for him to be her date. He suddenly realized Mary Ellen would be saving him from that fiasco.

"It's doable," he responded. He wasn't sure what the slang was here.

"Doable?" Mary Ellen lifted both eyebrows. "That's a bit archaic."

"Whatever," he tossed out. "I'll see you there. Gotta go." He grabbed Tempest's arm and steered her into the building.

A little farther on, Tempest dragged her feet, stopped, and regarded him with a frown. "What was that about? I counted on you taking me to the Rave."

Shaking his head, he answered, "You implied you consider me the same as a family member, so now she believes I'm fair game. You made the introduction; she made the move."

"I don't remember telling her she could date you." Tempest sounded upset. "You live with me. You should take me to the dance."

"Thanks to your special introduction, I'll be going to the Rave and hooking up with your good friend, Mary Ellen. You wanted her to meet me. You pushed me at her. Now I have a date. End of story. Anyway, it'll be a good way for me to be introduced to some older kids at the school. I want to get the lay of the land, and this is a good first step."

"I wanted to show you off," Tempest protested. "I didn't think she would grab you for herself. She's supposed to be my friend."

"We're going to have to be really careful with your so-called friend, Mary Ellen. I think that she has plans for us, and we better be on our guard." He looked at Tempest and suddenly felt a shiver of unease. He hadn't liked the calculating expression in her best friend's eyes.

Despite some concern regarding the whole set-up, he decided he would go through with it. He found out that Tempest, once realizing he was unavailable as a date, had arranged to spend the night with Jemma. Richard and Elise needed to go out somewhere and offered their automatic self-driving car if he would make sure to drop her off at Jemma's before going on. They showed him how to program the destination and put it in for him. Relieved that Jemma's parents would watch over her, he got ready for his date in a reasonable state of mind.

But as he drove up to Jemma's home, and Tempest prepared to get out of the car, she commented that she might see him at the Rave.

"What do you mean, you'll see me at the Rave?" he hissed at her, as she gathered her jacket off the car seat and picked up her overnight bag.

Giving him a sly smile, she said, "I don't want you to be shocked if I should happen to show up at the party, that's all. I've got my own date. Mary Ellen felt bad and set me up with a real hot guy."

She moved toward the car door, but he grabbed her arm. "You're staying with Jemma. You better not be showing up at any Rave. You're too young to go to those things."

"I am *not* too young. Everyone goes there to party. All *my* friends will be there." She pushed back a lock of hair. "Jemma and I really are going to study some, but then I might go on to the Rave. Someone should keep an eye on you and Mary Ellen. Someone has to keep you out of trouble."

"*You* keep *me* out of trouble? You gotta be kidding! Besides, you told your mother that you were going to Jemma's for the night."

"And I am. I just might not be there the whole night. If you tell mom and dad, I'll deny it and never speak to you again."

"Don't tempt me."

She whirled around, an angry expression on her face. "Maybe next time you'll take me, then." Waving over her shoulder, she sang out, "Bye now. Better behave as I'll be watching you." She admonished him with a waggle of her index finger.

Worried, he watched her skip jauntily up to the door.

Chapter 20

The moment Kayse entered the party; he knew there was going to be trouble. He also knew Tempest would be in the middle of it eventually, sooner if not later. The loud music, the frenetic atmosphere, the crowd of kids all jammed up against each other, made it a certainty she wouldn't miss it, if experience was any predictor.

Taking a deep breath, he plunged into the crowded room. Surrounded by an entourage of kids, Mary Ellen was easy to spot. She acted spaced-out already, and the chattering kids circling her looked as if they were on either drugs or drink or possibly both.

He didn't see a Terran in sight. It was just good old Alysian natives running amuck. Not the best environment for Tempest with Terran blood coursing through her veins. He peered through the flashing lights and the densely packed bodies, but Tempest was nowhere to be seen. He breathed a sigh of relief. That seemed a good sign, but he wasn't too optimistic. The night held a taste of inevitability about it.

"I see you made it," Mary Ellen slurred as she sidled up to him.

"Wouldn't miss it for the world." He glanced about and then smiled at her.

"Anybody with you?" She asked.

"No. Is it mandatory to travel in a pack? I got the impression only you and I were hooking up here. That's enough company for me."

She laughed, lazily flapping a hand. "Hey, Troy, get us a drink." She motioned to someone, and a tall, blond, jock tilted his head and veered off toward the bar. Kayse recognized the type. BMOC, or "Big Man On Campus" as students had called them in his time.

"Having people around does have its advantages," she answered, fluttering her eyelashes at him.

A short, dark-haired, muscular lad sidled into Troy's now vacant spot next to Mary Ellen and cast Kayse a belligerent glare.

Mary Ellen angled her head in introduction. "This here's Jeng. He's got some Ching T'Karre blood in him. He likes to order women around. I don't respond too well to the tactic, but he still tries. The culture's a bit archaic in his country."

Nodding in acknowledgement, Kayse watched him briefly dip his head in response.

"Those of the Ching T'Karre are known for their fanaticism." She gave him a tight smile. "Every group has to have at least one fanatic in it, I suspect. I'll bet your Terran friends have a few of their own, hmm?"

Before he could respond, the male under discussion broke into the conversation. "Mary Ellen says you're living with a Terran woman and her half-breed kid. Must be pretty weird living among aliens."

Well, that's not a polite way to start a conversation.

As if that wasn't enough, the kid continued, "My dad says Terran women are really hot. They consider sex just another sport and don't believe in marrying. You must be getting plenty with two of them at the house." He leaned in to leer in his direction.

Kayse snorted in derision at such a ridiculous notion. "Elise is married to Dr. Richard Steele, so I would say you're off base on that one. And believe me, he doesn't share—mother or daughter. I keep it at friendship only, believe me."

A tall, broad-shouldered kid with brown hair edged his way into the circle. Trying to gain their attention, he gave a bright eager smile and said loudly, "Pity that. They say she's a captain of a space ship, so maybe that makes a difference. We had a Terran working at our house for a while, and she was more than willing to oblige if dad needed a little sport sex. When dad put on special parties for his friends, she would put out for all of them. She actually encouraged it— so much so mom finally threw a fit, forcing the old man to send her packing. She knew how to please a guy, though. I know, since dad let me have a go at her." The kid took a sip and glanced at the group from over the rim of his glass. He winked at Mary Ellen.

What is wrong with this kid? Why is no one trying to rein him in? In fact, everyone is edging in awfully eager to hear my response.

Kayse frowned; his lips tightened. "Well, I don't know any Terrans like that, but I'll admit I don't know many. One bad one doesn't mean they're all bad," Kayse countered, trying to hold onto a fraying temper. Troy returned with drinks and handed one to Mary Ellen and one to Kayse. The circle widened.

Kayse felt really thirsty. The smoky atmosphere made his throat and eyes burn. As he took a sip, he realized their attitude about Terrans disturbed him. *Were all Alysians so prejudiced? Or were Terrans that immoral?*

"Drink up," Mary Ellen encouraged as she raised her glass. "Let's have fun and forget about the stupid Terrans." She glared at the group, warning them to silence.

The tangy taste, along with the chill of the ice, made the drink go down fast and sweet. He tried to figure it out, but he'd never tasted anything like it before. A warm glow suffused his body. He felt euphoric.

To add to the surreal atmosphere lights in the room started to strobe. Abruptly, they captured everyone in a freeze frame, which after a brief pause, released. Immediately after that, they flickered frantically. He would catch glimpses of couples frozen, then wildly fluttering, until finally, everything would return to normal. He became fascinated by this blinking pattern, gazing as if paralyzed by it.

"Hey there," Mary Ellen shouted. The lights flashed and froze three of her friends, catching them in mid-laughter. The strobe released and, in an eerie twilight, he saw her standing there with her hands waving up and down in time to the music. Some of the drink splashed out, but she didn't seem concerned.

A harsh, strident beat thumped out and reverberated up from the floor into his body, echoing his feelings of confusion and anger. Tension began building up inside of him, putting him on edge. The strobe flashed again, revealing Mary Ellen's face peering avidly at him as if she were studying him to see what he would do next. A red light caught at his peripheral vision, but he couldn't locate it on the dance floor.

"Dance with me," she urged as she grabbed his arm and tugged him out onto the dance floor.

"Okay." He needed to work off some of his nervous energy, so he followed.

Mary Ellen dragged him toward the center of a mob of gyrating kids. Once inside, he felt himself vibrating along with a mass of pulsing bodies. Mary Ellen edged closer in and rubbed up against him provocatively, causing him to feel an unfamiliar hunger stirring within him. She looked *so* sexy. He went to grab her, but she smiled coquettishly and danced backward farther into the crowd. He plunged forward after her.

He didn't understand this strange person he was becoming but, at the moment, he felt dynamic and strong, alive to the universe. Trailing after her, feeling the music, caught up in the moment, his whole body throbbed, driven by the rhythmic pulse that pounded at his very soul.

Mary Ellen leaned close into him and whispered indecipherable words that triggered a surge of lust, driving every thought out of his head but one—to touch her, taste her lips, feel her skin against his. The red light blinked faster. His heart beat to its tempo. He watched her lick her lips and shake her body, causing her breasts to rub against his chest. An overwhelming feeling of desire almost stopped his breath. Mary Ellen moved in closer; her hands rubbed his chest and then moved down his body, touching him there…and there…the agony was almost too much. In the background, the wild crashing music began a crescendo.

She reached up for him, pulling his head down toward hers. Their lips met, their bodies pressed together, as he crushed her roughly against him. The sweet, salty taste of her lips parched his thirst but left him longing for more. Lights flashed again, strobing as the music reached a climax. He pulled away from the kiss barely able to breathe. With a final cascade of light and sound, the music stopped, leaving the room in freeze-frame.

And there across the room, he finally saw Tempest, frozen in the glare of the strobe, staring at them with a look of anguish etched across her face.

Reality crashed in. He shook his head.

What's wrong with me?

The band announced they were taking a break, and those on the crowded dance floor halted to gape around at their fellow dancers as if waking from a dream. Slowly they dissipated to the edges of the crowd or went outside for fresh air.

"Wow, what happened to me? That's some music," he said, wiping the perspiration from his forehead. He scanned the room and spied Tempest as she disappeared into the crowd, pulled along by a big-shouldered, wavy-haired guy. He felt a spike of anger, followed by concern. Then he argued that it wasn't his fault. He had told her not to come. He had warned her, but she had not listened...once again.

"You're pretty hot there, stud. You can dance mighty fine. Makes me all tingly." Mary Ellen grinned at him.

He shook his head in a daze. "I need some fresh air. I feel strange," he responded.

"Hey, Mary Ellen, the stuff really works. You had him going there," Troy rumbled, coming up to them out of the crowd.

He frowned at them. "What stuff? What are you talking about?"

"Hush, Troy. Please go play somewhere else." Mary Ellen flicked her fingers at him.

"Sure, but remember you promised me some too."

"Shut up, Troy. Go away *now* and shut up. You'll be taken care of." Mary Ellen fired off a stern scowl.

The pack around Mary Ellen reassembled as if some magnetic force pulled them together once the music stopped. He saw their grins and noticed they were all studying him. He managed a smile, all the while thinking he needed to get away. He was overwhelmingly thirsty.

"I saw Tempest here," he said. "I think I'll go see if I can find her."

Mary Ellen waved a hand about nonchalantly. "Don't worry about her. She's already left to party with Carl."

"Who's Carl?" he asked with a feeling of unease.

"He's a friend. She mentioned she needed a hot date for the Rave. I think she wanted to make you jealous. His buddies, Arlyn and Jack, might join them."

Worry flared into full-blown fear. *She wasn't that stupid, was she? Hadn't she learned her lesson with Dan?*

"Did he say where they were going?"

Mary Ellen grinned. "Maybe, but you're not invited." She gave him a slight push. "She claims you're a prude. However, you weren't acting so shy a moment ago. I guess it just takes the right woman to start your motor." She wiggled her hips.

Before he could respond, Troy showed up with more drinks and handed one to him. Kayse noticed everyone eagerly watched him as he put it to his lips. Feeling uncomfortable with all the attention, he pulled the drink away from his mouth and gazed out over the dance floor. He should check on Tempest. The music started up with a slow tune. Moving over near a table, he put the drink down.

"No, no, drink up," Mary Ellen protested. "The night has just begun. It's going to be an interesting night for both of us, I promise." Her breasts heaved as she took a deep breath. She traced a butterfly fingertip over his lips, sending shivers through his body.

Hot sweat soaked his shirt. "I need fresh air."

A significant glance went around the group. Mary Ellen shrugged. "Suit yourself." Several hands reached for the drink.

He noticed that slow blink of red again out of the corner of his eye, although none of the lights on the dance floor appeared lit. He'd thought the aberrant flashing had been a part of the scene, but now he realized it couldn't be. Something was wrong with him. He rolled his eyes, trying to get rid of the annoying red pop and a woozy head. As he assessed the rest of his body it felt as if he were swimming under water using lead legs. Definitely time to get out. He edged toward the door.

"Now it's all going to waste," Troy complained roughly. "That's expensive stuff."

He stopped to stare at the upset kid. "What are you talking about? I only want some fresh air, and I need to find Tempest. I'm worried about her."

"I told you that she's already left," Mary Ellen repeated in an irritated tone. "Don't worry about her."

"What?" The comment alarmed him.

"She, Carl, and some friends went out for a bit of fun after that last dance." She waved her hand languidly off to some imaginary faraway place.

He grabbed her by the shoulders. "Where?"

"Didn't ask. Not my business. Hey, leave it alone, Kayse. Stop acting all jealous. You're here with me. I've got things planned for us tonight. Something you'll really like." She gave him a meaningful look, adding in a seductive lick of her lips. "Aren't you thirsty?" She surprised Troy by grabbing the glass out of his fingers and shoving the drink at Kayse. "You look thirsty. Feel how wet and cool this drink is. It'll ease your thirst. You're hot, I bet." She giggled as if she'd made a joke.

He pushed the drink back at her. "She doesn't realize that even if they're friends of yours, things can go bad. She's an innocent kid, Mary Ellen, and you know it."

"Hey, hey, it's just a game they're playing."

"Not a nice game, I'm betting," he answered grimly as he scanned the room once again. He dragged Mary Ellen along toward the door, plowing through a group of sweaty, laughing kids.

Outside, the air hit him like a cold fist in the face. His head cleared, and the damned red flashing stopped. He looked around for Mary Ellen's friends, but somehow, he'd managed to get clear of them. Inside, a pounding beat started up again, re-igniting the muffled stamp of what sounded like some tribal ritual dance.

The night settled around them. Mary Ellen looked frustrated, but before she could say a word, a dark form emerged out of the shadows. Mary Ellen gave a high-pitched yelp. In reaction, Kayse spun around into a crouch, his hands coming up in a defensive posture.

She stumbled backwards as her mouth dropped open. Then she squinted at the dark form a few steps away.

"Where's Tempest?" a voice asked. He heard an intake of breath from Mary Ellen as the intruder shook a dark hood off its head to reveal Angel's dazzling features. Not happy, the eyes lasered right at him.

Kayse groaned. He knew Richard and Elise were going to blame him for things going wrong.

The Enjelise gripped his arm and squeezed. The gaze became intense. "Answer me! Where is Tempest?"

Words fumbled their way to his lips. "Mary Ellen said she left with some guys. Look, I told Tempest not to come here. She lied to her parents about what she planned tonight. I don't know where they are, but I'm trying to find out where she went. This isn't my fault."

But, of course, it was going to end up all his fault.

As Mary Ellen stared stupidly at Angel, Kayse realized the "Angel Effect" had a hold of her. Being in Angel's presence, he felt the same wave of awe wash over him, but the increasingly painful grip brought him back to reality.

Mary Ellen made frantic motions with her hands. "Kayse, that's an Enjelise. I'll bet that's an Enjelise. I've never seen one up this close before." Mary Ellen leaned in, awestruck, her eyes as round as dinner plates.

"Yeah, I know." Kayse sighed.

"Tempest?" Angel insisted, shaking him.

Kayse lifted eyebrows at Mary Ellen. "Where is she?"

She looked distractedly at Angel. "I don't know, but Carl usually takes his girls to his dad's apartment. Jack and Arlyn might join them," she added in a murmur. Her gaze turned to the Enjelise. "What's your name?" She gave Angel one of her most dazzling smiles. "We haven't met before." She put out a graceful hand.

"This is..." Kayse started to say.

"Doesn't matter," Angel interrupted roughly. "We don't have time. We need to find Tempest. Come tell me how to find this apartment, and then I'm taking both of you home. We're going now." Angel gestured for him to follow, walked away, and was soon out of sight, expecting immediate compliance.

Just then, Troy and Joey materialized from the dance floor with several more of the group in tow. All were male, and none appeared friendly. Angel vanished into the dark, and Kayse started to follow him, but someone grabbed him by the arm.

"And where do you think you're going?" Joey questioned in a low, malicious tone.

Kayse looked around. It seemed that they were talking to him.

"Don't do this, guys," Mary Ellen protested.

"I'm not letting him slip away. I promised to deliver him, and I'm taking delivery right now before the stuff wears off. He didn't down that second drink." Joey sounded angry about something.

Through the noise of music starting up and the shuffle of feet from the partially opened door, Kayse heard an irritated voice start mumbling as Angel stopped, and then slowly began to move back toward him.

Kayse jerked his arm loose and whirled away, startling everyone.

The one called Jeng spat on the ground. "We'll teach you to mess with Terrans. I'm forwarding a message to them through you. You tell that alien bitch of a captain you live with to quit bringing her friends down here. This is our planet, and we don't want them polluting it with their ilk, you hear. You tell both her and Steele clearly, or we'll make an example of you."

"Yeah, you're at our school now, and you have a lesson to learn, alien lover." Troy grinned. He motioned for two of his friends to join them. They started to circle Kayse. Mary Ellen slipped into the background with a frightened look.

Kayse noted the menacing kids and felt sorry for the lot of them. They had no idea who they were messing with. Considering all his augmentations, he could take on these dumb teenagers easily. He wondered idly how he was going to explain any damage to Richard and Elise, not to mention to the kid's negligent parents. Someone was going to get hurt if they kept this up. How had they let their kids get this way, anyhow? Ah well, maybe he could teach them a few lessons on how they should behave better.

In the background, the music rose louder as the kids moved in on him. He whirled, kicked, and took one out immediately. The other three backed up, surprised by his agility. One tossed a glance over at a group of grown-up men lounging near the partially opened door. Kayse thought he'd try to get their attention. They looked like chaperones who'd stop this silliness. Sidling toward them, he kept an eye on the closing circle.

"Look, you really don't want to fight with me," he said. "Someone could get hurt."

Joey flashed a knife and grinned at him. "Yeah, you. You could get hurt. That was some fancy footwork. See if you can dance past this."

In relief, he saw two men break off from the group at the door.

"Put it away before someone gets hurt. Here come the chaperones. You're done now," Kayse countered angrily.

Instead, Joey lunged at him, laughing, but Kayse backed away with ease.

Troy's face took on an expression of cunning. "We haven't even begun. You're quick, but not that quick. There are four of us, and Eddie has a little drink for you, *Terran* lover."

A gangly teenager with wild iridescent hair and a crazed expression came out of the group, holding a sloshing drink that he threw all over Kayse. The cold liquid hit Kayse's face and dripped down his front.

"What the...?" Shocked, it dawned on him that they had spiked his drink. He tried to hold onto his temper, but it was fraying rapidly.

He looked at them and wiped his face with a sleeve. "If you don't start being more polite, you're going to make me mad, and I might to do something I'll regret," he warned them.

"I can take him," bragged the bright-haired kid. He put his head down and charged Kayse, who sidestepped him and watched him go down in a heap next to some garbage cans.

An appropriate place.

The kids laughed. "You'll have to do better than that, Eddie."

Two men from the outside door strode over.

Relieved, Kayse said, "These kids started this fight. You need to stop them and send them home before someone gets hurt."

A quick glance passed between them as one said, "You're right." He waved the kids off. "Never send kids to do a man's job." Then he pulled out a gun and aimed it at Kayse. "Okay kid, you're coming with us."

The second one tugged the other's arm. "The boss said he wants him alive and undamaged."

"Oh, this'll keep him alive and under control well enough." The first replied as he squeezed the trigger.

At that moment, Kayse realized the man was going to shoot him. He whirled away just in time to evade the dart as it left the barrel. He ducked and spun around behind the shooter before he could aim again.

"What the...?" The man swung around in confusion. "Where'd that kid go?"

"Get him, Jack. We don't have time to play around."

"I'm not playing around, you idiot. He's damn fast."

The second man yelled for more men to come over and help them.

Kayse got in front of his attacker and knocked the weapon away from his hand, landing a right palm-edged chop across his throat. The man's eyes rolled up as he went down, gasping and clutching his neck.

The second attacker scrambled for the gun, but Kayse arrived first, picked it up, and squeezed the trigger.

"Arrgh!" The second one dropped.

Two more men approached, and Kayse looked for an opening. He ducked in and out of the shadows as he watched them trying to locate him for a clear shot. Circling around, he came in behind one and knocked him down with a sliding sweep of his foot. The man fell hard and hit his head on a cement wall, then slid unconscious to the ground. The second man whirled around right into Kayse's waiting fists. Lights out.

Kayse surveyed the area. No one else seemed to be in the fight anymore. Anyone who had been interested before, now vanished. Inside music played on, lights flashed, but the area outside around Kayse stayed still.

Angel eased into view from the shadows and leaned over a dazed man. He laid something against his neck. Kayse heard a faint burp and the man went limp. He went to the second and did the same thing. Then the third. The fourth was out cold already.

"That should do it for a while," Angel commented wryly, staring at the unconscious men. "If you're done having fun, can we go now?"

Kayse shook his head dazedly and glanced at Mary Ellen who stood there with her back pressed against the wall. "Okay, tell us where Tempest is."

At that moment, a car materialized out of the dark, and Kayse grabbed Mary Ellen by the arm.

Joey groaned, but stayed down when he saw all the bodies littering the ground around him.

Kayse stared at the car, trying to figure out who drove it, and what would happen next.

Chapter 21

A familiar face peered out the car window. "Get in," Jemma ordered, her hand flapping at them.

Angel pulled Mary Ellen from Kayse, dragged her over to the car and stuffed her into the back seat. "Sit next to Jemma," he shouted at Kayse and slid in.

Hastily, Kayse clambered in and grabbed at the dashboard as the car accelerated into the dark street. The momentum of the car shut the door with a slam that barely missed chopping off his foot. Kayse turned to an angry Jemma Telluria. "What are you doing here?" he asked.

"I might ask you the same," she responded with a huff. "Tempest left my house, saying you were picking her up and her mom was back home. After thinking about it, it sounded bogus, and I suspected she might be up to something. When I called her, she sounded nervous. I asked her where she was, and she said that you were at the Rave with Mary Ellen where she planned to spy on you. That sounded like trouble, so I called Angel to go pick her up. Elise gave me his number, as a backup, in case there was trouble. So, where is Tempest?" Jemma craned her neck around as she sped through a yellow light. "Not here, huh? No big surprise there."

"Watch out," he croaked, as they barely missed a parked car.

Mary Ellen made a moaning sound.

"Directions?" Jemma asked tartly. "This car isn't in self-steer mode."

"Carl's gonna kill me if he finds out I told you where they are," Mary Ellen complained.

"Not before I do, if you don't," Kayse snarled.

"Okay, okay. They're at the Kantwell Towers on Second and Cliff Street."

"Big fancy apartments, white building?" Jemma shot out.

"Yeah, yeah."

"Underground parking off Second?" Jemma grunted as she turned onto Cliff Street.

"I think so," Mary Ellen answered hesitantly.

"And the room number is…?"

"Somewhere on the fourth floor. Four ten or two." Her voice cracked, "I'm not sure."

The car lurched, taking a stomach-to-the-throat leap down into an underground parking garage. Jemma pulled up in front of an elevator and looked back at Angel. "I should go get her," she said.

"Might need my help," Angel countered.

"Someone needs to stay with Miss Trouble here and watch over her. I'll take Kayse for emergency muscle. He can handle a couple of boys if things go south, but I want this quiet and not a big scene with bodies lying all over the hall. I'm going to be tiptoeing. You do understand what I'm saying?"

"Yeah, I get you." Angel nodded.

However, Kayse wasn't following at all. Why was Angel letting Jemma take on possibly three boys by herself? Tiptoeing around rowdy, drunk teenage boys? Were they serious? However, Jemma appeared totally confident, and Angel was agreeing with her. He, however, felt very nervous about this plan.

Jemma brushed her hair back, saying, "You know I can get her out without the commotion you two would create. That makes me the better bet."

Angel stared at her for a long heartbeat, and then smiled. "Yeah, you can handle this one best."

"No doubt about that," she said with a grin back at him.

"Let's go, Kayse," she said to him confidently.

He climbed out of the car, dazed and still confused about what might happen. He followed her into the already open elevator.

"Now, I'm going to keep this very simple," she said and keyed the elevator into motion. "I want you to stay with me and do exactly what I say. Do not, under any circumstances, take matters into your own hands. Understand?"

Still feeling disoriented and dazed from the drink, he nodded. Events were piling up on him and colliding into one another so fast he could barely think.

The elevator opened onto a corridor. Down toward the end, a young teenager guarded one of the doors, tapping his fingers and humming to himself.

Jemma swung around. "All right. That's probably the room," she whispered. "I'm going over and see if I can get in. Stay here by the elevator and watch out for anyone. Is that clear? Can you do that?"

Putting a hand on her arm, he cautioned, "Jemma, there's probably more than one guy in there. You can't handle them all alone. I should go with you."

She inclined her head, giving him an intense stare. "I'm going to say it just one more time. You are to stay here by the elevator and do what?"

"Watch for stuff," he gritted out.

"Exactly. That's what you do unless I say otherwise. Be ready to move really fast as soon as I give the signal."

"But Jemma..."

A finger went up.

"Yeah, alright." He didn't believe his words.

She pushed the elevator's hold button. Inside, he watched as she hiked up her skirt, unbuttoned her shirt low in front, and swept up her hair, letting a few strands dangle around her face. She pulled a bright red lip-gloss from her handbag, slicked it on, and then outlined her eyes in black, using the reflective walls as a mirror. Suddenly she looked like a teenager with too much makeup and an attitude. She fluttered her lashes at him.

He responded with an eye roll, followed by a headshake.

She tapped a finger on his lips, then turned, and sauntered out of the elevator toward the unsuspecting youth. Curious, Kayse leaned out to observe what would happen.

"Hey hot stuff," she said, yanking on the kid's earjacks.

Startled, his eyebrows rose as he slowly pulled out the jacks. "Yeah, mama," the boy drawled, looking her up and down with a silly grin.

"The guy inside called and wants me to join the party." She leaned forward slightly to reveal a generous chest for viewing, took a deep breath to increase the sight, and moved in close enough so that his eyes went wide as he looked down.

Catching his breath, the kid muttered, "Carl said no one was to go in unless he said so. And he ain't said so." His eyes kept staring at her chest. He licked his lips.

"Well, I'm telling you, he said so."

"Naw, girl." He lifted his gaze. "Carl said he'd tell me in person like. Until then, this door stays sealed." The kid patted his pocket. "And I keep the key."

Just then, Kayse heard a scream from inside the room. It sounded like Tempest. Next came loud shouting and a crash.

"The party's getting exciting," Jemma said, gazing around. "Be a shame to miss it."

"Carl likes 'em feisty," the kid replied nervously. "You go away now, and come back another time." He made a shooing motion with his hands.

"Naw, time is now." Jemma touched his forehead.

Inside the elevator, Kayse felt a strange shift in perception as the floor shimmered beneath his feet. He blinked and saw the kid now stood frozen with his mouth open. Jemma reached into the kid's pocket and pulled out the keycard. She tapped it with a nail and surveyed the area. Kayse stepped out of the elevator with a questioning frown on his face and walked toward her.

"Holy Shit, you're moving." Her mouth dropped open and her eyes went wide.

He stopped, puzzled.

"How come you're moving?" she muttered.

"What?"

"Never mind. Let's get Tempest." She gestured hurriedly at him, then cast a second glance at him over her shoulder as if to reassure herself she saw what she thought she saw. Shrugging, she added, "Since you're moving, you might as well help."

He sprinted down the hall and up to the door. No sounds came from within. She inserted the card and swung the door open. Kayse stared at the scene in front of him.

Three guys stood frozen in mid-action. Tempest sat hunched up at the head of the bed, staring at someone who wore his trousers around his ankles, showing off the family jewels. Meanwhile, her skirt was rucked up around her waist with her blouse pulled out and her fingers stuck in her mouth. The others looked excited, showing differing degrees of anticipation and sexual arousal, while Tempest's eyes stared wide open, filled with fright.

Jemma ran up and eased Tempest carefully to a standing position. She puffed out a breath. "Frag, I should just let her stay this way. It'll be easier than her screaming and wailing and making things more difficult." She turned to Kayse. "Can you carry her out of here like this?"

He stared at the frozen figures, not believing what he was seeing. No one moved. He touched one of the kids in disbelief, feeling the pliant flesh, but there was no reaction.

"We've only a short time before they unlock, and I don't want to be around when they do," Jemma commented as she slipped Tempest's arm into a jacket, pulled and straightened her skirt. "Here, take her." She pushed the stiff body at him.

Nodding, he caught and slung Tempest up over his shoulder. "Fate, not this again." Shifting her around, he managed a better hold.

"Don't worry, she's bendable and won't break. Just get her to the elevator." Jemma opened the door and dragged in the kid who'd been outside, so she could lock him in. As she wedged the card into the lock mechanism, she waved for Kayse to go on.

He carried Tempest to the elevator. As soon as he arrived, Jemma slipped in behind them and punched the down button. She was breathing heavily.

"What..." Kayse started.

"Can't talk now. We have to make tracks. Later." Jemma motioned him forward as the elevator opened onto the garage where the car waited in front of them. He felt the world shift again as he staggered against the car and lowered his burden. All went back into motion. Kayse could only imagine the shocked reaction of the teenagers when they gained consciousness and found Tempest gone. Tempest groaned as she slumped onto the car.

Jemma opened a door. Mary Ellen was rubbing her eyes as Tempest fell in. "What happened?" she blurted out. "Tempest! She's here already!" A puzzled expression crossed her face. "That was quick."

As they exited the garage, Kayse studied a world stirring with life. In relief, he saw trees swaying outside along the sidewalks. A car sped down the street next to them, and a bicycle rolled past going in the opposite direction. Thankfully, the scene reflected complete normalcy.

He shook his head. *What had happened back there? How far could she affect stuff?*

He turned to a dazed Mary Ellen, wanting other answers too. "What did your friends do at that Rave?" Kayse demanded indignantly. "You set me up, didn't you?"

She answered hotly, "No! How stupid do you think I am anyway?"

"Let me count the ways," Angel murmured.

"I know who her parents are, for Fate's sake. I wouldn't do anything to really hurt Tempest. Or Kayse."

Angel snorted, "Liar."

"Okay, when Troy heard that I arranged to be Kayse's date for the Rave, he got jealous. I didn't know his plan until later. I don't like it when he gets all possessive. I'm not anyone's woman, but I went along with his spiking the drink because I was interested in how far you would go with me. He said you would be so turned on, you would do anything I asked."

"That's a lie," Kayse countered indignantly.

"No, that's a truth," Angel argued. "I can tell truth when I hear it. My mother is a Truthsayer."

Kayse looked over at him. "A what?"

From the front seat, Jemma said, "A very rare type of Enjelise that's capable of knowing if someone tells the truth. Angel's mother is one, and Angel has a bit of the Talent himself."

"A Truthsayer?"

"I have a bit of the Talent, that's all." Angel shrugged.

"All?" Kayse looked at him, dumbfounded.

"Wow! Seriously?" Mary Ellen shifted uncomfortably and stared at Angel.

"So Mary Ellen is telling the truth," Jemma amended.

Mary Ellen nodded and smirked at Kayse.

Kayse frowned. "Still, who were those goons who attacked me? They weren't students. Those guys were professionals who wanted me delivered to someone. Their guns contained drugged darts."

"Yeah, well, Joey found out that you were going to be there and blabbed to his father, who got in touch with some people. They were the ones with the guns. We just spiked your drink as an innocent prank. At some point during the Rave, I would get you off alone into a compromising position, but Troy and his friends would come in and stop anything from happening. Then we'd all laugh."

A wave of anger washed over him. "I'm not laughing," he said. "In fact, I'm pretty pissed off."

"But, I didn't have anything to do with those men!"

"You're ark dung, Mary Ellen," Tempest shouted, finding her voice. "Those guys certainly planned to do me one. I'm not having anything to do with guys anymore. I've had it with men, boys, and their special toy. Did you have anything to do with what they tried in that bedroom?"

"You got what you asked for." Mary Ellen crossed her arms and glared back at her. "You kept wanting to see some guy's dick, so Carl said he would arrange to show one to you, up close and personal. You were getting obnoxious about it, by the way. Carl said he would show you several, since you were so eager. I said no. I didn't support that idea. I know you consider me a friend."

"Not anymore," Tempest retorted. "I'm done with you. Friends don't do things like that to friends."

"I told you it was a misunderstanding."

"You set me up with that snake, Carl." Tears started dripping down Tempest's cheeks.

"Hey, you wanted a hot date and a show. I didn't know he was going to bring his buddies along and turn it into an event."

"That's not the entire truth, Mary Ellen," Angel interrupted. "You had a hunch it might end up a gang rape, but you closed your eyes to the possibility."

Mary Ellen paused, frustration crossing her face. "Carl owed me a favor, and she *asked* me for a hot date who would make Kayse jealous. Carl fits that bill."

Tempest pushed back some hair and glanced at Kayse out of half-closed eyelids.

Kayse wanted to strangle her. "It's about time you think about the consequences of your actions, Tempest…before, not after, you get neck deep in trouble," he admonished her. "Next time there might not be anyone around to pull your ass out of the fire. If you keep this up, you're going to get seriously hurt."

"I know." Tempest hiccupped and wiped an arm across a tear and snot smeared face.

Smoothing down her blouse, Mary Ellen looked up. "You only brought this on yourself."

"Oh please," Tempest retorted, clapping her hands over her ears. "I've heard enough from you." She turned from Mary Ellen, fresh tears brimming and lip quivering. "I want nothing to do with you ever again."

Mary Ellen smirked. "You'll come running back. I have a lot of pull at that school. You'll need protection soon enough."

"Shut up!" Kayse retorted, now sure it was Mary Ellen he wanted to strangle.

Mary Ellen looked indignant. "Hey, I'm still a big shot around school, and she's a half breed Terran; so be careful how you talk to me. I said I was sorry and didn't mean it to happen the way it did. I only fulfilled her request."

"Time to get out," Jemma interrupted. The car came to an abrupt halt a block away from the Rave. "Mary Ellen, I'd be real careful how you treat my friend, Tempest," Jemma warned. "You don't want me any more upset with you than I am now. I have some pretty heavy influence around town, too."

While they were talking, Angel got out of the car and went around to open the door for Mary Ellen. He leaned in and softly whispered to her, "Count me in on that sentiment. And think on the fact that you can go to jail for aiding and abetting the rape of a minor, or drugging someone without their knowledge. There's also attempted kidnapping and assault. Let's say thirty years in jail if you should force us to press charges."

She glanced at him and slid out of the car. Then with a huff, she headed back to the Rave.

"Now, you two are going home," Angel commanded in a voice that brooked no argument.

Chapter 22

The rest of the ride home contained nothing but silence. Entering through the front door with Tempest and Angel, Kayse saw a knot of people break up and hurry toward them.

"Trey!" he said, then noticed his friend glowering at him. This wasn't shaping up as a warm welcome back.

"How is that beacon going to do you any good if you don't use it?" Trey demanded, striding toward Kayse. "Are you all right?" A hint of worry lurked beneath his rough reprimand.

"Yes, I'm fine. Sorry, everything happened so fast that I didn't think of it." His apologetic smile didn't erase Trey's frown.

"Next time use it. It might save your life."

Thankfully, everyone's attention shifted to Tempest, and Kayse felt relieved to be out of the spotlight.

Grabbing her arm, Richard shook it. "You put yourself in a bad situation, young lady. You need to start making better choices. I can't even begin to think of what might have happened…" A muscle clenched in his cheek as emotions of anger, horror, and guilt swept across his face.

"I know, dad. It won't happen again." She pulled her arm back, a pained expression on her face.

"That's for certain," he choked out.

Elise faced Richard. "She's coming out of that school."

"Mom," Tempest protested.

"Absolutely," her father agreed. "They're nothing but a gang of...of...juvenile delinquents. You're not going back." He hunched his shoulders.

Angel interrupted. "Richard, it's time to get her tested."

"I agree," Jemma added. "She froze when I stopped time." She frowned. "She may not have time Talent."

Dumbfounded, Kayse stared at Jemma. *Stopped time!* He thought it over. *Yes, that's exactly what she'd done. Of course, she was a Tellurian!*

"Oh, she has Talent," Richard countered. "I don't need to test her. I just need to give her a crystal to activate it. I've been holding it off because she hasn't proven she's ready for the responsibility yet."

Closing her eyes and grimacing, Jemma suggested, "You might consider getting her ready anyway. She'll need the protection her Talent might offer. I certainly wouldn't wait much longer." She opened her eyes and angled her head to one side, adding, "Kayse, on the other hand, wasn't stopped, which means he most likely *has* the time Talent. You should test him! Who *is* he? Does he carry a crystal already?" Jemma stared around the group in puzzlement.

Ignoring her questions, Trey interrupted, "Someone tried to abduct Kayse again? Who? Why?"

Shifting from one foot to another, Tempest replied, "Mary Ellen said Joey's dad set that part up."

Angel scowled. "Maybe we should press charges."

Giving a short shake of his head, Richard regarded the Enjelise. "The very last thing we need is for them to get Kayse on the witness stand....and they will if we press charges. That could disclose more than we want revealed right now. Whoever is doing this may be counting on that reaction. I'll get Trace to look into Joey's dad. I hope that they don't know everything about Kayse. This could be only a fishing expedition, which might lead us to who is after him or who killed his parents."

Angel frowned. "I see your point."

Richard smiled. "We need to tread carefully. They may have suspicions, but I don't think they know the extent of his abilities. They may only be interested in what he learned in that rebel camp, or maybe they just hate him for associating with Terrans."

"Who *is* Kayse?" Jemma interrupted again, a frown creasing her brow.

Elise put a hand on the girl's arm and shook her head. Jemma subsided, but her eyes narrowed in confusion.

"It's that Talent thing messing up my life," Kayse complained.

With a glance toward Elise, who was listening intently, Trey explained, "The fact they wanted him alive supports the idea that someone thinks Kayse can help them go back in time and stop the aliens from ever coming here."

Elise gasped, "Seriously?"

Snorting with derision, Richard countered, "They're wrong." Glancing at her, he explained, "I don't think it can be done. Certain events can't be changed. They're meant to be and if anyone tries to change them, somehow the universe works to make it happen another way."

Trey nodded in agreement.

Kayse's eyes widened. "You mean I might be able to go back in time and stop them from killing my parents?" Kayse sucked in and held his breath.

Trey held out a hand in apology. "No. If you go back to stop the attack, it'll happen in another way. Some actions are meant to happen no matter how we try to change them.

I already tried to change things several times, and this last scenario is the one where the least number of people get hurt. At other times, a car crash, a gas explosion, an angry mob…a lot more people die or get hurt. Still, there are times when events can be changed and should be changed. Your parent's death caused you to come here to us, and now that you're here, we have to protect you until you fulfill some particular destiny. It just works out that way." Trey shrugged.

"Oh frag! That's too much. I'm just a kid whose parents were recently murdered. For me, at least. I miss them."

Leaning forward, Elise said, "I'm truly sorry about your parents, Kayse. I know I'm not good at the parenting thing. I'm trained to be a ship's captain. What few children we had on *the Newfound Hope*, we kept in a protective crèche. I barely knew my own mother. They trained me for other than maternal skills, so I have no idea how a mother should act."

Richard stroked her arm. "It's my fault too. I should have kept a closer eye on our daughter. I kept getting distracted. Not a good excuse, though. I'll try to do better."

Letting out his breath, Kayse asked, "So, what am I supposed to do?"

Trey closed his eyes and grimaced. "Trace believes it involves the escalating conflict between Terrans and Alysians. If whoever is after you gets a hold of you and uses you, or kills you, you won't be able to do what needs to be done. The whole planet could be enveloped in war. So, you see why we are taking serious measures to keep you hidden and safe."

"He's not safe anywhere in Tygel now," Angel pointed out. "We need to find somewhere else."

Trey snapped his fingers. "How about that Sunglast friend of Richard's?"

Richard made a face. "Bashar now lives in the Ching T'Karre with a brand-new family. I called him when Kayse first arrived, and he said he couldn't take on any more kids."

Jemma whirled around to face Richard. "Madame Kat in Bogtown takes in homeless."

"Girls. They're all girls, and I don't want Madame Kat getting her busy fingers on Kayse. I.N.Sys has tried to shut her labs down, but has failed. She'd get a hold of Kayse and add him to her hybrid Enjelise/human experiments. No, not an option."

"Maybe Trace knows a place," suggested Trey.

"I trust Trace," Richard shrugged, "but someone high up in his division is working against us. Klaymore Townsend is building a power base, using someone in I.N.Sys to help bring down the current administration. Trace and I have been pulled away from the table and prevented from effective action by endless, bogus committee hearings. They are using the media to discredit the current government. I'm afraid turning Kayse over to Trace could be dangerous."

Breathing in slowly, Elise said, "I know a place where no one would think to find him." All eyes turned toward her. She shrugged. "My brother has a place in that's pretty isolated from everything. Elija might take him in for a while, until we find somewhere better."

Richard shook his head. "I don't know, Elise. I don't like handing him over to Terrans, especially your brother."

"Right now, he appears to be safer with Terrans than Alysians."

Stepping forward, Kayse felt a rush of anger at all the possible plans for him without his say-so. "Why would I want to go off to some deserted cabin to live with a Terran I don't even know?"

Richard scowled at him in response.

"No one would ever think to search for you there," Trey answered. "Trace just needs a little more time to find out who's behind the attempted kidnapping. With Joey's father as a fresh lead, we might wrap this up in no time."

"I don't like the idea of Elija getting his hands on Kayse," Richard repeated.

"So where exactly do you think Kayse should hide out to get away from the obviously dangerous Alysians?" Elise retorted. "Certainly not anywhere around here."

A shrug from Richard answered her. He sighed. "I've no idea, but Elija keeps saying he wants to be left alone to live a peaceful life in that isolated cabin of his, but I just don't feel I can trust him. Something strange is going on up there."

"Don't you think Trace Walker might also be curious about Elija?" Elise flashed a grin. "Here's an opportunity for Kayse to nose around the Homestead a bit. You know Trace has been trying for a while, with little success, to get someone he knows in there. Besides, Kayse has his medallion if he feels threatened."

Richard grumbled to himself as he thought it over. "At least it's not a military camp of armed Terran rebels who are targeting him." Richard paused, weighing the options. "It's obvious to me that I can't keep him safe here. I thought I could, but I can't. Also, Angel has his hands full with Tempest."

A grunt of agreement came from Angel.

Interrupting, Trey added, "He's probably safer there than here, at least until Trace can sort out who's behind these attacks. However, any public travel might tip off interested parties. There are ways to trace people when they need passports, identity markers and the like. Every monitor or surveillance system has flags on Kayse...bet on it."

"So we get bogus papers and disguise him."

"No!" Kayse protested. "No. I've been disguised enough."

"Kayse," Trey patted his shoulder, "You just need a few changes. Minor surgery only. Something simple. Maybe you could grow a beard."

Kayse grimaced, causing Jemma to laugh.

Richard took on a worried expression. "I can set up an appointment at the Med Center and get some bogus papers put together, but I have another committee meeting in two rotations. I don't think we can get him over there before then, or I'd take him myself. Also, I'll need some time to talk to Tempest. She needs to know…"

"I learned all about it, dad," Tempest interrupted him quickly. "Dr. Jay filled me in."

Rolling his eyes, Richard put up his palms, saying, "Evidently it wasn't as effective as we'd hoped. We need to revisit that topic and underline a few issues at some future date, but this is something different." Richard coughed, giving a grimace. Jemma nodded.

"I'll take him," Trey offered. Kayse noticed the strain in his voice. Something about the Med Center bothered his cousin.

Angel studied Trey, shaking his head. "No, I don't want you two over there together. I'll take him. Going there would be too painful for Trey, anyway."

Releasing a pent-up breath, Trey warned Angel, "Be careful there. Kayse mentioned a crazy security guard who accosted him recently. We should check up on him too. I'll call Ailey DeVey and have her meet you. We don't want our boy to get lost again. He may never find his way out.

There are lots of hidden labs and secret rooms deep in the Med Center."

Kayse only heard that he would get to see Ailey again. Maybe she would help him find out who he was. He nodded his head eagerly, acting the compliant young adult. Soon, the others moved into the next room, still arguing over the details of their plan, leaving the youngsters and Angel behind.

Angel cupped a hand under Kayse's chin, forcing him to gaze directly into his golden eyes. "Try to stay out of trouble until I come back tomorrow. I need the rest." The smile, when it came, was luminous.

Kayse could only nod speechlessly as Angel dropped his hand, turning to leave the room. Then he noticed Tempest glaring at Angel's retreating back.

Her eyes narrowed. "That's an Enjelise, Kayse. They're not human. Don't get emotionally involved, if you know what's good for you. Take my advice."

"Why, you sound jealous," he retorted, smirking at her.

She reddened in embarrassment and gazed away. "Just be careful with *it*," she bit out.

"Careful…now there's a word I didn't think was in your vocabulary."

"Gah!" She crossed her arms and gave him an angry glare. He stared back. A brief contest ensued with her finally turning her face away. "*Okay*, I'll try to be more careful." She whirled around and stomped out of the room.

His gaze followed her, as he smiled in triumph. Then, his thoughts went into a whirl. Ailey! The Med Center. Somehow, he knew the Med Center held the key to his true identity.

Chapter 23

The next morning, a car drove up to Richard's elaborate, front gate at the end of his extensive driveway. Kayse peered out the window and saw a jaunty Mary Ellen step out. Four shadowy figures stayed inside. She clutched a colorful bouquet of flowers in one hand and a gaudily decorated box in the other. Peering over her shoulder from time to time, she proceeded briskly up the lush landscaped path that led to the Steele's imposing front door.

Luckily, Elise was home, and Kayse went to find her. So, by the time the door chimes sounded, she was striding down the front hall. Kayse lingered in the next room just off the entry. Elise signaled Kayse to stay out of sight. Then, she opened the door.

Mary Ellen greeted her, wearing a bright smile on her face.

"Hello Mrs. Steele," she started out. "I've come by to see if Kayse's all right and to apologize for the other night. May I come in?"

"He's not available right now," Elise answered abruptly and started to close the door.

Mary Ellen put a hand out, stopping her. "Oh, I'm sorry to hear that. I brought him candy. Could you give it to him? Is he in bed, hurt?" Mary Ellen thrust the box forward. Elise eyed it and shook her head, not touching it. Frowning, Mary Ellen shifted the box back under her arm.

"After that drink you gave him, I doubt he'll want to taste anything you might offer," Elise spat out.

Mary Ellen shifted her feet. "I'm sorry for the misunderstanding. I wanted to see him to apologize…but if he's out, then maybe I can see Tempest. I brought her flowers. There's nothing to taste there." Mary Ellen lifted her chin and gave another plastered-on smile as she held out the bouquet of flowers, encased in a clear, sealed, plastic container.

"Tempest is also unavailable."

"They're just flowers to say I'm sorry, Mrs. Steele. Here, take them." She thrust the flowers under Elise's nose.

Elise pushed them away, turning her head.

Frowning, Mary Ellen asked, "Is Tempest home from the Med Center? I need to talk to her. She hasn't been at school for the past few rotations, and I'm worried about her."

"She's fine, but I doubt if she wants to talk to you. She's very angry at you," Elise responded. "Goodbye." She edged the door closed, but something stopped it from shutting.

"Ah, your shoe's stuck in my door, Mary Ellen," Elise said. Kayse could hear the annoyance in her voice and quickly stuck his head out.

Mary Ellen coughed apologetically through the opening. "It's just the guys and their parents are wondering what *exactly* happened. They don't remember Tempest leaving and, well, they have this idea she did something weird. They wanted me to ask her how she got out. They just want to understand what happened."

"You were there. Jemma and Kayse rescued her from a possible gang rape." Elise glared. "You do remember that?"

Shuffling her feet, Mary Ellen stared at a nearby bush for a moment. She looked up. "I know Kayse and that girl rescued her. But, I don't know how. I wasn't *there* exactly; I was in the car with Angel. If she didn't do anything, and I told them so, then Kayse maybe did something, hypnotized them or something. They said that he moves really fast when he fights. Therefore, of course, they're curious about him. He's a bit different, wouldn't you say? Everyone's just curious, that's all."

"Look, Kayse didn't hypnotize anyone or do anything wrong, so there's nothing to be concerned about. Just leave us alone."

Mary Ellen wrinkled her nose and made a face. "Oh, I doubt we can do that, Mrs. Steele. My friends have parents who are interested in what happened, and their sons aren't explaining things too well. I told them that I was a friend and could ask without a lot of trouble. I feel sure there is a reasonable explanation for what happened, but they keep asking us about stuff we can't explain."

She shifted the flowers and candy, smiling again. "I told them I would just ask Tempest about it. But if Tempest or Kayse won't explain it to me, then my friend's fathers are going to confront Mr. Steele in one of those very public committee hearings, and their questions won't be as nice. On the other hand, they might ask Kayse in some dark alley where he would be forced to come up with proper answers. You see what I'm saying? I just wanted to know if Tempest and Kayse were here so I could ask them to tell me what happened. These parents think Kayse is some sort of weapon, and that you're organizing a Terran takeover. I told them that was silly. I told them Tempest and Kayse are just nice kids and not dangerous at all. However, they don't believe me. I just want to talk to them and try to understand, you see. I don't want them mad at me. When do you think they'll be available? I can come back later."

With a white-knuckled grip on the doorknob, Elise responded, "I don't think they're ever going to be available for you or your friends." She gritted her teeth. "Besides, you're not trusted anymore."

Mary Ellen brushed her hair back with her right hand. "Oh, Mrs. Steele, you're making a great mistake. I want to be their friend. I don't think Tempest would be too happy to learn you sent me away." She settled her shoulders. "She's always liked me. She even calls me her best friend, and she doesn't have too many. She's half Terran and that makes things difficult for her at school without my help, you see. She'll probably want to talk to me. Don't upset her. If she returns, just let me know, and I'll come back. Here's my card."

Mary Ellen transferred the candy box again while she dug a card out of her pocket. It showed a smiling picture of her and a call number underneath. Elise took it. Mary Ellen offered the candy and flowers again, but Elise just shook her head. Mary Ellen shrugged and spun away, but then she turned back.

"It seems Jemma is off somewhere too. Maybe you know where *she* is? They're curious about her also."

"Nope, don't know where she is either."

A long stare from Mary Ellen greeted that remark. "That's a shame. She could be in trouble, and I'd like to help her. Call me if you change your mind, or she shows up." She swung around and strode back down the pathway to the waiting car.

Slamming the door shut, Elise stood heaving large gulps of air while she mumbled under her breath. She went to pull the curtains back so she could see out.

Coming over to stand by her, Kayse heard a motor start up and saw a car pull away from the tall wrought iron gate. A boy stood just on the other side, talking into a caller.

"They've left a lookout," Kayse informed her.

Startled at the sound of his voice, Elise whirled around, her frightened eyes wide open.

Tempest came down the stairs, slowly. "What does that piece of ark dung want now?" she asked.

"They're looking for both you and Kayse, and I don't want her knowing you're here." Elise rubbed her arm unconsciously. "Her friends are out there, and we're too vulnerable at the moment for me to let anyone into this house. Someone is either pretty bold or high up in the power chart and not afraid of us..." Elise stopped, a thoughtful expression on her face. "Or wants us to press charges and get into court. Richard may be right about that."

Kayse sighed. "What about Trace providing people to protect us?"

"Remember, the problem is Trace's I.N.Sys operation may be compromised. We don't know how, but someone is receiving inside information on our movements. However, now, they don't know what happened inside that room, and they want to know. We suspect an infiltrator. So, no, we don't trust them. Trace is trying to discover who it is, but keeps getting called into those damned government investigating committees. All the media commotion is weakening his position at I.N.Sys."

Kayse gazed down at the floor. "I keep thinking about the security guard I saw at the Med Center. Reminded me of my first attacker. The more I think about how odd he acted and his appearance, the more I believe he could be the deranged killer I saw at the Space Center."

"Really?" Elise looked interested. "You saw him recently? You're sure?"

"I think it's worth checking out," Kayse admitted. "He looked like he worked there, but it felt like a stakeout. I mentioned him to Richard. They' will research past employees. It might be a good lead."

Surveying the room, Elise murmured, "We'll have to pack everything by tomorrow night. The sooner you're out of here, the easier I'll breathe."

"I'm not too keen on being shuttled off to a remote mountain cabin for any length of time," Kayse complained.

"What matters more than your delicate feelings is your immediate safety. Besides, we're not talking about the rest of your life. We're talking about sanctuary for a few cycles and not much more."

"They tried to hurt Tempest too."

"Her problem is mostly stupid prejudice on their part. Still, they could use her for leverage against either Richard or me, so I'm taking her out of that school, and she stays close by. I'll put Angel on her full time."

Elise paced back and forth in agitation. "I also think the two of you need a break from each other. Keeping you together is just asking for trouble. She's now a young teen-aged girl with a crush, and you're a hormone-filled adolescent boy. It's a volatile cocktail at best."

"Then I'll help Kayse pack." Tempest blinked at him through tearful eyes. "I don't have to be separated from him until he leaves." She raised a stubborn chin.

Sympathy etched Elise's face as she waved them off.

"I'm sorry I brought this trouble on you, Elise," Kayse said, shuffling his feet and staring at the floor.

She smiled. "It's not only you; it's this sorry planet."

He was surprised to realize he would miss her—he would miss them all.

Chapter 24

"Well, Kayse Kiare, we meet again."

The twinkling eyes of Ailey DeVey met his gaze, but he didn't feel like he could cope with all that cheerfulness. He felt nervous and tense about this new plan. Leaving for some isolated hideaway and changing his appearance *again*, was all too uncertain and frightening. One thing for sure, though; he wasn't going back to that fricking school. Even being in the Med Center unnerved and disquieted him. He didn't know why, but he was beginning to suspect he was more familiar with this place than anyone might guess.

"You're early, really early," Ailey commented. Her eyebrows rose in question. Abruptly, her gaze shifted over his shoulder to movement behind him. "And you've brought someone special with you!" A glowing smile appeared on her face.

Kayse heard Angel behind him, fussing with a jacket and gloves. "Good morning," vibrated in the air.

They'd left under the cloak of early morning darkness. They'd sneaked through a secret exit in the kitchen pantry, emerging at the back of the house inside a stand of trees. On the other side of the foliage, a cleared space held a parked car and a hidden road out.

Then Angel had driven a route that had made Kayse dizzy. Traveling off the main roads, he'd backtracked and eased down side streets in a complicated itinerary that no one dared follow. Kayse had felt as if he was in one of those action vids with mystery cars tailing the hero.

Now, Ailey was looking past him at Angel, grinning at the Enjelise as if he was some special treat. The "Angel Effect" at work.

"This is Angel...er..." He looked questioningly at Angel as he realized he didn't know Angel's last name or even if he had a last name.

Inclining his head gracefully, Angel responded, "Avarric. My name is Angel Avarric. Pleased to meet you. Heard a lot about you, Ms. DeVey. Sorry Dr. Steele couldn't make it." The room brightened with his glow.

"Truly?" Ailey breathed. "You're *that* famous Enjelise, aren't you?"

"Yeah, most likely." Angel looked down with a strange expression on his face. Kayse almost thought him embarrassed or shy.

"Then you're the closest thing to a true Enjelise ever born on Alysia. Darius Avarric and Ariel Truthsayer are your biological parents, aren't they? Amazing."

Angel did a bit of a shuffle. "Yep, they're my parents."

"I heard they closed down Mother Kat's gene lab in Bogtown," Ailey mused.

With a shrug, Angel answered, "That's the official version, but knowing that group, I doubt it. Mother Kat is determined to produce a human/Enjelise hybrid that's space adaptable. I.N.Sys has tried to shut them down, but I'm betting they've gone underground."

"But you were born naturally, an almost pure Enjelise. They haven't been able to breed more males like you."

"One of a kind."

"Surely we have wonders here this morning," Ailey murmured. "You too are a marvel, Kayse Kiare." Ailey's bright eyes turned their dazzle on him.

"Me?" His voice squeaked upwards, expressing adolescent surprise. He hadn't considered himself anywhere near wonderful; nuisance was the first word that came to mind.

"There's an even greater mystery about *you*. Everyone's wondering where you came from and who you are." She gave him an intent stare.

"I'm a mystery to myself most times," he mumbled. "In fact," he looked up, brightening, "that's why I'm here early. Elise hinted that I might find some answers to questions about my background here in the Med Center. She recommended I talk to you, since you're one of their researchers. Do you have any information about gene projects that were done here about forty-five annuals ago?"

"We've done a lot of genetic programs. I can check on any of them for you, but first…." She rubbed at a small mark on her lab table, gazed at Angel, and murmured, "You know my mother published a paper long ago that suggested Alysia was a colony planet seeded by a space faring race."

Giving a nod, Angel explained, "My father told me that the Enjelise serve and protect the human race at the request of the Creator. To insure the survival of the human species, they brought some to this world to establish a colony. For our duty as their guardians, when we transform, we receive His blessing. Several annuals ago, they finished their task and most of the race transformed to another dimension to receive their glorious reward."

"That must have been an amazing thing to witness," she said with a sigh.

With a scowl, he replied, "It happened before my birth on another world far away." A frustrated expression crossed his face. "So, here I am, stuck, waiting for my own transformation, which may never take place unless I accomplish some act of true worth."

This line of talk startled Kayse. He'd read a little about the philosophies of the Enjelise, but hadn't given them much thought until meeting Angel. However, he didn't have time to ponder it all now. Time was running out.

"I really don't have much time," Kayse interrupted.

"Right." She tore her attention away from Angel and strode over to a computer console. She flipped a few switches and punched buttons as the board lit up.

"What are we looking for?" she inquired.

"I'm not sure." Kayse frowned.

Angel interrupted, "I came early because there are a few things I need to attend to before delivering you to your appointment. Will you be all right here with Ailey for a short while? Make sure you stay with her." Angel waggled a finger at him.

Kayse flapped a hand back. "Not to worry. See you in a while. Don't forget me."

"As if I could," Angel murmured as he left.

Kayse turned back to Ailey with a thoughtful expression on his face. "There's a man I want to find out about. His name's Arwoyn Telluria."

A shocked expression crossed Ailey's face. "Arwoyn? He's famous. Everyone knows about him. He's in all the history books. He founded the Institute for the Development of Human Talent and was on the Med Center's board for ages. Many suggest that he practically ran the government."

Shifting his feet, Kayse didn't want to admit his lack of attention during third class history. "Yeah, I read some stuff about him in school a while ago. Claimed that he traveled in time from the medieval past. Is there any medical data or reports that list blood type, DNA samples, tissue cores, stuff like that?"

Ailey regarded him oddly. "He lived here at the Med Center later in his life. I imagine I could find something along those lines." Her fingers flew over the keys, and a message popped up on the monitor:

Sealed Documents. Level One access required

"Lucky for you, I have a Level One access code," Ailey supplied. "But hmm…there's tripwire programs embedded in the data. I'm closing out the program."

"Can we do this another way without calling attention to ourselves?" Kayse asked. "Are there any documents or project reports where his name's mentioned?"

She hummed a little tune and tapped some more keys. Then, she gave a startled cry. "There aren't many, but this old paper may be interesting."

Edging next to her to see better, he read:

Cloning Procedures Leading to Replicant Variations.

He gasped. "He was doing experiments with cloning?"

She studied him intently and wrinkled her nose. He could practically see thoughts racing around in her brain. "There was some talk about a secret clone project here at the Center way back, but it was disbanded by none other than Brett Telluria. That's interesting." Ailey tapped her teeth.

"Is there any more information on the project? Any documentation on the clones themselves?"

She looked intently at the screen and drummed her nails on the table. "I'll see if there's a link off the document."

Straightening up, she frowned. "Tripwires again. This whole program is riddled with program tripwires and sealed access codes. Someone wants to know who's interested. Every click I make is tracked."

Pulling a stool over next to her, he stuck his elbows on the desk and leaned into the monitor to see better.

She leaned back and blew a piece of hair out of her eyes. "I would guess you don't want anyone to know that you're looking at this?"

"Right. Is there any other way to access the information?"

"We can go to the source. We keep some hard copies in a vault."

"In a vault? Here? How do I find it?"

"Be nice to me. As a level one researcher, I have, as they say, the keys to the kingdom." She dived into a nearby drawer and pawed through various items to emerge with a container labeled *Anderson's Breath Mints.*

"Here we are," she said with satisfaction.

"Breath mints?"

She unscrewed the container's lid and shook out two thin metal squares. "No, the keys to the vault." She held them up and rubbed them together in front of his nose. "Now follow me."

He followed her out of her office and turned right to go through an exit door off the hallway. They descended a long series of metal stairwells, burrowing deep into the Med Center's core.

All the ordinary sounds of people dwindled away. As they spiraled deeper, it got cooler and dimmer. Ailey pushed through a thick metal door and stopped at a security checkpoint. She stared into a retinal identity verifier and the door clicked open. They went through another long corridor until they came to another heavy door. There she put her finger to a disk. A green light clicked on, and she pushed through. Finally, they entered a reception area. At a large desk with a monitor on it, she swiped both cards through a reader and put her eyeball to another identifier. Nearby, a heavy vault door swung open.

With a glance over her shoulder at him, she said, "This place is environmentally controlled to protect the hard copy records. Everything's going to encrypted binary code nowadays. There's a big project to migrate all our records to digital before they disintegrate and become unreadable. A new holographic data storage program is expected to be beta tested here soon. Paper is so fragile that it's only a matter of time before we lose critical printed data, while our information base is growing exponentially. In addition to that, we're running out of storage space for hard copy. It's a problem." She pointed to a whole shelf of plastic boxes. "There's where most of his records are located."

Kayse looked nervously at his chrono.

"We'll never get through all those boxes," he groaned.

"Then you'll have to come back." She smiled brightly.

He frowned at her. "I may not be able to. I'm going away for a while."

"Seriously?" Ailey sighed. "I'd thought you might come here and work part time. I was really looking forward to it."

Breath gusted out of him. "Might have to take a rain check. I only have today to find what I'm looking for, but I think the answer is here."

"Then let's get started. That box is projects, and this is medical records." She pointed to a box, which he pulled out and slid to the floor. She grabbed the second one.

For a time, the only sound was the rustling of paper and heavy breathing. Despite the cool temperature of the vault, Kayse felt sweat dripping down his neck, and collecting under his armpits. Occasionally, he would check his chrono and mutter.

As he sorted through a new container, his eyes landed on a nondescript box entitled *Clone Project*. Two folders lay inside. One was entitled: *Deviations Derived Using Cloning Techniques* by Dr. Warner Straung and a smaller and much thinner folder with *Cloning Project Final Dispensation* scribbled across the front of it. Inside, a title page said: *Final Placement Papers*. Underneath the title, he saw the spidery signature of Arwoyn Telluria and the bold signature of an Elissandra Telluria. He pulled out some papers and read:

<u>Clone Derivation Results:</u>
Ten embryos per gene line

<u>Case#1</u>: Genetic line A: defective/all deceased. Adjust stem cell matrix/males
<u>Case#2</u>: Genetic line B: two alive up to one annual/all deceased/males.
<u>Case#3</u>: Genetic line C: one embryo surviving at current date/two alive for two annuals/remainder deceased. Adjust hormone levels/males
<u>Case#4</u>: Genetic line D: two embryos alive to three annuals/one to current date/males
<u>Case#5</u>: Splice in x chromosome, cloak y. Remainder deceased. Adjust endocrine levels/females
<u>Case#6</u>: Two surviving up to fourteen annuals/defect found causing death in one/corrected. One survivor past puberty/female.

Inside the other folder, he found copies of adoption papers. One contained his mother and father's names with an address. Curiously, there was another set of adoption papers with another set of names and an address. The two surviving subjects had been adopted and the program disbanded.

A further note scribbled at the bottom of the page in a cramped handwriting said: successful transition and insertion. Time travel program complete.

He wasn't sure what "successful transition and insertion" meant.

"I need to take these papers," he said, with shaking hands and a dry mouth.

Nothing proven yet his mind admonished, but his emotions were racing so hard he couldn't move.

What if…? How would it make me feel?

Right now, he was feeling almost sick. He couldn't get his head around the idea that he might be…

Putting the papers down, Ailey shook her head. "We can't. No documents are allowed to be removed from here, but I can scan any documents you want. I found a blood type and DNA genome data from Arwoyn along with his medical records. I'll scan that too."

He cleared his clogging throat. "I want to compare them with mine."

She looked at him, startled, then thoughtful. Putting a hand on his arm, she said, "Did you know Kiare means four? Your name translates to Case Four. One of the case four embryos lived, according to this report."

He cast her a distressful smile, running a hand through his hair, as he shook his head to fight off a dizziness.

Her hand slipped off. He watched her scan the papers. Then she neatly laid them back into the sealed boxes. After she finished, she pushed back her hair, rocked forward, and stood up. "I'll take this back and see if there's a match. I'll pull some data together while you're in your meeting and see what I can find out."

He nodded. They put the boxes back and straightened up, then he left on shaking legs.

Chapter 25

By the time they got back to Ailey's office, Angel was waiting for him. The Enjelise arched an eyebrow at him as if to say, "Where have you been?"

"You heard Richard say to be careful here, didn't you?" Angel chastised. "He doesn't want you roaming around the Med Center and getting into trouble. We have to be extra careful since that guard isn't showing up on any of the Center's current employee records." He brandished a handful of papers, most likely copies of Med Center personnel files.

"Ailey took good care of me." Kayse gazed over at her. "Please let me know what you find out." His voice cracked on the last two words.

She gave him a nod, accompanied by an encouraging smile.

He turned to Angel. "I guess we had better get on with it."

Casting a puzzled glance at Ailey, Angel gestured for Kayse to follow him. The Enjelise led him down the hall and entered an ordinary cream-colored medical room. Utilitarian, it had a sink, two chairs, an examination table and cabinets. Against the far wall, under a window, sat two carts, one full of stuff and the other with an empty bag on top.

Angel waved Kayse in. "I'll wait nearby until you're done." Then he closed the door.

Immediately, the door opened and in walked a Med Center doctor followed by a very peculiar looking individual.

The second person didn't look like your typical doctor. In fact, if Kayse were to guess what profession the man practiced, he would guess entertainment due to his garish outfit. He stood tall and lanky with a wild nimbus of dark brown curls that appeared to float around his head. A twinkling, mocha-colored face grinned at him. He was younger than Richard, but quite a bit older than Kayse, and that was all Kayse could figure out as far as how old he was. Kayse couldn't take his eyes off the white satin shirt and shiny silver slacks that sported a heavy metal belt covered with electronics. The guy wore more high tech jewelry than any medical doctor he knew. Blue earjack accessories winked from each ear, and a heavy necklace, also embedded with electronics, hung around his neck. No, it was hard to believe this apparition was a doctor. Kayse expected him to burst out into a song and dance number at any moment.

"Are you a doctor here?" he blurted out.

"Me?" The man laughed. "Naw, I'm just along as a special consultant for Dr. Steele. Call me Deuce, Deuce Card." He accented the pronouncement with a short bow and elegant hand roll.

Kayse snorted, "Deuce Card? That's a real name?"

The man chuckled. "Yeah, my pappy gave it to me. Said my ma won me in a card game. He would always laugh when he said it, so I think he was kidding, but with them, you never could tell. It was possible. They liked the game, and some folks will wager anything."

Kayse could feel the doubtful expression crossing his face, so he shifted to gaze at the other man, who did appear to be a real doctor. The man smiled and put out a hand.

"I'm Dr. Kane." He must have seen an apprehensive look because he put a hand on Kayse's shoulder, saying, "Don't be alarmed. I'm not going to be doing anything major. Just a mild anesthetic to implant a tracker and the rest of the time you'll be wide awake and alert."

Deuce started tweaking electronics and humming a tune as the doctor jabbed Kayse's arm. The next thing Kayse knew, he was rubbing his eyes, and Dr. Kane had left.

"Didn't take too long, did it?" Deuce grinned. "Practically painless."

"Did you change my eyes? What did you do?"

With a pat on his arm to reassure him, Deuce confided, "After talking to Richard, we agreed to implant a small tracking device under your skin. Once it saved him and he felt one for you, considering your history and recent abduction, would be a good idea. So, that's done."

Deuce motioned for Kayse to sit in a nearby chair and rolled over a cart filled with items. "Dr. Steele told me that you might need disguises and the means to implement them. That's where I can help." He pulled out a folder containing a series of documents: birth certificate, passport, medical information and bank statements for a person called Cameron Canfield. He had access to funds, it seemed. A quick glance revealed a substantial balance.

Reaching into the full cart, Deuce picked up a small box. "This box contains finger shields. If you need to draw money from your account or do anything that requires an identity print, then put these on."

He handed another compact box to Kayse. "This box includes tinted contacts. Use them when traveling or whenever you might run into the need for retinal identification. It's becoming more common, so be careful and use them. You pop them in like this." Deuce reached in and pulled out a wafer-thin piece of material. He tilted his head, and using a finger, transferred the contact to his eye. He blinked a few times and then looked straight at Kayse. "It's that easy."

"No surgery?"

"Nope. Makes your eyes pretty, too. Pick your color. These are a sexy blue."

He grinned at Kayse, showing one blue and one brown eye. Then he winked.

Kayse rolled his eyes and shook his head.

Unfazed, Deuce continued. "This is your palm computer, fully loaded and secure. It's off ASSIST and contains a secure link to both Dr. Steele and Trey, rock solid and unhackable." He tossed a small electronic device to Kayse, who flailed at the air to catch it. Luckily, he did.

Deuce executed a theatrical clap of approval.

"Dr. Kane has supplied an ointment that will lighten your skin. I have included hair dye in several colors. Pick the color you think will work best for the situation at hand. You might need to change your color several times. I also have a skin darkener if you need to go darker. You can go golden or select a chocolate mocha like my fine pelt." He smoothed his hands over his body. "Women love chocolate. Indeed, they do."

He paused momentarily for breath. "Now, if you need to alter your appearance even more, there are several ways to do it." Like a magician pulling a gibbet out of a hat, he reached inside the box and, with a flourish, pulled out a kit with various needles, bottles, and tubes inside.

Tapping a tube, he continued, "You can insert an inert material subcutaneously around parts of your face to change the shape of your chin, cheeks, or nose. The process is a bit painful, but effective. It will alter your appearance for awhile. Just be careful where you inject it and use it sparingly. Too much stabbing at your face can damage sensitive nerves. Here are the areas to be careful with." He poked a finger at several places on Kayse's face. "Don't forget. It's not fun to drool in front of people because you've damaged a facial nerve."

It sounded like Deuce had some experience there.

The items were emptying off the cart into the box at a rapid rate. Still, several more items remained.

"Here are some clothes to wear for different occasions." Deuce hefted a satchel off the cart and pawed inside. He drew out a pair of worker pants. "Never forget that the common laborer is seldom noticed. He can go everywhere and not call attention to himself. Here are shoes with lifts that will make you taller. Be creative and put together an outfit, which blends in with your surroundings."

Deuce sat back. "Any questions?"

"I can't think. It's a bit much."

A chuckle and glint of amusement from the man's eyes answered that comment. "Take your time and get to know what you got. It's a lot, I know. You'll be in an isolated place most of the time, so you won't need a lot of this stuff, but I wanted to be sure you were equipped. Dr. Steele said that it was important. Please be careful. A lot depends on what you do, and Steele is nervous about sending someone so inexperienced to a Terran he doesn't know that well. Unfortunately, you're our best opportunity right now to find out anything about Elija, so we're counting on you."

Heaving a sigh, Deuce stood up. "Okay, I've said my piece. Now if I.N.Sys drags you in for some reason, and I'm there, or vice versa, we don't know each other. Got it?

I don't want certain people in I.N.Sys to know we're working together until we resolve where the leak is."

Kayse nodded. This man was I.N.Sys in some way, but Trey had warned I.N.Sys might be implicated in his parents' murders. Appalled, he looked at all the stuff and decided his life had become far too complicated.

"You'll be fine, if you're careful. Deuce nodded. "You've resources you don't realize. Now I should leave. Good luck." He disappeared through the same door he'd entered, and Angel reappeared. "A lot of stuff you got there," he commented, eyeing the pile of items.

"Can you load the car while I say good bye to Ailey?"

"Let me escort you to her lab first." Upon returning him to Ailey's office, Angel left to load the boxes.

"You were right," Ailey whispered to him. Grabbing his arm, she shut the door. His heart skipped a beat when he saw her lock it. She turned to him, wide-eyed. "The data matches up exactly."

A shiver of fear trickled inside.

She dragged him over to her computer and pointed at the screen. "It's an identical match. Everything."

"A match?" he choked. His worst fears were realized.

"Arwoyn's medical data to yours," she exclaimed. "You must be one of Arwoyn's clones!"

"His clone?" He sat down with a thunk.

"That you have his abilities and his characteristics? That you can travel in time? I'd say very likely. However, there exist discrepancies. Keep in mind that environment also shapes personality and behavior. You're not an expert swordsman like he was, but I'll bet you could beat him at video games." She paused. "Although, I heard he was a good strategist."

"No wonder they want to make me look different. Everyone would recognize *him*."

"Yeah, but he didn't come here to the future until he was a lot older than you are now; so you don't resemble him that much yet."

He rubbed his face. "Someone must have seen that final report, put it together, and tried to find me."

"And they're still searching. There may be more than one person involved. Trey didn't want you to know who you were in case they had a mind probe."

"More like it's a *what* I am," he mumbled. "Arwoyn Telluria's clone. Makes me feel all weird and icky."

Her eyes softened. "Arwoyn was amazing. If you carry his genes, you should consider yourself lucky. Remember that fact when you feel 'weird and icky.' Figure out what to do with his talents, rather than resent what you are."

He mumbled, "Someone sent Mary Ellen around this morning. She tried to give me chocolates, and flowers were all wrapped up in an airtight container for Tempest."

Her eyebrows rose and her lips pursed. "Do you think they wanted a way to get into the house to find out if you were there, so they could make a snatch? Putting drugs in the chocolate, possibly a knockout gas in the flower container, would make it easy. If that didn't work, they would at least confirm you were there, and force their way in, or know that you weren't, and plan to come back later."

"Elise said that we weren't home, so they put a kid outside the house." He tossed a glance at the computer. "Make sure you delete that data. Whoever's interested, I don't want them knowing what we found."

"Here's a data chip. Put it somewhere safe." She slapped it into his hand and gave his shoulder a squeeze.

"Thanks, Ailey. I won't forget all your help." With an appreciative smile, he left.

Chapter 26

All the way home Kayse remained preoccupied, thinking about what Ailey had shown him. She'd matched his DNA, blood type, and various other markers to Arwoyn Telluria. She'd been very clear, that if he wasn't his clone, he was related closely to Arwoyn based on the test results. That opened a whole mix of problems but confirmed a growing suspicion.

"You all right?" Angel swiveled his head to cast a worried look at him.

"I'm fine," he muttered, and turned to meet Angel's golden eyes, narrowed and concerned.

Swallowing his irritation, he smiled. "Thanks, Angel...for everything." He didn't know how to articulate the appreciation he felt toward the Enjelise for all he'd done. Leaving him like this depressed him, and he vowed to concentrate more on the present with Angel nearby and think about the rest later.

As the temperature rose, Angel tossed his ubiquitous black jacket into the back of the car. Underneath, he wore a creamy white shirt with a collar that brushed up against his chin and reflected a glowing aura.

"You're going to watch over Tempest while I'm gone, aren't you?" Kayse asked suddenly.

"Always." Angel nodded, turning his attention back toward the road.

"She's constantly getting into trouble," Kayse added as he stared out the window.

"Seems to fall right into it, if it's anywhere in the vicinity," the Enjelise agreed, glancing over.

Kayse ran a hand through his hair and blew out his breath. "She doesn't mean to. She just gets way too enthusiastic."

"Is that what it is? Seems like she jumps first and thinks later."

"Yeah, she does a lot of that too."

"She'll be okay. I'll watch over her."

"Good."

They parked on a dirt road behind a stand of trees at the back of Richard's spacious home. Taking the secret passageway back, they entered an underground tunnel that came out into a pantry in the kitchen. Kayse wondered if sneaking in and out the back door was a Steele family pastime.

Angel managed a quick glimpse out the front. A lookout remained there, loitering about, but appeared not to notice their arrival.

Kayse wandered into the living room and dropped the bag of disguises from Deuce. Relieved that he wasn't staggering in from extensive surgery, he was surprised at how easily it had gone.

He heard Tempest call from upstairs somewhere. "Kayse, is that you?" She appeared at the top of the stairs. "Come up, come up and see what we got you." Excitement thrummed in her voice.

A feeling of apprehension fluttered through him. "What's up?" he asked, picking up the bag.

"I'm going to check out the house." Angel opened a closet door and closed it. Then he peered into Richard's office. "Where's Elise?"

"Mom's on the caller down in the office," Tempest offered as she advanced down the steps toward them. "She's busy."

"And left you wandering around?" Alarm tinged Angel's voice.

"Geesh! I'm not a baby!" Tempest retorted.

"You're a child, "Angel countered.

"I'm not." Tempest pouted, raising her chin. "I wish you would stop saying that. I'm almost fourteen."

Kayse jerked in disbelief at what he was hearing. "You *just* turned thirteen!"

"So, next I'll be fourteen. Already counting down the time. Besides, she said to call her if I needed her. Calm down and come see what we got you." She peeked over the railing as he trudged up the stairs, dreading any surprise that might be waiting for him.

Her face brightened as he arrived at the top. She grabbed the bag with one hand and his hand with the other and led him into his bedroom. There he stopped in amazement. Clothes and equipment lay strewn all over the place. He swung around with unspoken questions.

With a grin, she explained. "I suggested to mom that you might need some new clothes for your trip. You were getting scraggly out there at the Terran camp. I don't think she'd thought about it because she looked startled when I mentioned it. I figured that if I said something, I might get a clue as to where you're going. So, I hinted that if it was a warm place, you might need shorts, and if it was cold there, then you needed more sweaters and jackets. Look at what we got!"

"I already have clothes," he mumbled faintly.

"Yeah, and they don't fit you anymore. You've been growing so fast, you're already taller than when I first met you. All your physical labor at the camp has built up muscles so that the old clothes don't fit well."

He realized that what she said was true. Lately his shirts stretched uncomfortably tight, so he could hardly button them, and his pant legs were too short when he could even get into them.

"Mom's brother won't know you like I do, and you'll want to make a good first impression. First impressions are really important to Terrans. They just look at a person and leap to all sorts of conclusions about what a person's like when they haven't even gotten to know him at all. And then, that's what they think of a person for the rest of their life. So, while you were at the Med Center, we went shopping."

Kayse looked at all the clothes, and then his eyes alighted on a large trunk.

"And what's that?"

"That's the best part of all," she said excitedly. "While we were buying all the clothes, blankets, boots, and other stuff, I asked mom how you were going to get it all there. She looked at me funny and said that she had luggage. So I said it would be better to lug one major trunk, and a bag or two, rather than try to ride herd on lots of little bags. Too many bags make it too easy to lose stuff. I told her for you, that it needed to be simple, and she agreed with me."

Wearing an annoying smirk, she continued, "So I went online and ordered this trunk. We picked it up at the store on the way home. It has wheels and when you're not using it, it flattens out or can be used as a rolling table. Amazing, huh?"

She patted the monstrosity.

"Now here's the interesting part. Looks like you're going somewhere very cold. We didn't even look at shorts or swim trunks. She bought a thick coat with a lined hood and a pair of krell-furred snow boots. If I were making a guess, I would bet you're going somewhere in Islia or maybe the Diechwrathe," she concluded.

Angel stuck his head in. "What's going on in here?" His gaze swept over the pile of clothes. "Whoa, lots of stuff."

"All for really cold weather, too," Tempest pointed out smugly.

Angel frowned. "Not my style." Then he waved his hand as if to say he was going to check out the rest of the upstairs.

"There's something else I wanted you to see," Tempest whispered.

She motioned him over. Then she reached into her blouse and pulled out a necklace. An ornate pendant cradled a stunning crystal drop. The crystal winked and flashed brilliant colors at him.

"I have my own Talent crystal now. Dad psyched it to my aura, and I'm not supposed to tell anyone, but I have Tellurian Talent." Her eyes sparkled with excitement.

"Tellurian? They do things with time," he blurted out. The thought of Tempest being able to manipulate time terrified him.

She put a finger to his lips. "I said I wasn't supposed to say anything. Turns out dad carries the Talent and did some awesome stuff in his past." She grinned and slipped the necklace back inside her blouse while patting it. "Those boys better watch out if they plan to fool with me anymore."

"You are *not* to go anywhere near them, you hear?" he said firmly. "They are extremely dangerous, plus I won't be around to save you."

"You're sweet. I know. I won't try anything, but I've got Talent, Kayse," she said, her eyes sparkling.

"Just what can you do?"

She gazed down. "Can't say too much, but I'm going to work with Jemma starting tomorrow and get really good at whatever it is that I do."

"You don't have a clue, do you?"

"Hey, it's a secret, and I'm not saying another word."

But he just knew she had no idea what she could and couldn't do, and to his way of thinking—that was even more dangerous.

Popping in, Angel gazed around. "Everything looks okay inside."

"I told you it was," Tempest said indignantly.

Angel scowled at her. Then his caller rang. He pressed it to his ear and murmured, "Right. Right. They're here. Will do." He turned to gaze at them, a speculative expression crossing his face. "Your mom's finished, and your dad's going to be home soon. She wants the two of you to shower and get into nice clothes. They want to talk to both of you."

With that comment, he left the room. Kayse sighed and started unbuttoning his shirt as he headed toward the shower. Tempest came along behind him like a shadow. He stopped suddenly, causing her to bump into him.

"Excuse me," he said. "You have your own room and shower. I'm not a peep show."

"Just wanted to know what you were going to wear *first*," she said, gazing innocently at him. She firmed her lips. "Frankly, I never want to see another naked male again." She shivered. "I've learned my lesson."

"If only I could believe that."

"Now you sound like Angel!"

"You'll know what I'm wearing when you see me in it and not before. So get out of here and get yourself cleaned up in your own room." He edged the door closed.

She put a hand on the doorknob, pushing it back open. "Just want to say that you look a lot better than the last time when Dr. Jay tried to fix you. I'm glad they didn't do much this time. Last time you resembled someone who'd been in a bar brawl. I like you just the way you are right now."

"Alysians do things differently. They gave me lots of disguises so I can appear different if I want to," he said. "I'll show you what they gave me."

"I'll come by later tonight then," Tempest murmured. "Maybe you can show me someone different—someone nicer than your old grumpy self." With that, Kayse slammed the door shut on her and didn't even deign to discuss her threat of a late night rendezvous.

****

After dinner, Richard motioned Kayse into his office and gestured for him to sit down. Kayse fidgeted on the chair, not knowing what was going to happen. Richard pulled out his desk drawer and took out three pictures.

"I obtained a few photos off surveillance of the guy who posed as your guard at the Med Center. I want you to examine them."

"You mean Angel was right, and he's not a real guard there?" A shiver ran along Kayse's arms and down his neck.

"Nope, not any more. He was a guard at one time and got fired. Notes in the file claimed erratic behavior. I want you to tell me if you can identify him as the person who killed your parents."

Richard slid the photos over to Kayse. There they were. The grainy photo showed his terror-stricken face and the face of his parent's killer.

As he studied it without mind-blanking terror, he realized that it was the same person. "Yeah, that's him. He was a lot younger before, but it's the same guy. I remember those eyes..." Kayse shuddered, "What's his name? Have you found him yet?"

"No. Let me run this through a more extensive data bank and see what we come up with."

"You think you'll find him?"

"I'm optimistic. Next, maybe we can figure out why he's doing all this and if he's working alone or with someone. Someone tried to attack Trey too. It may be the same man or an accomplice. He didn't see who it was, but I'm fairly sure there's a connection."

"Maybe Arwoyn's cloning project is the connection," Kayse suggested.

Richard inhaled abruptly and stared at him. "What do you know about that?"

"I was at the Med Center and did a little research before Deuce came to fix me up with his box of disguises. By the way, is that guy for real?"

With a choking laugh, Richard nodded. "Afraid so. What did you find out?"

Leaning in, Kayse stared into Richard's eyes. "There was a cloning experiment Arwoyn was involved in, wasn't there? How would that tie in with this guy in the photo?" He paused to see what Richard would say.

"Back then, the lead scientist, Warner Straung, wiped out all computer data and burned most papers concerning the procedure. Then he killed himself rather than let his current government have the secrets of Arwoyn's cloning project. He was afraid of what they might do with it. So we have very little information about the procedure, and no one has tried to duplicate his efforts. Makes you unique in a way. A connection to that makes more sense than anything else. If we find out, then we'll know who's behind this and can neutralize them one way or another."

"I'm a clone, aren't I? Not even the one he wanted, apparently. Arwoyn Telluria's experimental by-product," he said bitterly. The result, the one he used, was the female. Right? "Successful transition and insertion. She was a time travel experiment. I was just a means to an end. That guard was right about me being a piece of garbage."

Richard caught his breath and put a hand on Kayse's arm. "If Arwoyn was the original, and you really are his clone, I can't think of another person's DNA I would rather have. It doesn't matter if you were first or last, you have a quality pedigreed. Many appreciated what Arwoyn did. I know I did. He was a great man who did amazing things...as you might too."

"Those at the Rave most likely know nothing about the cloning experiment," Kayse offered quietly. "They just hate me because of my friendship with Terrans."

"Elise and I are trying to work out that problem, but strong prejudice takes time.

"Me being Arwoyn means something? Will I do the same things he did?"

Richard pooh-poohed the idea. "You're nothing like Arwoyn. He was a prince whose family was brutally murdered when he was sixteen."

"Were they murdered in front of him like mine were?"

"No, but he found them right after it happened. It was very traumatic. He swore vengeance against their slayers."

"I understand those feelings, have them myself." Kayse raised an eyebrow.

"He became involved in a war between the Diechwrathe and the United Realm."

"Like between the Alysians and the Terrans?" Kayse inclined his head, a smirk now on his lips.

"Then there was the time travel…"

"Yeah, got that box checked off. There does seem to be several parallels in our lives," Kayse insisted.

"There are some differences too. He started in the medieval era, but after coming up the timeline, he did a lot with the Institute and the Med Center. But I will admit, like you, he had to adapt to a different and more advanced society."

"The Institute? What's that about?"

"He started the Institute to get the Talents and the normal Alysians to live together peacefully."

"Did it work?"

"Actually, it worked quite well for a time. Then it was disbanded because…"

"Because you didn't need it anymore. Everyone learned to get along without killing each other. Maybe someone should re-instate it. Teach everyone to get along."

"It's a thought," Richard admitted. "But first, let's keep you alive until we at least find who's threatening you and stop them."

"I'd like that."

***

"Kayse, take me with you."

Kayse jerked awake. He opened bleary eyes to see the earnest face of Tempest in the dim light of his bedroom.

"Gads, what time is it?" He struggled to read his chrono.

"It's late. Everyone else is asleep." She bounced onto his bed. "Take me with you. I don't like Mary Ellen, and mom and dad are too busy with their own lives to pay much attention to me. I could come live with you."

Groaning, he rolled over and put a pillow over his head.

She lifted an edge. "Kayse, I don't want you to leave me." Tears splashed against one of his cheeks.

Through blurry eyes, he saw a lip quiver. Her earnest face caused an ache in his heart until reality broke through. It just wouldn't work. Richard and Elise would never agree to it. "Tempest," he began and trailed off.

"Kayse," she paused, her mouth drooping downwards. "Kayse, I love you. You keep me safe." She buried her face in his pillow.

A safety net. Now there was a terrific basis for love.

"Look," he rose on one elbow and brushed a strand of hair from her forehead. "It will only be for a short while, and then I can come home. They have a picture of the man who came after me in the past, and once they locate him it'll be safe for me to come back here. You're too young to be thinking about love. You need to be thinking about getting through school and learning how to use your crystal. Before you know it, I'll be back and, by then, you'll have dozens of boyfriends I'll have to wade through just to say hi."

"I'll only love you." She wiggled closer to him.

"Your parents will throw a fit if they find you're here," he said feeling suddenly uncomfortable.

He smelled her flowery sweetness. A sigh escaped him.

"They won't and, if they do, I don't care."

And remembered her dangerous impetuousness.

He grunted. He was too tired to argue and, in the end, he was lonely and frightened too. He didn't want to go off again to be among a bunch of alien strangers where he wouldn't fit in. Tempest was a pest, but she was a familiar pest that he'd grown to care about. However, … He hugged her and closed his eyes in exhaustion. "You have a bed…you need to go."

"I will," she hiccupped and eased away.

***

In the morning, Tempest gave him a good-bye at breakfast, saying she had "things to do." A bit miffed at the brush-off, he took out the disguise kit and started to make changes. He put in brown contacts and dyed his hair a reddish color that Tempest would appreciate.

Only the muscles and physique gave away his Alysian heritage. He dressed in bulky clothes to hide his form and threw a large scarf around his neck that covered half his face. Checking the result in the mirror, he decided he would be hard to recognize.

After Kayse dressed, Deuce arrived with Trey. Trey had changed his appearance by growing a beard, or at least was making the attempt. Kayse brought down some of the luggage and started a pile near the door. Deuce handled the large trunk as if it were a puffball. Kayse searched for Tempest to say goodbye, but she didn't reappear. Probably didn't want to make a big scene. He frowned. *Tempest, not making a scene?* Somehow, that didn't feel right. She must have left earlier with her new tutor.

Richard was busy preparing for another committee hearing, and Elise was getting ready for an early meeting somewhere. They dashed to the door as he was leaving to say goodbye, gave him a hug and wished him well. Trey appeared, and then they were off.

A new chapter in his life was about to start. He felt like he had just jumped off a cliff.

Chapter 27

Kayse leaned his head against the window of the Maglev train and watched the landscape blur by. For such a fast moving train, it barely made a sound. All he heard was the sussing noise of the air vent and Trey's even breathing. Trey rested his head against the seat as if he slept, but Kayse could tell by the rhythm of his breathing that he was awake, planning their next move or, more likely, cursing the burden of a pain-in-the-neck teenage kid.

He stared at Trey's face with its charming dimples, now almost imperceptible under a beginning scruff but there nonetheless. Dimples, they were the giveaway. And there were other signs if you searched for them. He'd never really looked before because of the age difference. Now he studied the man with new eyes and new knowledge.

"Are your parents alive, Trey?" Kayse asked, idly running a finger along the bottom rim of the window.

Trey's eyes popped open. He gave Kayse an odd stare and then leaned back and closed his eyes again.

"No, they were killed in a car accident long ago."

"An accident?"

"Yeah, I miraculously escaped. I should be dead. After their deaths, my aunt and I moved across the country to a new home. She liked to move around a lot. Always had a new job, a new place to live. Great life for a kid. I hated it."

"The man who killed my parents…they have his picture now," Kayse commented.

Trey's eyes opened again. "They do?" Interest replaced the sleepy expression.

"He used to be a guard at the Med Center way back."

All pretense of sleep abandoned, Trey sat up, fully alert, "Are you sure? That's interesting."

"I thought so too. There were some cloning experiments going on back when Arwoyn was alive. I think you may be my twin brother or something like it." He wasn't ready to say "clone" quite yet.

"I'm a lot older than you are, Kayse. Twin brothers are usually the same age," Trey replied in a gruff tone. His eyes closed as if he wanted to avoid the conversation.

After a long pause, Kayse murmured, "Not when one travels twenty-eight annuals into the future. I'm betting you're about twenty-eight annuals older than I am. I didn't realize it before but, sitting in front of you and studying you, I can see we appear a lot alike despite my operations and this disguise. If you change me back to the way I used to look and add twenty-eight annuals, I bet we would appear a lot alike."

"You wish," Trey grunted.

Deciding to ignore the comment, Kayse continued, "You and Richard wanted to alter me quickly so I wouldn't notice the similarity between us. The other odd thing I didn't notice at first, but I do now, is that you've changed very little over all that time. You appear almost the same as when you last visited my house over twenty-eight annuals ago. There's a little more aging apparent, but not twenty-eight annuals worth. I'm betting you have the same Talent as I do."

"I'm younger than your numbers add up to. Call it clean living and a true heart. How about that? I've already admitted we are related, but I never suggested we are twin brothers," Trey huffed, shifting his eyes to gaze out the window.

Regarding Trey intently, Kayse added, "Okay, something other than twin brothers then."

Half-lidded eyes from Trey greeted this comment, and then they closed. "Maybe," he admitted grudgingly.

Just then, Deuce popped in and looked at the two of them. They both gazed back at him and cocked their heads at the same time. He stared at them for a moment and shook his head as he tapped his chrono.

"We're almost to Vandore," he said. "Trey, this is the end of the line for you."

Swinging around in his seat toward Kayse, Trey reminded him, "If you get in trouble, which you seem to do on a regular basis, don't forget the medallion with the crystal."

Deuce patted Trey on the shoulder. "I'll watch out for him, at least until he gets there."

Frowning, Trey answered, "Yeah, and you're I.N.Sys. That's enough to worry me right there."

A muscle jumped in Deuce's cheek. "Richard Steele saved my life once, and I haven't forgotten." With a fierce stare, he continued, "He's done a lot of things for me that I won't forget. There's no way I'd betray his trust. There's no mind probe that will ever get near this skull, but having the two of you together for too long is just too dangerous."

"This man that's after us is not so smart, Deuce. He's had annuals to catch us. What's I.N.Sys been doing?" Trey asked.

"Good question, I'll admit, but he's still out there, getting closer. Let me do my job and catch whoever it is."

"Kayse says Richard has his picture."

"Yeah, and I've seen it. Trace is working on it, but remember we believe I.N.Sys has been compromised, so I have to be careful and so does Trace. It's only a matter of time before we nail the culprit."

"It better be sooner, rather than later. There's a lot at stake here... my life, for example," Kayse retorted.

"On that we agree."

Deuce left them alone. Silence filled the compartment until Kayse said, "How come Deuce is taking me and not you?"

Trey shrugged. "If you haven't noticed yet, Deuce is high tech. I'm thinking that I.N.Sys is really curious about Elise's brother and his little hideaway. Deuce is the best man to scope out any technology that might be around the place. Even though Captain Elija Fujeint claims to be living a quiet, humble life, his cabin is built right up against a mountain. All flyovers so far have yielded a blank. It's as if the entire mountain is heavily shielded. Or maybe it's natural rock blocking our probes. Yet, it's too empty for what it is. We should see indications of certain metals and minerals, and there's absolutely nothing."

"Great, this isn't about sanctuary then; it's really about turning me into a spy."

Glancing away, Trey admitted, "Maybe a bit of both. You're the only person he's agreed to let in. In addition, you have surprising skills that will protect you. It's our first opportunity to check out the Homestead. Don't forget the Terrans have faster than light capabilities and other highly advanced technologies. They've indicated to Trace they might share some, if the Alysians co-operate with them. Trace is not sure how much is hype, and how much is truth. We think Elija is key to finding that out."

The train came to a stop just before Deuce returned trailing a pallet.

Trey groaned as he stood up and stretched. "Fate, I hate getting old," he complained, reaching up for some luggage.

Kayse snorted his disbelief at the comment.

They both watched as Deuce pulled the pallet in and began nonchalantly flipping their bags onto it. He barely strained as he added the massive trunk to the load. Kayse observed his actions with amazement. He thought he heard a strange noise, but it was drowned out by the commotion of other passengers coming out of their cabins and the banging of baggage as people prepared to leave.

Strange. A thought crossed his mind, immediately erased. Then it reappeared to niggle at him.

Outside, the air was cool, and the wind cut through Kayse's thin jacket. He wished that he'd put on his new heavier coat. He stared after the trunk. They would transfer to a large all-terrain vehicle and drive up to the hideaway. All around him, towering mountains ringed the area with their destination perched near the top.

"Well," they both spoke at the same time. Trey grinned. "It'll be okay. It's only for a short while, and then you'll be back. If you have any problems, activate the beacon, and I'll get someone in there to help you as soon as I can. You'll be fine."

"What about you?" Kayse worried.

"I can take care of myself. I have so far. Just watch your step and act happy to see me when we meet again."

"Thanks for everything," Kayse choked out.

"I'll miss you too," Trey echoed, giving him a rough hug and abruptly striding away.

***

Kayse stared morosely out the window as the four-wheeled transport began its long climb up the mountain. Behind the wheel, Deuce whistled and fiddled with his communication dials. Then he spoke into a throat mike and carried on a conversation with another operative while he adjusted the GPS screen. All the activity made Kayse nervous as they zipped around one hairpin curve after another.

The bright, breezy morning started to cloud up, and soon large drops of rain splattered the windshield. The wiper blades swished back and forth, hypnotically wiping away the wet. Kayse shivered in the dropping temperature and started to obsess about the heavy jacket packed in the trunk in the back. The jagged turns and steepening road did nothing to help his state of mind. He cast an eye over at Deuce who turned and raised an eyebrow while brushing back springy locks of brown hair.

"What?"

"Shouldn't you be paying more attention to the road? It's pretty treacherous out there." Kayse peered out his side window. Through the developing mist, he saw mostly deep ravines and switchbacks ahead. No guardrails, no wide lanes—just sharp turns and a dangerously wet surface.

"I *am* paying attention. I happen to be one of those people who can multi-task," Deuce bragged. "But if I'm making you nervous, we'll be stopping soon. I'll need to put on traction gear. Snow's starting."

Sure enough, the heavy drops of rain soon turned into fluffy flakes of snow. The blades groaned under the heavier load but kept on swishing back and forth. Ahead, the road grew dimmer, covered by a curtain of snow and rain. The higher they climbed, the steeper the road became. Deuce now diverted more attention to his driving and less to outside communications. A few times the tires slipped and spun, but then grabbed and gained back traction. Once the vehicle slid very near an edge, causing Kayse's heart to race in terror. He gave out a moan and clutched the seat in a white-knuckled grip, expecting imminent death. After that,

Deuce turned off the communicator and concentrated solely on his driving. Eventually, they came to a turnout where a few cars were putting on traction gear.

"We'll stop here," Deuce announced, as he pulled the car over.

Exhaling a sigh of relief, Kayse said, "Good, I want to put on a heavier coat. It's getting very cold. Do you need a carjack or something out of the back?" He opened the car door and stepped onto the slushy ground.

"Naw, I got this," Deuce answered, waving him away.

Kayse frowned at him. He didn't see how he was going to put the traction equipment on without levering up the car, but that was Deuce's problem. Right now, he just wanted to crawl into something warm. The cold wind whipped through his hair, sending chills down the back of his neck. He rubbed his frozen hands together. Errant snowflakes stung his cheeks and eyes.

He opened the back hatch and tried to maneuver the trunk around. The fricking thing felt heavy even with his augmented muscles. Deuce had made it look like a feather. The man must have arms of steel.

"Need some help?" Deuce asked, walking up to him with a grin.

"This thing's heavy," Kayse grunted, trying to work it around so he could open the latch.

"Here." Deuce moved him out of the way, then swung the trunk around, presenting Kayse with the front. Kayse couldn't believe the ease with which Deuce handled the thing.

He tapped in numbers, slid the catch over and opened the lid.

"Oh Fate!" Kayse exclaimed.

"Bloody Frag!" Deuce's mouth dropped open. They both gawked at the scene in front of them, not believing what they were seeing.

There, all nestled up like a gibbet in its burrow, lay Tempest. Kayse reached in to touch her.

Deuce muttered curse words Kayse knew that he shouldn't be hearing. Then Deuce shouldered him aside and leaned in to put his fingers against her throat. "Well, she's alive. I don't know whether to be happy or disappointed. What a fool stunt." He glowered at Kayse.

"Don't look at me," he said. "I had nothing to do with this."

"Oh please," Deuce snorted. "She's here because of you."

"Tempest! Tempest! Wake up." Kayse shook her shoulders roughly and slapped at her face.

What a stupid stunt.

Her eyes fluttered open. "Are we there yet?" she inquired drowsily with a small smile. "I'm really cold. Where's a jacket?" She grabbed at some nearby clothes and wrapped them around her with a shiver.

"What have you done?" Kayse shouted. "Your father's going to be livid and your mother...I don't want to think about what state of mind your mother's going to be in." Kayse reached in to pull her out. She rose easily, although a bewildered expression flicked across her face, as she turned to squint at Deuce who stood frowning at her. Kayse reached in and grabbed a jacket to put on her.

Deuce tapped his communication belt and began relaying the news to headquarters.

Kayse noticed some clothes missing. "Where are the rest of my clothes?" he sputtered.

Tempest shrugged. "I needed the room, so I put some back in your closet." She shivered. "I should have brought more for me, though. Girls need more clothes. No one cares what boys wear, but girls have to look good. If it's going to be this cold, I should have added more sweaters for me." She paused to survey her surroundings. "I thought we would be there by now."

"You're going home," Kayse stated. "You won't need extra sweaters there."

"Noooo," she wailed. "Let me go with you. You won't even know I'm around." She wrapped her arms around his chest and gripped him so hard he could barely breathe. He glanced over her head at Deuce and rolled his eyes.

"We've come this far, I might as well drop you off before I take her back," Deuce muttered to Kayse. "Elise's brother is expecting you today." He gave Kayse a brief smile. Kayse heaved a deep sigh.

"All right." He gave her a firm stare. "But you know you can't stay. You'll have to go home with Deuce after he drops me off," Kayse warned. "Take this jacket, put on these warm pants, and check out the roadside comfort station before we leave. We still have a long way to go, and I don't want you jumping around." He pointed to several small buildings lining the turnout.

Tempest gave him a bright smile and headed out, returning as Deuce snapped in the last link of the snow chains, and Kayse finished zipping up his jacket.

Back on the road, the wind whipped around hard and the snow fell thick. Abruptly, Deuce hit the brakes.

"What now?" Kayse jerked forward, staring out at a whitening world. Through the thick snowfall large dim shapes appeared.

Tempest muttered.

"Look ahead." Deuce pointed.

As they edged closer, Kayse noticed a pile of boulders hidden in the mist, blocking the road in front of them.

"Stay here," Deuce ordered as he parked the vehicle. He climbed out and trudged up the road toward the blockage. He started to push at the rocks. Several went bouncing down into the steep ravine alongside the road. Deuce jumped back from the edge and peered down.

Kayse turned to Tempest. "I'm going to see if I can help."

Her eyes widened. "Be careful."

By the time Kayse had clambered out, a large portion of the blockage had been cleared. The wind blew so hard, the snow slanted sideways. Strong eddies and whorls buffeted the rover. Kayse hugged his jacket and leaned into the driving snow and wind, his face burning with cold.

What was he doing? Kayse wondered. As he drew near Deuce, he heard a rumbling sound.

Studying the ridgeline, Deuce yelled, "Get back into the Rover." Immediately, a large boulder fell from the edge directly toward them. Kayse watched it arc past, barely missing them. Deuce broke out in a sweat and wiped his face with the sleeve of his jacket. "That was close!"

He waved angrily at Kayse. "Get back in the Rover, I said." Two more boulders slid sideways and plunged down the mountainside.

Kayse stared at him. "You're moving those rocks!"

"If I don't get this cleared soon, this whole section of the road will collapse. I can't let that happen," Deuce shouted into the wind. "Then we'll never get there. Do you want to be stranded here? I don't. Move back."

"I can help!"

"Not with this." Deuce eyed two boulders, as they began to rock back and forth. "Move away!"

Kayse turned. Now the wind pummeled his back as he returned to the Rover. Behind him, several more boulders plunged magically down the ravine.

Deuce gazed upward, as if assessing the precariousness of rocks overhead. One or two appeared and fell harmlessly through the air, just missing the road and ending up in the valley below. Finally, Deuce nodded, as if satisfied, and headed back to join them.

As Deuce climbed into the driver's seat, Kayse inched over. He handed over a towel, and Deuce wiped at a face dripping with sweat.

"How did you do that?" Kayse whispered.

Deuce stared at him. "It's *my* Talent. You've heard some Alysians carry the Talent gene, haven't you? Well, I carry the gene for telekinesis. I can move objects with my mind. When Trace Walker, the Director of I.N.Sys, found that out, he recruited me for his Special Unit. I don't like people knowing it because then they act funny around me and treat me as if I'm some kind of freak. Those who don't have Talent get edgy when they learn what I do, so I'd appreciate it if you'd keep your mouth shut."

"Sure," said Kayse, a little shaken. "I understand." He thought of his own special abilities and how he wanted to keep those secret.

Deuce noticed Tempest staring at him with an open mouth.

"Tempest?"

"Fine, I can keep a secret." Her mouth snapped shut and she glanced away.

Kayse and Deuce looked at each other in alarm.

Soon they headed out again. The snow swirled heavier and heavier about them until they were forced to stop once more.

Deuce sighed. "I guess we should wait here until this weather clears. I can't see the road with all this snow. I don't want to spend the night on this mountain, but I don't want to drive off the edge, either. It's going to get colder and icier, but it's too dangerous to drive in this if I can't see ahead."

"Move the clouds."

"What? I can move heavy objects, but I'm not the weatherman.

"Moving a few snow clouds should be easy compared to those heavy boulders," Kayse explained. "Give it a try. What have you got to lose?"

Opening the door, Deuce got out and peered up at the thick snow-laden clouds. He shook his head.

Kayse raised eyebrows at Tempest. She focused her attention out the window and then up at the overcast sky.

Deuce scrunched up his face in concentration. Eventually, a patch of blue appeared. The clouds began to drift off. The snowstorm abated. Deuce climbed back in. "The clouds will close back in soon, but we might be able to make it through this hole in the weather if we hustle."

"Not bad, Mr. Miracle Worker." Kayse smiled amusedly. "You learned a new trick today, I'll bet."

Deuce grunted. "Moving that stuff is harder because there's nothing to get a hold of. It's all flimsy and slippery. However, it's interesting that I could do it. May come in handy."

After a while, the clouds began to gather again, but Deuce pointed to a side road. "There's the turn off."

Soon they saw a good-sized cabin, sitting on the side of a mountain, nestled among tall firs and rugged brush. Smoke drifted out of a chimney and lights flickered from cheery windows, warm and inviting. Kayse thought, *Maybe, it won't be so bad.* Then he noticed a black helio tucked out back, and he knew Elise's brother had more company than he'd bargained for. They stepped out, heading toward the warmth and light.

Chapter 28

The door opened, and a fussy looking old man stuck out his head. "May I help you, sirs and ma'am?" He wore formal attire, consisting of a white shirt, black jacket, and dark gray pants. His hair was white, his eyes brilliant blue, but the smile came across as stern and a bit wooden.

"We're here to see Captain Elija Fujeint," Deuce announced, as he lowered various pieces of luggage.

"He's been expecting you." The man waved them in. "I'm Andrew." He turned to someone behind him. "See to the bags. Put them in the guest rooms."

Inside the vestibule the warm air felt wonderful, and Kayse's shivering muscles began to relax. As the snow and ice crystals melted, his face and hair began to drip. He banged his arms across his chest and stamped snow off his boots as the others followed in his winter dance.

"I'll take your coats," their doorman offered and stuck out an arm. Something about the way the man behaved bothered Kayse, but he couldn't figure out what. Kayse shrugged. *The man looks old. People get stiff as they aged, like Granddad, the Admiral.* The memory rippled a wave of grief through him, but he choked it down as he faced their greeter. Although he acted scrupulously polite, their doorman didn't exude the warmest of personalities.

Behind him, a young boy brought in the large trunk as if it was a small handbag. Kayse stared at his retreating back as another Terran picked up two more pieces and moved smoothly toward a back hallway. Kayse watched, startled. Maybe without Tempest's weight in it, it wasn't all that heavy, but Kayse found it hard to believe. How did he suddenly become the local wimp? He didn't think these Terrans carried Deuce's abilities, but they sure treated the heavy luggage as if it were stuffed with feathers, rather than winter clothes.

A squeal from Tempest diverted his attention. There, in a doorway to their left, stood Angel with his arms crossed. He didn't look happy, but a small smile tugged at his lips. The smile dissolved as a stern face took its place.

"Sugarpop," Angel growled, "you have caused all sorts of worry back home. Also, for me, navigating through these mountains in that storm wasn't the fun ride you might expect. Coming through weird weather in a helio tested my piloting skills as well as strengthening my faith. I swear I saw the face of the Creator laughing in the clouds. And our host is none too happy with you either. He doesn't relish all this extra company."

Kayse felt his face flood in a blush, but a surge of joy rocketed through his body as conflicting emotions warred within him. Delight overwhelmed him that Angel had come, followed by the embarrassment that there was a need. He stumbled toward the door as Angel backed into the room.

There, a man rose from a chair near the fireplace and approached them, wearing a disgruntled expression. As he drew near, Kayse saw how closely he resembled Elise. In fact, he could be Elise's twin brother. He featured the same fine bones and proportioned body with her auburn hair and startling violet eyes. At this very moment, he even recognized the "you're in trouble" expression Elise often bestowed upon Tempest. It was apparent he wasn't pleased with all the extra company. In fact, Kayse just bet Captain Elija Fujeint was downright furious by all the commotion.

Their host's next words gave truth to the belief. "I told Elise I would let one person come here. One! Now I've got four of you, and you in particular bother me." A long finger pointed at Deuce. "I swear, if I.N.Sys gives me any trouble, there'll be hell to pay. And you'll be the one paying it."

Kayse noticed the local welcoming committee slipping away and leaving the three of them, along with Angel, to face an angry Captain Fujeint.

"No, no. This is not official." Deuce tried to calm their host down. "I'm doing this as a personal favor for Dr. Steele."

"Sorry, I don't believe you. I've half a mind to send you all back out into that storm with the hope you'll wander about and fall off a cliff somewhere," Elija responded.

"Now Elija," soothed Angel, "Someone needed to transport Kayse here. Deuce isn't staying long."

"Damn right he's not!" Elija's fists clenched and unclenched. "I prefer to be left alone. I only took the kid because Elise asked me. I agreed to do a favor for her, but I didn't expect him to drag I.N.Sys and the rest of you here and violate my privacy."

"I'm taking Tempest home in the morning, if weather permits, so we won't bother you any further," Angel amended. "This wasn't our call. The girl did this all on her own."

"So I got her blabbing about my private location, too?" A glare from Elija passed over to Tempest.

Deuce shrugged. "She won't say anything. She's going home in the morning as soon as we can leave."

Kayse focused on the floor, holding still, trying not to do anything stupid. Tempest not blab? Who was anyone kidding? She was mouth personified.

"Let me stay here with him," Tempest pleaded. "Then you'll be sure I won't say anything you won't like."

Elija looked like he might consider the offer.

"Absolutely out of the question," Angel responded quickly. "It's not even on the table for discussion." Angel put a hand on Elija's arm and murmured something into his ear. Kayse could see his shoulders drop as he heaved an acquiescent sigh.

"No, of course she goes home." Elija shook his head. "I'll go check on dinner and see how the staff is coping." Their host headed for the door. "They'll need to set extra places now."

"Is there a lady's room where I can freshen up before we eat?" Tempest inquired sweetly.

"I'll show you the way." Elija gestured her forward as he headed out the door.

Left alone, Deuce looked meaningfully at Angel. Kayse watched them both. Something was up.

"So?" Angel muttered, casting a glance at the closed door.

"No less than fifty pings since I've been here," Deuce answered, eyeing Kayse. He fiddled with his heavy metal belt that now flashed small colored lights. "He's no rube hiding out in the mountains. High tech gear is all over this place. Moreover, Andrew...something's strange about him. I don't think he's human. I receive no biological read on him."

Angel's eyebrows shot up.

"I'd wager my first wife, if I had one," Deuce added, "that something's going on inside this mountain. Nothing I do gets past the back of the house. The whole mountain is heavily shielded." He waved a hand toward the back of the cabin. He tapped his belt and choker necklace. "This isn't going to cut it. I need something more sophisticated to penetrate what he has around here. Our Captain Elija is most definitely more than he pretends to be. So, we may have to rely on Kayse."

"Me?" Kayse choked. "I'm not a good spy. People just look at me and can tell if I'm lying or telling the truth."

"Don't worry kid, you'll be fine. Just act natural and have a good time. Be polite and use all your company manners. Something is bound to turn up. Keep an eye out for anything strange or different that we should know about." Deuce smiled at him, but Kayse caught the worried glance he shot Angel.

All swung around as they heard their host coming back down the hall. Captain Elija opened the door, saying, "Dinner's ready. Let's put aside our concerns for now and eat. You must be hungry. Driving up the mountain in our storms can be difficult and dangerous. There's nothing I can do now to get rid of you short of murder." He laughed nervously, as if he'd contemplated the idea. "The milk's been spilt. Yelling at you will do nothing to fix the situation. Some food and warm drinks might at least help everyone get along better."

So, with that, they went in.

***

During dinner, Kayse studied his new arrangement. When outside, Kayse had gotten the impression of a cozy bungalow built into the side of a mountain and surrounded by stately trees and lush greenery. It sat in an isolated region of the rugged Diechwrathe Mountains, southeast of Vandore, almost to the Penryn border. The steep road they had come through was called Rockridge Pass and had some historical significance as a famous battle site. Brand Telluria had stopped a barbarian invasion from atop one of its steep ridges. Ancient history flickered before Kayse's eyes, suddenly becoming real. Observing the peaked mountains made the boring, dusty past much more alive and interesting.

Inside, the place felt roomier than he expected. Part of the cabin most likely extended into the mountain itself. A cheerful fire lit the main living room. Comfortable, well padded chairs and recessed lighting bestowed an informal atmosphere. Stunning landscape paintings graced the walls. In the dining room, a large table supported a tempting spread of food. The salad appeared fresh and the vegetables newly harvested. Kayse wondered how such food could exist in this remote location until he remembered the black helio tucked up at the side of the cabin. Maybe Angel had brought in fresh produce as an appeasement.

With no further thoughts of décor, Kayse dug into the delicious meal. He went for the hot chocolate drink first, followed by a succulent slice of bovine. Soon he was removing his sweater and feeling a lot more comfortable.

He saw Tempest toss him a glare from across the table. She made fluttering motions with her fingers and tapped her elbows. He realized that she was commenting on his table manners; so he picked a moment when he thought no one was looking to make a face at her.

Next to him, Angel made a choking sound and gave him a sharp poke in his ribs. Kayse realized he'd been caught out, so he proceeded to adjust his behavior, thereafter watching Deuce and Angel for his dining cues.

Tempest shot him a smile and nodded as reinforcement for the better behavior, causing him to roll his eyes at her. He hated the fact that she thought she could control his actions. However, the meal was too good to waste any additional energy on Tempest and her etiquette tips; so, he decided to concentrate on the conversation around the table.

Using animated gestures, Deuce was expounding on the shift in Alysia's climate due to an increased axial tilt brought on by the consequences of a rogue comet hitting one of their moons.

Leaning in and raising his glass, Elija commented, "This region used to be frozen most of the time, but with the change in climate, we now enjoy a warmer season in which we can plant hardy high altitude crops."

Deuce rubbed his face and grimaced. "The patterns are finally stabilizing and, although many regions struggle to cope, at least they can predict their seasons now. Not that long ago, we couldn't even forecast the weather accurately." He shrugged. "Some areas have benefitted by the climate shift while others now struggle because of it."

Taking a small sip of his drink, Elija smiled at his guests. "Well, this area is benefitting as more and more hardy souls migrate here to an improving climate and away from more adversely affected regions."

Waving her fork at the table, Tempest chimed in, "You should bring down more Terrans from the space station. I'm sure they would love to live around here." She gazed across the table as Angel and Deuce exchanged disturbed glances.

A snort of laughter erupted out of Elija. "Out of the mouths of babes."

"I'm not a…"

Quickly interrupting any further outburst from the girl, Angel responded, "Captain Fujeint, as one of the captains of the fleet, I'm surprised you haven't taken a greater part in settling the Terrans here on Alysia."

Deuce nodded in agreement while cutting a particularly tender vegetable. He popped it in his mouth and gazed expectantly at Elija.

"Please, just call me Elija," responded their host with graciousness. "You can't imagine how difficult it is to acclimate to a planet when you've lived most of your life on board a spaceship. I'm doing the best I can. I often assist my sister with her work, but it's hard for me to get used to how open your world is and how vulnerable it is to weather and random events. The prejudice and animosity of the natives is also hard to take, so I retreat here to cope. Occasionally, if Elise needs me, I go help her."

He flourished a bit of leaf from his salad, nibbled on it, and continued, "Most of my work, however, can be done right here in the comfort of my own home through the ASSIST network. I write research reports, I distribute pamphlets, and I do important experiments here. I also recognize the fact that integration of our two cultures is going to take some time." He smiled benignly at them.

Kayse wasn't buying it. For some reason, he thought the whole thing sounded bogus. Still, the man was giving him asylum, and he wasn't about to forfeit his sole offer by antagonizing his benefactor. He wasn't going to become a total fool, no matter what anyone else might think or say aloud about him and his situation.

With the evening running late, all agreed to retire to sleep. Elija indicated those leaving in the helio should get an early start due to bad weather coming in later tomorrow afternoon.

Chapter 29

The next morning, Kayse awoke to find a stunning young girl arriving with a hot drink and pastries on a tray. Behind her followed a young man who could pass as her brother. After him, came another young girl who was identical to the first and smiled sweetly when she saw him.

Embarrassed, he quickly yanked up his sheets to cover himself, but his greeters didn't seem to care that he wore bedclothes. Tentatively, he sat up to receive the treat of a cup of a dark, steaming liquid and a plate of warm, sweet rolls. His mouth watered at the wonderful sights and smells, not all food.

"Good morning," the young man announced brightly as he flapped out a pair of trousers and a shirt and laid them at the foot of Kayse's bed. "I'm Ace, that's Bett, and there's Gami." He pointed to the girls, who sent shy nods in his direction.

"Aren't you having breakfast?" Kayse inquired.

"Oh this isn't breakfast; this is morning coffee and sweet rolls. So much better a wakeup than a blaring ringer." Ace smiled at him, and the two girls grinned in unison.

"We call it 'Hospitality plus' in here," chirped Gami, or was it Bett?

"Please enjoy your stay," Ace added, "We're excited to have you on our team."

"Welcome," they chorused.

Kayse felt confused and squinted at the two girls, who gazed mildly back at him. They were fantastically beautiful.

Flawless. Tall and slender, he admired both well-endowed chests, not wanting to slight either one. He noted long blonde hair that cascaded over pale, smooth shoulders. Perfectly etched eyebrows framed sparkling aqua eyes that flashed with humor. Pale blue, silken jumpsuits rustled as the girls moved about and finally settled at the foot of his bed.

He eyed each one with a glazed smile, but then his attention drifted to the bedroom door, and he almost spilled his drink. There, with a frown on her face, stood Tempest, taking in all the lovely ladies. He closed his mouth, wiped off the drool, and slammed a blank expression onto his face, while trying to appear innocent of any lust or desire. The expression on her face told him the attempt wasn't working very well.

"Hi there," he called out weakly and fluttered a wave in her direction. "Come on in. Join the group." He patted a place on the bed.

She refused to budge. Eyebrows scrunched together as her eyes traveled around the room. "You know, when he was a guest at my house, *I* let him get dressed before I intruded on his privacy." Tempest sniffed, "Alysians are taught to respect a guest's personal space."

What! Oh, really? Then what about all your midnight rambles into my bedroom? Not to mention…

"We really didn't mean to intrude." One of the girls hastily slid off the bed, jumping onto the floor, causing the bed to jiggle up and down so that he spilled coffee all over his lap. The girl glanced at him in chagrin, grabbed several napkins, rounded the bed, and began blotting up the dark liquid off his pajama's front. He helped by pointing out a few places she'd missed, and maybe a few places lower she needed to work on a little harder.

Tempest remained at the door, scowling even more at all the dabbing activity and the smile on his face.

Angling her face toward Tempest, the embarrassed girl tried to explain. "We just came in to offer a polite 'welcome and wake up,' considering he is a special guest."

"Alysians are a more private people," Tempest countered haughtily. "They don't like a lot of fuss."

What! Hey, I like it just fine.

"Oh! We're sorry. We didn't know. Watch out, Bett," said the eager dabber as the second girl leapt off the bottom of the bed, causing more jiggling. Kayse lifted his cup just in time to prevent any additional coffee from being spilled and aimed a grin Tempest's way.

Ace gave a shrug and gestured at the girls. "Maybe we should let him get dressed first before we bombard him with too much hospitality," he admitted.

"Oh no, I'm fine," Kayse protested, as he regretfully watched the shapely females head toward the door. He carefully placed the cup on the tray and slid his feet to the floor.

Tempest snorted in disgust and whirled around to leave. "Hurry up and get dressed, Kayse. Breakfast will be served soon. That's the real reason why I came here," she announced over her left shoulder. She ushered the others out ahead of her and practically slammed the door on him.

He eased out of bed to set the tray on a nearby table. Foremost in his thoughts was the comforting knowledge that Tempest would be leaving right after breakfast.

***

At breakfast, Kayse could sense Tempest was still unhappy about returning, but Angel remained adamant.

"I could use an all-terrain vehicle if you can afford to leave yours for a while," Elija suggested. "There's enough room in the helio, and I need better transportation than currently available to drive on these mountain roads."

"No problem," Deuce responded. "I'll check with Director Walker and see if I can get a new one for you to have permanently. If he has one available, I can return and swap them out."

Angel glanced over at Deuce and raised an eyebrow.

A pause in the conversation followed until Deuce asked, "Are you able to work the nearby mines at all?"

Nodding, Elija answered, "I've hired some locals, and we dig out enough ore to provide a bit of income. We hope to find one of those special diamond lodes that are highly prized by the Alysians, but so far, we've had no luck. No crystals yet. Also, as soon as any sort of spring arrives, we plan to plant a few hardy crops developed on board my spaceship."

"Really?" Deuced appeared intrigued.

"Oh, it's experimental, but we genetically engineered some rugged environment plants that might do nicely here."

Leaning forward, Deuce noted, "If you're successful, I'm sure lots of people would be interested. Alysia is currently experiencing a severe food shortage."

Elija's eyes widened. "We could sell the seeds and generate an income there, too. I'll inform the botany team of your suggestion."

Botany team?

Finishing breakfast and retrieving what luggage they'd brought, the returning few soon got the helio loaded. Outside, the morning sun shone brightly, and there was a snap in the air brought about by the passing winter storm. A sprinkling of snow covered the area, sparkling over the landscape. Against a deep blue sky, a range of mountains stood silhouetted in breathtaking beauty.

Deuce started up the helio, and a whirlwind of snow whipped about. Tempest clung to Kayse, shivering with bright tears, until Angel pried her loose. Then they were all in the big black helio, its blades whirring like a mad insect's wings. Tempest's pale face pressed against a window as she waved a tearful farewell.

Soon the helio lifted off the ground and climbed over rugged mountains blanketed by stately forests of green pines. Kayse lingered and watched until it became a black dot against a bright morning sky. Finally, he turned to Elija, who gestured him into the house. An attack of nerves hit him as he realized he was all on his own now.

Elija went through the front door and entered the sitting room. He gestured Kayse in. "Finally, we're alone," he said, settling into an overstuffed chair and motioning Kayse to a similar one next to him. Andrew followed them in with a tray containing two mugs and another pot of the drink everyone called "coffee."

"I really drink too much of the stuff, but I can't help myself," Elija admitted by way of apology. "Help yourself. I found it's very much like the Alysian equivalent of kauf."

Kayse hadn't planned on having any, until he smelled the delicious coffee fragrance and felt the warm steam rising from the mug. He whiffed the nutty chocolate aroma, changed his mind, and nodded. Andrew leaned forward to pour and stepped back to wait. Kayse frowned over at him.

Is the man going to sit down, leave, or hover about?

Kayse sipped at his drink.

Frag, he's going to hover.

"So here you are," Elija rumbled, ignoring Andrew and peering intently at Kayse.

Kayse tapped a few fingers on the arm of the chair and looked around. "Yep, here I am. I appreciate you taking me in." He took a sip of the hot brew. "I'll try not to be a nuisance."

A strange expression flitted briefly across Elija's face. He bent his head for a prolonged sip.

Despite the hot coffee, a chill traveled up Kayse's back. He shifted uneasily in his chair.

Elija noted his unease and put his cup down on a side table. He leaned forward. "Elise told me that you needed sanctuary, saying someone was trying to kill you and you were no longer safe at her place." Elija inclined his head at Kayse, a question on his face. "She seemed to think you were important somehow."

Kayse nodded. "I witnessed my parents' murder. My best friend was abducted because they thought he was me." Kayse rubbed at the arm of his chair, suddenly studying it intently. He looked up, tears glistening in his eyes. "They killed him when it turned out he wasn't. Elise thinks they're still out searching for me." He thought of the hospital, the attack, and all the things he'd discovered there.

"Some of my people think you came here to spy for the Alysians," Elija accused. Kayse felt Andrew sidle closer as if to evaluate his answer. His crowding presence made Kayse uneasy.

Putting down the coffee, he eyed Elija. "Why would Elise do that to her own brother, and what reason would the Alysians have to spy on you?" Kayse frowned. "Besides, Elise wouldn't rat out her own brother. She's an all right lady—unless you're doing something she disapproves of. You're not doing something she'd disapprove of, are you?"

Elija shrugged in response. "I'm not sure anymore. Ever since she married that Alysian, I've wondered whose side she's really on."

"Hey, Elise didn't want me in her life at first either. I was an inconvenience, but I was desperate, and there was nowhere else to go. So, she took me in. She's gone to a lot of trouble and expense because of me. The Alysians don't like me because of my friendship with Terrans, and now you're telling me the Terrans don't trust me because I'm an Alysian."

"Look, Kayse, we're not total backwoods morons," Elija answered angrily. He tossed him a menacing glare.

"I never said you were." Bewildered, Kayse reached for his mug, took a sip of the coffee, and frowned at the anger on Elija's face.

"I know you're more than you pretend to be."

Nervously, Kayse asked, "What do you mean?" He took another careful sip and eyed his host across the mug's rim.

"When you walked through my front door, our scans indicated a sophisticated ESA embedded in your brain and high grade augmentations throughout your body. Don't expect me to believe you're a normal person like you pretend to be."

"What?" Kayse jerked forward, spilling his coffee. "What's an ESA system, and what do you mean it's embedded in my brain?"

Andrew leaped to grab a rag and wiped vigorously at the spill, his face expressionless, while Kayse frantically patted his scalp with shaking fingers.

Elija studied Kayse as if ascertaining his truthfulness. He glanced at Andrew who nodded back. Then he answered, "ESA means Electronic Systems Assistant. It's a device, which enhances human brainpower and acts as an artificial assistant for higher-level tasks. You mean you don't know you have one?"

Kayse shook his head. "No, I don't know I have anything of the sort. Dr. Jay mentioned that he changed my eyes, my hair, and even accelerated my response time. He vaguely talked about a GPS and access to something that assisted me. What I remember most is that he said I would smell nice, but I don't remember anything about a *computer* in my brain. I *was* heavily medicated when he laid it all out to me, but I never thought... He said I would be augmented, but I'd have remembered him telling me if I had a computer in my head. I know it wouldn't have slipped my notice. And I have not been aware of anything assisting me at any time. I certainly haven't felt any smarter recently. Rather the opposite."

"Hmm, I see. So, Trace Walker didn't put it there?"

"Definitely not. They put me out briefly, but it was Dr. Jay Luttrell who did the surgery on me. I don't think the Alysians did much. I was sore for a long time after Dr. Jay's operations and, now that you mention it, I thought I was hearing things too. I assumed it was the drugs, not some brain implant."

Elija sighed. "Dr. Jay thinks that you carry one or more of the Alysian Talent genes. Actually, Jay also encouraged me to let you come here. I've heard and read about these so-called Alysian Talents, but I've never had the chance to study one up close. It interests me."

Kayse grew worried at what Elija implied.

Tilting his head, Elija assumed a thoughtful expression. "Let me study you and run a few painless tests and I'll give you your sanctuary. In return, you can stay for a while. And as a bonus, I'll activate your ESA for you. Right now, it's de-activated. It's the reason why you're unaware of it. I can show you how to use it. You'll find it incredibly useful."

"I don't want some computer messing about in my brain," Kayse gulped, upset.

"Electronic intelligence is far superior to biological intelligence," Andrew announced, calmly interrupting the conversation.

"Not always true, Andrew," Elija admonished. He held up a hand to make his point. "There are some functions we humans do better than AIs."

"I've not found that to be the case," Andrew retorted indignantly as he straightened up. Kayse would almost say he was miffed at the comment.

"Now don't get touchy about other opinions on robotic intelligence, or I'll have to lower your sensitivity paradigm," Elija countered.

Kayse stared at Andrew. "He's a cyborg?"

"Better than that," Andrew responded with what sounded like asperity. "I'm a fully integrated artificial construct. I contain far better analytical and computational skills than any biological being and can race rings around any puny unaugmented human mind or body."

Putting down his coffee, Elija harrumphed a bit. "Now Andrew, let's not get too full of ourselves. Kayse is not aware of all the sterling qualities you possess, and his attitude must be excused due to ignorance. Don't get your nose out of joint. I'll inform him about your extensive capabilities so he can fully appreciate you as much as we all do."

The statement seemed to mollify the android as he eased back and scanned his surroundings. Spying the empty mugs, he offered, "Perhaps you would like more coffee?"

"Yes, I would," Elija answered with a relieved smile. "There's the sensitive and competent Andrew I appreciate."

They both watched as Andrew glided out the door, back rigid and head held high. Elija gave Kayse a wry smile. "Be careful about casting any aspersions on artificial intelligence while you're around Andrew and the others. They might take it personally. They shouldn't take offense, but there is a degree of pride I've programmed into them, and you don't want to make them an enemy while you're here. You may even get to realize the tremendous value of both cyborgs and androids while living here. Alysians are a bit barbaric when it comes to their understanding of the value of advanced life forms."

Kayse stared at him opened-mouthed when he realized what his host was saying. He lived with human-looking robots that might get touchy, or possibly dangerous, if he didn't watch what he said.

Jesh!

"Is my team all androids, too?" Kayse wanted to know.

"Oh no, your team's *mostly* biological. They're not androids, not at all," Elija replied with a wave of his hand. "Cyborgs maybe, a bit, but definitely not androids."

Kayse startled. *Cyborgs!*

Straightening up, Elija concluded, "I'll contact Jay and get confirmation on activating your ESA. It has the design and installation pattern I use. I just wanted to make sure it *was* one of ours." Elija gave him a smile. "Can't be too careful nowadays. Then we'll call in your team and get you started in on the routine around here. Maybe we can mutually benefit each other."

Kayse wondered what that might mean. He wasn't too sure he liked the idea of being a lab rat for the Terrans. Been there, done that already.

Chapter 30

"The weather has turned warm enough that you might want to go outside and enjoy some fresh mountain air." Elija cut into a fluffy omelet and waved his fork around. Elija, Kayse, and "the team" sat at the breakfast table discussing the day's schedule. "I have to drive down the mountain on business, so I don't have any lab work that needs to be done this morning. You're on your own."

Fat chance. Kayse hadn't been "on his own" once.

For several cycles now, Kayse had been living and working at the Homestead. The Terrans considered from sunup to sunup a day, not a rotation like he was used to calling it, and ten rotations they called a week, not a cycle. It took some getting used to. Soon Kayse was settling in and beginning to adjust to his new situation.

It soon became obvious that there was more to the innocent log cabin than a first glance would suggest. Behind the main residence, a large lab facility burrowed deep into the heart of the mountain. Designated "Off Limits," it was protected by heavily locked and password encrypted doors found in various rooms. However, when Kayse indicated an interest in working in the labs, Elija surprisingly agreed. Working on procedures and data entry gave Kayse the opportunity to stimulate his mind and feel useful, not to mention the hope of an opportunity to snoop around and learn something useful. Meanwhile, Elija claimed to appreciate the help.

At first, everything proved new and exciting. Everyone acted friendly, which made for a change. Kayse occupied his own room next door to the Terran collection who called themselves "his team." They went everywhere he went, very seldom leaving him alone. They seemed to think he liked their company and, at first, that was true enough. Trying to be a good guest, he'd offered to help around the place with chores such as cleaning or laundry, but Elija waved him away, saying "Andrew's team" had it under control. That suited Kayse fine, especially since his mother always ragged on him about cleaning his room and helping with chores.

The thought sent a brief pang of grief skittering across his thoughts. He grabbed a half sob, half breath. Sometimes he missed her nagging, her soft voice. He also missed his father's stern lectures about proper conduct for a young man. He used to make fun of them behind his back...but never again. Then he remembered he was not their true son, but something far different. The grief ripped in with a sharp pang, sudden and unexpected, but gradually dissipated, as he willed it away and tried to breathe normally. That was the past; he needed to focus on the future.

Even though everyone tried to make him feel at home, he still felt like an outsider. They were all one big happy family, and he felt like some stranger among them that they needed to jolly along.

Ace and the girls did everything they could to please him. They woke him up in the morning, bringing him the Terran drink they called coffee. He was beginning to look forward to it. They shadowed him everywhere, especially when he helped in the labs. Often he could feel their hot breath on the back of his neck, as they stood close by, observing his every move.

Kayse's team also worked out at the gym every afternoon. Occasionally, others from the Homestead would join in. There, Kayse's accelerated performance made him the star. He began teaching others, along with Ace and the girls, how to move their bodies more efficiently.

And bodies they had! All three were stunningly beautiful and graceful. The girls had long blonde hair, bright white teeth, perfect features, and sunny dispositions. They never argued or frowned. Not one put a foot wrong, and all lived to please him. Yet, after a while, all that perfection, beauty, and good cheer set his teeth on edge. Next to them, he felt grumpy and awkward and isolated.

However, he found solace in the fact that Tempest would be wickedly jealous at the way they catered to him. More than once, he thought they offered sex, but he didn't know how to respond, so the offers dwindled amidst puzzled shrugs. They countenanced his existence with no sharp retorts, no arguments at his occasional ridiculous demands, and showed barely any annoyance over what an intrusive stranger might be expected to provoke. They accepted him with a grace that bewildered him.

In comparison, he remembered Tempest ranting and raving as she constantly argued with him. Here, he got bland smiles, soft words, and compliant responses. He found himself missing the sharp edges of Tempest's personality with her startling comments and spontaneous nature. Despite her difficult personality, he knew without a doubt, that she cared deeply for him, was engaged in his life, and might even be in love with him; while these agreeable beings only gave out indifferent smiles and complacent shrugs as a response to anything he did. He felt no real emotional attachment to them nor they to him.

Occasionally he would try to provoke them, but they remained calm in the face of outrageous statements and stupid actions. They never took him to a dangerous bar for lunch or maneuvered him into consorting with sex-riddled Alysians at a drug-soaked Rave.

Fate, he was bored!

With everyone always polite, always willing to please, he found himself becoming short-tempered and irascible. He never would have imagined he could miss Tempest so much. He often wondered what she was doing.

He needed therapy.

"But before I go, it's time," Elija announced, regarding him intently.

Kayse jerked back to the present, breakfast, and Elija's piercing stare. "Time for what?" Kayse's heart started to pound. He clenched and unclenched a fist while taking a deep breath.

Death? Disaster? Destruction? Tea?

"Time to try to find out what makes an Alysian Talent different from a regular Terran. You've been here long enough. Time to make it worth our while. I need something to take with me to evaluate."

Need something? What? A beating heart? A small finger? A lock of hair?

Kayse inhaled sharply at visions of vile scientific experiments while he was laid out on a torture rack. He swallowed hard, his stomach doing several flip-flops. He put on a bland, albeit nervous, smile and fingered his hidden medallion.

How fast could Trey get here?

"What do you have in mind?" he croaked aloud.

"I need to draw some blood, get a tissue sample, and give you a physical exam. I need to ask a few questions."

"It won't hurt, will it?" Kayse gave him a hopeful look.

"Not at all." Elija smiled as he put his napkin on the table. Simultaneously, Ace, Bett, and Gami did the same. Breakfast was over.

***

Soon after, Kayse sat slouched in Elija's office, which adjoined one of the science labs. A lighted screen covered a desktop where his host tapped at bright icons. "Do you have what the Alysians call 'Talent' and exactly what does that mean?" asked Elija, activating the desk's computer.

As Elija manipulated a hidden keyboard, Kayse noticed words begin to parade across the desk's surface.

Interesting.

"Well, they say I have a Talent." Kayse flipped his hand outward. "Because of it everyone acts as if I have a time bomb ticking inside of me. I sometimes feel like they think I might explode or do something dangerous."

"You might explode?" Elija's eyebrows shot up. He backed up his chair a bit.

Kayse puffed out his cheeks. "No, not really explode—or, at least, I hope not!" He laughed shakily and ran a hand through his hair. "I think it may have something to do with time travel."

Elija's eyes widened. "Time travel? I thought that strictly a Tellurian Talent."

"True, but I may have a Tellurian connection." Kayse winced as he said it.

"A Tellurian Talent? Have you ever time traveled?" Elija's eyes lit up, as he leaned forward eagerly.

Kayse squirmed in his seat and decided to stick with as much truth as possible. "Maybe. Two men killed my parents. One came after me and I panicked. Something happened and the next thing I know, I'm somewhere in the future."

"In the future? You mean as if you went forward in time? How far?"

"Maybe, about... twenty-eight..." Kayse shifted uneasily.

"Seconds?"

A significant pause. He wasn't sure how long that was.

"Weeks?" Elija's expression of amazement was comical.

"Weeks are like Alysian cycles?"

"A bit shorter, but essentially the same."

Sighing, Kayse admitted, "Annuals. I've come twenty-eight annuals into the future."

"You traveled here from a past nearly twenty-eight years ago?" Elija leaned back in amazement, his eyes gone wide.

Kayse nodded.

"A time jump of twenty-eight years?" Elija breathed out shakily. "Elise never mentioned it to me. She hinted, however, something about time travel and that I needed to ask you about it. No wonder you act so oblivious at times."

"Yes." Kayse nodded. "This future is fricking bewildering."

"That's quite an ability." Elija rubbed his face with his hands and stared at him. "Why didn't she tell me before?"

"About that." Kayse fidgeted uneasily. "I don't think Richard or Trey discussed it much until recently. I mean, the idea of living with someone who time travels can be freaky. They didn't want to upset her and.... that household carries an awful lot of secrets."

Elija's mouth hung open. He stared at Kayse. Then he licked his lips. His eyes narrowed as he tipped back his head, thinking things over.

"Secrets?" Elija unconsciously tapped his fingers on his desktop. "You're saying Elise has secrets?"

"Oh, come on," Kayse chided. "She's a Terran starship captain living on an antagonistic planet. Her husband is an influential leader of the local native tribe, so she can't disclose everything she might know. She's done a lot of things in her past that Richard wouldn't understand. She's not telling everything; you're not telling everything—and I damn well know Richard has a few secrets under his hat. She's fighting for the survival of her species. So is he."

"All of us are fighting for survival," Elija grumbled. He looked intently at Kayse. "Has this time travel experience happened more than once?" He raised his eyebrows.

"No." Kayse said the word abruptly.

Elija shook his head in amazement. "I can see now why you're considered so valuable." Elija stroked his chin. "Could you do it again?"

"I really don't want to." Kayse gave him a defiant glare, clenching his jaw. "You see, I don't know how to control it, and I really don't want to go sliding another twenty-eight or more annuals into the future. Getting used to this future has been hard enough."

"Can you go into the past? That would be interesting."

Kayse thought about the papers on cloning hidden away in the vault at the Med Center. He suspected one of the other clones had accomplished it. The words "successful translation and insertion" flitted across his memory. Then he remembered Richard saying that even if he were to go back in time, it might not change things. Or it might. Time travel was a tricky thing. Kayse had thought about going back to stop his parent's murder, but he didn't know yet how to do it or if it would even make a difference. Trey had said that most likely it wouldn't. He'd even indicated trying.

"I'm not sure, but traveling back in time can create serious consequences. You could change something you don't want changed. Besides, I said I don't know how to control my Talent. I might go somewhere I don't want to or change something that would cause an adverse effect on this present."

Nodding, Elija tapped his desk.

"I'll need a blood sample, some saliva, and a couple of tissue samples. Then let me see what the data says before we take it any further."

Elija gave him another hard stare and stood up as Ace came into the room. He held a syringe and a cup. Kayse spit in the cup and bared his arm. It didn't hurt. Still, he felt scared. What if Elija decided to do something experimental on him that he didn't want? He surveyed the lab and noticed a lot of fancy high tech equipment. He shivered. If that happened, he would stop it. It wouldn't take much to snap Elija's neck, given his augmentations, but he really didn't want to resort to violence. He rather liked his morning coffee and muffins served to him in bed.

Pushing back from his desk, Elija eyed him warily. "After I get back from my appointment, maybe we can talk more about this. Until then, enjoy the spring weather we're having. It may not last long."

***

Kayse was rummaging around in his wardrobe, searching for a jacket, when Bett burst into his room with the other twin right behind her.

"Can't you knock?" he asked irritably. He pulled out a black jacket. He was beginning to value personal space.

The two appeared startled at his comment and exchanged puzzled looks.

"Word is, the miners broke through," began one of the twins.

"And found a labyrinth that winds deep into the mountains," added the second.

"Come with us and check it out," they both finished excitedly in unison.

He threw on his jacket and followed them out the front door, where they joined up with Ace. In the distance, Kayse spied a commotion around a cave's entrance, and they all took off toward it at a run.

As he ran, he felt an invigorating sharp breeze slap across his face. Adrenaline pumped throughout his body as he gave a wild whoop, accelerating the step-up mode into full throttle. The others straggled behind in the dust.

He arrived at the entrance amid excited shouts and buzzing talk. Several miners gestured wildly at new arrivals. He hadn't realized so many people lived in the area. An unexpected number of Terrans mingled about. Where had they all come from? Excitement ran high.

Gami skidded up next to him, followed by Ace and Bett. She strolled into the dark mouth of the cave.

"Now be careful you A forms," a miner admonished her. "You aren't made to go poking around in caves."

"What'd you find?" Ace asked the man in charge.

The miner scratched at his short auburn beard and squinted at Ace. "We think it's part of a labyrinth that connects throughout the entire Diechwrathe Mountain Range. It abuts the Hammerslag holdings, so we're hoping to find those special diamond crystals somewhere inside. Our more sensitive equipment indicated unusual formations deeper in."

As Kayse listened to the chatter, he scanned the area. A tingling feeling ran over both arms and the back of his neck. At first, it tugged gently, but then became more insistent. He eased inside the entrance, and the feeling intensified. A group of newcomers full of questions distracted the miners, so he slipped farther in where he felt an even stronger pulling sensation.

He rubbed the rock wall, and it was like that time when his mother put out a batch of delicious cookies and asked him not to eat any. As hard as he'd tried not to, he found himself chewing on cookies without ever being aware of taking a bite.

So, before he knew what he was doing, he was in the cave, groping his way down a narrow tunnel. At first, the darkness disoriented him but, after a short way, the path opened into a large cavern with a hidden stream somewhere nearby. The sound of soft splashes echoed from hidden nooks and crannies. On his right, flashes of light came from a passageway and bounced off the cavern's immense walls, brightening that area.

He stumbled forward, yanked like a puppet on strings. At the mouth of the passageway, the light grew even brighter. Inhaling a deep breath, he plunged into the glowing tunnel. Toward the tunnel's end, shades of the spectrum began to strobe along its wall like a shuttle bay landing strip. He edged in closer and, as he rounded a corner, he saw a magnificent stack of glowing crystalline rocks. It resembled a small city all lit up and pulsed enthusiastically as if in welcome.

He stopped to stare as a brilliant blaze enveloped him. He grew dizzy and felt insubstantial. The walls started to waver around him and the next thing he knew, he was falling into blackness.

Oh, no, was his last thought as the darkness grabbed him, sucking him in. He knew this feeling. He'd felt it before.

Once.

Chapter 31

Kayse regained consciousness next to a heavy metal door on a cavern wall. Slowly, he stood and touched the door's massive handle. With a downward jerk, he opened it, falling through into a room that looked like a science lab. As the door ponderously slammed shut behind him, he studied the area, wondering where he was.

Rows of tall cylinders filled what appeared to be a science lab. Dampness sweated off smooth beige walls, and hard tile lay cold beneath his feet. Several metal lab tables snugged up against one wall, supporting stacks of mysterious electronic equipment. A sharp, medicinal odor intermingled with the smell of recycled air. Inside the cylinders, a thick fluid held floating bodies in various stages of development. He crept over to one and stared through the glass front, only to see his own face staring sightlessly back at him. Abruptly the body twitched, causing seaweed hair to waft about, and he jerked violently backwards.

Fate, what is going on here?

Fighting to gain control of stampeding horror, he leaned forward to examine the tank in closer detail. The viscous substance blurred the image, but the form appeared to be a male human. He stepped over to another tank and peered in. The limp body floated up closer to the glass front, becoming clearer. It was like looking into a mirror. He'd wandered into a room filled with a batch of clones that wore his face. Chills flowed down his arms and across his back as he gazed around the lab.

Frag! What was going on here?

Making his way across the room to a partially opened door, he discovered an empty carpeted corridor. The chemical smells intensified and mingled with the odor of mildew and ozone. He slipped through the door and sneaked down a hallway lined with glass windows that fronted various science labs. Peering through the glass into a different area, he saw a number of identical bodies, stacked in a row, like large dolls on an assembly line. A network of electrical cords plugged into each one. Studying the hard-bodied forms, the heavy musculature, and sharp features reminded him of military personnel. They looked like human super soldiers.

He crept down to the next door and peeked through a glass window into another room. There he observed a white-coated worker bending over a microscope. When the person straightened up and deftly selected a nearby vial to examine, Kayse recognized Dr. Jay Luttrell. Overwhelming relief swept through him, because in his recent timeline, Dr. Jay was on the space station and not anywhere on Alysia, much less here at the Homestead. That meant this was not currently happening. But was he in another alternate timeline or an inevitable future? He shuddered to think of a future filled with cloned versions of him.

Why am I here now? And, when is it? He would bet that stack of crystals had something to do with this.

I want out, and I want out now.

He'd seen enough. As he backed away, his hands shook and his body poured cold sweat.

Returning to the first lab, the floating bodies with their unfocused stares disturbed him. He swore that when he came close, their eyes sharpened and followed his every move. Goosebumps ran along his arms and the back of his neck. He couldn't help but stop to watch, mesmerized by the numerous tanks and their trapped occupants.

Transfixed by the gruesome familiarity of the drifting specimens, he felt something tap him on the back. He jerked around, startled. Panicked, he grabbed at the intruder and caught an arm. He made a quick survey to see if there were any others nearby and plunged for the exit, a body in tow to separate from them. He lunged out into the labyrinth's corridor. The door crashed shut. With his reflexes in overdrive and adrenalin flooding his body, Kayse whirled to face his captive as the body thudded against the rough wall of the cave. Breathing heavily, he leaned back to stare at him, —no, her! He inhaled sharply, only to find himself regarding a stunning woman who was also gasping for breath.

She frowned at him, rubbing an angry red welt that scraped one lovely arm. He stepped toward her as her hands went up into the air, indicating surrender.

For a brief moment, he stopped to take in her appearance. Dark hair curled in a wild riot around her face. She came up to his chin and featured a body that would make any man drool. Her eyes narrowed as she gave him an intense glare and reminded him of….

"Aargh, that hurt me!"

A jolt tore through him. The stance, the face, the tone of voice, all rang bells from recent memory. However, it was the violet eyes ringed with lush lashes that gave her away. He gaped at her as he began to realize who he faced.

Shaking her head, she coughed out, "Fate you're fast. I knew your reflexes were good, but Fate!" She leaned over, hands on knees, breathing deeply. Then she looked up, her eyebrows quirking upwards. "Must you treat a lady so rough?"

His mouth dropped open. No words came out.

"Gah! Stop staring at me. You need to get back," she admonished him. Her eyes narrowed. "You do plan to return to your own timeline, don't you? I sure hope so."

He gaped. *Wow!*

Brushing off dirt, she also smoothed out her clothes saying, "Pull your mind out of the gutter, kid, and stop leering at me like some sex-crazed lunatic. You need to get out of here. This is an extremely dangerous place for you."

Through his shock, he managed to stutter, "T...T....Tempest?" If this was Tempest all grown up, then he might have to re-evaluate their relationship. She sure looked good with luscious curves enhanced by a beautiful and elegant face, even though it was frowning at the moment.

Her violet gaze shifted to annoyance, as she seemed to read his mind. "Stop eyeing me like some...some..." She put her hands on her hips and rolled her eyes. "I can't imagine why I had such a crush on you, Kayse Telluria. You're an absolute idiot at eighteen." She shook her head at him and brushed back riotous hair.

Indignant, he replied, "And you? Do you know what a pain you are at thirteen?"

Her lips twitched as if trying hard not to smile. "I might have a clue," she offered. Then a smile curved her soft lips. "You certainly told me often enough. Ha, you still do. Part of your charm, I suppose. You can be terribly outspoken when you have a mind to be."

He sighed, realizing the futility of the argument. "What am I doing here? This is some future, isn't it? How am I going to get back?" He ran a hand through hair sprinkled with cave dirt and debris. He wiped at some blood from a scrape on a cheek. "What's happened? Why are there so many of me in there?" He pointed at the now-closed door.

"Did you see what was in there? Did you see the other labs full of android assassins? What's going on in there?"

Wrinkling an aristocratic nose, she said, "There? In this timeline? Frightening things. But this isn't my current timeline, either, I hope. I only came here to help you get away and scope out the inside of the Homestead. However, if you don't leave soon, it could very well become our future," she countered. "Fate help us if that happens. I need to get you back to where you belong so you can change this. What you see here is still only a possibility, but a terrifying one. This future is disastrous. You saw all those, those…" She shuddered.

"Yeah, I saw them. Too many of me is just too much of a good thing, huh?" He raised an eyebrow at her.

She coughed a laugh. "That's too right!"

"And the others? The military androids? Those things could be deadly. If Terrans use them in a war, the Alysians won't have a chance. So, how do I get back to warn them? Do you know? Because I sure don't." He hoped for firm guidance, but he received a distracted flutter of fingers.

"I can't hang around here much longer." She bent her head, frowning in concentration.

"No, don't go. Help me first."

She looked up. "The crystals are your best bet." Grabbing an arm, she tugged him down a rough cave tunnel, which soon took on familiar contours. Lights began to dance and flash against the cavern's wall as if signaling them in.

"Any mature crystal stack can serve as a gateway for those who can time travel. Select a piece to boost your Talent. You'll need more power than your mother's necklace can provide. You'll also need Elija to activate your embedded ESA. Get the procedure done as soon as you return so you can nose around a bit with it. Trace needs to know more about this possible Terran technology, and you're our best link to find that out. Get activated and record everything you see at the Homestead. Don't let this become our future!"

"Both sides keep trying to control me," he muttered. "I feel like a pawn in that game called chess your parents like so much. What was back there?" he asked.

"It looks like Elija and Dr. Jay are putting together an army of you cloned and military configured androids. If they successfully complete the project on time, they will crush the Democratic Union first and probably move on until they have taken over all of Alysia. There's going to be a horrifying war between the Alysians and the Terrans if you don't help stop it. However, you might give Trace enough warning that he can do something if you return with what you now know. Growing clones and building complex androids takes tons of time. And time is what the Alysians need. Don't let this happen, now that you know it's possible. Warn them."

"I can't do this alone."

"You won't have to. Mom's got her resources and ideas on how to use them," she said with a mysterious smirk. "And dad's never been helpless in a crisis."

She gave him a push toward the pulsing stack of crystal.

"Pick one," she said.

"What!"

"Make it a really good choice."

He reached out as a large chunk of crystal fell into his hand. Immediately, he felt the power of the crystal enter his mind and shuffle through his thoughts, ordering, revising, amplifying, and refining his brain. His eyes widened at the sensation. His body tingled and adrenaline surged through him as the crystal's power raised his abilities to a new level.

"Keep and protect that crystal. It'll help you control and understand your Talent. Don't lose it, whatever you do. Some of us believe the crystals are alive, even sentient, so treat it carefully." With that, she began to waver and fade.

"Don't leave me, Tempest. I don't know what to do. I need your help and knowledge."

"Sorry, I can't hang around here anymore. I must get back. I have things to do. People to see." A smile slipped onto her face, and her expression softened. She gazed at him with sudden affection. "You're the best, Kayse. I always knew it. Believe it yourself."

"I don't know what I'm supposed to do," he shouted frantically at a dissolving Tempest. Mist glimmered against the cave wall. He heard in his mind, "You'll know what to do when the time comes. We're counting on you, Kayse."

"Wait, I need to know…" But she wavered, faded, and was gone. Dizziness overcame him as the cave started getting hazy. The crystal hummed louder and louder in his mind as darkness closed in.

Going, going,

Gone.

***

He woke up with a splitting headache. In his hand, the crystal pulsed with a pale, red warning light. A feeling of nearby danger suddenly overwhelmed him. He groaned as he clawed himself up the wall to a standing position. Gripping the crystal, he eyed the vibrating stack. Blood oozed from between his fingers as he opened his hand to stare at the shimmering rock. Light leaped from it as if in response to his strange, churning feelings. He tore off a piece of his shirt, wiped down the crystal, wrapped it up, and put it inside a jacket pocket. He didn't know why, but he felt better.

Sentient. She'd mentioned something about it being sentient.

An incredible urge to leave overcame him. He must get out. He must get out now, before he became lost forever in this dark, forbidding labyrinth. He heard a shrill, alien shriek as if some monster hunted prey. It was a warning cry. He recalled stories of crystal spiders living down in dark spaces deep in the Diechwrathe. They were rumored to kill people and eat them. He'd considered it a tale by which to scare small children, but the noise coming out of a nearby tunnel sounded fearfully real. Another screech echoed off tunnel walls, and he began to walk faster and faster until he was running in full step-up mode through the tunnel toward a dim light. As he reached the familiar open cavern, a memory tickled his mind.

She called me Kayse Telluria. Telluria! I should think about that, study more about Arwoyn, learn what he could do, embrace what he was and use it… I'm afraid I'll need all of it to survive.

***

Elated, Kayse heard voices coming from the end of the passageway he'd chosen. One sounded like Ace. He ran to the entrance and stopped to study the scene before him, hoping he'd returned to the right timeline. Gathering his thoughts, he shuffled through what he knew or guessed.

So Elise has a plan. Is it for the Terran side or the Alysian side? A vague drowsy memory surfaced of Dr. Jay asking where Elise stood. She'd answered that she went where the ship went. She'd been a *Terran fleet commander*, after all. People tended to forget who she really was. What else might they overlook as she stood in Richard's shadow? What could she do? How far would she go to protect her ship, her people?

And whose side would he, Kayse Kiare, be on if it came to choosing sides? Alysians had killed his mother and father, not Terrans. However, he was Alysian and could not betray his own planet...or could he, if justice would be served?

Who wanted him dead? Was it someone who considered him an Alysian threat? Could it be a time traveler who knew some awful future that he might bring about? On the other hand, was there another reason?

Clone of the powerful Arwoyn Telluria, some people might consider him an abomination. They would see him as some concoction out of a test tube that threatened their human right to power. They wouldn't be wrong.

Maybe the killer was a strange lunatic out on a spree, with his parents caught in the cross fire of random insanity. The eyes of the Med Center guard flashed through his thoughts.

Terrans hadn't invaded yet in his initial timeline. They weren't to blame for his parents' murder. Or were they?

What or who had brought him to this future? Were others, existing in this timeline, interested in stopping him...from whatever he might do? And what might that be?

Questions, so many questions, and so few answers.

Relieved, he saw Ace and others pretty much as he'd left them. It looked like he was back where he wanted to be. Shakily he waved, and the three from his team turned simultaneously to wave back. In that instant, a piece of the puzzle clicked into place. Clones! Suddenly he understood what bothered him about his team. Not twins and a brother, but clones.

Just like him!

His world wobbled at the revelation. Immediately, his mind protested. *No, not the same at all.* He was from a different procedure and no longer resembled his original, much less any of his clone siblings. Fate, Terrans acted casual about the existence of clones, robots, androids...all things created and designed, never troubling to consider themselves immoral or abnormal. Very different in their thinking from the Alysians he knew who went to war over such differences.

Then he remembered another overheard conversation about a desperate convoy of spaceships whose crews were depleted and sterile. Dr. Jay had saved them—doing what? Cloning the survivors. What multitude of technologies and advanced science are the Terrans hiding? How many others were hidden clones?

Tempest was right. He should find out what secrets the Terrans were keeping and discover more about their technologies. What he saw here was chilling. What else might there be? He needed to stop the coming Armageddon. He shuddered at the image of an army of clones, all wearing his face, armed with his Talent, and carrying sophisticated Terran technology.

That might bring about the end of his world.

And somehow, they expected him to prevent it.

<u>Chapter 32</u>

He stood facing Elija in his lab. Back from his trip to town, Elija already knew about the breakthrough into the Labyrinth; however, no one had said a word about discovering crystal. Kayse knew that he certainly wasn't going to mention it.

Closing the door, a frown on his face, Elija said to him, "Don't go wandering through that dangerous labyrinth. We thought we'd lost you." A hand landed on his shoulder.

Images of what he'd seen sent a shiver through Kayse. Shaking his head, he stared down at the floor. "Yes sir. The Labyrinth is not a good place to get lost."

Elija touched his hand and pried it open. A long red gash crossed his palm. "You hurt your hand. Did you have the medical unit take care of it?"

"I'll be fine." Kayse pulled his hand back abruptly. "I'm fine. I just scraped it on a sharp rock."

"Watch it so it doesn't go septic. Those cave walls harbor lots of bacteria. So you found nothing of interest?" Elija asked, studying him. "Certain crystals, once found in there, are said to affect Alysian Talent types in strange ways. You said you didn't see any. Do you feel any different?"

He managed a smile, staring Elija straight in the eye. "Nothing there but some sharp rocks and lots of darkness. I did hear a loud shriek. I think those crystal spiders mentioned in popular horror stories really do exist."

"Do they? We'll have to keep that in mind as we explore the cave. Also, we can prevent you from getting lost again by activating your ESA. It's time." Elija patted a nearby chair.

Staring at the chair, he backed up. The thought of a computer in his brain disconcerted him, to say the least. "I don't like strangers messing with my head. I don't like foreign technology controlling what I think," Kayse croaked out apprehensively. "I don't want to change who I am."

He thought of the always happy personalities of his clone team. He shuddered, thinking he might turn into a happy-faced android.

A hand waved by his face to get his attention. "It's already there, and it won't change your personality one bit. You're going to love it. It will help you communicate so much better and augment your current intelligence. Think of it as a very sophisticated tool. It has a database you can assess anytime you need it.

Aloud, Kayse asked, "Will it hurt to activate it?"

Elija patted the chair again. "In all honesty, a little discomfort and some dizziness might happen, but that's all. Eventually, your mind will get used to a new way of operating. You'll be amazed at what you can do."

Kayse squinted in disbelief. "You won't like have mind control over me, will you?"

A rumbling chuckle erupted from Elija. "No, neither I nor anyone else can make you do something you don't want to do."

He sighed. He didn't see a handy escape route, except maybe to try to use a Talent that he didn't want to employ unless it became absolutely necessary. Besides, Tempest had insisted he activate the ESA as soon as possible. She'd stressed it was important. So maybe he should. Whatever she was, she wasn't dumb. Impetuous at times, but not dumb. He sat down.

A sigh of relief escaped from Elija as he moved around toward the back of Kayse's head. He held a lit probe in his hand. "It should be right here near your hairline. Ah, here it is." He touched a slight bump, which Kayse had noticed after Dr. Jay's operation, but had since totally forgotten.

He heard a zapping sound, and then a voice boomed out from within his mind.

Welcome to the Electronic Secretary Assistant. Do not be alarmed! Thanks to the ESA system, the voice you are now hearing is being generated directly to the hearing centers of your brain."

Great! Now I'm hearing a voice in my head. A loud voice.

He clapped his hands to his ears.

"Ah, too loud, I suspect." Elija slid into his chair behind his desk and opened a program. He fiddled with something, which caused the sound to diminish.

I am currently using a neutral male voice. Would you like me to sound female?

"Yeah," he choked. *Frag, I'm already talking to a voice in my head.*

Still, if he had to have one, he figured a woman's voice would be easier listening.

I can sound neutral female.

Gah! The voice sounds like mom. That won't do!

Or more sexy. The voice took on a sultry overtone, making Kayse's skin tingle.

"I kinda like that," he said with a catch in his voice. "Let's go with the sexier tone. Easier on the ears. Can I change it later if I want?"

Most definitely," the voice purred. **Your wish is my command.**

Wow! I might get to like having a female at my beck and call!

Elija chuckled. He tapped something into his desk computer and peered downwards.

To further facilitate communication, please respond to the following words. Once I integrate your tonal responses, you can turn the voice off whenever you want.

The voice then went through a short list of words and phrases while Elija monitored the results on the computer screen at his desk. Kayse repeated all of them back.

Perfect, the voice said when he finished the exercise.

Shifting in his seat, Elija rubbed his hands together. "Now you can vocalize commands to your ESA whenever you like. Would you like to move on to the text interface?"

"Okay," Kayse responded. It felt weird talking to empty air. *What will it be like to have a sexy voice talking in my head? Tempest would be livid about the idea.*

He grinned to himself just thinking of her reaction.

The words, **We will now proceed with the text interface**, floated across his vision. The text perfectly contrasted against anything he viewed. Even when he moved his head, the words stayed dead center in his vision, adjusting to any changing light conditions.

Elija nodded. "Good, good. Now you can personalize the ESA, if you wish. Do you want to do it now, and what do you want to call it?"

He tried to think of what would be a good name. Dickhead and Dumb Butt immediately occurred to him, but he realized that if he were in a situation where he needed the help of the ESA, those around him might not understand if he yelled out, "Hey Dickhead or Dumb Butt." They might take offense at an inopportune moment. Consequently, he named it Lola. The voice sounded like a Lola.

"Lola," he said satisfied.

Elija shot him a quizzical look and then shrugged as he returned to his computer. "Your choice," was all he said. "Now you need an activation word or phrase."

"Attend," Kayse suggested. "How about that?"

"That's fine. You probably should add 'Lola' to attend so anytime you say the word 'attend' she doesn't activate. She'll respond with 'Attending, Kayse,' to let you know she's activated. Now I need a deactivation word or phrase."

"Disengage, Lola," he answered.

"Okay," Elija agreed.

"What exactly can you do, Lola?" he asked the ESA.

A massive list of activities appeared before his eyes. Apparently, Lola could do a lot. She could send messages to others carrying an ESA, both in text or voice. Any kind of report was available to download. In addition, downloadable music and video from all over the ASSIST network could be streamed to him. She could provide games or call up any document from any known source. Immense amounts of data on any subject and high-level mathematics calculated in moments were at his fingertips. She was able to diagnose physical ailments and suggest remedies. A logic tree could solve numerous problems after he put in various pieces of data. Instantaneous translations of any language known to her database along with phonetic forms of speaking enabled him to communicate in most situations. There was more, but Kayse needed some time to assimilate what he'd just been shown.

"Wow!" he said. Elija grinned back at him. "Do you have one of these too?"

Of course. The answer floated in front of him. *Many here at the Homestead have an embedded ESA. You'll find it quite useful. Actually, until you showed up, we*

rarely used vocals. Most of our communication was
mind to mind.

"It's rather like telepathy," Kayse breathed.

"Oh, it's like that and much more," Elija answered excitedly. He rubbed his hands together and gave a clap.

Is he online yet? Kayse saw the words scroll across his vision.

"You might like to know how to block out unwanted communications when you want privacy," Elija muttered. "The team is enthusiastic about group participation. It takes some getting used to."

"Yeah, I noticed," Kayse grimaced. "How do you filter out what you don't want to receive?"

Elija tapped the air in front of him. "Focus on the red button at your lower visual field. That will block out all incoming messages or set a filter to them. Above it, the green button activates communications, providing a drop-down menu where you can set it to a certain voice."

On his desk, Elija ran a finger down a list of programs from the computer instructions. "You can also filter out what messages you do or don't want to receive and select special designated groups to which you might want to send certain messages. The blue button offers a way to send customized messages. Think the words and press the send button with your mind at the appropriate selection. You can drop down from the menu bar for more choices."

Kayse saw the green light and the menu bar. He thought of a greeting message, then pressed send.

Kayse felt exhausted by the time they finished. Elija stretched. "After breakfast tomorrow, I'll show you some additional things, but for now we are done."

Kayse closed his eyes, thinking of the power now at his fingertips. His life had dramatically changed once again.

Chapter 33

Later, while Kayse was experimenting with Lola and her capabilities, a red-flagged message appeared in the upper right hand corner of his viewing screen. He accepted it, and the words: ***You have a visitor in the front reception room*** scrolled across his vision accompanied by a headshot of Andrew in a white shirt and dark suit. Eagerly, Kayse made his way to the guests' receiving room and stopped short at the door.

In the entryway, Jemma stood talking to Elija. Kayse's heart clenched in fear. Then, a form shot around from behind them to crash into his arms. His arms tightened around her as he smoothed back the wild dark hair. His worry eased. Tempest squeezed back. At first, he felt surprise, and then delight, immediately followed by apprehension.

Why is she here with Jemma?

"Oh Kayse, I never thought we'd get here," Tempest gulped. "They arrested dad on some trumped up charges of treason, so mom took me to Jemma's, saying that if it got really bad we should come here. I don't know where she is. There's a whole anti-Terran rally going on in Tygel, led by Klaymore Townsend with the support of General Moore and most of the military. He invaded the New Earth settlement where many of the Terrans live and burned it to the ground." She was breathing heavily.

"Slower, Tempest, take a breath," he soothed as he glanced over at Jemma. She nodded back, her face grim.

Inhaling a deep breath, Jemma explained, "General Moore attacked the Terran rebels who were in the jungle near the camp. The fight became bloody, according to all the vid broadcasts. Both sides have declared war. The Alysians claim they're going to send a number of Terrans back up to the space station and quarantine the remainder in isolation camps here."

Tempest tightened her grip and shuddered.

Jemma continued, "A Terran riot started in Tygel when the announcement aired, and they've put the whole city in lock-down. Tempest and I just managed to get out in time. The whole country is expressing outrage over the whole thing and claim the Terrans plan to take over all of Alysia. It's getting pretty scary."

Kayse glanced at Elija who frowned back at him over the top of Tempest's head. Kayse's ESA lit up with activity. The news was spreading rapidly.

"Let's turn on the vid and see what's happening," Elija suggested in a tight voice.

He took them into the vid room and immediately left, saying he would return soon. They all huddled close to watch events unfold on the large screen.

A newscaster announced a recall to the Terran space station for all Terrans not sequestered or accounted for by sponsoring Alysians. Scenes showed many being rounded up and put in guarded areas until a shuttle could return them. The broadcast went on to say that Terran activists had escaped into a D'Ankanque jungle, and the fighting was halted there for the time being. Unfortunately, it was flaring up in other locations in the Democratic Union, most especially Tygel.

Several areas known to be Terran neighborhoods near Tygel now burned. Worldwide disturbances and general unrest had begun erupting. The heaviest concentration of violence, however, was still in Tygel. Klaymore Townsend's face plastered the vids, extolling the danger of a Terran takeover. It was akin to pouring fuel onto a fire. General Moore, and several other top ranking military officers, joined Townsend's call to arms. Under the guise of restoring peace, they poured military troops into Terran neighborhoods, bombing and killing innocent civilians. General Church didn't appear for comment, and there was no mention of Elise or Trace Walker.

Elija came back into the room, wearing a harried expression. Kayse noticed a flood of activity going on through the ESA. He tried to snatch pieces of conversations from the ESA, keep his attention on the girls, and listen to what the vids reported all at the same time. Ace messaged his ESA that Terrans from all over the Union had announced plans to head to the Homestead for sanctuary.

Twisting around, Jemma's voice quavered. "This thing could go global."

Elija scowled. "Kayse, you need to pack your things."

"Why?"

"Several contingents of desperate Terrans are headed this way seeking refuge and, since you're Alysian, that puts you in danger. I cannot guarantee your safety anymore. You'll be safer somewhere else."

"Oh yeah, just watching the vid reassures me of that idea," Kayse countered. "This thing is spreading all over the Democratic Union.

"And maybe beyond. I'm trying to contact Elise and set up a plan," Elija explained, "but she's off the grid. You'll have to trust me for now."

Kayse wasn't sure that would happen in his lifetime.

Overhead the *whop-whop-whop* of a helio could be heard coming in. He tossed a questioning look at Elija who returned a puzzled frown.

"Inbound helio. Friend or foe?" Kayse asked in a hoarse voice.

Sighing, Elija commented, "Eventually, the Union's military will come here. If they can't find Elise, they'll come after me. I've put this place on red alert." He stopped to attend to a transmission.

Kayse's ESA lit up. Lola flashed an urgent message.

"Good news for you," Elija replied with a grin.

"Then it's not a government helio?"

"It's from Elise. Go pack and get ready for transport." Elija waved him out.

Kayse shook his head. "I'm staying here to find out what's happening."

"No, you're not. Go get packed now. All three of you are getting picked-up."

"Attend, Lola."

Attending, Kayse.

"Contact Ace, or any in my team, and ask them to pack for an extended trip for me."

Acknowledged, Kayse.

"Disengage, Lola."

Disengaged.

If one had to have a team that hovered constantly over him, then they could very well pack his things while he analyzed the developing situation.

Andrew was at the door, letting someone in.

Tempest moaned, but he'd already figured out who it was.

Angel stood in the hallway, the light from the open door illuminating him from behind. Eyes glowered on a shadowed face; his hands clenched on his hips. He scowled at Tempest. "What were you thinking attempting to drive through that dangerous mountain pass?"

"We ran for somewhere safe," Jemma retorted, standing in front of Tempest. "Elise said if things got worse to head for Elija and Kayse."

"Angel!" Kayse strode eagerly toward him.

"I'm taking all of you out of here," Angel answered angrily. "Terrans are swarming here for refuge, and the military won't be far behind. Things are getting ugly. You three need to be gone."

"Where would you take them to ensure their safety?" Elija inquired, coming up behind Kayse.

Tossing a glance his way, Angel answered, "I have a place. Give the Democratic Union's army a little more time and they'll think to come here. Frag, all they have to do is follow the trail of desperate Terrans."

Nodding at Angel, Elija agreed. "We're pretty fortified here. I might be able to keep the kids and hold off the military, but they won't be safe from my own people who are very angry now. It would be better if these three left now. Can you tell me where you're taking them?" He appeared upset with the idea of Kayse leaving but resigned to the logic of it.

"You're not on a need to know basis," Angel replied, abruptly. Elija nodded, but he didn't look happy. Kayse figured it was because Elija was losing control over him and couldn't do anything about it.

"Stay in touch." Elija tapped his head. Kayse nodded. They'd know where he was going soon enough. Just then Ace and the girls arrived all a-twitter with his bags. They looked inquiringly at Elija, who nodded.

"Angel, please keep him safe," all three voiced in unison.

"He's Tempest's guardian." Kayse replied stiffly. "He doesn't watch over me."

Elija shook his head. "Wrong, Kayse. I'd wager you're as important to him as she is." Angel nodded and tossed Kayse an enigmatic smile.

"You're putting both of us in the middle of your stupid war, aren't you?" Kayse accused.

Elija smiled at him. "Smack dab. You're my trump card with the Alysians. And Angel is the neutral species who will aide us if it comes to that."

"Stop there," Angel interrupted angrily. "Why would I want to do such a thing? Why would I want to be involved in your ridiculous interspecies war? I have my own mission, which is quite enough." He glared at a Tempest and Kayse. "Why should I help Terrans?"

"Because of the future." Elija smiled. "You and Kayse come with me."

"What about me?" Tempest intervened. "I want to go with Kayse."

"You go clean up and get some food, young lady," Elija ordered. "You're leaving with him soon enough. Ace, take care of her." Ace motioned for her to follow him and the girls. They departed with Tempest glancing over her shoulder and dragging her feet.

Elija gestured for Kayse and Angel to follow him. He went to his study where he slid open a panel. Behind it stood a heavy door with a keypad and a security sensor. He tapped in some numbers, peered into the optic scanner, and led them into a long hallway. Glass windows lined both sides, revealing rooms that contained scientific instruments and frantic lab workers. These were those labs from that future!

Terrans hurried everywhere. Amber lights flashed overhead. Elija ignored all the commotion, strode down a well-lit corridor to a glass wall, and gestured at it. On the other side sat incubators. Ten in all.

Studying the small metal containers, Kayse heard Angel suck in his breath. The incubators contained growing embryos.

Grinning at Angel, Elija said, "You think you're the last of the true Enjelise here on Alysian? Oh, there are hybrids scattered around the planet, and even up on Alysia Station, that Madame Kat decanted; but you, you are considered the purest of the pure." Elija regarded Angel. "Not anymore. I collected the DNA that you left behind when you were here the last time. We've been force growing several viable embryos. We expect to stabilize several ninety-percent male Enjelise—your clones."

"We don't have stable sexes," Angel murmured, staring at the developing fetuses. Tiny wings fluttered gently from a few backs of rolled up embryos wafting lazily in the tanks. Next to him, Angel caught and held his breath as he studied the tanks. Kayse noticed the normally stalwart Enjelise blinking rapidly, fighting brimming emotion.

Kayse contemplated what he saw, overwhelmed at the thought of Angel having clones. Somehow that made him feel more valuable as a clone, because he knew he felt he would cherish even Angel's clones.

Elija was still talking rapidly. "I believe you can become stable if the circumstances warrant it. Your father stabilized after he met your mother. During the breeding stage, Enjelise often stabilize to a particular sex if the conditions are right. You don't have to be the last Enjelise on Alysia anymore. All you have to do is help protect this installation. Negotiate with the Alysians. Stop them from using nuclear bombs or missiles to destroy the Homestead. Explain that we don't want to dominate their planet; we just want some land to live on and are willing to do anything to get it...anything. We haven't found any other habitable planet in over a millennium of searching. If a part of the old human race from Earth is to survive, our best chance is here—but not against a full-blown war with mutant Alysians who can time travel." He cast a glance toward Kayse with his last comment.

Elija placed a hand on Angel's arm. "Help us, Angel. They might listen to you. Otherwise, your species will also die on the war-blasted planet that Alysia will become. We can let that happen, or we can learn to live together in peace. We're a more formidable enemy than Alysians realize. Think of Darius and Ariel. Terrans will fight to survive if we are forced to, but some may go too far with the weapons we have available. The whole planet will suffer if that happens. I don't want to go that route; I'm betting you don't either."

Angel contemplated the scene through the glass window. A hand caressed the hard, cold glass as he turned a now composed, but pale face toward Elija. "I'll do what I can, but it may not be much. Would you be willing to sit down and talk with Steele?"

"If they let him live, and if he is able to offer reasonable terms...of course. But we have little time left before this gets out of control," Elija warned.

Angel's gaze returned to the incubators. A soft glow suffused him. He murmured, "I'll contact Elise to see what can be done. Right now, I have to get Kayse and Tempest out of here."

"No argument there." Elija agreed.

Angel turned one last time to stare at the lab as they left chaos and, now, flashing red lights.

Chapter 34

For a time, the helio bucked and whirled its way through snowy mountain passes and over dense green trees. Kayse's last trip had been mostly during the night when he'd been preoccupied with Tempest's critical condition and in a disoriented state. This time he could observe the awesome landscape of jagged mountains and thundering waterfalls. Several times, he gripped the arm of the seat, as a touch of acrophobia overwhelmed him, and he swallowed hard to keep everything down. A sudden air pocket caused all three of them to gasp.

Angel tossed him a look and then spoke into the radio. Frowning, he turned to say, "Director Walker seems unavailable. Jak Fields insisted, as currently in command, he could take my report, so I signed in and relayed my orders and destination to him." He shifted in his seat, but kept a firm, white-knuckled grip on the helio's controls. "Elise said it was important to let Trace Walker know, and Jak will deliver the message personally. So, Walker is alive at least."

At Angel's request, Kayse closed his ESA system, blocking out Elija and the Homestead. Idly he thought that maybe more than just Elija might be trying to follow him. Most likely, his body was riddled with trackers. He knew Deuce had inserted something also, probably putting in his own leash.

Then there was the crystal. That had changed him too. He rubbed his pocket where a chunk of crystal lay wrapped in a soft material. Its throbbing warmth oozed through his jacket, transmitting a calm that soothed him.

To his amazement, Tempest kept quiet. Jemma also said little. Both sat behind him and stared out of side windows at the passing scenery. Not saying much either, he admonished himself to be grateful for the silence because most likely it would end soon.

Once, Jemma gestured out the window, and he noticed a strange mass inching its way along a winding mountain road. He quirked an eyebrow at Angel.

"Terrans are leaving Tygel, headed for Elija's place. He's offered them sanctuary, claiming he can hold off the Alysian army if they attack."

Tempest jerked in her seat, moved to speak at last. "He lives in a small mountain cabin. It'll never hold all those people, much less hold off an attack."

Kayse snorted. "Small cabin my foot. There's an entire complex built deep into the mountain behind that seemingly innocent cabin facade. The Terrans have a much more advanced technology and are better prepared to defend themselves than the Alysians realize. If it comes to a fight, the Alysians better be careful. I think they have underestimated their enemy."

Angel gave an abrupt nod.

Kayse pressed his lips together as he remembered the sight of cyborg soldiers in the lab all designed for battle in some horrific future war.

Farther on, as the helio approached Tygel from the north, the glass bubble of the helio revealed dark smoke that eddied and twirled up into the sky, dancing funnels of destruction

"What the…" Kayse choked out.

A charred landscape soon rolled out beneath them, the result of a large fire burning northwest of Tygel. Homes smoldered, leaving people to scatter like fleeing gebbits.

Farther east, soldiers attacked the western edge of the city. Bright lights from lasers and explosives sparked and lit up certain Terran neighborhoods. As Angel flew them lower, they saw a home explode and the resulting sparks caused a nearby cluster of trees to catch fire. People ran everywhere in the streets, trying to escape the heavy artillery fire, but they were killed left and right as heavily armed soldiers swept through the area. A massacre was in progress and chaos reigned.

As they flew past, Kayse couldn't believe the devastation. "Klaymore Townsend is doing this?" he questioned. "Some of those down there are innocent civilians; not all are attacking Terrans."

Angel growled, "Vids are blaming President Courtland and Richard. In a surprise move, General Moore and a large part of the military threw their support to Townsend. That's the reason they were able to charge Sean Courtland and Richard with treason. Klaymore claims he's the interim president now. With the military behind him, no one dares dispute him. Director Walker's gone to ground and cannot be located. Through his contacts in I.N.Sys, Trace may have received an early warning of the arrests. The situation doesn't look good. We need some military might to counter attack."

"Military might?" Kayse sneered, "We're out of luck there." He observed the disturbing landscape beneath him. *Had it come to this?* No wonder Elija considered cloning super soldiers. Still, world war conflagration wasn't good for anyone, anywhere. Besides, he didn't want his face on mindless battle soldiers whose main mission was to kill his own people.

Other helios appeared in the sky as they drew closer to the city proper. A weight pushed down on him as their helio rose sharply and banked to the south in an evasive maneuver. He could feel Angel tense with apprehension as several military aircraft swooped across the air space now below them, heading east. But, they were charging out to the firefight and ignored the black helio whirling its way south overhead.

A premonition as to where they were headed flashed into his mind as they entered the northern edge of Tygel. Sure enough, the tall building emerged directly in front of them as they soon began descending toward the Med Center's heliopad.

"There's a safe place you three can stay for a while." Angel gestured toward the Med Center.

Kayse bet he knew where. They were going deep into the bowels of the medical complex where all things secret hid. His skin tingled at the thought. Great, just what he needed to confront after seeing all those clones at the lab. He felt his stomach churn at the prospect.

Echoes of memories stirred as they slowed to land, and he glanced over toward the rooftop garden. The helio touched down, and whirling blades slowed. As the hatch opened, he paused before disembarking, feeling the wind toss and slap at his face. His eyes caught dancing trees in a far corner of the roof. However, no phantom emerged from the flickering shadows and, better yet, no soldiers challenged them with guns at the door.

Descending the shaky metal stairs of the helio, he turned to offer his hand to Tempest. Jemma followed with Angel. A gaunt, elderly doctor materialized from one of the rooftop doors, frantically waving at them. As the blades wound down, the wind settled, and they followed the doctor into the Med Center, leaving the empty garden to stillness and silence once more.

Inside Ailey DeVey waited. She smiled at him and gave him a hug under the baleful glare of Tempest. Then she put out a hand to Tempest. "Welcome. With all the confusion and influx of casualties, we haven't had time to provide the accommodations I would wish for you. However, considering the circumstances, I think you'll find them agreeable. Follow me. Klaymore Townsend and company most likely won't consider searching the Med Center for you. They're too busy outside killing Terrans." She sniffed, showing animosity

With a sigh, Tempest hefted one of her bags, and Kayse lifted his.

Jemma tapped Angel's shoulder. "With you and Kayse protecting her, Tempest should be safe here. I need to check on Jahn and my own family. I just got a message to stand by from Deuce who says your mom is safe but may need me. She's working on trying to stop this madness, so I'm going to say goodbye for now."

"You've heard from Mom?"

"Yes, she's safe and will contact you soon. Get some rest, she says. I have to go." She looked over at Angel.

"Be careful out there. It's dangerous."

A fierce expression crossed her face. "Angel, *I'm* dangerous."

"Too true."

After waving goodbye to Jemma, they descended into the bowels of the building. Certain passages began to look familiar. Kayse wasn't even surprised when the elevator door opened, revealing Deuce with a grim expression on his face.

"Richard said that when Arwoyn needed to hide his secrets, this is where he came," Deuce announced, leading the way through several heavy, steel doors. Security cameras rotated as they passed.

Now they're hiding his secrets here, all over again.

A modest suite of rooms opened before them. Tempest perked up when she noticed an adjoining room with bed and bath. She shrugged off her bags and flopped into the nearest chair with a gusty sigh. "Jemma said that Mom's okay."

Locking the door behind them, Deuce said, "I just talked to her. She's alive and trying to get your father free." He nodded at Tempest. "Townsend is saturating the vids, blaming Courtland's regime for the riots. He's declared a state of emergency and taken control of the government."

No one asked about Trace, and Deuce didn't offer any information.

Heaving a sigh, Kayse faced Tempest. "I don't know about you, but I'm beyond exhausted. There's nothing we can do right now, but get some rest."

Ailey gestured toward a corner where there was a table set with covered trays. "I took the liberty of fixing you something hot from the kitchen. It's not gourmet, but it'll fill you up. Get a good night's sleep, some food in your bellies, and decide tomorrow what happens next." Then with a nod at Kayse, she left.

Deuce tapped Kayse's shoulder. "Here's a caller for you. Contact me if you need me. I'm on speed dial #1. Angel's on #2. If neither answers, you're on your own, and things have gotten dangerous. Angel and I plan to be somewhere close by in the building. There's something we need to take care of while we're here. It shouldn't be long."

Angel swung around to Tempest and waggled a finger at her. "I expect you to behave, Sugarpop," he admonished. "Absolutely do not step a foot outside this room. Stay right here. Both of you." Strong eye contact followed the comment as his brows furrowed together. He swiveled around to glare at Kayse. "And do not let her talk you into wandering anywhere. Stay put!" A strong poke of his finger hit Kayse's chest.

Kayse and Tempest nodded simultaneously.

Then Angel and Deuce left, locking the door behind them.

Kayse faced Tempest. He studied her face for traces of the extraordinary woman he had met in the future and saw hints of them. He smiled. Maybe he should make an effort and remember her better attributes. Maybe she might be worth the trouble, seasoned with a little maturity.

"What are you smiling at?" Tempest glared at him. "When you smile like that, it always means a lecture is coming, or you're going to laugh at me." She lowered her head.

"Did you know I really missed you?" he said softly.

The head snapped up. "That so?" Eyes went wide.

He gave her cheek a caress. Then, he chuckled. "Hard to believe, but true."

"With all those beautiful slave girls at your beck and call, you missed little old me?" She gave him a searching stare, which slowly became a mirror smile to his own.

"T'is true. I need a sanity check."

"Yeah, well, I need a reality check." She shuffled a bit and then eased closer. He put his arms around her and laid his chin on top of her head. "You're a pistol, girl. I never know what you're going to do next," he murmured.

"What I'm going to do next is get some food and then get to bed." At his grin, she put up a finger, tapped his nose and said, "To sleep."

"And dream sweet dreams," he rejoined solemnly. "Me too. Don't wake me up in the dead of night either, like you usually do. Promise?"

"Yeah, yeah. You wish," she said as she dragged him to the table of food. "Not going to happen."

***

So, of course, he woke up in the dead of night, not knowing what roused him. Listening closely, he magnified his hearing and extended out his awareness. Someone was moving out in the corridor just outside their door. He first thought of Deuce or possibly Angel. Someone had said that the Enjelise didn't sleep much. In the next room, Tempest turned over in her bed and punched a pillow. He eased out of bed and tiptoed into what served as a small living room.

"Kayse, is that you?" murmured a sleepy voice.

A scrabbling sound came from the other side of the door. Someone was trying to jimmy the lock or insert a rough key.

Gliding into her bedroom, he put his fingers to his lips. Her eyes widened in the dim light. He mimed for her to stay put, but she trailed after him, stopping at the bedroom door.

Kayse eased into the living room and watched as the lock clicked and the doorknob slowly turned. Tempest put her hand to her mouth. He waved her back into the bedroom. As he motioned his hand to his ear, she nodded understanding. Positioning himself behind the door, he watched it cautiously open and pulled out his medallion to activate it.

Slowly, a dark head of hair appeared at the edge of the door. A man dressed all in black eased his way quietly into the room, holding a gun in his hand. Scanning the room, he headed toward the bedrooms. With a shift of his weight, Kayse caused a board to squeak underfoot. The intruder whirled around pointing the gun right in his face. "Who are you?" he growled.

Kayse inhaled a sharp breath. *It was him!* Here was the kid, now grown, who had murdered his parents. The rough face revealed familiar contours, even though age marked his terrifying, nightmare features.

"You killed my parents," Kayse accused him.

"You! It's you. You're the reason for my father's suicide," the man spat back.

"What are you talking about?"

"My father worked here in this section of the Med Center. He was the lead scientist on Arwoyn's fragging secret clone project." The gun waggled in Kayse's face.

"Your father?" Kayse couldn't believe what he was hearing. Then, things began to make sense.

"I was ten when he killed himself because of you fragging clones."

"Your father was..."

"Dr. Warner Straung. He spent most of his time here in these labs." The man gestured about him with his left hand while still holding the gun in his right. "Many nights, my mother and I sat alone while he remained here to watch over his *precious* clones. I vowed I'd avenge his suicide. I've waited annuals for you to resurface. Now, I've found you."

"He worked on Arwoyn's clone project?"

"Yes. It was *his* project. He did all the work. All are dead now, but two. Only one left alive after you, and I know where he is. You're all abominations...some...some piece of DNA garbage cooked up in a petrie dish and incubated to be called human. None of you should be considered human; you're not worth all the concern and attention he spent night after night here. You're nothing! Nothing! I was his son! I was his *true* son! And all he did was spend time fooling with his experiments! How dare any of them be left alive to breathe the same air as me."

Spittle lined his mouth, a glazed expression fixed on his face.

Kayse stared at a crazed fanatic.

The man rubbed his eyelid, the gun waving in Kayse's face. "Oh yeah, I killed the others. Made it look like accidents. Only two are left now, and soon, no more mutants will contaminate Alysia. Dad will be able to come back home and spend all his time with us."

Kayse shook his head, thinking of the Homestead and everything this man didn't know. He wondered how many others might agree with his sentiments, if not with quite the same fervor and reasons. The man was insane, but others might see the argument. A chill passed through him.

"Who is the other clone?" Kayse asked intently. He suspected he knew; he just wanted confirmation at this point. "The one that's still alive besides me?"

He's talking about Trey.

The man paused in his vocal rampage as he thought over the question. Obviously, it was an obsession with him, and the question diverted his emotional outburst to rational thought. His eyes narrowed. "I'm not telling. He was here for a while, and I almost had him, but then he was gone. The time traveling makes it difficult to track either of you. When I first tried to kill you, I didn't know where the frag you went. I thought you were cornered for sure, but you disappeared. Vanished into thin air."

The man turned an accusatory expression on Kayse. "For a long time I waited, thinking you were out of reach. Then I learned you were back. I found you but, before I could kill you, you vanished again. It took me a while to realize you were still here, just altered. Then, I realized maybe the other one had done the same thing. I almost got him once, and I think it scared him." The man smiled at the thought.

Kayse shuddered.

"I'm not telling you the name. You'll just warn him and he'll get away. Fields said he would help me if I just let him know where...er...uh." The mouth snapped shut. The eyes narrowed. "It's time for you to die, and me to quit talking. I've waited too long as is." He raised the gun.

The lights snapped on, startling Janos, His gun jerked up into the air, discharged, and flew out of his hand.

A screech came from Tempest's bedroom, and she appeared at the edge of the door.

The attacker swung around, scrabbling for his weapon, grabbed it, and dived for the door where Tempest cowered. Reaching the door, he knocked her down and they tumbled into a heap. He raised the gun to her face...

"Janos!"

Involuntarily, the guard looked over toward the voice.

Bam! From the suite's entrance, Deuce fired, hitting him between the eyes, and Janos slumped dead to the floor.

"Nice going there, Deuce," Kayse commented. "Just in time." He inhaled a breath. "Glad the medallion worked."

"*I* used that caller he gave you," Tempest retorted, brushing herself off and struggling to stand up from her sprawled position. She edged away from the dead body, but continued her nervous chatter. "While you two were discussing stuff, I snatched the caller off the nightstand and punched in Deuce's number. I told him to hurry." She glowered at the tardy agent.

"I hurried as best I could, given that Jak Fields arrived with a team to kidnap Kayse." Deuce glared back at her. "Angel and I went through the Med Center records earlier this evening and matched Dr. Straung's name to a Med Center worker. Then we crossed checked to see what the relationship was. That's when Janos' name popped up as his son. We obtained the picture of the man who attacked Kayse the last time he was here and matched it to Med Center personnel records. He's been working here at various jobs, lurking about, waiting for you to show up again or hoping to get information on your whereabouts. A couple of incidents led to him being fired a while back, but it seems he copied critical access keys. Then Tempest sent her message, and it all fell into place—except I didn't realize he was working with Jak Fields until I wondered how he knew you were here. Only Fields knew you were coming here. Then it all made sense. Jak Fields is working for Townsend, who believes he can use Kayse's ability to prevent the invasion from happening. Fields manipulated Janos all along to get help in locating Kayse."

"You used me as bait!"

"Not deliberately. We didn't know until tonight who was behind everything," Deuce protested. "We suspected a high level I.N.Sys agent; we suspected Fields, but had no proof. Hey, I saved your life, your killer is dead, and we know who the traitor is and stopped him. All's good."

Tempest whirled around, glaring at the group. "Good? Not by a long shot. My father is still in danger, and the world is falling apart outside, if you'd care to notice."

Deuce cleared his throat, but no comment came out.

Kayse stared at the dead man lying on the floor. His breath heaved in and out as realization crashed in on him.

He almost killed me.

He started to shake with the aftermath of events, adrenaline still coursing through his body.

Noticing his agitated state, Deuce took his arm. "It's all finished. You'll be safe now. We got the guy."

Until the next clone hater shows up. He jerked away. Then Kayse regretted his childish action toward the man who had just saved their lives.

Deuced dropped his hand and stared at Janos.

"Thanks, Deuce," he choked out. "You saved my life."

Deuce nodded.

Tempest took his hand and led him to the couch where she sat him down and rubbed his knee until he got himself under control. Finally, Kayse stopped trembling, passed a hand over his face, and turned a weak smile toward her. He started to breathe normally again.

He was glad the killer was dead, but revenge didn't feel as sweet as he'd hoped. There was just an empty hole in his heart for those lost. He was still angry at what Janos had done, but now he understood why. Deep emotional pain made a person act differently…not that it was right.

In a short while, two young men arrived. Deuce introduced them as Thomas and Joe who proceeded to wrap up the body and cart it away. Deuce exchanged whispered instructions with them.

A caller buzzed, and Deuce answered, "Yeah. No! Frag! I had something I had to take care of first. You need to know that Jak Fields made a kidnap attempt on Kayse, and I had to use killing force to stop him from harming Tempest. Yeah, Fields. Surprise! Janos Straung showed up to kill Kayse and Tempest. No. Don't worry, they're fine. Okay, I'll tell her. Right sir, I'll come." Deuce gazed up at them. "Doesn't appear like I'm getting any sleep tonight."

Deuce faced Tempest with a sigh. "It's been a busy night. That was Trace. An Alysian mob tried to blow up your home. Your mom wasn't there so she's okay."

"Where is she?" Tempest snapped out of her daze and grabbed at Deuce.

"Trace didn't say, but she's somewhere safe. Angel's on his way back here to watch over you two. I need to tend to things. We'll meet up early. Pack your bags and get rest."

"Where are we going?"

"I'll tell you later," was all the answer she got.

What that meant, Kayse didn't know. He'd been attacked, and the man who'd been trying to murder him was dead. He should feel relieved, but a mob had burned Richard's house, and now, he and Tempest headed somewhere else. The situation was getting ugly between Terrans and Alysians, while the Alysians really didn't know what they faced. They thought they knew, but they didn't.

So, weary, he fell into the bed while still dressed because he was too tired to change. Also, exhausted, Tempest lay down next to him. Barely conscious, except to feel her comforting warmth, he wrapped his arms around her to protect her and fell asleep.

He woke to hear the outside door open softly. He tried to rally some energy and prepare to defend against, or greet, whoever it was. He struggled to wake as her weight lifted off the bed. Coolness wafted over him as her warmth evaporated away.

Forcing bleary eyes open, he saw Angel standing over him, cradling Tempest in his arms.

Waggling his index finger from side to side, Angel shook his head. But then Angel smiled, and his whole face illuminated, bathing Kayse in a glory of light. "Just taking away temptation," Angel murmured as he turned to leave. Pausing in the open door, the two blended outlines stood in silhouette against the living room's light.

"I'll be on watch in the next room." Dark returned as the door shut softly behind them.

Kayse sighed. With all the bad things happening all over, he finally felt safe knowing that Angel watched over them. That knowledge let him fall into a deep sleep.

Chapter 35

As an early light rose over the city, Kayse and Tempest silently followed Angel up the back stairs of the Med Center. An antiseptic smell permeated even this back corner of the building, triggering shadowy memories in Kayse's mind. The hard steel stairs echoed their hurried steps. Up above, Kayse picked out the sound of whirring blades from an incoming helio. The trio burst out onto the misty rooftop at the same time as the helio danced in like a large black insect, whipping up the winds until it settled delicately nearby. Kayse gazed out over the rooftops of Tygel. The normally sharp outlines of the city's buildings emerged, softened by the morning fog. Deuce gestured frantically from the pilot's seat of the helio.

Angel tapped Kayse on the shoulder, disturbing his reverie. "Inside," he murmured. They all climbed on board the helio, and it lifted off and headed south.

Kayse watched the sun swim upward into morning, shedding a golden glow over the cityscape while dispersing the covering mists. A cup of hot kauf, thrust into his hands, helped him struggle to wakefulness. He stared at the steam curling out of the cup and took a satisfying sip. The warmth trickled down his throat to his chilled soul. He was going to miss the Homestead's morning coffee ritual but, for now, this sufficed.

"We're going south," Tempest announced loudly over the noise of the helio. She pointed at the sun and then toward the direction they flew. "There was a big fight recently near that camp where we stayed. I saw it on the vids. I bet we're headed there." She glanced inquiringly at Deuce who grunted and tried to ignore her.

The pale morning light reflected off her excited face and cast highlights over her dark curling hair. Kayse smiled a sleepy smile at her exuberant energy while taking another sip, clarity finally arriving.

Angel leaned forward to peer out the glass bubble.

Tempest turned her head sideways. "I'll bet they hid the stolen shuttle somewhere there, and Mom is on it," she said excitedly. "We're going up to the space station, aren't we?" She swung triumphantly around as if she had just solved the world's problems.

Everyone pretended to ignore her.

Kayse sat up suddenly, as he realized that the Alysians had several shuttles to ferry them back and forth between the two space stations; yet he didn't recall any mention of an Alysian spaceship. He hadn't paid much attention to his history, except he knew Braden had taken an Alysian ship to accompany the Terran armada when it had gone back into space, and there had been no mention of building a subsequent spaceship. Did the Alysians have any spaceships like Elise's? He'd noticed Elise's ship welded to the station upon approach, but now he recalled the distinctive smell of a welder's torch and the clanking of steel when he had been in Dr. Jay's operating room.

"The station first, but then the ship. My money's on us going to the ship," he said aloud. "But do we have a shuttle?"

Everyone went still.

Deuce frowned. "We're on a tight schedule. Director Walker originally had the shuttle diverted from the camp to another base so it couldn't land there. Now with the current confusion, he has arranged to get that shuttle crewed and flown to the camp. With General Moore reforming his military and heading north to the Homestead, it will give us a window of opportunity in which to launch and head for the Earth2 Space Station. All the commotion in Tygel will act as a diversion for us. Timing is critical so get in the shuttle as soon as I touch ground."

Silence engulfed the cockpit, except for the steady *thwap thawp thawp* of the helio's blades. Kayse stirred a leg that had fallen asleep. His mind sorted through the scenario.

And then what, he wondered. *What were they planning to do next? What was Elise going to do with the ship? Would they just leave? Would she abandon Richard?*

***

It seemed like forever, but finally Kayse saw dense jungle and a large charred wound that gouged into the land. The rough airstrip he'd helped widen emerged beneath them and extended off into the distance. The helio made a circle and Deuce muttered into his mike. They slipped sideways so fast toward the ground that Kayse's ears hurt from the change in air pressure. As he looked out, he saw the shuttle, which resembled a large metal beast, lurking under dense foliage.

"Tygel Military Base knows that an unknown aircraft left the Med Center, and they're sending a helio after us," Deuce warned, tearing off his headset and flicking switches rapidly. "Let's get moving."

Before the wheels even touched the ground, Angel leaped off with Kayse right behind. They both raised their hands to swing Tempest down as Deuce locked down the board. Jungle vegetation and dirt kicked up all around them and then drifted to ground as the helio shut down. They

raced to the waiting shuttle, now sitting at the end of the
runway. It stood there, engines revving as Elise emerged at
the entrance, waving wildly at them.

"They suspect I'm here," she shouted. "Hurry!"

Up the ramp, they clambered, grabbed seats in the
cockpit and snapped buckles shut.

The shuttle's engine went into a high whine, and the
shuttle lurched forward. Kayse heard the engines open up
with a roar and smelled burning vegetation. Their speed
picked up. Elise took second seat and started flicking
switches and punching lighted buttons while nodding to
the pilot. He was the same one who had piloted the
hijacked shuttle.

Outside, the landscape blurred by faster and faster.

"You don't think mom would take us away from
Alysia forever, do you?" Tempest interrupted his staring
out the window. Her voice wavered on the last few words.
"I don't want to leave Dad. And where would we go?"

Ah yes, where would they go?

Her troubled eyes turned to Kayse. "She wouldn't
leave dad; she just wouldn't."

Kayse remembered Elise's words, "I'll go where the
ship goes, if it comes to that." A cold chill ran through
him. She wasn't above abduction either.

"Don't leave me, Kayse. Even if it means going out
into space." Tempest shivered against him. He thought of
the starvation, the rioting, and the desperation in the ships
that had happened before out in that dangerous void. This
time there was only one ship and, not a protective convoy
surrounding them, if space proved difficult.

She clutched his arm as the shuttle roared down the
runway and leaped into the sky. It lifted higher and higher,
until it reached a point where the blue sky turned black,
and stars winked into view.

"Tempest, I..." His words stuck in his mouth. Whether gravity forced his words back down his throat or his own hesitation, he wasn't sure.

"Mom won't let you go back now," she said as she canted a chin at him.

They entered low orbit and the engines quit firing. He lifted in his seat as weightlessness took hold. Fluids began to re-position themselves. He felt strands of hair float and his arms flailed upwards. Suddenly, he felt trapped by other's choices for his life. Angel came floating forward from the back part of the shuttle, followed by Jemma.

"Jemma," Kayse said relieved. One good thing among many disconcerting events.

"Are you going into space with us?" Tempest asked brightly.

"Depends on what your mom has planned," was Jemma's enigmatic answer. "Hold on to your hats, girls and boys, things are going to get interesting soon enough."

<u>Chapter 36</u>

There was nothing Kayse could do to change things now, so he decided to relax and see what happened next. Vaguely, he heard excited voices coming from the back of the shuttle. Luckily, they'd evaded the other helio and, so far, no other shuttles had launched. He was just beginning to breathe easier when he realized that other people were on the shuttle with them back in the cabin.

"So who else is onboard?" he asked Jemma as he heard voices murmuring behind him through the cockpit's hatch.

"Some of Commander Brock's soldiers volunteered to round up the Earth2 stationers and herd them onto Elise's ship," she answered brightly. "They're going to help evacuate the station."

"Are we really going into space?" he asked, flicking a frowning glance at Elise.

"We'll be moving everyone off the station into the ship," Jemma answered. It was an evasion of his question.

Elise fiddled with the ship's controls, ignoring the discussion.

He turned around as curiosity got the best of him. Something bothered him about her comment. He wondered who else might be on board, so he stood up, stretched, and casually suggested he wanted to take a stroll to the back.

"Too much excitement," he said to her. "I need to find the refresher."

"Back that way." Jemma pointed out the exit that led from the cockpit into the cabin area.

He floated out casually, felt his way through the cockpit door, and stopped, abruptly.

There, in the middle of the cabin, packed in amongst several grimy soldiers, sat Dan Smith. Their eyes made contact.

Smith gave him a feral grin as he nudged one of his comrades. "Looky there," he said. "Surprise!"

Kayse froze. He was trapped on a shuttle with a man who had threatened to kill him. He supposed the man wouldn't make his move until after they reached the station, but then amid all the excitement of an evacuation, who could tell what might happen? It would be all too easy to put a knife into his back accidentally while everyone else was preoccupied with crowding onto the ship. Kayse's stomach contracted and his muscles tensed.

Dan made a cutting motion across his throat accompanied by a devilish smirk. Two seats over, Commander Brock narrowed his eyes and caught the byplay.

Kayse decided worry wasn't going to help...Yeah, tell that to his emotions. He inhaled a deep breath. He needed to warn Tempest and ask Elise what in Fate's name had she been thinking to let the man on board.

He went into the refresher, did his business, tried not to throw up, failed that, and searched for an idea of what to do. Edging his way back to the cockpit, he tried to ignore the sadistic laughter coming from Dan Smith, followed by a sharp word from Brock.

Before he even sat down, he said to Tempest, "Dan Smith's back there." He nodded toward the back and saw the startled expression on her face.

"You're kidding," she said with widening eyes.

Elise frowned at her. "Dan Smith came on board? I didn't see him. Frag!"

"He's the soldier who tried to rape Tempest," Kayse answered angrily.

"I told you about him, Mom."

"Yeah, I remember. I told Jeb about him and thought it was all taken care of...Jeb said he was behaving."

"Well, he just threatened me again!" Kayse jerked his seatbelt tighter.

Angel scowled over at Elise, who shook her head.

Kayse rubbed his face with his hands. "He's a pretty bad one," he answered. "He'll probably try to get at me sometime during all the boarding commotion. I'll just have to keep a watch on him. If I see him coming, I can take him down easily. It's the not seeing him sneaking up behind me with a knife that I'm worried about."

A look passed between Angel and Elise. Angel nodded.

"Okay," she said. "Deuce, go to the back with those station blueprints. Make sure each group knows what area they're responsible for. Tell them that everything depends on the schedule, and anyone too slow will be sucking vacuum. And see what you can find out about Dan Smith and any of his plans? Understood? Send Jeb Brock up here now."

Deuce nodded.

She turned to Kayse after Deuce left. "I want you to avoid this Dan person and go with Angel to bring Dr. Luttrell on board. Leave this package behind in his lab." She pointed at a bulky case. "Move fast. We don't have much time. The Alysians will come after us in their shuttles to stop us. I'm counting on your accelerated speed to get your group back in time."

"What are you going to do?" he asked.

"I'm going to evacuate everyone in the station onto this ship."

"Why?"

"Because you're going to blow up the station."

"What?"

"Jeb's soldiers are going to bring everyone here. As soon as they do that, I'm taking the ship away. I'll leave this shuttle in the docking bay in case you encounter any problems, and I have to disengage the ship before you return."

"You're kidding! Blow up the station?" Kayse couldn't believe what he was hearing.

A stubborn expression settled on Elise's face. "The Terran Station has been our prison. As long as it exists, Terrans will never integrate into Alysia. If we blow it up, then there will be no other choice but for us to go planetside. Then, the Alysians will be forced to deal with us."

She stared at Kayse. "I'll need you on board along with Jay as soon as possible. Timing is everything. In addition, you're my backstairs link to Elija. Can you connect to him from here?"

"I can try. I blocked everything after I left." He closed his eyes and muttered, "Attend, Lola."

Attending, Kayse.

His internal screen lit up. Message icons swarmed across it. He mentally touched Elija's and a blast erupted.

Where have you been? Alysian army marching here, but having difficulties. They're on the way. Time

is short. The message ended with a red exclamation mark. ***Stay online.***

He quenched all other incoming messages and cleared the board except for Elija's icon. Then he put Lola on standby. Swinging around, he said to Elise, "He says the army is marching toward them, but they're having some trouble." He smiled over at Tempest as they both thought of heavy boulders blocking the road and snowstorms raging in the mountains that would slow them down. The delays would give Elija's people more time to prepare before the attack, but the escaping Terrans were in trouble.

Brock edged his way into the cockpit. A disgruntled expression covered his face as if he knew he faced a problem.

Elise whipped around to glare at him. "Okay, Jeb. We're now on my turf, and you brought that piece of ark dung on board with you. He's just threatened Kayse again, and he's the one that tried to rape Tempest at the camp. I'm done with him. Here's my deal for you because you brought him on board and let him get out of hand. I'm blowing up the station. If see him or his cronies heading back to this ship, I'm kicking you off to suck vacuum with them. So you make your decision about what happens on that station because I'm tired of dealing with him, and your negligence."

Jeb Brock paled. He gazed at Angel's stern face and then Kayse's angry one. His lips thinned and his eyes tightened.

Elise turned back to her board. He nodded and staggered back to the cabin.

Chapter 37

The shuttle approached Terran Station like a lover unsure of welcome. From afar, the station looked like it always did. Up close, it appeared deserted and locked down. Elise had a hard time finding station hands to guide them in and secure the shuttle, but eventually threatening and pleading brought a skeleton crew to get them safely docked.

"Point out Dan Smith to Angel when he goes by," Elise ordered as she finished closing down her side of the board. Kayse nodded glumly at her and flicked his eyes when Dan arrived at the exit door. Dan turned to glance at him and winked. Kayse only grunted. Elise caught the byplay and frowned. She signaled Angel, but Angel already had already caught it.

Elise regarded him grimly. "Now Richard hinted that you have some kind of ability, which enables you to jump ahead in time. I suggest you control it. Jumping ahead here, if all goes as planned, might leave you in open space with the rubble of the space station around you and inhaling vacuum. Not suggested."

Kayse choked at the idea. Right, control what he hadn't been able to so far, but if he didn't, he would be stardust for sure.

"Tempest, you're with me," she said.

"I'm going with Kayse," the girl replied defiantly.

"You're coming with me. If you're with me, he's bound to stay alive and finish quicker," Elise argued, glaring at the two of them.

"I wouldn't bet on it. More likely an incentive for him to stay," Tempest mumbled.

"Go with your mom," Kayse ordered. "I'll be along shortly." He gave her a quelling look. "I'm not suicidal."

"We don't have much time," Elise insisted. She pressed a com into his hands as he donned a space suit and helmet. "If you hear anything from Elija, or Jay gives you trouble, contact me. It's a direct and secure link."

"Let's go." Suited up, Angel nodded his head toward the cockpit's exit. He waited until the bulk of Commander Brock's group had dispersed away from the loading dock. Kayse noticed Brock tracking the group.

Bypassing the usual protocols for decontamination and inspection, Kayse and Angel came into the main hub quickly. The outer area appeared eerily quiet. Except for a few hurried Terrans ahead of them, it was just Angel and him.

"What's Deuce doing?" he asked.

"He's got a job," came the terse reply. "Elise has Jeb's men out planting explosives and herding stationers. We're to make sure Jay's lab is evacuated and rigged for detonation."

"Oh," Kayse answered, eyeing the package in Angel's arms. "Are you sure this is the right thing to do?"

"The station is a prison. If this is the only way to free the Terrans from it, then I agree with Elise. It's been too long, and they need to get planetside. She's taking everyone off, so no one gets killed...except now, maybe, Dan Smith and friends." Angel tossed him a grim look. "But that was your call."

Once through the airlock, they removed and clipped their helmets to their suits, skirted past the main receiving area, and jumped into an empty Travel Car that trundled toward the science labs. Closer in, they noticed a stream of Terrans headed toward the ship's boarding tunnel. Coming to a section of entrances, they jumped out. Kayse stumbled as he tried to adjust to the different gravity. A light flickered on his monitoring screen, indicating a worried Lola. He paused and inhaled the metallic tang of the station air that hit the back of his throat.

Angel grabbed his elbow. "It's through there." He pointed to their right and slid open a door panel.

They shuffled and lurched down a smooth walled corridor until they came to another set of door panels. "Elise says this is Dr. Luttrell's lab." Angel gestured to a large locked metal latch. He pressed the latch down as Kayse scanned the area to make sure they were clear.

"Go away," said a voice from within.

"Dr. Luttrell, it's me, Angel." Angel eased the door open.

"The station's going to explode," Kayse announced. "You have to leave."

The panel slid open to a harried looking Dr. Jay. The place was in shambles. Golden brown hair danced and tumbled around his head. He waved a hand at them. "Too busy. Found the Talent gene. Big breakthrough. Can't leave. Have to record my results."

"Time to go," Angel insisted, gesturing at the exit.

"I can't. I'm about to make a big breakthrough in my research. Can't go now; some other time," Dr. Jay answered as he moved back to a microscope and his lab table. He bent down to peer through a large scope, dismissing the intruders.

"You can work on it at the Med Center. They'll take you there," Kayse offered, trying to persuade the man to leave.

Jay gave a vigorous shake of his head. "I'm not going to turn over my precious research to those idiots. Oh, no, I'm not letting ignorant Alysians get their hands on my hard work. It's our only leverage against those savages. We can use our technology as a bargaining chip, or even as a weapon if we must fight to survive. Besides, once they realize what we are, what we can do, they'll never accept us. They'll fear us; then try to kill us. Now they think of us as human, possibly distant cousins, but we're more than that. None of you have any idea of what we've become because of my work, because of what I've accomplished."

"Do you want to lose everything you have here? Didn't you hear what I said?" Kayse shouted in frustration. "Elise is going to destroy this station whether you come or not. Where will your science be then? Floating bits and pieces, most likely."

"She wouldn't tear up my life's work. Hell, it's several lifetimes of work. I've made us almost immortal. And now, with the Talent gene, we'll transcend time."

That thought appalled Kayse.

Angel moved forward. "Here, where is the important stuff? We'll help you move it. You can find a place at the Homestead, but we must get out of here. We haven't much time left."

Choking, Kayse remembered what he'd seen in the future at the Homestead and knew what such a lab might produce. He could stop that future right here. He could leave Luttrell to die and change everything. He could turn around and just go.

But, he suddenly realized, he wasn't the kind of person who could abandon a man like Luttrell to die if there were other options.

Kayse's com rang. He heard Elise say, "The Alysians have launched several shuttles. I need you here ASAP. Those are captain's orders."

No, he couldn't do it. Not cold-blooded murder. Not Elise's closest friend. He put the com on speaker so Jay could hear her, and she repeated the message.

"Elise, I can't leave now. I've made a big breakthrough here," Jay protested.

"Captain's orders, Jay. I'm blowing up the lab whether you come or not. Do you want to save your work or destroy it all? This is an order from your captain. Bring what you must, but get here now!" The com clicked off.

Kayse observed a stricken Jay as Angel began gathering up equipment. Jay shook his head and looked around. He closed his eyes and then opened them. Resignation crossed his face as he turned to pull out software and equipment to load into a box. Angel headed toward the door carrying an armful of stuff. Kayse picked up some boxes and joined him. As the door slid open, they stood face to face with a grinning Dan Smith and two of his buddies.

"So here is where you're hiding, boy. I thought I spied you going in this direction," Dan crooned, pointing a gun at Kayse. Angel put down the box; Kayse followed suit.

"Don't move, fella. Stay right where you are," Dan said angrily. "I've dreamed of this moment for a long while now."

Suddenly, sirens screamed throughout the station.

"There's the final warning. Too bad, you won't be able to board Elise's ship. I promised you payback, and I like to keep my promises," Dan snarled.

Around Kayse, the world started to shimmer. *No! I can't jump. Not here, not now.* Angel said something and put a hand on his shoulder. The darkness cleared and the room came back into focus.

"You're dying and I'm leaving," Dan flipped the gun back and forth in front of him.

"Elise knows about you," Kayse countered. "She'll know who did this."

"So what."

"You won't leave this station alive."

"Wanna bet?"

Dan's gun swung up, and Kayse saw the bullet fire. He toggled into step-up mode, but it wouldn't be fast enough with Dan so near. Next to him, he felt Angel fall forward.

Idly, Kayse knew he was going to die, and then a blur of motion intervened. A body blocked the bullet headed straight for him.

Jay yelled, and Kayse turned toward him as Jay raised his arm, firing at the intruders.

Dan reeled back as he was hit, exposing the other two, who stared open-mouthed as ion beams burned a hole in the center of each of their foreheads.

Kayse stepped-down, and time flicked back to normal speed. Angel's body came crashing against him. "No!" he shouted as he moved to catch the falling Enjelise. "No, no!"

A bullet lodged in Angel's chest over his heart.

"Argh..." Angel moaned.

The stench of burning flesh bloomed and saturated the room as Dan and his cronies smoldered at the door, brought down by Jay's ion blaster. Jay leaped forward.

"Angel, no," Kayse sobbed as tears poured down his face. "Don't die!"

Angel's eyes closed as a smile appeared. "A bright light," Angel murmured.

"Angel…" Kayse choked.

Dr. Jay bent over and gazed down at the dying Enjelise, shocked.

Deuce's face appeared at the door. "What the Fate is going on here?" He stared at the prone bodies, and his eyes flickered up toward Kayse. Then he saw Angel in Kayse's arms. "Oh no, not the Enjelise," he said, coming over.

Jay looked up. "An Enjelise?"

"They're coming for me." Angel coughed.

"No, you have to live." Kayse choked on his words. "You just have to…"

"No, what I wanted," Angel whispered. "To be with the others. I see them." He reached out his arms.

"We need you here, Angel."

"I'll always…be…. nearby in spirit. Just pray and I'll answer." A weak squeeze on Kayse's arm and his eyes fluttered closed. A glow began to suffuse his body.

"He's ascending," Deuce murmured.

In the background, Kayse could hear the wailing of the sirens as Angel burned brighter, lost form, and the body in his arms became insubstantial. It coalesced into a glowing ball. As the ball of light flickered, growing dimmer, they heard a voice saying, "Be joyous for I ascend to join my own. Promise to protect those left behind, so my kind may continue." Then the diminishing ball of light winked out, leaving a stunned group alone in the dim light of a dying station.

"I promise, Angel," Kayse whispered.

Close by explosions shook the lab, sending equipment and boxes tumbling. Gravity began to shift and breathing became dangerous as outside vacuum rushed in at various damaged areas.

Deuce shook his head and grabbed Kayse. "We have to get out of here," he said. A shudder thundered through the station. Detonations sent shockwaves from cascading explosions through the corridors. Lights flickered on, and then off again.

Kayse's com crackled. "Kayse, where the hell are you? I'm taking the ship out. It's too dangerous to hang around any longer. Get your group to the space dock and get into the shuttle. Get away! You're running out of time."

Unclipping space helmets from their suits, they jammed them on, as Deuce levered up the boxes and equipment. The lifting gravity helped him. "Let's go, Doc," he said through the helmet's com. A mound of equipment and file boxes lifted to encircle them as Deuce grabbed one arm of the doctor, and Kayse grabbed the other. They fitted him into a suit and stuck on a helmet. Apparatus and containers from the lab now floated around them, raised by Deuce's telekinesis Talent.

They stepped over the sprawled bodies of Dan and his companions and made tracks toward the shuttle as fast as they could drag Luttrell and his possessions. Deuce leveraged the jumble of belongings and equipment into the TC, dropping them in the cars behind them as they took off. More explosions shook the station and they prayed the track would stay secure.

They unloaded the cars, emerging through the service port's airlock out onto the station's loading dock. There they saw three shuttles, trying to maneuver into berths without stationside assist. One shuttle floated partway into a slip and hung there. A door opened and a soldier jet-packed out over the open span to the dock's edge. He landed and began securing their shuttle against a docking platform.

"Alysian soldiers at three o'clock, Kayse," Deuce barked in a strained voice through his com.

"See them."

Two other shuttles arrived and eased partway into loading slips. Doors on the second two opened and followed the actions of the first shuttle.

Straight ahead, their shuttle clanked against its mooring.

"Speed ahead, open the shuttle, and unmoor us from the dock," Deuce commanded. "I'll come right behind you with Jay and pilot her out." He slapped the shuttle access coder into Kayse's hand.

Toggling into step-up mode, Kayse felt the adrenaline surge through his body, accelerating him. He took off. Deuce propelled four lab containers after Kayse, vainly trying to provide a shield for him. They looked like small quackers bobbing after a mother hen.

Kayse reached the shuttle's hatch and opened the door using the coder. Then he tended to the grappling hooks. Soldiers began racing toward them, closing at a rapid rate from the right side across the plascrete, shooting laser fire. Shots missed due to the change in gravity disrupting the soldiers' aim. He accelerated some more, and the world took on a strange blur.

A quick glance revealed soldiers moving in slow motion. He could see laser beams lazily stitch themselves across the air heading toward him. From another angle, Deuce and Jay moved at a tangent as if swimming under water. He unhitched the first grapple; finished the second and third, but was unable to reach the back.

As he fumbled to reach the last tether, a barrage of gunfire punched through one of the swaying containers next to him, creating a decorative pattern of gaping holes. Pieces of cardboard and liquid matter puffed and bubbled out in lazy swirls, filling the air around him. He grabbed arriving boxes and began throwing them in the back of the shuttle.

Finally arriving at the shuttle's hatch, Deuce gave a slow motion high-diving leap into the open cockpit, executing a perfect four-point landing into the captain's seat. A line of fire etched itself across the shuttle just above Kayse's head, as both projectile and laser fire spewed from the advancing soldiers.

Out of nowhere, Commander Brock appeared, firing at the attacking soldiers and thwarting their progress. With Deuce and Jay's arrival, more boxes and lab equipment joined him and crowded the shuttle's entrance. Kayse grabbed at the remaining bouncing boxes and containers, heaving them back toward the cabin through the open cockpit door.

Two soldiers pulled ahead of the others and, in slow motion, dangerously approached the shuttle. Commander Brock cast aside a spent weapon and fired a second, hitting one of the attacking soldiers who dropped dead. The second, however, hit Brock, and the Terran collapsed mortally wounded and floated mindlessly about in the now absent gravity.

Dr. Jay reached the shuttle's hatch and squeezed in, clutching a microscope and canisters.

Deuce tapped intently on the ship's controls, fingers stroking surely across the board.

Near the shuttle's entrance, Kayse ducked behind a large plastic container as a closing soldier fired at him. A case of tightly packed data cubes exploded outward in slow motion, causing a unit of soldiers to slow and flail blindly through a hail of attacking software.

The remaining mound of boxes and paraphernalia butted against the shuttle as Kayse stood at the entrance, ducking weapon's fire and pushing equipment and containers at Jay. They bunched up so tight around him, they almost blocked Kayse's ability to enter. He pushed through the crowding cases in the cockpit and slid in next to Deuce. Exhausted, Kayse powered down to real time as chips flew in from the explosion, and Jay frantically pulled the rest of the containers into his arms as if gathering in great treasure.

"My research," he moaned. Escaped data cubes bobbed randomly about the cockpit.

Deuce angrily swatted them away from his board as if they were pesky insects.

"Help me pitch everything into the back," Kayse ordered Jay.

One of the soldiers outside found his footing and wedged himself through the closing hatch. The shuttle shuddered as the engines ignited and strained toward increasing power building up to departing velocity.

Kayse stuttered, exhausted, "The far grapple…I couldn't reach…We're…"

Deuce threw a glance to his left, staring past him with widened eyes. Kayse swung sideways to see what he looked at as a soldier edged in and stuck a gun against Kayse's helmet.

Jay erupted from behind a box, and a large power stapler snapped down on the man's wrist. The man screamed as a staccato of staples rattled across the back of his hand and punctured his suit, causing him to leak air. He dropped his weapon in surprised pain. Kayse scrabbled to retrieve the gun from between his knees.

Deuce turned back to his board as the engines whined into acceleration mode. He motioned for Kayse to secure the cockpit hatch. Unable to eject the intruder, Kayse reached across the now gasping soldier and sealed the hatch shut.

Air flowed in, letting Deuce shake free of his helmet to concentrate on the ship's board. Kayse yanked his helmet off and tossed it behind him.

The shuttle tugged against the still attached mooring line like a wild animal trying to escape it leash.

Practically in Kayse's lap, the soldier thrashed around, hitting an array of electronics on the panel.

"Fragging hell! Get him away from me!" shouted their pilot, forced to do a reset. Outside, soldiers drew closer to the shuttle, looming into view at the shuttle's window.

Jay dug around in a box, while Deuce waved a warding arm and barked, "Secure that man."

Kayse gripped the soldier and wrestled him away from Deuce and the controls as blood droplets floated in the cockpit, leaking from the soldier's wounds and splattering Kayse's face.

Jay gave a satisfied grunt and flailed a roll of duct tape in his hand. At the shuttle door, they could hear the ping of weapons' fire hitting the shuttle and caught the smell of the engine burning as the shuttle strained against its mooring.

Jay rapidly rolled the tape around the man's wrists to secure his hands and then attacked his feet as the soldier frantically kicked at them. Kayse pinned his feet; Jay wrapped them up.

The man stared at the stapler that bobbed next to him in the low gravity, almost kissing his helmet.

Kayse yanked off the man's helmet and stuck the gun in the soldier's face. "Stay still or I shoot. A little more blood around here won't bother me."

"A Fate-wracked stapler!" the man shouted at them in disbelief as he jerked his face away from it. "You captured me with a fragging stapler and *duct* tape?"

Jay leaned forward, ripped off a piece of tape, and slapped it across the man's mouth.

Deuce muttered at the boards as the shuttle gave a violent lurch and broke free, tearing off a piece of the dock as it launched.

Outside, men fell off the station's edge, through the open breach and into the dark void as the shuttle shed them like pesky fleas. A dangling cable trailed off the shuttle's back.

The shuttle's com crackled with Elise's voice. Kayse couldn't make out the words.

"We're on our way, Captain," Deuce shouted into the com.

Angry sounds mumbled back. Kayse didn't need a translation to understand.

"Fragging cable's making it difficult," Deuce complained.

Deuce tuned the ship's com clearer, and Kayse heard Elise say in exasperation, "Pull the orange undock lever, you idiot."

"Fate, curse me for a fool," Deuce responded as a clank sounded, and the ship lurched from a canted path to an even one and burst forward. A long cable writhed out into space and disappeared into the void behind them.

"Er, affirmative, Captain," he muttered. "We're on our way at top speed,"

"Roger that," returned the sarcastic reply.

***

The ship soon loomed ahead in the shuttle's viewport, swelling in size. As the shuttle drew near, the ship's outside docking bay doors opened like a large animal snatching up a tasty morsel. Deuce half-crashed, half-landed the shuttle onto one of their landing pads. The outside doors clanged shut behind them.

So exhausted he could barely move, Kayse noticed Dr. Jay's pale face along with Deuce's sweating one and figured they felt the same. Deuce flicked levers and switches on the board and swiveled his chair as a loud klaxon began blaring outside. The shuttle bay was in an uproar with Terrans scrambling everywhere.

"Take hold, take hold! Fifteen minutes until transition," blared throughout the shuttle bay. People rushed frantically about. As several Terrans locked the shuttle down, arms waved at them urgently.

"Shit," said Dr. Jay. He unwrapped a new roll of tape and whipped it around the prisoner and then to a nearby stanchion.

"Let's get out of here. We'll be like loose eggs in a glass bottle if we stay here. Put on your helmets and activate your suits. Shuttle bays have very little breathable air."

The tethered soldier jerked about violently, his eyes wide with terror.

Kayse jammed the man's helmet on and patted his back. Staggering to his feet, he followed Dr. Jay and Deuce out the shuttle's hatch.

"Find a grab bar and pull yourself over into a pod," Jay shouted through his com. He gestured across the bay where several men and women were securing themselves into what Kayse decided were coffins.

"Take hold, take hold," sounded the loud speaker. "Ten minutes until transition. Secure all decks."

They swam like fish in the low gravity to a series of empty pods. Pods began filling up as workers raced to get secured. Some floated, bewildered, trying to find a vacant pod. As most pods filled, those left out became frantic.

They reached a row of empty pods. Jay unlatched and pushed Kayse into one, slamming the hatch shut on him. Kayse peered out of his cushioned cocoon.

"Five minutes to transition," blared the loudspeaker.

Kayse was finding it hard to breathe. "What's happening?" he muttered.

He saw Jay scrambling into a nearby pod. "Count down now, ten, nine, eight…"

As Kayse craned his head over, he saw Jay's case close. Deuce was nowhere to be seen.

"Transition now!"

A giant hand slammed against the ship. Lights went dim and flickered. Kayse felt himself pushed against one side of the pod so hard he lost breath. Then as that released, another push came from a different direction. Everything around him became insubstantial. Light went black and then a misty gray. Kayse felt as if everything was falling away from him, and he drifted in a nether region of not being. After a brief span of time, everything started to reform. The cozy interior of the pod became solid again. Lights flashed back on. His fluids repositioned themselves within his wracked and bruised body.

Jay emerged from his pod as the klaxon blared, "All clear! All clear! Jump complete. Space normal. Stand down."

Green lights blinked on, brightening the shuttle bay as mechanics and technicians began to emerge. Those who hadn't made it to safety were either groaning or floated, limp and silent.

Kayse's com beeped. "Report to the Bridge ASAP."

Kayse waved at Dr. Jay who nodded in acknowledgement and pointed to a nearby exit. As Kayse emerged from his shelter, he was relieved to see Deuce stagger from a pod and gesture at them. Kayse pointed to the exit.

Jay pointed at nearby grab bars, indicating the way forward along the wall.

They made their way to the shuttle bay exit and stumbled into an airlock. As they took off their space helmets and clipped them to their belts, they passed through to spray radiation sterilization, finally emerging onto the main corridor of the ship.

There, they noticed crowds of confused Terrans milling about. As soon as one recognized Dr. Jay, she grabbed him. "My daughter took a hit, Dr. Jay. Her leg's broken. Can you fix it?" a woman implored him.

"Martha, you know the take hold rules. Com the infirmary. Tell them to send someone. Until then, keep her quiet and still." Dr. Jay shook his arm loose. "She'll live from it and learn what a take hold means," he added.

The woman gazed down and nodded.

Facing Deuce and Kayse, Jay pointed up the corridor. "There's the way. Go up that corridor and take a right. Follow it up to the Bridge. Anyone can point the way for you. I need to get to the infirmary, get that girl taken care of, and see who else needs me."

Deuce's eyes widened as he stared up the long narrow corridor.

"You'll find it easy enough," the doctor soothed. "Tell Elise that I'm helping with the injured. She'll understand."

A strong odor of Terran sweat and the ship's recycled stale air choked Kayse's breathing. Curses, yells, and muttered words bombarded his hearing. A curser blinked red across his line of sight. He'd been too busy to check in. Elija was demanding an update and had activated an emergency override.

Kayse keyed the cursor as he followed Deuce's stumbling steps along a corridor that soon had several people staggering by them. Some wore small stitched white crosses on a shoulder and headed in the same direction Jay had gone.

A faint line of words paraded across his line of sight as the ESA overrode his hold commands with the emergency message.

Alysian military approaching Homestead with heavy weapons. Where are you?

Kayse keyed the response scroll. "Attend, Lola."

Attending, Kayse.

He gathered a breath and thought, "Message him that I'm in the ship and headed for the Bridge. And stand by."

Message received and sent. Standby mode activated until further notice, Lola purred.

A few intervals later, they reached a guarded door. The men mumbled into their coms, letting the door whisk open to reveal Elise in the Captain's chair. She swiveled around and snapped, "Took you long enough. Where's Jay? You did get him out?" Her eyes filled with apprehension.

Kayse looked past her to the captain's monitor, which showed a faraway expanding debris field where the space station had been. He shivered. They'd barely made it out in time.

A lone shuttle tumbled at its edge, but the rest was twisted metal and bits of blown apart scraps. An entire space station blown apart. Debris coasted toward them. Kayse stared.

"Have you heard from Elija?" Elise demanded.

Kayse nodded dumbly.

"And what's his status?"

"They're at his door," he mumbled, still staring at the view. "Knocking loudly," he added. "Apparently with heavy firepower."

"Okay, tell him I'm on my way." She waved to two empty seats and turned to Deuce. "Where's Jay?" she asked louder. He could hear her voice quavering a bit.

"He's at the infirmary. Said you'd understand."

She smiled a wry smile and nodded. Her shoulders slumped with relief. She gathered breath and swung back around, concentrating on her board. "Set course for plan A, helm. Announce heavy speed and give a 'take hold' warning."

Kayse could already hear the groans that would accompany that announcement.

One of the Bridge personnel muttered, "Fragging bitch thinks she's a Wild West cowboy."

Kayse wondered what that was, but by now knew that when the speaker said, "Take hold," he was going to grab on for dear life and not worry about anything else.

"This one's sublight, city slicker," snorted Elise.

The take hold warning sounded again and gave a countdown. The ship shuddered as the screen went white and flashed before Kayse's eyes as it made the short jump. He made sure he was strapped in tight. Again, all dissolved into white mist, but after a brief time shuddered back into solidity.

Elise appeared frozen in concentration at her boards. An officer sitting next to her gestured as the screen cleared and panned to a large and very close Alysia.

A satisfied huff of breath came from Elise. "Jaren, get me Tygel Tower STAT," she ordered.

"Roger, Captain," he answered. "Querying Tygel Tower now." The man stabbed at lighted buttons and switches.

Elise studied Kayse. "All right?" she asked, angling her head toward him.

"I'm alive."

Swiveling around, she frowned. "Where's Angel?"

Kayse gazed at Deuce who stared out the viewport. His eyes filled as he shook his head.

"No!" she said angrily. "No, tell me no. How in hell could you let that happen?"

"I'm sorry, Elise," Deuce answered. "It was Dan Smith. Angel was just protecting Kayse and got in the line of fire. Saved Kayse's life."

"Sounds like something he would do." She stared off into the distance, a welling of tears in her eyes. She smiled sadly and murmured, "Farewell, bright and blessed."

Kayse could swear he heard a murmur near her, and a kiss brushed against his forehead. He rubbed at his own cheeks that dripped with uncontrollable tears.

"If it helps, he seemed glad at the end," Deuce offered as solace. "He transcended. It was quite an experience."

"I'll bet it was," she said softly. "I would've liked to say goodbye."

Kayse leaned close to whisper, "I think you just did."

Elise caught her breath and slowly let it out.

Jaren spoke into his mike. He turned to Elise. "Tygel Tower is on the line."

She straightened. "Tell Tygel Tower that I want an immediate patch to General Moore or Klaymore Townsend. Tell them they have one hour or an equivalent duro to put it through before I level Tygel, beginning with them." She swung around, assessing her board.

"How are ship's personnel doing?" she asked her com officer.

"Shaky, but most survived," he answered. "Luttrell's in charge at the infirmary."

She laughed shakily. "True to form. At least he made it out—thanks to you guys." She nodded at Kayse and Deuce and then, tiredly rubbed her face with a hand, pushing a strand of waving hair out of the way.

Another nearby officer interrupted, "We don't want to do too many more high speed transitions. It takes too much energy for those short sublight bursts. The energy levels are dropping rapidly," he warned.

"Get them back up," she snapped. "We're not done yet. Divert all light speed energy resources to weapons."

"Affirmative, Captain," they both answered simultaneously and bent busily to their boards.

She tossed a glance over to Kayse. "Tell Elija to hold out a little longer. The cavalry is on the way."

"What's a cavalry?" Kayse asked.

Elise smiled at him. "It's an old Earth saying that means rescue is near."

Kayse frowned at her, but thought out the message to Lola and gave it a send.

"Wiping out Tygel seems extreme, Elise."

"Go along with me, Kayse. You, too, Deuce." She cast a glance at a worried Deuce who sat with a white-knuckled grip.

Jaren started waving and pointed out the viewport.

Kayse noticed that the ship was now flying above Democratic Union territory, right over the Diechwrathe mountain area where Elija's Homestead sat.

"Captain, they're launching jet fighters and missiles out of Tygel's military base," said a nearby officer.

"Stupid, stupid Alysians," Elise muttered. She rubbed a hand over her face and shook her head.

"Target a nearby missile silo. Let them see what we can do. What are they thinking launching silly planes?" she wondered aloud.

"Aye, Captain. How many do you want to explode?"

"Pick one for now. I don't want to waste the energy. I just want to make a statement."

"Ready at your command, Captain."

"Fire at targets."

Kayse craned his neck, trying to watch out the viewport. Elise saw him and waved him over. "Unbuckle and come over here," she ordered.

All three Terran officers looked worriedly at each other as if he were some raging assassin. He edged over so he could observe the spinning world out the larger viewport.

A bloom of smoke appeared rising from the planet into the atmosphere, a smoky tower of destruction.

The com board crackled.

"Tell them they have a half an hour now to get me patched in, or I'll start taking out every missile silo the Union controls and continue until either I'm speaking to one of them or Alysia is burning," she grated out.

Jaren started talking rapidly into his com. He nodded at her. "I have a line."

"Put it through," she ordered.

There was a crackle, and then a voice boomed out saying, "Elise, we have your brother bottled up in his little mountain cabin, and if you both don't surrender now, we'll wipe out every Terran on this planet." Kayse recognized the noticeable drawl of Klaymore Townsend. "General Moore has a rather large army at your brother's doorstep, and he is cleared to use deadly force."

"Senator," began Elise.

"Actually, I'm the President now, Elise," he chided arrogantly. "I'm in control."

"Not really," she answered with equal arrogance. "I don't remember any election. Here's the deal. You order

Moore's army to pull back, then have Townsend release my husband and President Courtland, or I'll raze Tygel. Do you understand? You might want to check with the Tygel Missile Base for confirmation of what this ship can do."

Kayse's eyes widened as he cast a glance over at Deuce, finding his face furrowed in a frown.

Raze Tygel?

Kayse could hear some crackling of static and then voices behind Klaymore urgently speaking to him.

"The base says you just took out a missile silo. I hardly believe it, Elise," Klaymore choked. His voice had a more concerned note in it and not as much arrogance this time.

"Believe it, Senator Townsend. Fact is that your planes and missiles won't reach this far up. You can't touch me. Plus, you have no armed space ships available that can attack us this far out."

"President. President Townsend," he corrected.

"No, Courtland is President no matter what you say. What you are doing is treason and genocide. And if you don't start doing what I say and command General Moore to withdraw his troops, I'll wipe out every last one of you."

There was an intake of breath and then an angry yell. "Listen, you fragging alien. I'm the one in charge here, and we're going to annihilate your ilk from the face of this planet. You just signed your brother's death warrant. I'm ordering General Moore to attack now. I'll bomb that brother of yours into oblivion."

Over the com, they heard Klaymore shout, "General Moore, order an attack!"

Elise shook her head. She swiveled her chair to face Jaren. "Okay, plan A continues. Lieutenant Shipley, fire on targets A at my command, then B. Tell me when you're ready."

"We're ready, Captain," the answer snapped back.

"Fire."

Outside, a fine laser beam left the ship and headed to Alysia. The ships' monitor tracked it as it streamed toward a highly decorated figure who was waving his arms around in front of a humble cabin at the base of the Diechwrathe Mountains. From the speaker, Kayse heard a gurgling sound and a strange sizzle as it hit its target.

Another beam shot out and targeted an ambitious political opportunist who thought he sat protected in a vehicle, but it melted around him trapping him in a deadly, liquid, metal puddle.

"Okay Jaren, tell Tygel tower to patch me into the next in command down there. Maybe he'll listen to reason better than those two."

"I hope so, Captain. We can't go through their military one man at a time, or we'll soon run out of fire power."

"Oh, I don't think it will take that long before the Alysians will be willing to bargain," answered Elise with a wry smile, nodding at both Deuce and Kayse.

She was right. The next in command was more cooperative.

Chapter 38

With the death of General Moore and Klaymore Townsend, the army surrendered and withdrew. The takeover collapsed with no military behind it. The surviving leaders capitulated to Elise's demands, freeing both President Courtland and Richard Steele who immediately took charge of restoring order.

Elise held her ship in a stable orbit while President Courtland re-established control of the government.

Richard Steele and President Courtland went on the worldwide vids dressed in somber suits and wearing haggard faces. In serious tones, President Courtland announced, "The goal of *this* government is a unified and just society. No one species will be encouraged to dominate the other."

Then, Richard leaned in with a wink and a smile. "Everyone needs to learn to get along just as well as my wife Elise and I get along. Although government, like marriage, has its good times and bad times; so we should all continue in marriage and government to work on getting along for the good of all."

President Courtland continued, "With that in mind, I plan to schedule a conference where both Alysian and Terran leaders can sit down together, listen to grievances from both sides, and hammer out agreements and procedures. I plan to make needed changes."

Richard nodded. "To demonstrate good faith, President Courtland has agreed to appoint Elija Fujeint to a special position in his cabinet to handle alien affairs."

Surprisingly, the committee hearings, when all was said and done, agreed that President Courtland and Dr. Richard Steele had accomplished miracles in the face of critical crises. They had downplayed the roles they'd played in saving Alysia, but overwhelming evidence surfaced that corrected that misconception.

Hostilities calmed, cleanup commenced, and order was restored once again.

In a quiet moment on board the ship while waiting for Richard and the government to restore order, Elise and Kayse found time to talk.

"Well, Kayse," she replied, leaning back in her chair. "First you need to finish school. Richard has suggested the Academy at Sunpointe. He can get you in there. Pull a few strings. My guess would be political science." She grinned as she said it.

"Political Science?" he asked puzzled. "Never considered that."

"Yes, well, after you marry Tempest, you'll want some sort of job, and we think you should consider a political office. You see, Kayse, it isn't the time travel gene that interested the Alysians half so much as the other quality that Arwoyn possessed."

"Other quality? What was that?"

"He was first and foremost a leader of his people, a king first, and then a powerful politician. His skills at governing were exceptional. In addition, after traveling here from the past, he organized the Talent Institute and brought together the Talents and Naturals so they could live together in harmony. He went on to run the Med Center, and quietly from the background, guided the

Democratic Union government to peace. Richard indicated that maybe you could do the same thing in your own way."

"Whoa! Back up there to the 'after-you-marry-Tempest' comment," Kayse protested.

"Caught that, did you?" Elise grinned at him. "If you ever tell Richard that I said anything to you, I will deny, deny, and deny it. Do you understand?"

"Yeah, yeah, but do you think I'm crazy, Elise? I know her. She'd make my life insane. You *have* met the girl, haven't you?"

"I've met her, but you haven't met the woman that she will become. I suggest you consider the idea." Elise winked. "Besides, I think that you would make a nice son-in-law."

Rather than correct her, Kayse let the comment pass as he remembered the stunning woman from the labyrinth. "Let me think about it," he murmured. "I want you to know that I appreciate all these wonderful ideas, and I'll give them serious consideration. However, Richard's life choices for me so far have been almost fatally exciting, so I need to take a hand in deciding my own future. Although, some of your suggestions do sound interesting, and I would like to talk about those choices later at the appropriate time."

Smiling wryly, Elise shrugged. "Richard has a lot of Talent also. More than I suspected. In fact, he and Trey are forming a group that Jemma calls the Time Cops. He's putting it together, but he wants to turn it over to someone younger like Trey. It would seem that Trey also has some of the time Talent, since he is also an Arwoyn clone. Right now, Trey is in charge of the Timelab, but that's another skill that Arwoyn had. He ran the Timelab for years. Richard worked for him as his assistant and evidently did a bit of time jumping himself. The Alysian Talents are very interesting to Jay and Elija. They believe that using Talents combined with their technology will make a better future for all of Alysia."

"Do we really want to manipulate the future? And who gets to choose what it will be?"

"Richard says it's like sailing a boat and watching out for the shoals and snags of future occurrences. Sometimes you don't realize what's critical until you examine possible consequences. Haven't you mentioned some experience along those lines?"

He thought of the rows of incubators containing his clones and shivered. "Yeah, made me think about what could be down the road if we aren't cautious." He sighed. "But I wish I could go back and save my parents."

"Okay, there's a perfect example. Trey considered that possibility and found out that without your parent's death, you would never have leaped ahead to our timeline. We need you to be in this timeline where you're the right age for Tempest, where it's the right time to groom you for leadership, and in a time of crisis, where you get to save Dr. Jay and blow up the space station."

"Wait! First off, I didn't blow it up! You did."

"History may make you and Deuce the heroes of that event. It'll give you national exposure so you can win the Terran vote, or possibly the Alysian vote, depending on how you spin it."

"Let's think about that later down the road. I'm willing to listen but, from now on, I decide what I want to do with my life. At this moment, I'm taking it one step at a time."

"Fine. Give yourself time. Sean wants to step down and Richard thinks he can persuade Trace to take on the job of President. After all, Trace's father was president before and the committee finally showed that he did a good job of getting the Union through several crises. In time, I believe most people will realize that Klaymore

Townsend manipulated the investigative committee. He used it to be a whipping horse that would discredit Courtland and elevate himself into office. Too bad it backfired." She gave him a smug look. "Meanwhile, we'll protect the government and the President's office until you take charge."

"I appreciate the enthusiasm, but that consideration is a long way off still…"

"I know. You won't have to make that decision for another ten years or so. Meanwhile, you'll need to learn how to use that ESA more effectively and work with Jemma to control your time Talent. Then school will be enough to keep you busy for the next few years until you decide what you want to do." She smiled at him.

The com beeped with a message. Her shuttle was waiting in ship's docking bay, now ready to go.

"I want to go kiss my husband again, Kayse," Elise explained. "And smell the green grass and watch the trees sway in the breezes. I promised Jay that he wouldn't have to wait much longer to enjoy our glorious planet. The man is impatient. But, I kept my promise. We go now at last."

"You never planned to leave," he acknowledged.

"Oh heavens no! I was ready to fight until my last dying breath in order to live on this amazing world. I was willing to wait years for them to assimilate us, but when it became apparent that it was taking too long for others, well, I was willing to sacrifice everything to insure we would stay. Alysia is a very livable and beautiful place compared to what else is out there."

"I am beginning to appreciate it more and more."

Elise stretched, working out some kinks. She sat back and tilted her head as she glanced at him through narrowed eyes. "Fortunately, the Alysian people forgot what I really am—a starship captain. They only saw the cold, alien wife of a famous and powerful Alysian. To them, I was an unimportant female, a negligent mother. Richard and I used those stereotypes so I could quietly do my work with the Terrans. There aren't many places like Alysia out there in the vast universes, Kayse, so it's important to cherish this world and protect it. It's truly unique. I want to give my people, and yours, a happy life here."

She rose to leave the Bridge with him as they joined Dr. Jay, and several others, now cleared to return to Alysia. Jaren would keep the ship in orbit because there was no place on Alysia for it, and because it was still necessary to maintain order. It would provide the Terrans insurance until things settled down even more. There were still a lot of Alysian hotheads who feared the Terrans' power and planned on ways to get rid of them. There were also Terran hotheads who swelled with newfound liberty and took it too far, too often. Both needed a not so gentler reminder of the ship in the sky if they ever tried to threaten the planet with their squabbles again.

As they were leaving, Elise received an urgent message that an Alysian shuttle approached the ship with a hail. The ship fell into a tense silence while she answered.

She didn't have to go all the way down to the planet to get her kiss. Richard had taken a shuttle up to meet her to ride back together, despite his gut wrenching space phobia. She threw out her arms to greet him as he jumped out of the shuttle and bounced over to her where they embraced in front of a cheering shuttle bay.

Kayse felt a smile emerge on his face and his shoulders relaxed and leveled out as he headed into the shuttle. He was finally going home at last, free of fear and full of promise, with a bright future ahead that only he would determine.

Thank You for reading the seventh book in the Alysian Universe Series.

And... **please**, if you liked it, leave a review on Amazon.com. I would appreciate it.

You can email me at shmccartha@gmail.com.

If you want to find out about the development of Alysia's space program and how the crew got selected for The Seeker, read *Cosmic Entanglement*

If you want to read the adventures of Braden and his crew in space as they went through the stargate and battled aliens, read: *Past the Event Horizon*

Richard's experience building the space station and uncovering a secret genetic program is the story in *Space Song.*

To understand the impact of the alien crystals and learn of the arrivals of aliens that changed Alysia forever, read: *Touching Crystal.*

A follow up to this book that goes into the romantic story of Tempest and Kayse can be found in *Time's Equation*. Kayse is accused of murder and both end up in an unexpected future that they have to change…a little math is involved.

A whole new series called the **Terran Trilogy** begins with **A *World Too Far.***

However, although it has a whole new cast of characters, except one, it still takes place in the Alysian Universe on a starship and eventually dovetails into the Alysian Series.

For ideas on other science fiction/fantasy novels and all things science fiction, including the challenge of being an author— go to http://www.scifibookreview.com

For a complete list of all my books
www.amazon.com/Sheron-McCartha/e/B0045K0HD6

For more details of character descriptions, a map, and news: go to: http://www.AlysianUniverse.com

or Tweet me at Twitter.com/Sheronwriting